ALSO BY JAMES BRADY

Warning of War

The Marines of Autumn

The Coldest War

The Press Lord

Fashion Show

Holy Wars

Superchic

Nielsen's Children

Designs

Paris One

THE HAMPTONS NOVELS

A Hamptons Christmas

Further Lane

Gin Lane

The House That Ate the Hamptons

▪ THE MARINE ▪

THE MARINE

A NOVEL OF WAR FROM GUADALCANAL TO KOREA

JAMES BRADY

THOMAS DUNNE BOOKS / ST. MARTIN'S PRESS ✖ NEW YORK

BrA

THOMAS DUNNE BOOKS.
An imprint of St. Martin's Press.

www.stmartins.com

Book design by Jonathan Bennett

Map © 2003, Mark Stein Studios

Library of Congress Cataloging-in-Publication Data

Brady, James, 1928–.
       The marine / James Brady.—1st ed.
          p. cm.
       ISBN 0-312-29142-6
       1. United States. Marine Corps—Fiction. I. Title.

    PS3552.R243M36 2003
    813'.54—dc21

                                      2003041353

First Edition: June 2003

10 9 8 7 6 5 4 3 2 1

This book is for my daughters, Fiona and Susan,
and for my grandchildren, Sarah, Joe, and Nick.

It is dedicated to the United States Marines and other Americans
who fought the Korean War, 1950–53.

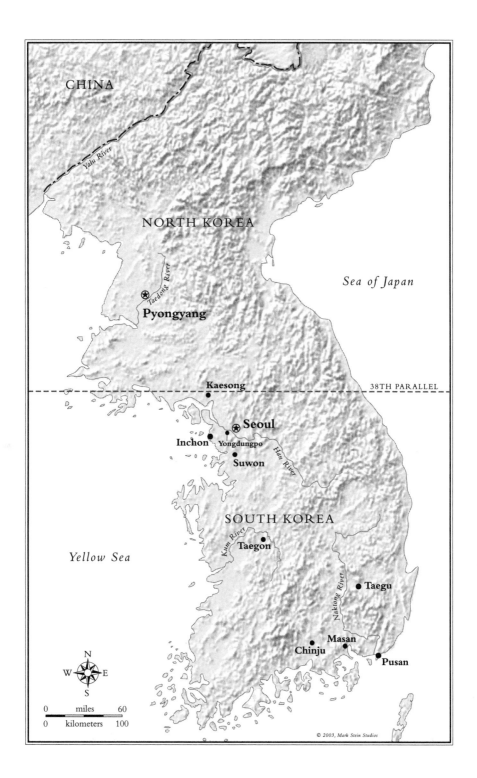

CHINA

Yalu River

NORTH KOREA

Sea of Japan

Taedong River

⊛ Pyongyang

Kaesong

38TH PARALLEL

⊛ Seoul

Inchon Yongdungpo

Suwon

Han River

SOUTH KOREA

Yellow Sea

Kum River

Taegon

Naktong River

Taegu

Masan

Chinju

Pusan

N
W ✦ E
S

| 0 | miles | 60 |
| 0 | kilometers | 100 |

© 2003, Mark Stein Studios

PREFACE

■

Early in that bleak first winter of our Revolutionary War, the American colonial army was falling apart, plagued by desertions, cowardice under fire, short enlistments, and slack, undisciplined troops who campaigned when it was convenient: when the year turned cold, the sky darkened, or the crops had to be brought in, they simply packed up and went home. Volunteers fetched along their own muskets or fowling pieces, or they went into battle without firearms, hopeful of scavenging a weapon on the field, from the dead of either side. Few enlisted men had actual uniforms; some lacked shoes. Rhode Island troops sassed officers from Virginia, and insolent York Staters refused to obey orders from Carolinians. Unity under fire gave place to petty, provincial differences and snobberies of caste and place. Clearly, the rebellion that began to huzzahs at Concord and Lexington and on Bunker Hill wasn't going well. It was against this despairing background that essayist Tom Paine wrote a few lines that General Washington would read aloud to his troops before they crossed the Delaware by night to surprise and attack the sleeping, drunken Hessians at Trenton on Christmas Day of 1776:

"These are the times that try men's souls," Paine wrote in his little pamphlet. "The summer soldier and the sunshine patriot will, in this crisis, shrink from the service of their country; but he that stands it now, deserves the love and thanks of man and woman. Tryanny, like hell, is not easily conquered; yet we have this consolation with us, that the harder the conflict, the more glorious the triumph."

Aristocratic British officers were amused, snobbishly regarding the colonial irregulars as an "impudent rabble." Lord Howe and Gentleman Johnny Burgoyne and Cornwallis and his generals, veterans of historic European battlefields, preened and flaunted imperial power and early victories over traitorous rebels who, quite clearly, had no stomach for a long campaign and would soon argue and bicker and bad-mouth their own army into collapse.

But in the end it would be those same undisciplined Americans, those contemptible "summer soldiers," who would become an army to defeat Gentleman Johnny at Saratoga and hound Cornwallis and his red-coated regulars to their deaths and to humilating capitulation at Yorktown. It was this "rabble in arms" who would win our country its freedom and establish a nation.

Two centuries later, on a distant shore, another flawed and unready American army, its surly rank and file unfit and insubordinate, its officer corps smug and feckless, was hammered and falling back under enemy attack, throwing down its weapons and fleeing in panic. Would these latter-day summer soldiers, these crapped-out sunshine patriots, also be inspired somehow to pull themselves together, to embrace the warrior's trade, and to rally in a righteous fury and turn on and rend the enemy? Could American troops again respond to the martial call?

Would Tom Paine's words still resonate in 1950?

• THE MARINE •

BOOK ONE
THE MARINES

■

▪ 1 ▪

In ways, young James T. ("Oliver") Cromwell would later conclude, Notre Dame wasn't all that different from the Marine Corps.

South Bend and the Corps both revered tradition and the past, shared a positive passion for winning, and each had a fine and famous fight song that men sang with a rollicking spirit and something approaching love. And they had their heroes. When the eighteen-year-old Ollie Cromwell arrived at Notre Dame for his freshman year in September of 1933, men still spoke in hushed tones of the Four Horsemen, of George Gipp, and of the legendary Knute Rockne, much as Marines did of Lieutenant Presley O'Bannon at Tripoli, of Lejeune at Belleau Wood, and of Uncle Joe Pendleton in the Banana Wars. Rock was dead a couple of years, an American icon killed in that 1931 plane crash into an Iowa cornfield, but his shade both haunted and illuminated the university and its famous football program, and, indirectly, got the freshman Cromwell in trouble. Or maybe it was Ollie's own father's fault for insisting the boy go out for football. "Just give it a try, son."

"There'll be a dozen high-school and prep-school stars trying for every position, Dad. I'd love to be able to play the game, but I don't know how, not at this level. Not after four years of high-school basketball. I haven't played a game of tackle since the eighth grade at Saint Ignatius Loyola scrimmaged in Central Park."

Mr. Cromwell, who'd played halfback on one of Rockne's better Notre Dame teams, was a good lawyer and a persuasive advocate.

"Notre Dame's a football school, Ollie. You'll regret it forever if you don't at least go out for the squad. You're fast on your feet, and they certainly can't teach speed. You've got good hands; you can take a knocking around and bounce back. I've seen you on the basketball court in tough games. And you can run forever. To matriculate at Notre Dame and waste all that . . . ?"

The boy continued to argue, but when he got to South Bend and they posted a notice for freshman football tryouts, Cromwell was there, queuing up with 150 others. Maybe his father was right, and he wrong. An eager undergraduate assistant had him fill out a form.

"You didn't play at *all* in high school?" The assistant made no effort to mask astonishment.

"Regis is a small school. Didn't have a team. I played basketball."

The assistant screwed up his face. The nerve of this kid. And with a home address on Park Avenue. Did he think this was the Ivy League? Notre Dame played Southern Cal and Army and Ohio State. The football powers. Not Cornell and Brown.

"Well, okaaayyy . . ."

They issued him cleats and pads and helmet and a faded uniform laundered too many times. One of the coaching staff, professionally cheerful, sternly square-jawed, middle-aged men in baseball pants and caps who were forever shouting at people, made a brief speech in which the sainted name of Coach Rockne figured prominently. Then a whistle sent the freshman candidates off on a two-mile run, round and round the great stadium. Here, at least, Oliver Cromwell could hold his own with anyone. As he did when they began actual football drills—blocking, tackling, throwing, and catching. Someone had heard about his home address, gossiped about it. Which meant he was not only a basketballer but probably a spoiled rich kid, so they nicknamed him Park Avenue. Cromwell was accustomed to nicknames, like the "Oliver" bestowed on him by roughneck Catholic schoolboys who thought it amusing to brand one of their own with the name of the famous Roundhead general who'd slain Irishmen by the thousands and transported Irish wenches as indentured servants. Despite nicknames, Ollie actually survived the first two squad cuts, being especially useful when it came to hitting the tackling dummy.

"Head on and low, boy! Take his legs out from under him! Hit 'im and hit 'im low!"

He even got through the freshman scrimmage and almost caught a pass. As he wrote home with a wry realism, "Compared to you, Dad, I realize 'almost' grabbing a pass doesn't count, but it felt pretty good."

Then, in a scrimmage against the varsity, Ollie met Jack Ballard. Met him head-on and low!

This wasn't going to be a great Notre Dame varsity year anyway, and Hunk Anderson's critics were lining up early. Hunk had succeeded Rockne as coach (they would certainly never *replace* Rock!), and after a so-so season they were cutting Hunk very little slack. And by 1933 there was already talk of dropping Anderson for Elmer Layden, lean and handsome, one of Rockne's legendary Horsemen. This was Notre Dame, where they were accustomed to winning, and before the season opener, before they'd won or lost a game, you heard the talk: in the Chicago dailies and the big metropolitan papers, especially in New York, with its thousands of zealous subway alumni who'd never even seen Indiana. Here on campus, where the critics really knew whereof they spoke, you heard comment along the lines of, "If only Rock were still here." While this might not be much of a Fighting Irish team, it had its charms. Jack Ballard, for one, their star tailback. Jack was the best they had, rangy and elegant, with a turn of speed in an open field. Jack might win a game or two all by himself the way he ran the ball. Everyone said so.

And now, as they carried him off the practice field by stretcher, even the paid-to-be-cheerful assistant coaches were hushed. And careful not to look at Oliver Cromwell.

Too careful. Far too careful. Coach Anderson made it a positive point of not looking at the freshman who had just ruined his best player and, quite probably, a season that would start in two weeks against Purdue.

When they whistled practice short that afternoon, Ollie was uneasy, nervous, unsure. He tried to understand what he had done wrong. His freshman squad teammates were no help, patently edging away from him. Perhaps they felt, irrationally, that they shared his guilt, that they, too, were somehow to blame for what happened, for the tragedy of Ballard's knee.

Only his roommates, who weren't footballers and hadn't yet heard what happened, were still speaking to Ollie. Others, talking about the young man behind his back, didn't bother to use his name but sneered at him as Park Avenue, injecting class hostility into an already-angry situation.

Then, two days later, after a tense forty-eight hours, Ben Sweet came for him. The two met, Sweet having waited for him to pass, in the gloomy, smoke-smelling autumn dusk at a treed and isolated corner of the campus behind the big chemistry building. A dark and empty place.

"Park Avenue!"

The words crackled on the evening still, not so much an address as a snarl.

"Yeah?"

Ben came toward him, a large young man and menacing, shuffling through damp leaves.

"Look, fellow, this wasn't my idea. The squad picked, and it came up me."

Ollie knew who he was: Ben Sweet, a big, good-looking fullback from Oak Park, vital, broad shouldered, and brimming with life; a popular young man on campus who played varsity football, hardly a star but a useful player, one of the most powerful men on the entire squad. He was about six-two, close to Cromwell's height, perhaps thirty pounds heavier, two or three years older; a rather pleasant junior with a potential for bullying lesser men.

"Picked you for what?" Ollie asked, a younger boy confronting an upperclassman and not understanding.

"How you wrecked Ballard."

"That was a fair hit. No one can say it wasn't."

"Sure, if you say so," Sweet agreed affably. No point haggling with the boy.

"Well, what's the problem?" Ollie was getting angry at indictments being brought without counsel. A little of his lawyer father had rubbed off.

"There's no problem," Ben Sweet said, "only the varsity would feel better about things if you didn't get clean away with hurting Jack."

Cromwell stared at him, not really believing this was happening at the wonderful little Midwest college that the sportsman Rockne had made famous.

"I told you, kid. Not my idea. The team just lost their tailback. Jack was the key to our season. They think it'd send a message to other wiseguy freshmen out to make a name if you were made an object lesson, roughed up a bit."

"By you."

"Yeah. They decided to send a big guy. But," this smugly apologetic, "don't worry. I'll go easy."

"Okay," said Cromwell. Ben was in sweats after practice, and Ollie wore a tweed jacket and tie, taking off the jacket but leaving his tie in place (which an amused Sweet took as evidence this bird was no fighter) as he put down his books carefully to the side where they wouldn't be kicked, and the two squared off.

Ollie knocked Sweet down three times.

When he helped him up the last time, Ben staggered unsteadily on his feet, and Ollie knew he couldn't just leave him there in the dank evening. So he led Ben gently by the arm into a campus men's room, where he dampened an old towel to swab him down, rinse away the blood.

"You okay?" Ollie asked.

"Where the hell did you learn that?" a bruised Ben asked, sore, embarrassed, but still curious.

Knowing the inside jokes, the cutting slights, Ollie said:

"A Park Avenue street gang I used to run with."

If Ollie thought that put an end to it, he was mistaken. From that moment on there was trouble. Not from Ben Sweet but from other players who resented the very idea of a basketball player trying to make the football squad. Scrimmages became tougher, the hits on Cromwell harder. Head Coach Anderson, so aware of the Rockne mystique, didn't demean himself by speaking directly to a freshman player but had the freshman coach do the deed.

"Football is a team game, Cromwell. You're trouble. We don't need disruptive elements."

Ollie was cut shortly after that. He sulked about the inequity of it for a day or so, and then, being a positive sort of kid, he put it behind him to concentrate on classwork and study, doing well academically with his first monthly grades, As in Latin (that was the Jesuits); history, which he loved, and English. Math was a challenge and chemistry a puzzle. Religion—well, at Notre Dame no one flunked religion. Then, in October, when notices for basketball tryouts were posted, he showed up with his shoes and shorts from Regis High. Here, in the college gym, there were none of the psychological adjustments he'd had to make on the football field. Basketball was his game, on a tiny high-school court or in a university field house.

"Hoop's still ten feet high."

His old man, sensible and loving, hadn't beaten up on him for not making the football team. Ollie gave him a full report on what had happened. "I agree you were poorly treated, son. Maybe it's my fault. Getting you to try out for the team while you were carrying my record on your back. I'm disappointed in Hunk."

"It wasn't Coach Anderson. It was the freshman coach. . . ."

"Anderson knew. The head man is paid to know such things."

"Yes, sir, I guess."

He didn't last much longer on the hoops squad than the freshman football eleven. At least here the coach leveled with him.

"You handle a nice ball. Shoot pretty well. And you'll mix it up under the boards. But once the football season ends, a few of their players come out for varsity basketball, Oliver. Play the second half of the season when we need a few boys with heft to get in there and bang. Having you scrimmaging against them as part of the freshman team—well, it might get nasty. You understand?"

"I'm not afraid, Coach."

"You can't fight them all, son."

"I fought Ben Sweet."

"Beat him, too, I hear."

Mr. Cromwell was an intelligent man who'd lost a wife young and who had no intention of losing his boy just out of love for his college and its traditions. What did such things matter when measured against your only son's future? So Ollie received no judgmental letters from his father and had no hectoring waiting for him at home during Christmas break. He knew how fortunate he was on both counts. And then, as into each life some rain must fall, along came an unexpected ray of sunshine in the unlikely form of Syd Ketchel.

■ 2 ■

STANLEY KETCHEL, THE MICHIGAN ASSASSIN, WAS HAVING BREAKFAST
WITH A MAN'S WIFE.

Come see me one of these days, Cromwell." That was the extent of the
note, on Notre Dame athletic department stationery, shoved into Ollie's
student mailbox and signed with a name he'd never heard.

"Who's Syd Ketchel?" he asked his roommates.

Whittle, who seemed to know something about everything, but few
things deeply, answered.

"Coach of the boxing team. Half brother or something of the late
Stanley Ketchel, the famed Michigan Assassin."

"Oh?" Cromwell wasn't all that up-to-date on prizefighters.

Coach Ketchel had a small office off a small gym stinking of sweat,
jockstraps, arnica, and vinegar-heavy pickling brine. *Why vinegar?* Ollie
wondered. And—oh yeah—cigar smoke.

"I'm Oliver Cromwell, Coach."

A small, solid man with broad, sloping shoulders, a broken nose, scar
tissue over both eyes, and gnarled hands that looked as if they'd been broken, set, and broken again, looked up from a beat-up leather armchair
positioned behind a cheap, unpainted pine desk with a telephone, a yellow-
lined pad, an ashtray, and a couple of pencil stubs. Thumbtacked to the
wall were faded fight posters, curling at the edges, and the sort of giveaway
calendar they hung in gas-station garages.

Coach Anderson's office was in a large, bright admin building and was
sleekly staffed by dozens. So said campus talk.

"Ben Sweet says you can hit. Can you?"

"Well, I dunno. I hit Ben pretty well."

"That ain't difficult. I once had hopes for Sweet," the coach said. "They
got dashed."

Jesus, had Cromwell injured yet another team's star?

"And now?"

"Oh, I realized long ago he wasn't much. Strong, but that was it. Can't
move his feet. Like most young men, Ben's read too much Hemingway.

Hemingway did a little boxing and wrote stories about it. Bullshit mostly, the few that I read, but that's what got Ben coming down here to learn to box. He weren't the only one, neither. College boys do better reading books about boxing than they do boxing, hitting and getting hit. That's why I left that note for you. Thought you might be different. That maybe you was a fighter and didn't just read up about it."

"And?"

"A fellow can learn to box. Plenty do. Like learning to dance, doing the fox trot. But knowing how to hit, that's instinct; that comes from deep down. Can't teach hitting. You can hone it, but you can't give it to a boy if he ain't got it natural. Like soaking a boy's hands in brine toughens the skin over the knuckles, but you can't toughen up a fellow's insides. He got gizzards, or he ain't. What d'you weigh?"

"One-seventy, about."

"You got height."

"Six-two."

"I like them shoulders. You'll fill out, I'd say, given time. Make a nice cruiser-weight. Maybe a heavyweight if you live that long."

"Look, Coach, I've just been fired off two Notre Dame teams. I've taken a lot of ribbing about it. I don't need any more."

"I ain't ribbing, kid," the older man said furiously. "Us Ketchels make jokes, but not about boxing. We take boxing serious."

He was so solemn about it, Cromwell thought he ought to say something to mollify the man's rage.

"Your brother, the Michigan Assassin . . ."

"Second cousin once removed. I never claimed Stanley as a brother. Much as I loved the bastard, God bless his troubled and immortal soul."

He blessed himself, and Ollie thought he'd better go along. Out of politeness, if nothing else. That, too, was part of the Jesuit training and of being a Catholic.

"God bless the late Stanley Ketchel," he murmured.

"And so say all of us, boy."

Ollie was now caught up in a vinegar-scented miasma, intrigued and curious. "What happened to him, to Stanley Ketchel?"

"He got shot," Syd said.

"Who'd shoot the Michigan Assassin?"

"A husband that came home unexpectedly from a business trip and found Stanley having breakfast with his wife."

"You mean he and this lady were . . . ?"

"I draw no conclusions, sonny. But it was that fellow which shot Stanley as the Michigan Assassin departed through a bedroom window."

Coach Ketchel put Ollie into a ring with another undergraduate, a big sophomore, so he could see how he took a punch, if he had a chin. "Let's see who's got the best whiskers," was what the coach said. He liked what he saw.

"You take a good punch, kid. And you hit that guy a ton. You put on a few pounds, I'll have you fighting heavyweights. They'll be slower than you, most of them. Combined with your height and reach and how you hit, that could be interesting, you know? Not that you know much yet, but I'll learn you."

Until now the only fighting Ollie had done was in the gym at Regis High School and on the street in Yorkville, where there were plenty of tough mick kids from the tenements along First and York Avenues and German square-heads who hung out along 86th Street. Those were street fights that ended when one boy quit or a cop broke it up. The bouts at Regis were gentlemanly affairs, two-minute rounds, and refereed by athletic director Don Kennedy, who coached basketball and baseball, taught PT (physical training), and was a sensible, solid family man with a mustachioed, pitted face and a nice smile. A man who understood sport. And recognized a sportsman.

"I don't believe every boy was meant to be a fighter, but I do believe that everyone ought to know the rudiments. And I include the bespectacled and spindly. None of my young gentlemen will close their eyes when they spar; they'll learn not to run away and how to move their feet. Also how to punch off a good jab. Even if, after that, they're sort of on their own. I'm better at teaching basketball than boxing, to tell the truth."

Though, if a kid were really being shellacked, and this being a Jesuit school, Don Kennedy would call "Time!" short of the two minutes.

He could never recall calling "Time!" for James Cromwell, only for the youngsters Ollie fought. And now, during Cromwell's freshman year at Notre Dame, Syd Ketchel picked up the tutelege of the young man where Coach Kennedy and the Jesuits had left off.

That year Ollie easily won the university's light-heavyweight championship and got to the Midwest regional intercollegiates before being outpointed by a Minnesota boxer three years older. He won his varsity letter as a freshman because there was only a varsity boxing team, no freshman squad. Then he was voted in as varsity captain for next year, when he'd only be a sophomore—something unprecedented at South Bend.

The football team lost to Ohio State and to several other elevens. The basketball team was fair. Only fair. Could have used a big, speedy guard, it was said.

Ollie Cromwell wasn't a gloater, but it would be inaccurate to say he drew no pleasure from such ironies. Then Sweet came around, cheerful, outgoing, and yelling "Halloo"s.

"You calling me out again, Ben?" Ollie asked with a smile, knowing he wasn't.

"Nah. Coach Ketchel said it'd be okay. Thought we might work out together, spar a bit, if it's all right with you."

Ollie was learning more than boxing. Such as, let's not have a confrontation over *every* damned thing. "Sure," he said pleasantly. But he went to Syd while he was taping his hands.

"What's this about Sweet? I'm not going to learn anything sparring with him."

"I know, Ollie. But don't be so damned hard on people. Give a man a chance. You beat Sweet bad last fall. He's big and strong enough that it probably never happened to him before, and he's trying to get a little pride back."

"He's not stupid; he'll know if I'm going easy on him."

Ketchel gave him a cold look.

"Then don't go easy on him."

They went two rounds, Ollie moving the bigger man around the ring, slamming him hard to the body mostly, then dropping him halfway through the second with a left hook.

Oddly, Ben thanked him when they finished, and he seemed to mean it.

"That was great, Cromwell. I never saw that left coming. Maybe with a little work I could learn moves like that, too."

"Sure, Ben. You take a good punch."

"Thanks. I wish I was better at it. I'm not really that fanatic about football, but we're not supposed to say that at Notre Dame."

"What are you good at?" Ollie asked, just being accommodating.

"Writing. At least I think so. I write for the school paper, and the literary magazine may publish some of my stuff."

Ollie was apologetic. "Sorry I haven't seen any of it."

"Doesn't matter. I can't say this to most guys without being kidded about it. But what I really want is to be a good writer, maybe the best writer we have in this country since Hemingway. I'm going to get a news-paper job when I get out next year. Then write books."

Sweet had clearly decided to make Ollie his confidant, to share his dreams.

"Well, that's fine, Ben," Ollie said, the younger boy encouraging the older.

And from then, Ollie was conflicted about Ben, who didn't like football very much but played because he was expected to, and who had only a single fiercely held ambition: becoming a writer; and about that, except with Ollie, he was too shy to talk, even with his teachers, and especially with teammates on the varsity.

Sweet was one of the boys who boxed just because Hemingway did.

Ben thanked him again and went in for a shower.

As Syd said, "Don't cost nothing to be be polite to a guy after you beat the crap outa him. Stanley liked to take the other fighter out for a beer and a friendly shooter afterwards—unless he had a car and a dame waiting, that is."

Ollie had the impression Coach Anderson's lectures to his young men weren't quite this earthy. As he took his own shower, he wondered if Rockne talked to the team more like Syd Ketchel did and suspected, yes, he might have. Might very well have.

Syd's office door was ajar as usual, but Cromwell backed away when he saw the coach had a visitor. Lounging on the tired old chesterfield couch with the broken springs was a peppery, bespectacled and business-suited, fedora-wearing gent, a spiral notebook and pencil in hand. Syd beckoned Ollie in.

"Arch, this is my new hitter, name of Oliver Cromwell. Don't know much yet, but he can wallop. We're working on the rest of the stuff."

This was Arch Ward of the *Chicago Tribune,* not only the leading sports-writer in town but, through his syndicated column, a national figure. It was Ward who was pushing the idea of a baseball all-star game as a promotion for the newspaper, and it would catch on. Ward, himself a Notre Dame graduate, had functioned for years as Knute Rockne's personal press agent and as propagandist for Notre Dame football. He was a dreamer, something of a politician, and had a lively, quotable writing style and a reputation for pettiness.

"You the young man who broke Jack Ballard's leg?"

"Yes, sir. Ripped up his knee, actually."

"Well, the Irish weren't going to be much this season anyway. Even with a healthy Ballard."

"No, sir."

Ollie wasn't going to start explaining himself to the reporter or issue additional regrets. Nor, though he enjoyed Ward's pieces, did he entirely trust newspapermen. The few published accounts of Ballard's injury, and of how a "reckless" young player caused it, had turned Cromwell gun-shy.

Even if he suspected it wasn't reporters who'd branded him reckless, but the varsity coaches.

Ben Sweet, freshly showered, was there, eager and waiting, when Ollie came out.

"That was Arch Ward from the *Tribune,* wasn't it?"

Ollie nodded.

"You and him talk?"

"A little."

"If he comes back and I'm around, Ollie, would you introduce me? It would mean a lot. . . ."

"Sure." How could you dislike a guy so open about his ambitions? And Ollie was trying to follow Syd's advice, giving a man a chance. Especially one you've just beaten.

A couple of days later Ward dropped Ollie's name into a column. "This Cromwell is the kind of kid who puts the fight into 'the fighting Irish,' " Ward wrote. Ollie tried not to be pleased but was. And Ben Sweet made a positive thing of it.

"Imagine, knowing a newspaperman like Arch Ward."

Sweet was two years older, but from then on it was as if Ollie were the senior man. And could be trusted, relied on. With other undergraduates Ben threw his weight around, but not with Ollie. Shyly, at first, Ben asked Cromwell to read a story he'd written for the Lit. It was pretty good, actually, and when Ollie told him so, Ben seemed more than grateful. So much so that he and Ollie double-dated once with two sisters from Chicago, pretty girls from Lake Shore Drive. Not even with the girls did Ben talk about wanting to be a great writer, wanting to be Hemingway, only with Cromwell. Then, the summer he graduated, Ben phoned Ollie back at home in New York during vacation to tell him he'd been taken on at the *Trib* as a cub reporter.

"Mr. Ward put in a good word," he said, "thanks to you."

That next year Ben called Ollie a couple of times at the college, inquiring if he knew any dirt that might make a story.

"Arch says I'm doing a good job," Ben Sweet said.

"That's fine, Ben."

So it was "Arch" now and not "Mr. Ward." And Ben was not above pumping college friends for story ideas, for dirt on the old alma mater. He was boxing now in a Chicago gym, he said.

"Where the real pugs work out. I get to go a few rounds with them. Handle myself pretty well, too."

"Wow!" Cromwell responded, not knowing quite what to say and wanting to be amiable. Ben took it for praise and went on.

"I'm working on a novel nights. It's a swell novel. This winter I might go to New York and find a publisher."

"A swell novel." Even the idiom was Hemingway's.

Ollie liked Ben, and, in ways, he envied his focus, wishing he himself knew what he was going to do after college (even his dad was inquiring how a history major with a minor in Latin lit might play in a Depression job market), so he put this down as a phase Sweet was going through.

■ 3 ■

While he was still an undergraduate at Notre Dame, Cromwell had won an AAU light-heavyweight championship and two Chicago Golden Glove titles and had begun campaigning as a heavyweight, filling out not with flesh but with muscle and bone. He'd even made the cover of the newly issued *Life* magazine with two other Americans who came out of the Olympic trials: a blonde girl swimmer and a Negro track star, Owens. His one regret: having broken a right hand on the hard head of a wonderful Senegalese light-heavyweight fighter in the quarter finals of the 1936 Olympics in Berlin and missing out on a medal in the semis, where even the losers were assured of a Bronze. His dad sailed over on the *Normandie* and was there for the final week of the competition and two of Ollie's bouts, a knockout win and then the fracture that left him fighting one-handed for half the fight and narrowly losing on points.

"Don't ever again listen to my tales of Rockne and the Gipper," Mr. Cromwell said over their final dinner together at a rollicking *brauhaus* on the Ku Damm. "I never saw a guttier performance, Jim. I was proud of you, proud as I've ever been in my life."

"Thanks, but a medal would have been nice."

"The deuce with the medal. Everyone in the arena was on his feet yelling for you at the end. And even one-handed, you darn near beat that fellow. Sometimes, the cheers are better than gold."

His father could be starchy, but now, as he reached over and patted his son's broken hand, a discernible tear was working its way slowly down the older man's cheek. Mr. Cromwell tried to get out the word "Congratulations . . . ," but got only halfway through it before tugging out a handkerchief, and he contented himself with another wordless pat on the boy's hand.

"I know, Dad," the son said softly, "I know."

Ollie's hand was in a cast, but he and his father put away the bratwurst and the beers with the best of them, even joined in the drinking songs, especially that one that went "Du, du. . . ." This although Cromwell senior was a bourbon drinker who never sang, unless it was "Happy Birthday" at home or a Christmas carol at midnight Mass.

He didn't even try living Ollie's life for him anymore, which, for his dad, was something.

"I'd like to see you go to law school after South Bend. You've got the grades. But that's your call, Jim. I badgered you into football, and it didn't work out very well. So you'll get no pressure on law school. Have you thought what else you might do?"

Ollie had expected the question—assumed it was coming sooner or later—and he had thought about it for a long time now, back to Regis High, where the Jesuits started him off right away in freshman Latin on Julius Caesar's *Gallic War*. They followed up with other tales, some in Latin, others in English, of Rome's famed Tenth Legion, of their epic fights against Gauls and Belgians, and especially of Vercingetorix, noblest of the barbarians and a favorite of young Cromwell. It was Vercingetorix who got the boy to ponder soldiering, who set him on a path to the boot camps where soldiers were made. What the "noblest of barbarians" didn't do, a close perusal in history class of *Lee's Lieutenants* did. And when he began Greek, Ollie realized that he preferred the Spartans, rude fellows who were forever waging war, to the Athenians, philosophers and aesthetes.

"Yessir," Ollie said now in the smoky Berlin dive; he had been thinking ahead. "Not many jobs out there waiting, not in hard times. I thought instead of three years at law school, I might go in the service for three or four years. No war on right now that involves us, and I can just wait out the Depression. Then try whatever comes along with my newfound maturity and store of globe-trotting adventures." All this offhandedly, poking fun at himself.

Mr. Cromwell had never been in the service, and Ollie had the impression his father disapproved of the military, so he was diffident, coolly choosing his words, careful not to mention boyhood dreams of soldiering. As we get older, some dreams are better kept quiet about.

His father laughed at his self-mockery. "I've read the Army pays privates twenty-one dollars a month and all the potatoes you can peel."

"I've heard that, too. Thought I might try the Marine Corps. I joined the college NROTC to mess around in boats, and they've got a new officers' candidate program for the Marines. I could get myself a reserve second lieutenant's commission."

They both then, in the glow of the beer and his dad's warmth, drank to that. "To the United States Marine Corps and all those who serve . . ."

Vercingetorix, the young man was convinced, would have been a Marine. But that was something else he didn't tell his dad.

Almost as good as that last night together, he and his dad over beers in a Kraut bar, was a staticky overseas phone call from the seedy South Bend hotel where his boxing coach had a room.

"Syd Ketchel here, kid. The morning papers got your picture. Page one in the *Tribune*. Arch Ward wrote the story. They said you did great. Damned shame about the hand. That other boy must of had some hard head to take your right and not go down. Wish I could of been there to see it. If you run across that Hitler bum at the parade, tell him the Michigan Assassin's cousin Sydney says hello."

"I will, Syd."

Now that it was all over, the pressure off, Ollie realized how much he'd enjoyed the Games. Even the repetitive *Sieg Heils* and all those Germans forever jumping up to toss off that stiff-armed salute. But how could he not enjoy the cheers? He'd been in Europe before with his parents, but that was London and then Paris, and he was only a kid. He'd never seen Germany before, had never been abroad on his own, had met and gotten to know some fine people, including one girl, a real honey, an American swimmer from Coral Gables whom he thought he'd like to see again; they both promised to write. She wasn't the girl he'd been with on the cover of *Life* but was really nice. So was Jesse, who won all those track medals. He'd actually seen Hitler once, at a distance, and he resolved to read the papers more closely when he got home to try to figure out what *der führer* was up to.

The Germans were interesting people, some of them awfully good-looking, but Ollie wasn't quite sure of them. Not sure either of a country that had so many uniformed soldiers around without being at war.

▪ 4 ▪

"NO, HE'S NOT A SAILOR," SAID BULL HALSEY. "GOD SAVE US, HE'S A
MARINE."

It was Arch Ward's story of Cromwell's gallant, though losing, Olympic
fight, syndicated nationally, that caught the eye of Captain William ("Bull")
Halsey and that he recalled later when he heard that James T. Cromwell
had chosen the Marine Corps over the Navy after graduation from Notre
Dame with an NROTC commission.

"We don't have a heavyweight in the Pacific Fleet who can stand up
to Bruiser Wells," a glum Halsey reminded the officers' mess.

"Nossir, we don't."

"I'm fed up with losing to the Army."

"Yessir, we all are, sir."

"We need a heavyweight who's a hitter."

"Yessir."

Other naval officers, senior to Halsey and not quite as measured in their
response, went further.

"The Army's got Bruiser Wells. Wells *kills* people in the ring! Who
have we got who kills people? Name one. Just name me one!"

"Yessir, you're right, sir."

"Our boxers don't *kill* anyone! It's embarrassing!"

It may be difficult to appreciate how seriously American officers, Army
and Navy, along with the Marine Corps and the Army Air Corps, took
intramural sports during the 1920s and '30s. There was no real war on, and
they needed something to entertain the troops, maintain morale, and satisfy
the egos of the brass. Boxing—prizefighting—was the sport of choice.
Football cost too much for equipment and big squads, baseball was boring,
and track meets too complicated; no one played basketball except in Indiana
or industrial leagues with teams like Phillips 66. Polo was British and elitist.

"Boxing, that's the sport!"

Man on man, plenty of action, a winner and a loser. And what did it
cost for a pair of gloves, a mouthpiece, and an athletic supporter and cup?

Plus—and this was always a bonus—fighting men liked a blood sport, wanted one; maybe *needed* a blood sport.

Wherever there was an Army base, a naval station, a military airfield, a Marine garrison, there sprang up a boxing team. The best action was in the Pacific. More men in uniform, better weather, lots of big Army and Navy bases, far from Washington and congressional snoops. In the Pacific you found ambitious, aggressive officers anxious to make a reputation. In peacetime, how did you flaunt your leadership skills and motivational strengths? Well, you put together a successful boxing team.

Promising recruits were sought out.

Halsey, not yet an admiral but a very senior captain who had commanded famous ships such as the cruiser *Juneau* before learning to fly and transferring to aircraft carriers, was an intelligent man who thought things through.

"Look, the Army has an advantage going in. They're based onshore. They can do roadwork. They have the space to build and maintain large gyms. Sailors are cooped up on ships. And not every one of them an aircraft carrier. How does a promising welterweight do roadwork on a destroyer? Never mind a damned submarine!"

The admirals heard Halsey's screed.

"What do we do, Bull? It's one thing to bitch and moan. And let Bruiser Wells beat the crap out of our boys year after year. But what in hell can we *do* about it?"

"Admiral, you may object, sir, but I'd like you to ponder on it. Suppose we stopped training sailors to go up against Bruiser?"

"To do what?

"Recruit a few people with a nasty frame of mind, ill-tempered men who train on land, run up and down hills, and get into fights all the time, anyway. Because it's in their naturally sour disposition to do so."

"Yes?"

"Gentlemen, I suggest the Pacific Fleet recruit a few Marines."

Halsey wasn't yet thinking solely of Ollie Cromwell when he suggested this. But what he said was: "Get us a Marine who's as good as Bruiser Wells. And if Bruiser beats him, then we get the hell out of the prizefighting business and start playing the Army in contract bridge."

The admirals looked at each other.

"All right, Halsey. Then do it! Find us someone to beat Bruiser Wells."

"I may need SecNav to pull it off."

The admirals goggled. SecNav? The secretary of the Navy? You had to take your hat off to Bull Halsey, not yet promoted to admiral.

"He's got balls."

He soon, some months on, also had Oliver Cromwell.

When Ollie's name first arose at those exalted levels, a skeptical Navy secretary asked Halsey just who he was.

"Sir, he was AAU champion and fought in the Berlin Olympics as a light-heavy."

"Win the Gold? I don't recall it."

"Didn't even win Bronze. Broke his hand on a Senegalese head and fought a brilliant bout one-handed. You'll like this boy."

"Oh?"

"Yes, he takes considerable killing."

"A good sailor, then."

The response, for a Navy man as loyal as Bull Halsey, was painful.

"No, Mr. Secretary, God save us.

"He's a Marine."

▪ 5 ▪

If you've never seen San Diego with the fleet in, then you've seen just another postcard of another pretty California coastal town; you haven't really seen Dago.

And when Second Lieutenant James T. Cromwell, U.S. Marine Corps, arrived at San Diego early in Christmas week of 1937, the fleet was definitely in. All the big battlewagons bristling with sixteen-inch guns and those erector-set towers, and the cruisers, the heavies with their eight-inch guns, the light cruisers built for speed, with observation seaplanes perched cocky on their fantails. There were the slim, gray, tigerish destroyers, and low, lurking, slightly ominous subs, even the new aircraft carriers, the *Lexington* and *Saratoga,* moored out there at anchor in midstream or lying inshore at the piers, quays, and docks lining both banks of the vast bay. On the water the patrol boats and launches busily scuttled about like waterbugs, shiny blue biplanes droning overhead, with Coronado Island there in all its glory with the big wooden turn-of-the-century resort hotel, a sometime movie set, its towers and cupolas and shaded porches gracing the beach, and the big North Island Naval Station, all business with its derricks and hoists and steam engines and machine shops bustling and cranking and grinding away. And, to top it off properly for Ollie, the pleasantly haciendalike barracks and administrative buildings and well-watered green parade grounds of the Marine Corps base facing the ocean, facing out toward Japan and China and the islands, with eight thousand miles of Pacific Ocean just beyond the palm trees and shelving golden beaches and the lazy surf sliding up and slipping back down the sand.

That was San Diego with the fleet in, which Lieutenant Cromwell was seeing for the first time. And falling in love with, without even realizing that he was doing so. It was something to see: Scapa Flow with sunshine; the Bay of Naples with Capri thrown in; San Francisco Bay before they built the Bay bridge. And with the finest weather in the world, barring a morning sea mist. Even now, in the first week of winter, it was sunny shirtsleeve weather, and, for the girls, fresh silk and cotton dresses. Summer afternoons the temperature might top seventy-five; nights it fell to sixty-five, and it almost never rained. Go a few miles inland in summer, of course, and a baking heat shimmered off the parched hills. But along the waterfront and the beach, and on the bay, with the fleet in—ah, there was a sight. And not too many miles to the east, brown coastal mountains rising dramatically above the emperor palms, the higher peaks already bright with snow.

It was at Marine headquarters that Dago really began for Ollie.

"Second Lieutenant James T. Cromwell reporting, sir."

"James Cromwell? Thought your name was Oliver. Aren't you the boxer?"

"In college, sir, I boxed a little. Oliver's a nickname."

Ollie wasn't being modest: he was a newly minted second lieutenant in the U.S. Marine Corps, and this was the adjutant, a captain, asking the questions, and he wanted to be precise in his answers.

He handed over his orders from the Basic School at Quantico—orders that had not made the young man very happy.

The captain, who shuffled papers and second lieutenants with equivalent disdain, seemed to take pleasure in Ollie's drab assignment.

"The cruiser *Juneau,* San Diego Naval Station, Marine detachment shipboard."

Cruisers and up, through battleships and carriers, rated a Marine officer and a small seagoing detachment.

The captain enjoyed the look on Ollie's face.

"That's right, young man," the adjutant sarcastically agreed, though Ollie hadn't said a word. "Seagoing bellhop. The nearest thing the Marine Corps has to a Black Hole of Calcutta, commanding the Marine guard aboard an old cruiser that once sailed under a skipper named Bull Halsey. My, my, on some few of us, good fortune casts its glow."

Cromwell had a temper but cut off a retort, not wanting to provide amusement to this sour, desk-bound cynic. Had men like this plagued Caesar in his day?

"Thank you, sir. I've heard good things about Captain Halsey, and they tell me the *Juneau*'s a fine ship."

He was rewarded. The adjutant's face fell.

"Oh?"

Truth was, Cromwell had never heard of Halsey, and as far as he knew, Juneau was the capital of Alaska. Or was that Nome?

And here he was in California, reporting in to superiors whose sole interest in him was boxing.

Only San Diego didn't disappoint. To an Easterner, the place was gorgeous.

The Marine Corps young Cromwell had joined was in 1937 quite small, only seventeen or eighteen-thousand officers, NCOs, and enlisted men, and still very much a Corps remembering yesterday rather than looking ahead to tomorrow. The men of the 5th and 6th Marines who fought the Germans at Belleau Wood and Soissons and Château-Thierry, earning from the enemy the epithet of Devil Dogs, were quite senior by now, officers and NCOs both, many retired if not dead, and the barracks and bar talk tended to be less of France and the Hun, and more of smaller wars in the Caribbean and Central America during the twenties and into the thirties. Those were the days of the Banana Wars, of martial reputations earned by men like Evans Carlson and Red Mike Edson and Chesty Puller, of fetid jungles and ferocious firefights with *bandidos,* of adversaries such as the Caco leader Charlemagne in Dominica and the Nicaraguan rebel Sandino, of hard campaigning in Haiti, and of the infamous Benoit Batraville, whom Colonel Joseph H. Pendleton, Uncle Joe to his Marines, hunted down and killed.

It was Batraville, men recalled with a perverse relish, who had the nasty habit of roasting and then eating the hearts and livers of dead Marines.

"The Banana Wars weren't always that lively, Cromwell, you understand," an aging major might remark ruefully at the bar of the officers' club, "but the slack times were brief and fleeting."

And, according to the accounts, might be relieved by *cigarros* and rum, hunting wild boar, diving for shellfish amid the barracuda and the big reef sharks, trapping alligators, and infiltrating the camps of the *bandidos* in sombreros, mufti, and greasepaint and shooting it out with the occasional *pistolero.*

"As well as, if you were so inclined, Lieutenant, learning Spanish with the encouragement of a *señorita bonita, sabe?*"

Moments like this, stories like those, caused Ollie to feel pity for men studying torts and contracts in law school and confirmed him in the belief that at age twenty-one, soon to be twenty-two, he'd chosen absolutely the right career. Let Ben Sweet and Hemingway scribble their adventure stories; Ollie would be living one.

■

He arrived at San Diego just as Bull Halsey was recommended for admiral commanding a carrier task force. But never daunted, the Navy had its procedures, and Halsey's handpicked Marine boxer was efficiently passed along to yet another impressive and high-ranked naval officer.

"I am Captain Raymond Spruance. Are you the prizefighter?"

"Second Lieutenant James Cromwell, sir, United States Marine Corps."

Spruance gave him a dour look.

"Wasn't what I asked, mister."

Ollie's self-assurance started to ooze away. It wouldn't do to launch his career nitpicking a Navy four-striper.

"Yessir, I'm the fighter."

Spruance, a fiery sort who exploded easily but didn't nurse grudges, stuck out a hand.

"Good to have you here, Cromwell. We need a heavyweight."

"Thank you, sir."

Though Ollie had no way of knowing it when he reported to San Diego, he was joining the great captains, the men who would command the American fleet and win the Pacific war against the Japanese: Spruance himself, Fletcher, Halsey, Nimitz. These and a handful of others would become legends in their time, much as Drake and Frobisher and Hawkins did centuries before against the Spaniards; the buccaneer captains who sank the Armada and saved England. Although, at the moment, Ray Spruance had more-pressing issues than war on his mind.

"The Army's got a hell of a boy, Cromwell. Name of Wells. Bruiser Wells. You ever see him fight, mister?"

"Nossir. He wasn't on the Olympic team, was he?" he inquired innocently.

That was wiseass stuff, and Ollie knew it was. But, hell, Spruance asked for it.

"Touché! They said you were a corker. Kicked you out of Notre Dame, did they?"

"Nossir, just off the football and basketball teams. I graduated with my class."

"By damn! Cromwell. What do they call you, 'Jim'?"

"Nossir, 'Ollie.' As in 'Oliver Cromwell.' "

Captain Spruance seemed to like that. Among the brass he had the reputation of an intellectual and he decided to test this Cromwell.

"The boy that chopped off King Henry's head and started the Protestant Reformation, right?"

"King Charles, sir. Charles the First. And the Reformation had been on for some time when Cromwell and his Roundheads came along to fight the Royalists. But they certainly did a job on the Catholics—priests and nuns especially—and sending young Irish girls to the Barbadoes to be married off to planters."

Sometimes, though he strove against it, the Roman Catholic in Ollie came out. A touch of the Jesuit pedant as well.

"Close enough, mister," said Spruance huffily. Being a Protestant, he didn't think they needed an entire rundown on the English Civil War. "Now tell me about the Berlin Olympics. You get to meet Hitler?"

"Well, sir," Ollie lied, "there were certain opportunities. Quite unexpected. In the second week of the Games . . ."

Ollie glibly conjured up a couple of intimate cocktail-party, conversations, one visit to Berchtesgaden, and a film screening hosted by Goebbels at which Leni Riefenstahl . . .

Spruance enjoyed the stories, didn't believe them, and concluded that when he'd been an ensign, equivalent to this Cromwell's rank now, he would not have been capable of such imaginative fiction. Maybe the young officers they were turning out now were smarter than they were.

I hope he can fight, Spruance told himself. He meant against the U.S. Army's Bruiser Wells, of course. At least, Ray Spruance thought that's what he meant.

Juneau was in dry dock, so they billeted Ollie ashore in the spartan bachelor officers' quarters, the BOQ of Marine Barracks, San Diego. But, aware of his youth and potential as a boxer, they didn't leave him on his own.

"Come on, Cromwell, you got to see this town, see the girls. Prettiest stuff you've ever seen, the town *and* the ladies."

His guide to San Diego was a regular Marine, a commissioned warrant officer named Homer ("Gunny") Arzt, a salty guerrilla fighter with fifteen years in the Corps and a reputation for ferocity earned mostly in the Banana Wars. Despite his wild ways Arzt was an old-school Marine, very spit and polish, uniforms tailored and crisply pressed, knife's-edge pleats, brightwork gleaming, hair cropped and skin tanned and taut, even at a certain age and despite long nights. Halsey, or someone, maybe Spruance, wanted an impressionable young man like Cromwell to have a keeper, and Gunny Arzt was it.

"Myself," said Arzt (who mispronounced his own name as "Arts"), "I would of assigned you to some nice polite and gentlemanly naval officer instead of a crude fellow like me. But I'm it, and you're stuck with me."

Cromwell, who liked or disliked most people on first impressions, was delighted.

"Chief, I'm in your very good hands."

"That's well, mister, since you don't have anything to say about it anyway."

It turned out neither Halsey *nor* Spruance came up with the idea of a baby-sitter for their prize heavyweight, but Commander Kronstadt, who along with additional duties, such as running the brig, was athletic director of the North Island Naval Station.

"You meet Kronstadt yet?" Arzt inquired.

"Nossir, not yet. I think Kronstadt was where German sailors mutinied in 1918."

"Knowing Kronstadt, I ain't surprised," said Arzt. "He's a Kraut, of course. Probably on the kaiser's side in the Great War. But he's a sports nut, which makes him okay with the brass. He runs the local boxing tournament, and he captains the Navy boxing team at the All-Pacifics. They hold those every winter at Pearl Harbor, and they're sort of like the Olympics except bigger. At least to the brass. When you were over there in old Berlin, you meet Hitler?"

Everyone wanted to know about Hitler, but to Homer Arzt, because he was a Marine and an old-timer, Ollie told the truth. "Saw him during the parade around the stadium, up there in the royal box from a distance, is all."

Beyond that, and boxing, Gunny didn't pry. But he was fascinated by the boxing. Ollie told him about the spare beginnings, at Regis High.

"Never heard of the place," admitted the warrant officer, "but then, I been sheltered."

"It's a wonderful school really, small and endowed anonymously some years ago by a rich woman who admired Jesuits. Only four hundred boys, and all of us there on scholarship. All you paid for was the books. Four mandatory years of Latin, three of Greek, and no chemistry or physics. They tolerate math, but barely. Regis is where I first read about Caesar's wars and the fights they had with Vercingetorix."

"Never heard of the gent," Arzt admitted. "He a Bolshie, was he?"

"I don't think so. But he gave the Tenth Legion plenty of grief up there on the Rhine."

He completed his rundown on Regis High.

"Lots of reading and writing, and they're big on debating. About a thousand boys take the competitive written exam each spring, the top students from Catholic schools all over New York and nearby Connecticut and New Jersey, and only one hundred and fifty are admitted. And of those, seventy-five boys will flunk out before graduation."

"Sounds like the Marine Corps," Arzt said, impressed.

"It is."

"And they taught you to box."

"Coach Don Kennedy. He's a great man. He got me started. But it was really Syd Ketchel who . . ."

CWO Arzt, who knew about the Michigan Assassin, was impressed all over again.

"By the Christ! You gotta meet Carlson. Anyone who's seen Hitler and is a pal of the Ketchel family he's gonna like, mister. And if he don't, I'll convince him of error."

"Who's Carlson?"

"Didn't them Jesuits and Regents High tell you? . . ."

"Regis, named after Saint John Francis Regis."

". . . Well, damn their eyes, they didn't teach you much if you never heard of Evans Fordyce Carlson, who's maybe the best Marine officer we got and—if he don't get killed—is bound to be commandant. He's my age or a year older and just a major. But he's got the president's ear, or claims he does. And I never yet knew Carlson to lie about important matters."

"What president's ear?"

"Oh, hell, I dunno, right or left. Who you think I'm talking about? President FDR Goddamn Roosevelt hisself. Carlson's got him sold on the notion there just might be new ways to fight wars invented since the hollow square and the Gatling gun."

"And I'm going to meet him?"

"Well, not right away. Soon as he leaves Washington, he's off to China to spend a year or so living in the hills with the Communists that are fighting both Chiang Kai-shek *and* the Japs. Carlson's got an idea that when it comes to fighting, we might learn something from these people. Even if they are Reds and don't believe in God. So the Marine Corps, which on rare occasions does something smart, gave him the okay to go over there in civvies and hang out taking notes on new and imaginative ways to kill people." Then Arzt paused. "Keep this to yourself, mister, since I don't want people to know what Carlson's up to and get him in trouble or his travel plans canceled."

The Gunny had a car, a sun-faded Studebaker with bald tires and a star crack in the windshield, and he and Cromwell drove from the Marine barracks into town and down to the waterfront.

"You like fish?"

"Sure," Ollie said, thinking filet of sole or maybe a nice trout.

"There's a Jap joint here on the water with a view of the harbor and the ships coming by where we can get raw octopus. Lace it with enough Tabasco sauce and wash it down with beer, it's a hell of a dish. If you can keep it down."

"Sounds wonderful, Chief," Ollie said uneasily.

"Call me Gunny."

"Yessir."

Like most young lieutenants, Ollie wasn't all that comfortable with commissioned (or even uncommissioned) warrant officers. Neither fish nor fowl, it seemed. Not quite an officer, but more senior than other senior NCOs. Over the meal Cromwell got up the spunk to ask. Arzt didn't seem offended by his curiosity.

"Don't let it bother you, mister. Master and gunnery sergeants, a sergeant major even, great men all, are also confused by the status of a warrant officer. Far as I can see, becoming a commissioned warrant officer means a few more bucks in the paycheck, enlisted men salute you, and you get to drink at the officers' club. Other than that, the rank ain't worth a bucket of warm piss."

After dinner they visited several waterfront bars, and Arzt attempted to pick up two girls who said they taught school at Point Loma. They let the Marines buy them a Tom Collins, but when Arzt told them he had a Studebaker outside and why didn't they drive up the coast to a beach he knew that was pretty nice this time of night, the schoolteachers took off.

"Back where I come from in Yakima, Washington, an invitation like that brings the schoolteachers running. But no one hits a thousand," Arzt said complacently, "not even this kid DiMaggio the Yankees brung up."

So instead of going on a double date on the beach with schoolteachers, Arzt made up for it by buying a fresh round and telling Ollie more than he really wanted to know about Major Carlson:

"At the tender age of sixteen, the son of a Congregationalist minister in upstate New York, Evans Carlson joined the goddamned army, served in the Philippines and Hawaii, fought under Pershing in the Mexican Punitive Expedition, served in France, got wounded, was commissioned second lieutenant, and then in December of '17 was made a captain of artillery. After the war Captain Carlson come to his senses and quit the army, enlisted in the Marines as a private. Imagine that, Mr. Cromwell: from captain down to private, and work your way back up! That's what hatchet-faced, Bible-pounding Evans Carlson did and never looked back, being commissioned second lieutenant all over again as a Marine in '19 and '23. Served in the Pacific Fleet, learned to fly at Pensacola but washed out. They liked him fine except he kept wrecking airplanes. He was great in the air, but landing and taking off complicated matters. Went Chinaside for two years at Shanghai and then it was off to Nicaragua as an officer of their Guardia Nacional, where he earned his first Navy Cross leading ten Marines against one hundred bandits. Ended up as the chief of police of Managua. Kill a bad guy soon as look at him. Have another drink, son?"

"Yes, I will, Gunny."

Commander Kronstadt, when Ollie met him, was something else again: guttural, Teutonic, overbearing, everybody's favorite stereotype of a promising candidate for the German general staff. Inevitably, he'd picked up a nickname: the Kaiser.

"You staying in shape, Cromwell? You working out? I don't see you around the gym. You doing the roadworks? What's your weight?"

"I've been getting to know the Marine detachment and visiting the shipyard. The *Juneau*'s still in dry dock."

"I'm talking about the important matters, Cromwell. You're here to box. Not to hanging around drydocks."

"Yessir."

The Navy commander seemed to resent any number of things about this brand-new second lieutenant who spoke, airily, of Stanley Ketchel, had been on the Olympic team, and came from New York money, the *right* side of the tracks; who . . . well, you get the idea.

Ollie didn't take offense. Rank had its privileges, and Kronstadt had a little rank. Besides, some of the Kronstadt harassment made sense. Ollie ought to be working out, sparring, pounding the heavy bag, doing roadwork, and not hitting the waterfront joints with Warrant Officer Arzt quite every night. What he did resent was the Kaiser's assumption that Cromwell was a prizefighter, period. That his Marine duties, the shipboard Marine detachment, were somehow derisory, that even the *Juneau* itself (about to emerge from dry dock), a fabled warship with an honorable history, didn't count. Was that also the attitude of those senior to Kronstadt, officers like Spruance and even Halsey? Did the captains and admirals of the Pacific Fleet view life as a prize ring where, if you beat an Army pug named Wells, all would be right with the world?

He tried Arzt on it.

"Is that how they think, Gunny? A big war in China, civil war in Spain,

Hitler makes noises about Austria, Mussolini invades Ethiopia, and our brass talks boxing. I know I sound stupid, a kid lieutenant just out of college, but is everyone *that* nearsighted?"

"No, you ain't stupid. You've traveled the wide world; you've seen Hitler; you've had beers in Berlin and boxed fellows from Senegal. You've got advantages, Ollie, but, yessir, right now if you're a rising officer in the Pacific Fleet, it's a hell of a lot more important to kayo Bruiser Wells than to save Ethiopia. And that's why Evans Carlson, who is only a major, is heading for China instead of wasting time with Kronstadt the boxing expert."

The *Juneau* finally came out of dry dock, but before Cromwell could move his gear aboard from the BOQ, he was summarily pulled from the Marine detachment.

"San Diego Fleet Finals are next month, mister," Commander Kronstadt informed him.

Ollie groused to the adjutant at Marine barracks, only to be told, "A Navy matter, Lieutenant. We can't interfere."

"But I'm not in the Navy."

"You are now, mister."

He went back to the gym, to the ring, to roadwork along the beach, but took time out to meet a girl, who picked him up at the BOQ in a nice Olds. The mere fact of which inspired Kronstadt to accuse Cromwell of shirking. But despite the Olds, and the girl, his workouts were sufficient for Ollie to win the heavyweight title of San Diego, going undefeated, pretty much untested in three bouts leading up to the championship, and then knocking out a big Swede of a gunner's mate in the first round.

Bull Halsey, watching from a good seat, enjoyed the show—so much so that he went backstage afterwards, visiting a locker room packed with enthusiastic Navy and Marine Corps brass shaking hands and yelling at each other and slapping backs. Dewey at Manila wasn't this worked up, nor Farragut at Mobile Bay. Kronstadt, whose star athlete had just impressed the brass, led the cheering. The only man in the room who wasn't celebrating was the big Swede. He just sat there on a rubbing table, shoulders hunched, swathed in towels, with fresh stitches in one eyebrow and his trainer with an arm slung around his shoulders and talking low. He was consoling his boy but with his eyes enviously on the winner's circle, on Cromwell's side of the room.

It was different there: the crowd around Ollie, the rankers and back-slappers, men who believed success rubs off on you. Ollie, still in his trunks but having had a navy blue sweater that said "Navy" tugged over his head, also sat on a rubbing table. That was the only similarity to the Swede.

"Nice work, son," Bull Halsey said. "You're a hitter."

"Thank you, sir."

Men with braid on their sleeves and shoulders fell back to let Bull Halsey through, to let him talk privately to the fighter. Halsey wouldn't be promoted to admiral for a few weeks yet, but everyone knew he'd been selected, knew he was one of the Navy's comers.

"I've been following you since Arch Ward wrote that piece from Berlin. What I can't understand, how the Notre Dame football team didn't get you first. You look like you'd have made a good end."

"I went out but didn't make the team, Captain. When I was cut, our boxing coach, Mr. Ketchel, thought I might make a fighter."

There was no point rehashing Jack Ballard with Halsey. But since Halsey had brought it up, Ollie took advantage of the opening.

"I've been assigned to the Marine detachment on your old ship, sir. The *Juneau.*"

"Oh, yes. Good ship, fine ship."

"But I was pulled off to box in the San Diego Finals. I'd like to get back to the *Juneau,* Captain. To the Marine detachment and start learning my trade, sir."

Halsey's flat mouth went tight.

"The Pacific Fleet Finals are coming up. You'll rejoin the ship eventually, I'd expect."

He saw something in Cromwell's face.

"You probably think there're more important things for a young officer to be doing than boxing, right?"

"Well, yessir."

Halsey nodded.

"And you're right. Except that when you're trying to get ready for war, slugging it out man to man isn't a bad way to go about it. Even we old farts know about the Nazis and the Empire of Japan and Stalin's commissars. But they're not in the ring with us. Not yet. Right now there isn't any enemy out there more important than Bruiser Wells. You beat Bruiser for us, and we'll be one step closer to a bout with Hitler. Or Mussolini or the Japanese. After Wells, we can step up in class. Except we've got to win that first bout before moving on. I don't like to see the United States Navy on a losing streak. Which is what we're having with Bruiser Wells and the Army. I don't like losing streaks; they carry over. Get me, mister?"

There was an avuncular twinkle in Halsey's blue eyes, but Ollie didn't let it fool him. He knew his pitch had just been turned down. Cold.

"Yessir, I get you, sir."

"Good. Now let's win another one at Pearl. You do that, and the U.S. Army, and Mr. Wells, will be next on the card."

"Yessir."

Gunny Arzt, who shunned the cheering section locker-room scene, was waiting outside with the Studebaker.

"He's right, y'know," Arzt said, driving home after Ollie told him about Halsey.

"Yeah, but . . ."

"In this business you can order people around, Ollie, and no one's offended by it. But don't preach at 'em. People resent holiness."

▪ 6 ▪

In March of 1938 Austria caved in to the Nazis and "agreed" to be occupied. Its chancellor, Schuschnigg, himself an authoritarian hardly blameless for the crisis, but a courageous veteran and a pious Catholic and an intellectual, was soon arrested and confined to a dungeon where, with the same towel he used for bathing, he was set to swabbing clean the toilets of his German warders. A few months later, Germany declared it could no longer sit back and watch its German *volk* in the Czech Sudetenland being tormented, even killed by the Czechoslovaks. German men castrated? Women raped? One concocted tale followed another, had Berliners in a righteous frenzy, Londoners digging trenches in Hyde Park, and the French considering mobilization, the whole leading to appeasement at Munich.

Which didn't mean the U.S. Navy, our most powerful military arm, was sitting idle. Hardly that.

They flew Cromwell and his keeper, Comissioned Warrant Officer Gunny Arzt, to Honolulu for the Pacific Fleet Boxing Finals. Commander Kronstadt, at his most bumptious, shared the plane.

"You don't know how fortunate you are, Cromwell. Never before are they flying the San Diego boxers to Pearl. Always by ship we go. By ship, you lose three days' training, four days even. The legs, they going."

"That's awful, the legs going," Arzt remarked pleasantly. "Who was it, Ollie, that lost a war when his horse went?"

"King Richard, 'My kingdom for a horse.' Can't remember if it was Richard the Second or Richard the Third, but it was one of the Richards."

"When the legs going," continued the humorless Kronstadt, "a boxer got nothing. Not even a puncher. Without good legs under him, no power. No knockouts. Remember that, Cromwell, and don't cheating on the roadwork, yes?"

"Yessir."

"You can be be sure Bruiser Wells, he don't cheating on the roadwork."

When Kronstadt went aft to the lavatory, Gunny just shook his head.

"I thought the Kaiser was going to have you running laps up and down the aisle."

Bruiser Wells wasn't even going to be in Hawaii, and Ollie was already fed up with him. To the Navy, Bruiser wasn't just worse than Hitler, he was bigger. Cromwell was anxious to get these Pacific Finals out of the way so he and Wells could finally meet. This was dangerous thinking. Syd Ketchel warned against it: looking ahead to a future bout instead of the guy you're fighting tonight. Cromwell could still hear the voice, the words.

"That's how guys get taken, Ollie. Concentrate on the boy in the opposite corner. He's the one can hurt you. Not the fellow you're meeting next month. With heavyweights, it takes only one punch."

So Ollie ran miles on the beach and jumped rope and hit the light and heavy bags and sparred. He liked the sparring best, in there against another fighter, and not just whacking away at bags or at those oversized catcher's mitts Kronstadt donned to catch the punches.

They put the boxing team up in barracks at Pearl Harbor except for Cromwell, who was the only officer on the team. He and Commissioned Warrant Officer Homer Arzt and Commander Kronstadt had rooms in bachelor officers' quarters. The enlisted boxers didn't seem to resent this since it was the way of the Navy, and besides, they all knew Ollie was the best fighter on the squad.

"You ever meet Heil Hitler over there, Lieutenant?" a welterweight asked.

When they weren't working in the gym or running, the Navy laid on lunches at the Outrigger Canoe Club at Waikiki, sightseeing tours, boat rides, and pretty girls draping the fighters in leis. Gunny Arzt, who'd been stationed on Oahu at the barracks of Pearl Harbor, knew a few joints. In San Diego, the two had done considerable bouncing, so much so that Cromwell asked, "Should we really get drunk every night, Gunny?"

And Arzt, just as solemn, said, "Yeah, I think so." Now, with Bruiser Wells looming, it was different.

"Since you're in training, Ollie, I'll have a drink for both of us."

Kronstadt tried to keep track, but without a leash the two Marine officers were too much for him. They were less successful in eluding the brass, all of whom wanted to meet their "tiger," the Marine lieutenant who'd fought in Berlin and was one day going to handle Bruiser Wells and put the Army in its damned place.

Then, over breakfast on the patio of the Royal Hawaiian Hotel, while

Arzt's eyes followed the women and Ollie read the morning paper, a story bylined by Ben Sweet jumped out at him.

"Hey, Gunny, I know this guy. We were at Notre Dame together. Look at this—a story on the front page about the war from Spain, written by Ben."

"My, my, a pal of yours a war correspondent."

Gunny wasn't as excited as Ollie, but then he'd never knocked Sweet down in a campus fight, had he?

"Boy, that's something. He wanted to become a newspaperman, and by God, here's Ben in Madrid covering the war. With the *Chicago Tribune* syndicating his stuff all over the country."

"Oh, I dunno, Ollie. A fellow I knew from the 6th Marines who was in France in 1918 said the war correspondents never went near the front. That they all interviewed one another at the Crillon Bar or some such tony joint and put it in the paper the next day. The bloodthirstiest yarns ever, and all they were was a lot of drunks talking saloon talk."

Cromwell laughed.

"I don't think Ben Sweet'd do that. He was forever talking about wanting to be the new Hemingway, to cover wars and write books about them."

Gunny Arzt nodded. He knew what was biting Cromwell. This college boy pal of his was living through an actual war over there in old Spain, and Ollie was in Hawaii getting ready for a half-assed boxing tournament that didn't matter to anyone but Navy brass.

Ben's dispatch was good—far sleeker, slicker too, than he would have expected. And it was very first person: Sweet there in the trenches, Sweet going over the top, Sweet helping get the wounded back into friendly lines, Sweet's hotel being shelled, Sweet under fire. Much of its style, the brief, punchy sentences, was lifted from Hemingway, of course. Ben's hero worship wasn't subtle; he was doing everything Hemingway did except driving an ambulance on the Italian front.

But the stuff was good, really good, wasn't it? That rankled Ollie, though he knew it shouldn't, realized he was jealous.

The Fleet Finals were a joke. One big able seaman off the battleship *Arizona* gave Ollie a tough first round, using his forty-pound weight advantage to muscle him around the ring, only to be stopped on cuts in the second when Cromwell found himself some punching room. The other bouts were no test. Ollie was heavyweight champion of the Pacific and Asiatic fleets.

As the brass celebrated, chanting Cromwell's name and uttering terrible threats to poor Wells, Ollie again marveled at their undergraduate enthusiasms: grown men, senior officers, in command of great warships and strategic bases, capering like sophomores at a pep rally.

Gunny Arzt scowled. "To hear them talk, it's hardly worth you even showing up for the bout. Bruiser don't stand a chance."

That week the Nazis issued their ultimatum to Czechoslovakia.

Ollie sailed out of San Diego aboard *Juneau* for the first time as CO of its Marine detachment. His duties were mostly handled by the platoon sergeant, a Marine ten years his senior, but one who didn't box. *Juneau,* a tanker, and three escorting destroyers were on a sort of goodwill tour of the western Pacific, with ports of call at Hong Kong, Singapore, Manila, and Batavia in the Netherlands Indies. Hitler rattled swords, Prague was calling up the reserves, the Germans moved up to the Czech frontier, and the American Navy went sightseeing. Liberties were pleasant, barring the occasional waterfront brawl or whorehouse nastiness that ship's officers, including Cromwell, had to square with local authorities. But at least they were at sea, sailing to foreign ports, mastering gun drills and calls to quarters. Still only playing at war, but better than lolling about Dago.

When they sailed into Pearl Harbor and Ollie saw his first American newspapers in weeks, Ben Sweet was still writing from Spain, despite, as an editor's sidebar indicated, "shrapnel wounds suffered by Mr. Sweet during the recent fighting on the Ebro."

The lucky stiff!

HiS RIB WAS BROKEN, MIGHT PUNCTURE A LUNG. NO GOOD FOR A
FIGHTER. OR ANYONE.

Neville Chamberlain, Daladier of France, Mussolini, and Hitler met at Munich in October of 1938 to carve up Czechoslovakia.

"Peace in our time," the British prime minister called it at the airfield on arriving back in England. Daladier, who feared he might be stoned by French antifascists, was instead cheered. Churchill, churlishly, called Munich "an unmitigated defeat" for England and France and their abandoned allies the Czechs, whose thirty-five regular army divisions and vaunted defensive positions in Sudeten Czechoslovakia had now been outflanked and rendered useless. (Commons hooted Winston down.)

Early in the new year, 1939, German foreign minister von Ribbentrop suggested to the Poles it might be helpful if the two countries met to talk about reconfiguring their borders to provide Germany with access to the Baltic port of Danzig.

Premier Josef Beck, who knew what happened to the Austrians and more recently the Czechs, was wary.

Through early '39 the Poles hung tough, turning the Germans toward the bizarre notion of cutting a deal with Stalin, acting before the Brits and French cut their deal. While in the Pacific, where the Japanese rattled sabers of their own, the American Navy scheduled the usual sea maneuvers and prepared to produce an all-Navy team capable of challenging the all-Army squad and its champion, heavyweight Bruiser Wells. Except that the Americans, Army and Navy both, were hung up on an even trickier business than Hitler and Stalin.

Should their respective boxing teams continue to include officers? Or should the squads be restricted to enlisted men? Since the Navy's top heavyweight was a Marine officer, this posed a problem. When Arzt, no longer a baby-sitter but by now a friend, asked how Ollie felt about that, he wasn't surprised by the answer.

"Doesn't bother me, Gunny. I see their point. Officers and enlisted men mixing it up in the ring? Surprised it hadn't long ago caused trouble."

"That ain't why the Army's pulling this, Ollie. They're protecting their boy Wells, knowing you're the only heavyweight the Navy's got that's any good."

"Oh, hell, what does it matter?"

Cromwell had been an officer for almost three years now and was starting to think of himself as a grown-up. More so than some of the officers he served under. As a result, some of the joy and sheer physical satisfaction had evaporated from boxing.

"Right now there's a kid with muscles at the Brooklyn Navy Yard or down in Norfolk who's coming along. Kronstadt or some smarter Kronstadt will hear about a new hitter somewhere and track him down. Bruiser isn't getting any younger, y'know. One day a big sailor or Marine'll catch up with him. And who knows if I could handle Wells if we *did* box?"

Though not yet articulating it very clearly, Ollie was ready to move on from prizefighting. To just plain fighting; wasn't that what being a Marine was all about, where the world was heading?

Arzt was still declaring loyally, "My dough's on you over the Bruiser, Ollie." But he wasn't agonizing over it, either. Arzt, too, had bigger game. Major Evans F. Carlson was back in the States and promoted to lieutenant colonel.

"Carlson's full of crazy theories that'll turn out pure genius. You watch. They're grilling him right now in D.C. about what he learnt there in Old China, and how they can make a dollar-fifty off of it. He sent me a post-card, making it into a joke. Said they got this ancient thing that they're modernizing up, a way of fighting called 'martial arts.' And Old Carlson, he made a joke out of it. Said the chinks named it after me but couldn't spell, called it 'martial Arzt.' "

Arzt laughed, enjoying his joke. Then went on about Carlson:

"Half the brass really wants to know what he learnt; the other half is suspicious, not sure if Carlson's turned Commie or just what."

"What do you think?"

"They're probably both right, Ollie. Carlson, he's a pisser. Never stops learning, never stops thinking. And he's got the president's ear, or used to." Arzt permitted gloom to seep into his manner. "They got a new secretary of the navy coming aboard so you never know."

"Do I still get to meet him?"

"I'll fix it. There's times Carlson don't do squat less'n he first discusses it thoroughly with me. Course, there's other times he keeps his own counsel."

Before anyone could meet Carlson or the brass decide if he were in-spired or a nut or had gone Red on them, on September 1, 1939 a hundred German divisions and a thousand planes crossed the Polish border, and World War II began. The Russians and Germans carved up Poland, and and before autumn was out Stalin had invaded another smallish neighbor, Finland.

The following spring, in 1940, Denmark and Norway went. And in June France collapsed. To homebound Ollie's envious chagrin, Ben Sweet evacuated Paris just before the Germans marched in, getting front-page stories out of the debacle for his *Chicago Trib* syndicate.

We weren't in it yet, of course, although with Roosevelt pushing for a military draft and making no secret of his support for England, Americans had at least a rooting interest. And when U-boat attacks on Allied shipping in the North Atlantic drew first blood (the destroyer USS *Reuben James* was sunk and another U.S. destroyer damaged by torpedoes), a distant war began to rattle cages far away in the Pacific. Where even for theater commanders Admiral Kimmel and General Short the Army-Navy boxing championship had become less of an obsession.

Then Ben Sweet published a book.

Ollie read about it in *Newsweek*—a brief note on their book page, but nonetheless, there it was:

> *Chicago Tribune* war correspondent Ben Sweet, 27 years old and a former Notre Dame football All-American, captures both the subtle complexities and the raw feroc-ity of the Spanish Civil War in a gripping first novel, *Fiesta,* written not so much from the objective posture of a reporter covering the fighting but as one of the com-batants, a young Spanish infantryman caught up in the siege of Madrid. An impressive debut for Sweet, who in Spain was said to have been taken under the wing of a somewhat older (40) correspondent/turned novelist, also a Chicagoan, Ernest M. Hemingway. Sweet's choice of title for his novel seems part-irony and part-homage to Hemingway's own first novel (*The Sun Also Rises* was issued in England as *Fiesta*).

Barring a chuckle over the description of Sweet as an All-American, Ollie was impressed. Here was Ben, covering wars and writing books.

Give him credit. Sweet knew from the first what he wanted and went out and did it. And Ollie? A Marine officer who didn't fight wars but just other pugs.

In June of 1941 the war stepped up in class when Hitler invaded the Soviet Union. Global insanity. Would the United States remain immune?

■

Admiral Husband Kimmel, commanding the Pacific Fleet, also knew what he wanted. Or thought he did.

"I've talked to Short about it." Short was the top Army general in Hawaii, Kimmel's alter ego.

These would be the two officers court-martialed for dereliction of duty following the Pearl Harbor attack. Yet in 1941, with Europe dominated by the Nazis and the Empire of Japan waging brutal war in China, General Short and Admiral Kimmel were haggling over the terms of engagement for a prizefighting competition.

"Short's not happy about the restrictions, either. But he can't do anything about it. Stimson won't let him."

Henry Stimson was Roosevelt's new secretary of war, a distinguished Republican chosen by the canny president to bolster bipartisan support for peacetime universal military conscription and heftier military budgets. Stimson, a stuffy sort, considered some of his generals to be idiots and made no secret of it. Navy secretary Frank Knox, also a Republican but of a more cordial breed, pretty much left things up to his admirals to sort out. They knew what a sailor wanted and how to navigate a ship.

No one knows (or will say) whether it was Bull Halsey or Fletcher or parties unknown (the introspective Chester Nimitz?) who came up with the inspired idea that would eventually allow Marine lieutenant James T. Cromwell, an officer and a gentleman, to fight Army sergeant Bruiser Wells, decidedly an enlisted man and of the crudest cut.

A venue was swiftly chosen. The flight deck of one of the big new American carriers berthed at Pearl, maybe the *Hornet,* the bout to be staged at night under floodlights.

"Just picture it," admirals and four-stripers told each other over cocktails at the club, "a great ship of war moored under the Southern Cross, the harbor lights, scurrying pilot boats and tugs and *avisos* sending up their courtesy wakes, the shoreline off to starboard, starlight above, a cooling breeze off the ocean past Diamond Head, ruffling and rattling the palm fronds along the beach, on the flight deck thousands of cheering sailors and a few hundred khaki-clad soldiers sitting glumly on their hands."

Well, not all the officers' club talk was *that* poetic, nor could you see the Southern Cross from Hawaii, but such minor items did little to curdle the general enthusiasm.

"Yeah, but can Cromwell really handle Bruiser?" the rare doubter asked.

"Ketchel trained him. . . ."

"Rockne personally recruited him. He made the Olympic team. . . ."

"Met Hitler. Stood right up to him, the way Chamberlain and Didier never did. . . ."

"Daladier."

"The froggie. You know the fellow I mean."

Here was the decidedly ingenious scheme cobbled up by the brass:

Instead of trying to get the rules changed, the Navy would come up with a challenger who was neither fish nor fowl. Just Navy. Neither an officer nor an enlisted man.

"Oh, shit, we've only *got* one hitter. And that's Cromwell. An officer."

That was what they had to do something about.

Admiral Kimmel called Ollie in for a chat. He had to be sure the young Marine would play. The admiral hit him with it right away—no sweet talk.

"If it came to it, Lieutenant, would you fight under a nom de guerre?"

Ollie had anticipated questions, but not this.

"I don't understand, sir."

"In England, when there's a cricket Test match, a really big deal against Australia, they hand in a batting order at the start of play with all the names. Except that if they're unsure of just who's physically fit, they list a player to be named later, called simply 'A. N. Other.' "

Cromwell, still puzzled, said, "And . . . ?"

"Don't be dense, Lieutenant. If we can't nominate a commissioned officer against Wells, why can't we submit someone called 'A. N. Other'?"

Ollie stared at him. Admirals and generals playing games like this?

"So I'd fight Wells not under my own name and rank, but as simply 'Another.' "

Kimmel smiled broadly. At last this boy seemed to get the message. "Precisely."

Cromwell thought for a moment.

"May I ask a question, Admiral?"

"Of course."

"Is this country going to war one of these days?"

Admiral Kimmel was stopped by that.

"What the hell does that have to do with beating Bruiser Wells?"

"Nothing, sir. Absolutely nothing."

If the irony was intended, Kimmel either missed it or decided against picking up on it.

"Just concentrate on Wells, mister. The rest of it can wait. He's problem enough."

"Aye aye, sir."

There were separate dressing rooms aboard the carrier, spacious officers' cabins, for Ollie and Wells.

"So the fix is in?" Arzt asked. "The Army is going along with this dodge?"

"That's what Admiral Kimmel tells me. . . ."

"And him and you is just like brothers."

"Yeah," Ollie said, "unless Wells kayos me. In which case the admiral really *won't* know my name."

"If Wells wins, kiddo, you get keelhauled."

There was one other thing, also previously agreed upon. This wouldn't be the usual three-round amateur bout. This one was to be fought to a finish. Arzt liked it.

"You're younger than him and ain't carrying as much weight. This fight goes past five or six, and you're still on your feet, I figure you'll breeze. Can't really see ol' Bruiser going ten."

"Sure, Gunny, sure." Ollie loved Arzt and trusted him, but he didn't take anyone's predictions seriously.

Cromwell had no idea what it was like over there in Wells's dressing room, but at least he was spared the usual prefight brass. There was only Kronstadt, solemn, silent for once, overcome by the enormity of the occasion, a trainer who doubled as cut man, two sailors to run errands if need be, and Gunny Arzt. The fighter was already in his trunks and shoes with a towel draped over his shoulders, a five o'clock shadow evident under the bright overhead lights. Ollie never shaved before a fight, not wanting to offer his opponent a cut to work on, no matter how small.

"Wear a robe going up there, kid," Arzt said. "There's a nice November breeze off the Pacific, and you don't want to go in the ring cool."

Kronstadt broke his silence.

"They even got women up there, Cromwell. Navy nurses off the hospital ship, even."

"Gee, that's swell, Commander," Arzt said, mouthing an aside to Ollie, "What an idiot."

Things had been arranged by a coin toss beforehand—which fighter came on first—and as Cromwell and his little entourage headed down the companionway and toward the ship's ladder to the flight deck, he could hear the yelling and then the band and finally the singing, "On Brave Old Army Team," followed by "The Caissons Go Rolling Along."

He looked over at Arzt and grinned. Ollie liked martial music, corny songs like that. Even if they were "Army."

When he first came out onto the open flight deck, he blinked under the glare of the overhead floods. Wow! Nine at night and brighter than midday. The sailors and Marines saw him now, and as they began their yelling, the band took it up again, "Anchors Aweigh" and a good rousing "Marines' Hymn."

When he got up into the ring, he saw Wells for the first time. He was big, but Ollie expected that; not taller but certainly heavier, though with long, lean greyhound legs and skinny ankles. *So the Bruiser can move; he won't just plod around,* Ollie told himself, half-nodding. Wells didn't look at him at all. Maybe that was part of how the Bruiser intimidated people. Didn't even bother to look 'em over.

"Well, hello there, Mister Bruiser Wells," Ollie said to himself, less disdainful and starting to be caught up in the event. "This night has been a long while coming."

The referee, a professional hired for the occasion, beckoned them toward the center of the ring. Ollie still had his robe on, but Wells wore only trunks. No light sheen on his chest and shoulders. Maybe that was the cool night, or else, he hadn't shadowboxed or limbered up as Cromwell had. Was the Bruiser taking Ollie lightly?

Arzt, for one, surely hoped so. As much as he believed in Cromwell, he didn't like Wells's big, sloping shoulders or those beefy forearms.

As they waited for a glib lieutenant commander to welcome everyone and for the introductions, Ollie allowed his eyes to roam across the scene. He'd fought in the Olympics, but he'd never, ever, seen anything quite like this—the flight deck a couple of football fields long, the rows of Navy and Marine brass, the Pacific Fleet band, the thousand or more sailors in white, the khaki-clad soldiers, Honolulu's lights way off in the distance, the loom of Diamond Head, the smell of the sea carried on the cool breeze, the rival factions chanting, cheering, the shouts and occasional bursts of song. He thought he saw Admiral Kimmel. And was that Halsey with him? Vandegrift, the Marine general—he recognized him. And the Navy nurses promised by Kronstadt—there must have been more than a hundred of them in their pristine whites, some of them young and pretty, others, well, who might have been to sea before.

"And now, for the heavyweight championship of the Pacific, in this corner, weighing two hundred and twenty-four pounds . . ."

Bruiser Wells was given his due and loudly cheered as he shuffled to the middle of the ring, raised one great arm, and then retreated, chin down, scrutinizing the ring canvas, pointedly not looking at his opponent.

". . . and in this corner, weighing one hundred and ninety-five pounds, representing the United States Navy, the Marine Corps' very own, A. N. Other." *Other!*

They all knew who he really was, of course, and there welled up an even louder cheer. Which Ollie acknowledged with a brief wave and a sort of grin. If others pitied him for having to go up against the formidable Wells, Ollie didn't feel sorry for himself. This, the great moment just before the opening bell of every bout, was something he relished.

Arzt and the trainer, just outside the ropes now and positioned behind him, took the robe, and Ollie could feel the Gunny's hand, kneading the back of his neck as . . .

"Bong!"

For perhaps the hundredth (could it be five hundredth?) time in his young life, Oliver Cromwell stepped forward, the left hand pawing ahead of him, as he prepared to battle another strong and presumably dangerous rival.

And he no longer saw admirals or Diamond Head or the harbor lights or the Navy nurses, but only Bruiser Wells shuffling purposefully toward him, shoulders hunched, hands held high, his legs, skinny as Babe Ruth's, carrying him with surprising swiftness toward the Marine.

And now, for the first time, Wells looked into Ollie's eyes, a terrible look.

From that very first minute of the very first round, it was a good fight.

If you're a fighter, there's something reassuring about that first stiff punch you take. If it doesn't knock you silly or hurt too bad, you've taken his shot and shrugged it off, you've shaken those early nerves, and you've gotten into the rhythm of the fight. But when it occurred to Cromwell to think back on that first hit from Wells, he realized that if he took too many of those, this might turn out to be a short evening.

As for Wells, he knew he'd hit the Marine a good shot, and that Cromwell had taken it and was firing back.

Only a minute into the first round, both men suspected this was going to be a fight.

By round six Ollie was pretty sure he had a broken rib, and his left eyebrow was swollen but, fortunately, not bleeding. Bruiser Wells's nose had been broken (how many breaks does that make, Wells?).

"How you feeling, kid?" Arzt inquired after the sixth.

"Great. Except one of my ribs feels broken."

"Try not breathing too deep. It won't hurt so much that way."

There was a novel medical theory for you.

Arzt looked around at the crowd. "Kronstadt looks worried."

"So am I, Gunny."

In the seventh Cromwell knocked Bruiser down for the third time. Trouble was, Wells got up. He just kept getting up.

The eighth started fast for the Bruiser, who came out with a bull rush that knocked Ollie back against the ropes, where Wells pinned him for a few seconds and hit him hard with both hands.

Cromwell felt his knees buckle for the first time, and when Bruiser caught him on the ear with a roundhouse right, the Marine went down.

". . . four . . . five . . . six . . ."

Ollie was up but not feeling all that perky. Wasn't the theory that Wells, the bigger, heavier, and older man, would be tiring by now and that the younger Cromwell would gradually be taking charge?

In between rounds Ollie found himself confused. This, too, a first.

"What round is it?"

The trainer gave Arzt a look.

"Nine coming up, Lieutenant." When they lost track of the round, it bothered you.

"Okay," Ollie said. He wasn't okay, but what are you going to say? Arzt sneaked a look at Bruiser. He didn't seem to be breathing very hard, but one eye was nearly closed. The right eye, handy to Ollie's left jab.

"His eye's going, Ollie. Keep jabbing at it."

Admirals and generals in the ringside seats looked either anxious or smug. But what the hell did they know? They weren't the ones getting hit. The admirals saw Wells's eye. The generals—well, they knew Cromwell was hurt.

Gunny Arzt was sore at the smug ones, sitting there fat and happy. And sore too about the anxious fellows, as he labeled them: "Oh, ye of little faith."

"The hell with those bastards," he snarled into Ollie's ear.

"What? The hell with who?"

"Forget it, champ. Just keep after Wells's eye."

In the ninth Bruiser went down twice. He couldn't see Ollie's jab coming and kept walking into the right. The Navy brass and the sailors were going nuts. The Navy nurses, even. They were jumping up and down, and not just the frisky, younger ones but the sedate and senior among them, women who had crossed that International Date Line and then some.

Army generals, including the lugubrious Short, ground their teeth and looked thoughtful. Had they ridden their horse one race too long?

Out of somewhere Bruiser found a reservoir, and as the tenth began, he hit Ollie with a right that almost caved in his cheekbone and that knocked him to his knees. But when Cromwell got shakily to his feet and stared into Wells's one good eye, a point seem to have been made. As many times as Wells got back up, the Marine was going to do the same.

Over Diamond Head a moon rose, only a slivered crescent, but it set the sea to shimmering in its light.

Some sailors began to sing. They weren't very good, but at least they were singing. And they were loud; the couple of hundred soldiers were silent.

"You gonna be able to go out there, sir?" Arzt asked. What had Gunny worried was that rib. A splintered rib could cut into the lungs. And that wasn't helpful to a fighter or to anyone else.

"What?" Arzt never called him sir. Never.

"You okay?"

"No."

Arzt had never heard a no like that out of Cromwell. It startled him, and, without knowing what else to do, he asked, "You wanna quit, Ollie?"

Cromwell, spitting blood, wasn't up to speech making, so he just bobbed his head up and down a couple of times.

That meant "yes," that he was finished, but Arzt chose to misunderstand, reckoning his warrior was confused. So he said, "Of course you ain't quitting, boy. Bruiser's finished."

"He is?"

"Would I bullshit another Marine, sir? Let's finish off this meat."

The eleventh round was pure nightmare.

Then came the twelfth, which opened with a blinded Wells staggering clear past Ollie without actually ever seeing him.

◾ 8 ◾

Hearing them counting over Bruiser, Ollie knew his arm was being lifted. He heard the roar, the singing; was it "Anchors Aweigh"? After that, nothing.

Not until he woke in a hospital bed in a small private room, customarily reserved for flag officers, in the big naval hospital at Pearl. It was daylight, he knew that, and Arzt was there, crouched in an armchair reading the newspaper.

"Sleeping beauty!" said the Gunny cheerfully.

> *"Wakey wakey, lash and stow,*
> *The sun is up, the moon's below."*

"What happened? When is it?"

"You whipped Wells. You remember that?" Cromwell nodded. "There's a nice story in the local paper about the Army and Navy having a sort of church social, but without no names. They don't mention that before you left the ring, you just keeled over. That boy gave you one hell of a beating. You got a couple broken ribs for starters. And you've been pissing blood. That's a bruised kidney. Maybe you got concussion. Otherwise, they think you'll live. How do you feel?"

Ollie didn't answer, not yet. "But I won?"

"Hell, yes. Was there any doubts?"

"How long did it go? Did it go the distance?"

"It sure did, mister. You was in the twelfth round when that damned Wells finally went down and stayed down."

"I knocked him down?"

"Seven times that I counted. He kept getting up. That soldier can fight. I don't want to hear no Marines disparaging the Army no more. Not while Bruiser Wells wears the uniform."

"So I won. In twelve. Arzt, I never went more than three rounds before. Never."

"You also got knocked down your own self, too. Remember that?"

"I think so. Not sure."

"Well, you was down. Three times. You got up, too, so the Bruiser didn't have no exclusive on guts."

Ollie shook his head. "What day is it?"

"It's tomorrow. The fight was last night. You been asleep about fourteen, fifteen hours, I figure. You feeling better now?"

"Yeah, except being tired. And I hurt when I breathe."

"That's got to be the busted ribs. That's why they got you on intravenous."

"Yeah."

CWO Arzt went serious, his voice falling, confidential.

"Those last few rounds, Ollie, they scared me, those last rounds. I was thinking they ought to stop it then. Maybe I should of throwed a towel. It wasn't just you; it was the Bruiser, too. Do you remember anything about them? Those last few rounds, Ollie?"

Cromwell didn't answer right away. Then, "Yes, I do, Arzt. It was like dying."

Doctors and nurses continued to come by. Along with a few senior officers who dropped in, quite deferential, not as rah rah as they usually were after a fight, but almost as if they'd seen something they had never expected to see, something sacred, a memorial service, or a rite in church. As if they, like Gunny Arzt, were frightened by what they'd seen, by the spectacle. Most of the uniformed visitors were Navy, including a surprise guest in Admiral Nimitz, not one of the usual cheerleaders. Plus one full colonel of Marines. Who remarked, by the by, that Ollie "should have coldcocked that dogface early" and "not carried him" into the twelfth.

"Yessir," Cromwell said, lacking energy to debate a man that stupid. And when Arzt asked the doctors to close down visiting hours, the patient went back to sleep.

Ollie still hurt next morning, and they told him there was some residual blood in his urine, but otherwise he was feeling better—not as tired.

It was then, with Arzt settled in and flirtatious, telling nurses about his Studebaker, that an apparition manifested itself at the door of Lieutenant Cromwell's room.

"Sir, it's me, Bruiser Wells. How you feeling?"

Wells, except for the broken nose, mirrored sunglasses shielding a black eye, a lumpy face, and with some fresh black-thread stitching above his right eye, actually looked smashing. He was in civvies: a chalk-striped business suit, a starched shirt, and floral tie, with a straw boater cocked jauntily atop his large head and a boutonniere in his lapel. He held and gestured vigorously with a large bouquet of cut flowers in a left fist the size of a Virginia ham.

"The business hand's broke," he explained. "The fingers can't close."

Behind him, just tentatively inside the hospital room door, were a couple of doxies.

"Wait outside, ladies. The dancing can wait until me and the Marines exchange compliments."

"Sure, Bruiser. Whatever you say, honey."

Wells came over to the side of the bed as Ollie tugged himself to a more upright position aganst the pillows.

"Gunny, I guess you know Sergeant Wells."

"I do, sir, and proud to say so."

Wells shook Arzt's hand gingerly, and then, even more gently, he took Cromwell's.

"You okay, sir? Man, for an officer and a gentleman, you are some hitter."

"Me, a hitter? Which one of us is in the hospital, Sergeant?"

"Yessir, well, you got yourself a point there. That's why I brung you some flowers."

Ollie gestured him to a chair, and the big man sat down.

"They tell me you got trained by Ketchel."

"Syd Ketchel, boxing coach at Notre Dame when I was there. Great man."

"I figured. The way you cross a right off the jab. That's pure Ketchel. Pretty move. Most fighters never get it. You did, sir. I never my own self seen the Michigan Assassin fight, but the old-timers all tell you that was a trademark, the hard right off the stiff jab."

"Thanks, Bruiser, and the name's Ollie."

"Yessir, Ollie. And you went to the Olympics. By God, that must of been something—Berlin and the beer halls and the squareheads parading and all them blondes. I wished I could of gone, too."

Bruiser paused, perhaps still thinking of the blondes and tugging his tie loose at the mere thought of it.

"You would have done our country proud, Sergeant. Maybe even got the medal I didn't."

"Oh, I heard about that. How you broke your damned hand. You gotta hit coloreds in the belly. They don't like it down there."

"That was a Senegalese gentleman, Bruiser. Son of a chief, in fact. And deserved his medal. Though he did have one hell of a hard head."

"I stand corrected, sir."

Then he inquired, "You get to meet that Hitler?"

They released Cromwell the next day, and the Navy sent him off on a fifteen-day leave. Ollie didn't even pretend to protest on grounds the ship and its Marine detachment needed him. "The platoon sergeant does all the work, anyway," he admitted to himself. Arzt told him there was an offer to fight Joe Louis in Madison Square Garden (the Gunny pronounced it as "Joe Looie" and thought they ought to explore what kind of money was being offered), but Cromwell took his leave alone (Arzt made noises about possibly coming along but was not encouraged) at a resort hotel on the beach at Maui, where he swam, slept, drank a little, and actually started to read Ben Sweet's novel. There was an attractive woman staying at the hotel, and he bought her a cocktail one evening. But when she asked why he was there ("recuperating from an accident," he said vaguely, not wanting to get into the boxing), and she began to narrate her own life story (a failed marriage plus other tragedies hinted at), Ollie drew back protectively. When the woman proposed they talk more about it over dinner, Ollie invented a long-distance call he was expecting, and, feeling sheepish about it, he bade her an early good night.

Ollie was twenty-four years old, and he was beginning to wonder just how you went about this falling-in-love business. He'd liked that swimmer from Coral Gables he met at the Games, had picked up girls in Rush Street joints in Chicago, and had dated a few met in bars in San Diego and an airline stewardess at the Outrigger Canoe Club at Waikiki, and that was about it. It must be comforting to be as casual about women as Arzt, as self-assured. Well, maybe he'd grow into it. He was maturing about boxing's place in the priorities.

One of these days he might do the same with women.

As for Ben's book, it was really pretty good. Then, on his third morning at Maui, as he lazed sunning in a beach chair, Oliver Cromwell abruptly stopped pondering Sweet and his sudden rise in the world when he saw Darcy bodysurfing smoothly up onto the sand and coming gleaming up out the water in her white swimsuit.

Darcy was in her late twenties and did fashion illustration for the advertising department of a chic store called I. Magnin, working for a brilliant merchant named Hector Escobosa, and she owned a little waterfront house north of San Francisco in a small town called Sauselito, from which she drove into work each morning over the Golden Gate Bridge. Suddenly Oliver Cromwell had this new perspective about the bridge and about driving over it mornings. Since he had never been in love before, he did not completely understand this. Darcy, who was quite intelligent, did not push. Besides, as she reminded him on the second morning they woke up together in his room, their idyll in the islands was about to end. She was due back at work Monday and had a plane reservation to San Francisco the next afternoon.

"That's okay," Ollie said. "There's no rush. I'll call the airline and get another ticket and go with you."

"Yes," she said, not at all astonished or turning coy, "we can do that quite easily, I'm sure."

With a candor that surprised him, Ollie found himself telling Darcy everything: about Jack Ballard's knee, about Syd Ketchel, about that swimmer from Coral Gables, about the Marines, and about prizefighting and how Bruiser Wells came to his hospital room with flowers.

"That was sweet of him, Ollie," she said. "I'd like to meet Sergeant Wells someday."

"Yes, well . . ."

"And I do wish I'd seen you fighting out there on the aircraft carrier under the Hawaiian moon," she added, quite surprising Ollie, who didn't realize there were women capable of crafting a lovely, if simple, poetry out of a stupid prizefight.

■

Because of his convalescent leave, Lieutenant Cromwell missed the Thanksgiving cruise. Two heavy cruisers, his *Juneau* and a second light cruiser, screened by six destroyers and a scatter of minor craft, were to escort three American carriers, *Saratoga, Lexington,* and *Hornet,* on a ten-day sweep east and north of the Hawaiian Islands. The exercise was intended to ready a carrier task force for action in case things suddenly got worse with the Japanese. An official, coded "warning of war," signed by Navy Secretary Frank Knox, had gone out. Action by the Japanese was expected somewhere in the Pacific and/or Indian oceans. No one knew precisely when or where. The Philippines, Malaya, the Dutch East Indies had been put on the alert. Kimmel, it may have been, or Nimitz or Halsey—one of them—thought the carriers might benefit from a little sea duty. When they came back in, it would be time for the battlewagons to go out, as many as four or five of the eight capital ships moored at Pearl along battleship row.

The carrier task force with *Juneau* was scheduled to return to Pearl December 9, 1941, with plenty of time to arrange Christmas leaves.

At Darcy's house at Sauselito, with an opportunity to ponder his future, Ollie concluded the Navy better find itself another heavyweight. Unless he was going to turn professional and fight Joe Louis, he'd done enough boxing, and, in fact, he was ready to stop fighting completely.

"I'm quitting," he told Darcy over dinner that Saturday evening in the St. Francis Hotel. He might phone his dad in New York on Sunday to tell him.

"I've been boxing since my freshman year at South Bend, staying in shape, doing roadwork, sparring, watching my weight. Here I am almost twenty-five years old and still doing it. I want to be able to take a drink, smoke a cigarette, go out with girls. Anything wrong with that?"

"Not a thing," Darcy assured him, eyes laughing. "If I'm one of the girls."

"Let's go home," he said.

"Oh, yes, let's."

The night Ollie announced he'd quit fighting was Saturday, December 6 of 1941.

BOOK TWO
THE RAIDERS

■

▪ 9 ▪

After Pearl Harbor Sunday, nothing and nobody in the United States naval service, or the country, would ever be the same.

Along the West Coast, for obvious reasons, it was just plain nuts. A Jap submarine, or that was the popular assumption, shelled the Long Beach oil fields. Streetlights were blacked out a hundred miles inland at Fresno. Japanese farmers, in the country for years, were arrested. Coast Guardsmen on horseback patroled the beaches at Santa Monica, at Malibu, at Big Sur. Recruiting offices were thronged. Hundreds of American soldiers, sailors, and Marines married local girls on very short notice. It took Cromwell more than a week to get on a flight to Honolulu, and then, when he thought he had a seat, he was bumped by a rear admiral—a week spent not so much with Darcy but mostly hanging around the Navy air station at Alameda, hoping to get on any sort of plane heading west, and feeling guilty he whole time because he'd missed the fight at Pearl. Now frustratingly, he seemed at risk of missing the entire war.

While Ben Sweet, a civilian with a press card, was dispatched by a great newspaper to cover his third war.

Ollie was already five or six days over leave, but every time he reported in to some Navy or Marine Corps desk officer in the Bay area, he was shooed away and told to get back to his own unit and his own ship, and to stop fer chrissakes causing trouble.

When he finally reached Arzt in Dago (long-distance phone calls were also at a premium, and you booked hours ahead in hopes of getting your three minutes), he asked if any of his exalted connections could pull a helpful string.

"I've gotta back aboard *Juneau*, Gunny. With the beating the fleet's taken, she'll go into action while I'm in San Francisco waiting for Santa."

"Gimme that gal's phone number. And don't go nowhere. I'll call you back soonest."

"Just get me a flight out of here. . . ."

"I might do better than that, champ. Just wait by the phone."

What Commissioned Warrant Officer Arzt did was hook up with Evans F. Carlson, the Marine guerrilla warfare expert who "had the president's ear."

He called back.

"I told Carlson about you. How you damned near killed Bruiser Wells. How I took you under my own wing and vouch for your character and such. I even told him you speak Latin and Greek and wrecked half the Notre Dame football team and got poor Coach Rockne upset. . . ."

"Rockne was dead by the time I . . ."

Arzt told him to just shut the hell up.

"I hope you don't never go into the advertising business back there in New York, Ollie. Bashful don't sell shit."

"I guess not."

"Anyways, it worked. Carlson wants to see you. They're giving him a command. Don't say nothing about it because it's top-secret stuff. Biggest thing since the Boxer Rebellion. I and him are gonna put together some other crazy fellas that think like us and go out after dark or in the rain killing people. You don't often get an opportunity like that, and you don't want to miss out, do you, Ollie?"

"But *Juneau* will be . . ."

"Oh, hell, they'll find someone else to play seagoing bellhop. You wasn't never cut out for it; you'd get seasick. What Carlson wants you for there ain't no one else can do. Less'n he's Bruiser Wells, maybe."

There were no available flights to San Diego, and there was a three-day wait on railroad seats, and in the end Darcy drove him the six hundred miles south down the strangely, but understandably, blacked-out California coast along Highway 101 in her little MG with the top down.

"Magnin's will just have to handle Christmas without me."

They broke the drive for one night and maybe four hours' sleep on the lumpy bed of a motor court near Santa Barbara. Then, at the main gate of the San Diego Marine Corps base early the next afternoon, they said good-bye. He was saluted and waved through, and she, as a civilian, though an inarguably very pretty one, was saluted but turned away, facing the six-hundred-mile drive back alone.

"Now *that*," said Arzt, when Ollie told him about Darcy's driving with the top down in the MG, "is a keeper. You find a girl like that, you keep in touch with her."

"I will," Cromwell said, and meant it. But it would not be soon.

■

Lieutenant Colonel Evans F. Carlson was operating temporarily from a newly erected raw-wood barracks on the San Diego main base with a couple of very senior sergeants; a tough-looking hombre with a highfalutin name, Wilfred S. Le François, who was a Chinaside enlisted man promoted to lieutenant; another lieutenant, Plumley, whom everyone called Plum; a clerk typist; a tall, balding executive officer squinting nearsightedly through thick eyeglasses; an Armenian lieutenant out of Fresno named Victor Maghakian who, because of his size, was called "Tractor"; and CWO Homer ("Gunny") Arzt, plus a half dozen privates whom Arzt kept hopping.

"I want to get away from main base soonest," said Colonel Carlson, "and set up camp in the boondocks. San Diego's too handy, only a cab ride away. Too many bars, too many sailors to fight and girls to chase. These new men aren't going to be altar boys, and I don't want them around civilians. You get civilized in this business and start holding doors for people and tipping your hat, you get yourself killed. Which isn't what this command is going to be about. The idea is we do the killing, and the others do the dying."

"Now that makes sense, doesn't it?" Arzt said, grinning, proud of Carlson for putting things so neatly.

They were bringing in the first batch of a thousand volunteers (another thousand would be checking in at Quantico on the East Coast to serve under Red Mike Edson), all of them already Marines and lusting to become Marine Raiders. With trucks and trains arriving on the hour and men just wandering in, with physicals to be taken, forms to be filled out, and credentials checked ("We don't need no ringers!" Arzt announced), the little office, the small parade ground out front, and the few canvas tents adjacent to the barracks were already humming with activity and grinding with confusion, shouted orders, queries, and a deal of cussing, with men counting off and being sent places that no one had any notion of how to get there.

Evans Carlson insisted on interviewing every volunteer personally. He began with motivation: Why do you want to be a Raider? What do you think Raiders do? Then, just as offhandedly, "Can you march fifty miles in a day?"

Early on, it was Ollie's turn, with Arzt as sponsor.

"Sir, this here is Cromwell, what kills people in the ring, that I told you about."

Carlson looked up calmly from behind a cheap raw-wood desk, just about the only man in the place who wasn't agitated. Arzt, for one, never spoke if he could shout, never asked if he could demand, never urged if he could threaten. But that was Arzt, *not* Carlson.

The colonel went through the usual catechism with Cromwell about why men wanted to join his Raider battalion. And then, without further preamble, he asked, "Think you could kill me in a ring, son?"

"Well, no, sir. Maybe knock you out. Gunny exaggerates the killing stuff a bit."

"One of these days we'll try you. Let you knock a few people out."

When Arzt, inevitably, brought up Ketchel, Carlson laughed—a hard, harsh, rasping laugh that didn't convey much humor.

"Lieutenant, we're going to teach you things not even the Michigan Assassin knew."

And they proceeded to do so.

From Arzt's accounts Cromwell recognized Carlson's "hatchet face" but had expected the colonel to be loud, profane, and marginally vulgar, much like the Gunny himself. Not so. S. E. Smith, who knew and wrote about him, called Carlson "a devoutly religious and dedicated officer." Lieutenant Colonel Carlson began Marine life as an enlisted man and never forgot it, preaching to his officers: "It is necessary that you live close to the men, study them and teach them not only military techniques and maneuvers, but basic ethical doctrines as well."

Carlson's mantra from the start: "Live clean and fight dirty."

A reluctant Arzt acknowledged that the commander had his saintly moments. "Kinda like your favorite gramps back home, y'know. Like he wouldn't hurt a fly, And following which, he'll lecture his men on strangling with the garrote and the stopping power of a load of number-four bird shot fired into a man's groin."

Take bayonet-fighting. There were plenty who considered the bayonet a joke, suitable for opening a ration can, or something obsolete out of the Zulu Wars—those Welshmen battling Zulus at Roark's Drift. But Carlson knew its usefulness.

"Slash! Parry! Thrust! You run the point of a bayonet across a fellow's face, he's blinded by the blood and scared he's dying. You parry and get him off balance. And when you thrust, don't run him through. That stuff belongs in the movies. You shove that blade through a man, and you'll get stuck on bone or something, and you waste time tugging free. Leaves you vulnerable to someone else. Just jab it into his belly three or four inches. A wound like that'll give anyone indigestion, y'know."

Colonel Carlson's years serving in China inspired a slogan that became that of his men: "Gung ho," meaning, "Work together." Carlson had taught himself Chinese, gotten close enough to Mao Tse-tung to persuade the Communist leader to let the American campaign with his Eighth Chinese Route Army up in the mountains of Yunnan for nearly a year, and was something of a mystic, a student of feng shui, the Chinese art of positioning objects according to the flow of spiritual energies (a theory behind the invention of the magnetic compass).

His men, observing Carlson's sleight of hand, firmly believed their colonel could levitate, peer around corners without the aid of optical devices, and breathe underwater through hollow reeds; he had reputedly raised a man from the dead. He was celebrated for eating meat and eggs raw and fish still alive and wriggling, never taking vegetables if he could get rice, and wherever he was, even in combat, kneeling in prayer last thing before sleeping (which he preferred to do on the bare ground).

Some of the top brass thought Carlson a madman or a Communist. The men both loved and feared him.

As to peering into the future, he early, and quite unofficially, dispatched a handful of Marine officers and enlisted men, who would become the cadre of the Raiders after Pearl, to train with British commandos in the United Kingdom, and, once we were in the war, he sent others to accompany the commandos and Canadians on the August 1942 raid on Occupied France at Dieppe—a bloody failure, but one that taught hard lessons a successful operation might not have taught.

No detail was too small for Carlson's notice. When on actual raids or surreptitious recon patrols, Raiders didn't wear issue field shoes but softer, supple, ankle-high athletic sneakers. The usual herringbone tweed design fatigues would be supplanted by issue khakis died black. The cloth itself, he said, was "quieter," didn't rustle. A Raider stiletto was being designed. As a decidedly Gung Ho fan of the Raiders wrote breathlessly of their operations, "They carried machine guns like pistols and a knife tempered in hell."

That was a part of it—the bouyant, antic capering, the cheap music-hall abracadabra of a stage illusionist. Their work would be lethal, dangerous, dead serious. But, oh, the wicked, gritty fun of learning at Carlson's knee, competitively striving for the Old Man's grudging favor.

And whether he "had the ear" of President Roosevelt as Arzt boasted, Evans Carlson might have had something even more precious to FDR. The tall, balding, bespectacled captain (about to be promoted to major) who was exec of Carlson's new command was the eldest and arguably the class-iest of the president's four sons, James ("Jimmy") Roosevelt.

Who would end the war a colonel and commanding a Raider battalion himself.

▪ 10 ▪

MARINES LEARNED TO EAT SNAKE. AND, IF THEY HAD TO, DOG AND RAT.

Not everyone in the Corps was buying Carlson's message. Some officers resented what they considered his elitism, his "putting on airs." Weren't all Marines "swift, silent, deadly," storming hostile beaches, scaling dizzying heights, squishing through swamps, stalking the enemy, and killing by stealth?

"Damned right!" more-traditional officers declared profanely at the bars of "O" clubs from Quantico to Panama.

Not true, of course. Even the Marine Corps had its yardbirds. Not every Marine soared high and plunged swiftly to the kill like a deadly, hunting hawk. And nobody else in the Corps was training his men these newfangled, yet ancient, Oriental martial arts. Only Carlson was hardening troops to be on the move for twenty-four hours with pack, ammo, and weapon, living on swamp water and a cup of cooked rice stuffed into a clean sock. No other Marines learned to eat snake, and, if they had to, dog and rat. On some marches Carlson's people carried no food and ate only what they took off the bodies of Japanese dead. This inspired stories of actual cannibalism—none of them documented, not one!

And the core element of Carlson's command, the men? Well, they were a piece of work, a bunch for whom the word *colorful* fell inadequately short. Career Marines who'd fought warlords in North China or Central American *bandidos* in the Banana Wars and newly minted second lieutenants melded with steelworkers, professional pugs, cowboys, salesmen and blacksmiths, oil wildcatters, loggers, lifeguards, farmers (invariably referred to by fellow Marines as "shitkickers"), Harvard undergrads and coal miners, football players, language experts, especially those with a working Japanese, and reform-school alumni. Among Carlson's early volunteers: a Ringling Brothers circus roustabout, a deep-sea diver, three Apaches who got drunk and enlisted together, the gardener off a Beverly Hills estate, a preacher, a dozen cops, forest rangers, prison guards, a Salt Lake newspaper reporter. Inside of a week a thousand young toughs poured into a camp that was still being built—roads graded but not paved, latrines dug, water wells sunk, a tent city going up—in the hills north of Dago, southeast of Oceanside, a couple hundred thousand acres leased (or confiscated, depending on your view of the right of eminent domain) for Marine training. And it was some training:

Run a mile with rifle, ammo, canteens, knife, and field pack in eight minutes; swim a mile in fatigues and wearing shoes (this wasn't so much timed as survived, with half-drowned Marines being dragged up on the beach and pumped out); rappel a sheer cliff with pack and weapon; build and then cross a rope bridge over a dizzying five-hundred-foot drop; master the garrote, knife fighting, and dirty tricks, how to booby trap an enemy latrine to explode when a man sat down, fist-fighting, shooting, shooting, and more shooting. And, yes, there actually were fifty-mile hikes. Of the thousand men in camp, 10 percent flunked out every week, with Gunny Arzt, nicknamed "the Turk," put in enthusiastic charge of notifying the failures and parceling out humiliation.

"You might sugarcoat it a bit, Gunny," Cromwell suggested. "After all, these guys are pretty disappointed."

"Hell with it. If they were any good, they'd still be here. I ain't wet-nursing men old enough to wipe their own asses."

That makeshift rope bridge didn't flunk out a single trainee, all of whom sprinted without hesitation across the madly swaying, decidedly ramshackle affair. Leading a vertigo-challenged Lieutenant Plumley to remark:

"We're all a little crazy."

And Arzt to nod in cheerful agreement. "Plum's right, y'know."

Strong-willed and wild young men were encouraged to freelance in combat, to cut corners, cheat, fight dirty, and break rules so long as the objective was taken and the enemy dispatched.

"I know it ain't Markers-of-Queens-Berries rules, Ollie, like what you had in the Olympics. But it sure makes sense. You grab a fellow by his balls and twist, you get his attention. He's too busy screaming and begging your pardon to do no damage, I can tell you."

Cromwell had to agree it sounded effective. And there was, just as in boxing, a sheer manic jubilation in being able to brutalize the other fellow into crumpling and crying, "Quit!"

The Raiders were also very big on gouging, a personal Carlson favorite. "There's a technique to it," Carlson or one of the instructors might say. "You get the old thumb in there and swivel, you pop it out like peeling grapes. And a fellow with his eyes hanging down his cheeks, he gets discouraged pretty quick. Stay alert now while we put on a little demonstration of preferred gouging technique." Maybe a hundred Raiders would be sitting crossed legged on the ground listening and waiting, eager for the demonstration. Lectures they could do without; Raiders hated to miss a good demo.

From the start, with only a cadre of officers and NCOs to lecture at, Carlson stressed short-range gunnery. He wanted a few sniper marksmen handy for the occasional telescopic-sight assassination. But mostly, he preached, "our fighting's going to be close-in stuff, jungle or village firefights. When you surprise the enemy with a good raid, you're right in there among the other fellows before they know it. You don't need fancy shooting at six hundred yards. More like twenty-to-fifty yards, you'll discover, or even closer. Point-blank. That's where a Thompson submachine gun does the job. And we'll have a batch of good twelve-gauge shotguns. You hit a fellow in the belly with bird shot, you open a hole right through him. Hit the thigh, you take his leg clean off at the hip. Hit a shoulder, that arm just drops off, nice as you'd like."

He still looked harmless, but Ollie was no longer thinking of his commanding officer as genial, lovable old "gramps."

As for motivation, Carlson didn't deal in patriotism and airy generalities. The Raiders weren't fighting for some vague notion of country and the Bill of Rights or to make the world safe for democracy. The trainees were told that the enemy, if not defeated and destroyed, would rape their sisters, murder their parents, burn down their homes, crap in their churches, and force their girlfriends into brothels to service Japanese regulars.

So it was that pious old Evans Carlson intended to yank his young men out of a civilized and law-abiding life and plunge them into the dog-eat-dog culture of the forest primeval. It is hard to overstate the enormous energy thus unleashed in this super boot camp.

Not all of Carlson's young lieutenants met his standards and got platoons to command. Ollie did. How much of this was due to Arzt's promotional blarney, Cromwell was unsure. But he'd seen the colonel watching when he worked with small groups on hand-to-hand combat, and he thought he'd made something of an impression. Whatever the facts, Ollie Cromwell was assigned a short platoon of promising young roughnecks, most of them trained athletes, all of them volunteers, not a one bashful or retiring.

The usual Marine rifle platoon in 1942 was made up of three 9-man squads, a lieutenant, platoon sergeant, platoon guide, and corpsman—33 or 34 men with three Browning automatic rifles (BARs) among them, the rest carrying Garand M-1 rifles. Carlson was going in a different direction: more chiefs, fewer Indians, more automatic weapons, more weapons of every sort. Instead of a squad with seven rifles and one BAR, his squads had 10 men, the leader and three of what Carlson called fire teams, 3 men each, armed with one submachine gun, one BAR, and one Garand, three times the usual firepower, and each man armed with a specially designed knife. Some men lugged privately purchased handguns, jammed into a waistband or holstered, a few sporting two guns Wild Bill Hickok style.

For the first time, Cromwell had men to command (his shipboard detachment, beyond close-order drill, really didn't qualify), and he set out to get to know them, assess their strengths. And especially their weaknesses, if any.

Ape Lombardi was a hulking twenty-eight-year-old wrestler out of Neenah, Wisconsin, where a "guinea" had to fight a Swede every day after school or let himself be chased out of town. Told he might be too old, Ape challenged Carlson himself: "I ain't near as old as the colonel, sir. The day I can't go no further than you, wash me out."

Canuck Fleurie, who played Juniors for Camloops in the Montreal Canadiens' hockey system, had a right ear sliced in half by a Saskatchewan skate and held together by a copper ring. He wasn't even an American. "How the hell'd you get into the Marine Corps then?" Arzt asked.

"I lied, Gunny."

That at least was honest, and Arzt okayed him. Arzt flunked them out on the basis of one-armed push-ups. Match old man Arzt in push-ups, you might make the first cut.

Ollie's favorite, being a boxer, was Bobby Swing, a welterweight who'd fought at Madison Square Garden and of whom *Herald Tribune* sportswriter Red Smith wrote, "He fights with a Texas drawl." Except that with Bobby, you might get nailed by the business end of the drawl . . .

Corporal Inge, a relation of the famous Dean Inge of the Church of England, whom a pessimist dubbed "the Gloomy Dean," was an instinctive and deft knife fighter but gloomy himself, earning from fellow Marines the title Black Cloud.

There was Earl Dash, a Norman Thomas Socialist who'd fought in Spain with the Lincoln Brigade. A Jew in the Marine Corps of the time was a rare bird and a Red was even less likely, but Dash won over Ollie and the platoon with his fists and readiness to duke it out, his combat savvy, and a battered old guitar. During those first months Earl Dash relieved boredom with Spanish Civil War songs to the tune of "Red River Valley," but full of mellifluous Spanish battle sites.

> *"I am leaving the Red River Valley.*
> *To the war, that is where I am gone.*
> *"If I die on the Rio Cabrera,*
> *From now on that is where I am from."*

Flynn Cortez was a diver from Key West whose Cuban daddy rolled cigars and whose mother was an Irish girl who had waited tables at Sloppy Joe's when Hemingway, and not tourists, still went there. Flynn brought up conch and sponge and occasionally a doubloon, working the green waters off Marathon and Sand Key. For Carlson, a swimmer who could stay underwater like Flynn Cortez was born a Raider.

And there was Walt Harrah, a cowboy from Reno whose family owned a small hotel, and who had, until Pearl Harbor, been wondering aloud over family dinners if the state might allow them to install blackjack tables and a few slots.

There were fifteen others plus Ollie's top kick, a staff sergeant named Stoneking, a big, rawboned Oklahoman who at eighteen drove a bootlegger's truck in a Dry state. And now Stoneking was helping a green officer put together a Marine platoon.

All of them Marines drilling to be another kind of Marine, a super Marine, so to speak—being trained as professional killers by a religious fellow named Carlson who lived on live fish and rice and of whom the description "unconventional" seemed understatement.

Officers and men both went through the course. The three doctors seconded to the Raider Battalion, even the two chaplains and several naval officers (considered by fellow sailors to be insane but possessing specific skills) were welcomed into the Raider battalions. Ollie not only went through the course but was pulled aside to help in the instruction in hand-to-hand combat, in the Chinese martial arts via Colonel Evans Carlson.

"The theory is very simple: use your opponent's strength against him, find the vulnerable killing points, and use the hardened hitting edges of your own body, feet, knees, top of the skull, and elbows included.

"You can do all this weaponless, using your bare hands, and other parts, and will be so taught."

Then, pausing, Carlson manifested a small, rare wit:

"Of course, if you have a BAR aimed at a man's belly ten yards in front of you, shoot him and save your best moves. A celebrated New York nightclub owner named Texas Guinan was once quoted as saying, 'Never give a sucker an even break.' Miss Guinan might have done well in the Raiders."

Because he was an athlete, Cromwell was quick to catch on to the moves, though Carlson himself, even at his age and rank, facing off against Ollie and other Marine huskies half his age, handled them with little apparent effort. Ollie, lacking the older man's subtlety, had to work harder to equivalent effect and found himself reverting to throwing a punch.

"No, no, Oliver," Carlson would chide gently, "a move like that could get you killed. And more importantly, sir, your men."

But when you put a thousand young men of violent persuasions in a tent city in the badlands with rattlers, scorpions, and tarantulas, deprive them of alcohol and sex, wake them at 4:00 A.M., and run them up and down hills in the black of night and the stultifying heat of midday, you might expect a few rebellions, desertions, and attempted homicides. Especially when, as happened, supply broke down and men in the field actually went hungry for a day, and on one occasion were reduced to gnawing hard tack smeared with cosmolene, the thick grease used to protect stored weapons against rust.

Arzt proved himself a regular Torquemada in rooting out the second-rate and the malingerer.

"Combat's a Marine's meat and drink, Ollie. And he's gotta earn the right. We ain't handing out free passes to the big show, Carlson and me. I don't take no crap, Ollie. You may have noticed that, even back in Dago during peacetime."

The few really incorrigible men, hard cases too ready to go for a knife or the jagged end of a bottle over the most trivial dispute or matter of barracks protocol, were turned over to Ollie. It was a court-martial offense for an officer to strike an enlisted man (Marine sergeants of the time labored under no such restrictions), but there were no rules against the lieutenant's taking a malcontent behind the barracks, stripping his blouse, and squaring off for a boxing lesson, one in which the troublemaker swiftly had his lights punched out by the heavyweight champion of the Pacific Fleet.

Some of what would become the battalion's best men were Marines taken behind the barracks by Lieutenant Cromwell.

As Carlson remarked privately to Jimmy Roosevelt, "I don't want to court-martial folks, Jim. I want to make them Raiders."

"Yessir."

"And that Cromwell does have a way of reasoning with people, doesn't he?"

"Yessir," said Captain Roosevelt, "he surely does."

By the time these youthful and untried Raiders had moved on to finishing school on Oahu, the first legends were sprouting about their eagerness to fight, specifically to fight for Carlson. Lieutenant Tom Jolly dined out on one story:

"When we came out of submarine class, someone passed some crazy scuttlebutt that the Old Man was starting a catapult school to teach us how to catapult over the Jap lines. We took it so seriously fifty men went to the First Sergeant to volunteer."

Cromwell himself had a new distinction. Shortly after he began using his fists to discipline the insubordinate, Ollie was promoted to first lieutenant. "My my," said Arzt, mock-impressed.

"Passage of time, is all," said Ollie, modestly but accurately, having been a second lieutenant now for almost four years.

In the meanwhile, Raider training continued and meticulously so, even down to the manner in which an old latrine would be disposed of for sanitary purposes. An officer of engineers gave this lecture:

"You use a light charge of dynamite. Light!, I emphasize—half a stick or less. Drop the sunovabitch down the drain with the fuse ignited so the shithole exolodes, collapses upon itself, and vanishes."

One Marine, ignoring the stricture about the dynamite charge having to be light, was believed within the tight community of Raiders to have inspired the popular expression "The shit hit the fan!"

And then amid all these preparations, there came the inevitable day when, during a break on a fifty-mile hike, Carlson asked of Ollie, "In Berlin, did you happen to meet Hitler, Lieutenant?"

▪ 11 ▪

FIRST BLOOD ON MAKIN ISLAND.

Difficult now to realize, but from that December morning at Pearl in '41 until halfway through the summer of 1942, the Japanese won every battle they fought on land against Americans: Wake Island, Guam, Bataan, even, Attu and Kiska in the Aleutians. All over the Pacific the enemy seemed irresistible. Thousands of American soldiers, sailors, Marines were dead. Other thousands had been prodded at bayonet point into death marches and the POW camps. Except at sea, the Japanese just beat hell out of us.

Early in August of 1942 U.S. ground forces would launch their first offensive against the victorious Japanese Imperial Army, invading Guadalcanal and other islands in the Solomons, east of Australia, northwest of the Fijis.

The two Marine Raider battalions, the 2nd under Carlson himself and the 1st under Colonel Merrill ("Red Mike") Edson, were to see their first combat. Clearly, in a war this large, a couple of battalions of foot soldiers, which is what the Raiders really were (whatever their egos insisted), would be spear carriers nowhere near center stage.

But like Jimmy Doolittle's raid on Tokyo with a few B-26 medium bombers, this first nothing raid on a nothing enemy garrison on Makin Island by U.S. Marine Raiders would convey a psychological and political message to the Empire of Japan and to millions of Americans at home. On August 8, 222 men and officers of the 2nd Raiders departed Pearl Harbor aboard two submarines, *Argonaut* and *Nautilus* (even the names were portentous), arriving August 16 off Makin Atoll (its main island was narrow and about twenty miles long and, according to the friendly local Aussie coast-watcher, occupied by 250 Japanese soldiers). After eight days in cramped submarines that traveled most of the way submerged, the Raiders, wild and physical men, were happy to be getting off the subs, even if it would be in the dark and meant piloting rubber boats through the surf and fighting their way ashore under fire.

The rubber boats, it turned out, weren't really going to be good enough.

The trouble began on the submarine decks, pitching and rolling, wallowing in the heavy swells and awash with waves deep and powerful enough to swamp or capsize a small boat and drench its outboard motor. Lieutenant Le François, "Frankey" to his men, helmed the first boat, lugging along a big brass compass that in the climb up the ladder clanged against the sub's hull so loudly that Le François cringed, thinking every Jap on the island must have been alerted. Ollie, less experienced than Le François, skippered the second boat. He wasn't as noisy but was no more adept at getting himself and his men off the sub's deck and their rubber boat headed toward the roar of the surf and the beaches beyond. All this would have been tricky in broad daylight and calm seas; at night and with swells it was chaos. Men were disoriented, queasy, unsure. From the peak of a swell Le François could see by starlight a line of trees, so that, for all their problems, they were making progress. But a fierce current ran this close to the beach, and the submarines, at risk of grounding, had to pull away, their wake sending the little boats pitching, tossing—nearly swamped. Carlson, by now aware their intended two-pronged assault was too complex in conditions like these, passed the word for everyone just to "follow Frankey." Which simplified Ollie's task.

Good thing, too, they would later realize in light of day. The Japanese had eight machine guns along the beach on which the Marines originally planned to land.

For men not previously under fire, the rough surf, the problems of navigation, were helpful, keeping them so focused on staying afloat and on course, they didn't worry about how they would react when the fighting began.

Le François nearly capsized riding a big wave up onto the sand and shouted back to Cromwell:

"Tell them to paddle like mad! Don't get sideways! You'll go over."

As heavily laden as the Marines were, "going over" meant drowning.

Ollie's men heard Frankey, and there was no need to tell them. Once on the sand, they dragged the heavy rubber craft into the underbrush, stripping palm fronds for camouflage. As a third boat safely made it ashore, someone let off an accidental discharge, the characteristically heavy *rrrrippppp!* of a Browning automatic rifle.

"Oh, shit," cursed a man near Ollie. "The Japs don't hear that, they don't deserve to win the war."

Carlson and all of them were safely ashore now, and still no enemy came for them. Reconnaissance patrols were sent out, the men crawling or hunched over, trotting along drainage and irrigation ditches. Still no firing. "Did we catch the Japanese that much off guard?" Ollie asked himself aloud. A sergeant kneeling in the brush looked over.

"Don't rush it, Mister Cromwell. They'll be along."

Ollie grinned his thanks. As an officer he ought to be more sure of himself. Not fear, but lack of knowledge, made him uncertain.

He wondered how Arzt was making out, back there in the dark with Carlson.

Taking a lead from the veteran Le François, Cromwell carried a Riesing submachine gun, very simple, light, and fast-firing. Most Marines despised the Riesing, claiming it was stamped out en masse from old Gillette razor-blades. Frankey swore by it, and, anticipating a water-soaked landing, he had oiled the gun heavily, urging Ollie to do the same. Cromwell also carried a holstered .45, a sheath knife, and four fragmentation grenades hooked to his cartridge belt.

Now, with dawn coming, runners came back from the patrols to report the way was clear to the opposite side of the narrow island. The Marines set off through the forested terrain at a quiet trot. After that scare in the surf, Ollie was very calm. Of course, no one had yet taken a shot at him. In the East the sky brightened. Without encountering the enemy they crossed to where a long concrete pier jutted out into the green water; it was lined with small warehouses, and, moored to it, were a few native canoes and a battered old harbor tug. Some natives emerged for the first time, tall, dark-skinned men mostly, with a few boys gamboling about. No women to be seen. Were they afraid of being raped by either the Japanese or these new people, the Americans?

Without prompting, the natives confirmed there were plenty of Japanese soldiers on the island, eighty of them not far from here along the coast. The Marines went from warehouse to warehouse, bashing open doors and dashing inside only to emerge shaking their heads. Copra, burlap sacking, wooden shipping palettes, dust, a few rats. Nobody, nothing more.

Someone's shotgun went off—again an accidental discharge and harmless. Where were the damned Japs? Even Carlson was getting antsy. And he'd been around for twenty-five years. A new boy like Cromwell was mystified.

"Maybe they heard we were coming."

A corporal smiled, as if to reassure the lieutenant, but a salty sergeant just shook his head.

"The Japs let the point man pass; then they come at you from both sides and the rear."

How could the sergeant be so sure? Ollie asked himself. None of them had yet seen a Japanese soldier. Carlson had, but that was in China.

Two Marines came out of one of the buildings with a Japanese flag, and, to Ollie's astonishment, they began a tug-of-war over the souvenir, pulling at it and cursing each other. The scuffle turned nasty, and before anyone could react, the two Marines were duking it out. Other Marines, ready for diversion, rooted for one or the other until a sergeant snarled an order to stop the damned grab-ass and shape up!

Just then a foot patrol of about twenty Japanese soldiers led by a young officer strolled nonchalantly out of the jungle toward the pier, blissfully unaware the Second World War had come to Makin Island.

There was a brief moment of stunned surprise when neither side moved.

Then firing broke out, and within a very few seconds the Japs were down, except three or four running away as fast as they could back into the trees.

"Get 'em. Don't let them boys get away."

A dozen Marines took off after them, some firing from the hip as they ran. Twelve-gauge shotguns loaded with buckshot, they were the thing for close-in combat. You didn't have to aim, just throw lead in their general direction, and you were bound to hit them somewhere.

For a firefight, it didn't last long. Carlson was shouting now at his officers. "Come on, too much time wasted here. They're not deaf, y'know; they'll have heard that. Let's get moving, up the coast road. There are a couple hundred Japs on this island, and we've taken care of twenty. Let's go. Let's get the rest." He called the captains to him and is-sued orders.

Cromwell hadn't yet fired his Riesing gun, slippery and oil-soaked against seawater. But he'd been in his first firefight, had seen his first men die, had heard return fire whistle past, hadn't frozen or done anything stupid. That was something. None of his men had been hit. For a first firefight that was fine.

"Okay, Sergeant," Ollie said, leaning on a savvier Stoneking, "get them ready."

"Aye aye, sir."

Ollie was wondering which of the two Marines had won the tug-of-war over the flag when a captain came up.

"You, Cromwell, take your platoon and find us some natives who know where the Japs are. Where they hide out, and how many."

"Aye aye, sir."

In combat, you have to know where the other fellow is. It was Ollie's first meaningful, direct order since he was told to beat Bruiser Wells.

And before this patrol was ended, he'd lost his first man.

There had been no firing during the night they came ashore, and the Raiders, with perimeter security posted, were able to sleep under bushes and hedges. There were lizards. And a few land crabs. But except for mosquitoes, sleeping wasn't bad.

Cromwell's patrol wasn't bad, either, until they came under sniper fire about a mile inland on treed ground around a small clearing and a few palm-frond huts. It was only one sniper, and he got off a couple of shots before the Marines located him halfway up a big tree and a volley of small-arms fire brought him crashing heavily to earth. "Good work, Stoney," Cromwell said.

The platoon sergeant was less enthusiastic.

"The Jap scored first, Mr. Cromwell. Got Corporal Gallatin with his first shot right through the damned head."

Gallatin was a Princetonian who'd written lyrics for Triangle and played on the football team the year they shut out Yale in the sleet at Palmer Stadium. Since he was a college boy, the Marines offered him officer candidate school, but the poet in Gallatin drew him to the exotic Raider battalions. Now he was dead, and Cromwell had no time to grieve or remark parallels to Rupert Brooke. Other firefights broke out.

Lieutenant Le François was also hit early, and it looked as if Cromwell would have to take command. Somehow, after several bouts of treatment by Raider corpsmen and a Navy doctor, Frankey was able to keep going. His sergeant, Thompson from Atlanta, firing his shotgun to great effectiveness, had quickly been hit by return fire and was dead. Lieutenant Holton was next. Dying, they said. Someone was calling for a corpsman, calling for help for Holton. Then, the words, flat, dismissive: "Never mind."

By now there was fighting all over Makin, one firefight following on another.

About 10:00 A.M. about thirty Japanese infantrymen came down the road, led by a large flag of the Rising Sun, and when they saw the Marines, they swiftly, not panicky but fast, melted into the forest bordering the dirt path and began firing. Le François, surprisingly alert, deployed his troops, directing fire. Cromwell, just to the rear, could see Frankey doing this and noted how cool he was. Then Le François, weakened from blood loss and hit a second time, went down again. It was becoming confused now, especially with Frankey down. Cromwell moved up at a trot. Should he take charge? Or would one of Frankey's sergeants do it—someone who knew his men? Ollie'd been a Marine officer four years, but what with the boxing and sea duty, he'd never puzzled out an infantry dilemma as simple as this.

Behind the first thirty Japs came four light machine guns and a flame-thrower. It was one of the machine guns that got Le François a second time through the arm. When Cromwell galloped up, a Marine had ripped off his own web belt and tightened it high on Frankey's arm to stop the bleeding. It must have hurt like hell. Cromwell asked, looking down at Le François:

"You want me to take over?"

"No, Ollie. If it don't get worse, I can work one-handed."

There were ten dead Japanese sprawled about, on the little road or just off on the shoulder or visible at the edge of the forest. One man was stark naked, as if, in pain or in his death throes, he had torn off his clothes, wanting to die the way he came into the world.

Corporal Earle was hit through the face by a sniper. There were Japs in depth now, plenty of them back in the trees, some of the snipers scrambling up the lower branches to get a better angle at which to fire down at the Marines out on the road. It was one of them who got Earle, and it seemed to drive the corporal crazy. Blood streamed out of his mouth, and he was running around shouting, while men tried to stop him so he could be treated. They knocked him down, and, flat on his back, Earle went delirious, bleeding and shouting. Then he jumped up as if miraculously healed and took off for the woods, firing and yelling.

"I'll get those heathens by myself!" Earle shouted. "Just show me where they are!"

He was firing at anything—trees, shrubs, men—but not for long. The Japs, able to focus on this single target rushing at them, all got into it. They just murdered him, and Earle fell.

Another sniper's shot hit Fred Kemp, a San Franciscan, in the cartridge belt, and by some fluke it ignited a tracer round so that smoke began to rise from the belt and his uniform. Kemp beat at it until, almost fully aflame, he dove into a pond in the swamp.

Le François was back on his feet and issuing orders. What kept Frankey going? Ollie wondered. But he was glad the old China hand, and not he, was in charge.

Only the Japs weren't finished. One of them had a bugle and sounded a call the Marines didn't recognize, which drew more enemy infantry out of the trees and toward the Raiders. But, cooler now, the Marines had settled down, no longer startled to be in a firefight, and, taking their time, they took aim and cut down the Japanese as they came. Cromwell was firing too, and he found the Riesing easy to aim and efficient enough despite its crappy reputation. With it, he'd just killed his first man.

When the last Japs were down or had run, Lieutenant Le François said, "Let's get back to where Carlson is and find out what he wants us to do next." He was blood soaked but didn't look too bad. Cromwell wondered if, during a firefight, no matter how bad you'd been hit, it really didn't hurt because of the distractions, the excitement. Sometimes it was like that in the ring: you didn't know how badly the punches hurt because you were intent on the fighting.

"You okay, Ollie?" the wounded Le François asked.

"Fine, Frankey. Fine."

What the hell do you say when people are being killed all around you but not you?

"Fine" seemed to cover it. He realized he wasn't even mourning Gallatin, his own man. Maybe he'd think about Gallatin later. And about the Jap soldier he'd shot.

There were a scatter of huts and a barn of sorts about a mile away, and that's where they found headquarters and the colonel. Later they pulled back to a big warehouselike place called Government House. But for now, it was these huts. Doctor Cantrall cut off Le François's bloody sleeve and removed the web belt to prep his arm for Dr. MacCracken, who cleaned the wounds himself and applied sulfanilamide, telling the wounded man, "Frankey, this isn't so bad as it looked at first."

"You don't have to cut it off, Doc?"

"Shit, no."

"Good."

Carlson was out trooping the line and adjusting his men's positions. In the big, echoing, barnlike building where they'd set up the aid station, you could hear sniper rounds bouncing off walls or coming through and exiting the other side, but they didn't hit anyone. Just ricocheted around. Nice, jolly pinging sounds actually, if you didn't get in the way.

Ollie left Frankey and went out to organize his men and await orders. He, too, was pretty cool now and felt good about things. A hundred yards away he watched a small Raider named Julius Cotten strolling about under the trees, pulling the pin on one grenade at a time, counting aloud, "One, two, three," and tossing it up into the tree as high as he could. Every grenade or so, a Japanese sniper, blasted from his perch, would fall, landing with a thud not far from the resourceful Cotten.

▪ 12 ▪

THE JAPS WERE ZEROING IN ON JIMMY ROOSEVELT'S BALD HEAD,
GLEAMING IN THE SUN.

Jap fleet coming!" someone shouted from the beach, and a flat trajectory shell followed quickly, screaming in overhead to land harmlessly back in the bush.

They'd traveled eighteen hundred miles into Indian country, gotten ashore without disaster, surprised and killed some Japs, blown up several of their objectives, including a radio tower, and they had started feeling pretty cocky. Too soon. Makin Island wasn't going to be simple. Japanese infantry and now ships. And the planes wouldn't be far behind.

Through a gap in the palms, Cromwell could see the lagoon, where a patrol boat slowed to a stop abeam of what looked like a supply ship or small transport disgorging enemy infantrymen. They were climbing down cargo nets into boats, lots of them, infantrymen heavy with packs and weapons slung. The patrol boat, with its forward gun, anchored, and the gun crew began scanning the shore for Marine targets.

Which was when Cromwell noticed Major Roosevelt.

Jimmy was sitting under a clump of brush, his helmet off in the heat and his bald dome glistening, sleek with sweat. The Japs could see it as well, and from the gunboat small-arms fire was coming in. Cromwell couldn't help himself:

"Major! They're zeroing in on your damned head."

Roosevelt, owlish and embarrassed, grabbed his helmet, squashing it down hard on his head, and he acknowledged Ollie with a grin, a little wave.

Just then one of the two American subs surfaced a half mile seaward of the Japanese vessels and unlimbered its own three-incher. In less than a minute it was firing and scoring hits. At that range, over open sights, the swabbies couldn't miss. First the patrol craft exploded, its magazine hit, and then the transport lurched to starboard, the last of its infantry jumping heavily into the still waters of the lagoon, its white-suited sailors on deck running about in considerable alarm. The Japanese infantry, weighted down with ammo, packs, and helmets, drowned right away. Their sailors took longer, flailing about in the water until Marines, who enjoyed a good shoot, began picking them off, taking their time, leisurely lining up their targets.

"I've got that fellow swimming on the right. He's mine."

More natives were hustled up to be grilled.

"They say there's eighty or a hundred Japs living on the On Cheong pier."

Carlson was back from his reconnaissance. "Show me the pier on the map."

"Aye aye, sir."

The radios didn't seem to be working ("Seawater, most likely," the communications officer defended himself against Carlson's withering stare), and Roosevelt beckoned Cromwell. Both crouched in Jimmy's clump of brush.

"Colonel wants you to check out the On Cheong pier, Ollie. Natives say there's Japs all over the place. Maybe a hundred."

When Cromwell did a double take on that, Roosevelt said, "Well, they exaggerate. Make themselves important." But he didn't say there *weren't* a hundred, and Cromwell had a thirty-man platoon. Ollie looked over the map with Roosevelt and Sergeant Stoneking and got the detachment on its feet. Just as they saddled up, along came a single enemy soldier pedaling a bike from the other direction. "Now what the hell . . . ?" someone muttered before a half-dozen Marines fired and the fellow fell from the bike, which kept rolling, tumbling, riderless, for another ten yards.

When Cromwell's Marines got to the On Cheong, they paused at the land end of the long concrete pier sticking way out into the blue-green Pacific. No Japs swarmed. Not a one. Maybe the natives really did make up stories to ingratiate themselves with the Americans, earn some smokes? You could see all the way to the end, and there was nothing there but a couple of small lighters moored and a big corrugated tin warehouse halfway along and a few similar, but smaller, huts. Ollie half-turned to the Marine kneeling nearest him.

"You see anything?"

"Nossir." It was Lombardi, the big guinea from Wisconsin who beat up Swedes, and who they worried was too old, too slow. He wore a half-grin on his hard, battered wrestler's face.

"Okay, let's go look. And move fast," Cromwell told the men. Lombardi was on his feet as quickly as any of them.

The platoon covered the first seventy-five or hundred yards in a sprint without drawing fire. Then, on the nearest lighter, two Japanese soldiers or maybe sailors appeared on deck, lugging rifles and scrambling up the ladder to be on the same level as the oncoming Marines.

"Get 'em! Get those guys!" Ollie shouted.

Half of Cromwell's Raiders fired simultaneously. One Jap just fell; the other, hit by a shotgun blast, was propelled backward and overboard, dead but still clutching his weapon.

"The warehouse!" Ollie ordered Stoneking. "Go for the warehouse." *That's where all those Japs must be.*

Flynn Cortez and Bobby Swing were the first Marines through the big sliding doors and inside, blinded by going directly from brilliant sunshine into the dusty gloom. As Cromwell followed, he heard Cortez: "Nobody, sir. Not a freaking soul. . . ."

Then there *was* someone, and Bobby wheeled and fired. Just inside the doors Ollie heard a scream and then the metallic rattle of twelve-gauge pellets bouncing off the tin walls.

"Sorry, Lieutenant," Swing said in embarrassment. "Only a native boy. Must of been crapping out. The twelve gauge sure woke up the poor bastard."

Bobby had the youngster's long black hair in one hand, lifting up his head trophylike to show Cromwell.

"Yeah, I see," Ollie said. The native's big brown eyes were still open and staring, and his face bore a surprised look. But it was his chest that Cromwell would remember, the gleaming white ribs exposed by the shotgun blast against the dark skin, and the bloody froth still bubbling from the left lung.

As a fighter, Ollie was accustomed to seeing blood, facial blood mostly, but this was pinker than that. Maybe it was the air in a man's lungs made it look pink, was that it?

One thing for sure: old Carlson was right about what a shotgun did up close. Damned shame about the kid. But he was pleased Bobby had fired first; didn't wait around until someone shot him.

By the time they cleared the rest of the pier, an enemy mortar off there in the bush was chunking in shells onto the pier and along the shoreline, and Roosevelt with Gunny Arzt had come up to get a report. When he was told there was next to no fighting on the pier, Jimmy Roosevelt ordered Cromwell's Marines into the forest to root out the enemy mortar. Ollie nodded and called for his sergeant to roust the men. Arzt, sweating and grinning, a shotgun in one big hand, saw Ollie and called to him.

"Meat and drink, boy. That's what this is, meat and drink." Arzt was very happy.

"If you say so, Gunny," Cromwell said, more restrained.

"Absolutely," Arzt assured him. "Just like Bruiser in the last round, kid. These boys is ready to cave, too."

"Sure, Gunny," Cromwell said, not quite that sure. He hadn't been scared advancing up the pier in sunlight, but after Gallatin's death he was a little nervous about going back into the dark-shadowed forest where the Japs were waiting, and unable to think of anything clever to say to Arzt.

▪ 13 ▪

Back inside the barn-turned-hospital, Le François was puzzled by how well he felt. When he was first shot and saw all the blood, he thought he might bleed to death. The second wound wasn't as bad. Then came lassitude. Now there was only a little pain, and a man could handle pain. Morphine helped. Being a man helped.

"Lieutenant!"

It was one of Frankey's corporals.

"Yes?"

"We found their officers' club, sir. Nobody to home, not even a mess boy, so we grabbed ourselves a couple bottles of cold beer outa the reefer. Figured you might be able to use one after getting shot and all."

Le François looked around; didn't see the straitlaced Carlson. *What the hell.* "Sure, can't hurt me, I guess."

"Nossir. All that blood you lost, do you some good."

Then, apologetically, the corporal reported, "We scavenged for some drinkin' whisky, but there weren't none. Pretty crappy officers' club if you ask me. Not a pint of Four Roses on the shelf. If them's the standards their officers' clubs set, we oughta win this war."

Ollie's second patrol was busy, you had to say that, but it worked out fine.

They found the mortar right away, caught them swabbing out the tube, and took the three-man crew out with a first volley and a couple of grenades. But every half mile or so after that, there was another small clearing, cultivated and with a couple of shacks, a few natives, dozing or scared, depending, and in some of them the enemy had set up behind a light machine gun, just waiting for the Marines. There, in the villages, and in the surrounding bush and forest, all that afternoon and into the night, there were a half-dozen running gunfights, and it was becoming clear that if the Marines weren't completely in charge, the Japanese were falling back every-where. So much so, the higher-spirited among the Raiders had begun looting. Other Marines were asking about a withdrawal. Carlson himself checked with his officers.

"Come on, come on. I need a count of working rafts with motors that'll run. Cromwell says there's a big motor launch tied up at the On Cheong pier. Some of these native outrigger canoes are pretty big. We could use those. We may need all the boats we can find getting out to the subs."

The problem now was getting away before Jap reinforcements came ashore. If they could get out tonight, they might just pull it off. So far, this was a winning ballgame. Tomorrow, well, that might be different. The two submarines lazed on the surface a mile out. The Marines could see swabbies sunning on the hulls. Pretty cushy. Wasn't that just like the Navy?

But every time you get comfortable in a war, some damned thing happens.

Now it was the turn of the planes. A flight of Japanese Kawasaki light bombers appeared in the high blue sky without notice, and both subs had to crash-dive. So the planes, deprived of one target, came back again for a second run over land, bombing every building in view. A couple of fighters followed, strafing individual Marines twisting and dodging and sprinting for the trees and cover. Even a torpedo plane got into the act, dropping a thousand-pound naval torpedo, propellor uselessly spinning, on some poor Marines in grass huts. And wasn't that some damned nerve!

It was then that Ollie's outfit returned, intact but for a couple of walking wounded and that was about it. But here at the base there were men dead and others not likely to make it, a few looking stunned, vague, out of it. That was the bombing. Ollie had not yet been bombed. He'd seen men react like that in the ring, after taking a hard punch. Did you get used to it after awhile, he wondered? Strafing he understood. That was just machine guns that flew. When he reported to one of Carlson's captains that they'd taken out a mortar and its crew and gotten two enemy machine guns, the captain took it down. Carlson gave Ollie a quick nod. The Old Man wasn't much for speech making. Fine with Cromwell. If God nodded, that was sufficient.

After the enemy planes vanished below the horizon, a work detail of a dozen men, with some natives conscripted, came in lugging cases of good American canned corned beef and other treasures they'd found in a general store on one of the other piers. The spoils included big cardboard cartons of Japanese-made men's silk underwear—shorts and shirts in pink and sky blue. It didn't take long for the Americans to begin tugging on the shorts and undershirts over their uniforms, the pink and the blue mixed or matched. Depending on a fellow's fashion sense.

No one stopped them, and Major Roosevelt was laughing, but a few of the other officers just shook their heads while Gunny Arzt cursed steadily, looking sore. About half the Marines, a few of them Cromwell's, now had Jap rifles slung, part souvenir, part supplement to their own weapons. A fortunate couple of men had samurai swords strapped on, and Arzt had already broken up a fistfight over one especially handsome sword.

Lying in the shade of huts so they wouldn't swell and stink in the heat were maybe six or seven dead Marines, Corporal Gallatin among them. While other men sported in pink underwear and swapped souvenirs and the major laughed.

"Roosevelt!" Carlson called out just as the sun sank toward the western ocean, hurriedly as it did at this latitude. "Take a motorboat and a couple of men and go out to the subs. Tell them to expect the entire battalion coming aboard tonight starting as soon as they give us the all clear and we can launch."

Roosevelt saluted and went off. Another firefight raged at King's pier, where a small Jap unit was holed up under heavy fire and pressure from a Raider detachment.

"Sea's getting up, sir," a scout reported to Carlson. "Oh, shit!" said a captain who heard. Carlson didn't curse. He snapped:

"Get Roosevelt back."

The major, yanked from his motorized rubber boat just before setting off, was as calm as ever. Ollie, thinking about it, would have been sore, exasperated.

"Yessir?"

"Major, ask the subs whether, with a big sea running, they can circle the island and pick us up off the lagoon beach tomorrow rather than the oceanside tonight. The lagoon side should be calmer. Let me know by radio soonest. Maybe our radios can receive if not send."

Major Roosevelt was off again, his bald head gleaming, his helmet lost or again discarded. Well, they couldn't use him as an aiming stake in the dark, could they?

Roosevelt had just reached the first sub when another Jap plane came in, strafing and dropping small bombs, hundred-pounders maybe. The sub crash-dived without the Marines, who scrambled back aboard their rubber raft, but when the plane returned, they dove into the water and swam ashore, leaving the raft to be sunk by the strafing Japs.

Carlson took the bad news about as well as a man could. This getting off Makin Island was going to be a project.

The shamed comm officer had rigged one radio that worked. Carlson ordered, "Raise the subs by radio. I'll talk to them direct."

Using slang and arcane Navy terms, nicknames for officers he and the skipper might know, so as to confuse any English-speaking enemy listeners, he made himself understood about moving to the lagoon shore of the island. Or thought he had. But the planes came over yet again twice more during the night, and the Raiders lost more men, with several more of their boats damaged beyond use. In the aid station, Le François was bleeding again, having been hauled out into the forest and dumped every time the planes returned and then carried back inside after their run. "Jesus," he growled at the corpsmen, "better the Japs kill me than you bastards."

There was renewed ground fighting toward dawn, and then the Marines set out carrying weapons and their wounded, some of the casualties still sporting silk underwear, to cross the narrow island to the beaches of the lagoon, where they intended to board the few rubber rafts still seaworthy, a couple of canoes, and a beat-up old sloop belonging to a Makin Island trader long gone. They fought two more firefights crossing the island, lost a few men.

At the beach, with no Jap air in view, the subs were clearly visible three-quarters of a mile away where the lagoon let out into the open sea. Trouble was, the damned wind had shifted, and out there the seas ran just as high as on the windward shore. Cromwell was deputized to Le François and carried the wounded officer, bleeding again, on his shoulders and onto the deck of the little sloop.

The Japs had set up what may have been their last mortar, and they harassed the departing Raiders all the way cross the lagoon, sinking two of the rafts, so that about a score of Marines reached the waiting subs by swimming to them. The sloop, without Le François but with Cromwell, returned to the beach for another shuttle.

It was during the night that Colonel Carlson panicked. Or so people said. While Arzt and a few said it was a damned lie from the very first.

▪ 14 ▪

SOME SAID THE MARINES WERE SHOT. OTHERS, BEHEADED. THE JAPS
ENJOYED A GOOD BEHEADING.

As good officers do, Carlson kept sending out patrols. No one knew just where the Japs were or how many of them were still alive. One patrol would come back and report all clear. Another would have to fight its way home under heavy fire. Some officers felt the Japanese were down to their last few dozen men. Carlson insisted there were still a hundred of them, maybe several hundred. Another patrol went out and triggered what came to be known as "the battle of the breadfruit trees," the sudden and rather gallant dash out of a grove of breadfruits of maybe a score of Japs, all of them shot down. Cromwell took out one of the patrols and came up void in trumps, not a shot fired. Who was he to question Evans Carlson, who'd been fighting in Nicaragua when Ollie was playing high school hoops?

But how did Carlson let a handful of Japs steal from him the initiative of battle? Maybe it was the heavy casualties his command had taken, with the nearest replacements eighteen hundred miles away. Surely, it wasn't lack of physical courage on the Old Man's part.

"Lookie there," a crouching Marine would marvel as Carlson, pipe between his teeth, strolled past, erect and oblivious to sniper bullets whistling by.

Firefights continued along the entire skirmish line, strengthening Carlson's belief that the Japanese were still a cohesive force. It was then that an enemy flying boat, escorted by fighters, appeared over the lagoon and began strafing the Marines on the beach and up in the pasture above. The two U.S. subs, of course, had again vanished. Then, impressing even the Raiders, the seaplane cheekily set down on the lagoon, taxied in to within a quarter mile, and turned its machine guns on the Marine boats shelved up on the sand.

"Bastards! We *need* those boats!"

One of the colonel's favorite Raiders was a former communications sergeant, Murphree, who'd deserted from the Army to join the Marines as a private, and who was now provided with a powerful flashlight and ordered to shinny up a palm and signal the *Argonaut* to pick up Marines at one the next morning at the reef sheltering the lagoon. The message got through, seen by periscope, and the submerged sub acknowledged. But in war nothing ever happens the way you lay it out. Not Murphree's fault, of course.

When the *Argonaut* failed to appear and the 1:00 A.M. rendezvous didn't come off, the "deserter" Murphree and his pals, Corporal Red Ricks and Private Sebock, went to Carlson directly. Savvy enlisted men sensed that the operation, which had begun so well, was stalled and in fact falling to pieces. Raider after Raider asked, "What the hell do we do now?" Was a failure on the Old Man's part filtering down to the lowliest private soldier? Colonel Carlson gave Murphree a hearing.

The three wanted permission to escape on their own, hiding in village huts until the next nightfall and then, in a native canoe, making their way, island by island, to Australia.

Carlson, who had a weakness for Murphree, told him, "I would rather have you with me in combat than any man I know. But out of combat, you and Sebock break every regulation in the book."

Nonetheless, he gave them his blessing. "If you make it and we don't, tell them what happened."

Maybe that despairing instruction to a couple of career troublemakers signaled the doubt eating at Carlson's soul.

The colonel had reason to doubt. Rubber boat after rubber boat, laden with Marines and weapons, was launched in darkness into the big Pacific rollers. Some rafts managed to make it over the first roller and the second, only to be swamped or capsized or tumbled over backwards into the roiling surf, the men helpless, retching in the shallows, sobbing their fatigue, cursing the Navy, damning the enemy, the strewn wreckage of men become the flotsam and jetsam of a hostile sea, cursing the cruel Pacific itself. Once they regained their breath, driven by officers and NCOs equally as drained, the men relaunched and tried again, intent on the subs. But the boats were no good; the surf was too rough; the men were overladen and tired; the submarines had been forced by enemy air to crash-dive, swamping the boats or abandoning the Marines to float idly and vulnerable, being strafed when they weren't drowning on their own.

"The surf beat us," Carlson himself would later say in his report.

Ollie Cromwell was among the stronger swimmers who jettisoned boots and belts, everything but their trousers and shirts, and twice made it nearly to one of the subs before being again forced back to shore.

By now platoon leaders such as Cromwell had lost control of their commands. Some men were dead on the island, some drowned, a few already aboard the submarines. Others still manned the skirmish line protecting this last foothold of the Marines on Makin; some were wounded; others wandered lost elsewhere on the island in little pickup detachments. The only men still attached directly to Ollie were Bobby Swing, the Spanish Civil War vet Dash, Sergeant Stoneking, and Cortez the diver.

"Try to keep them together, Stoneking. If we can all get in the same raft, let's do it."

Stoneking nodded agreement, but he was staring at Cromwell's feet, bloody from the coral.

"Jesus, Mister Cromwell, them feet of yours is in a hell of a shape."

"Yeah, I know."

No one looked very good by now. Shirtless men who'd stripped in the night to swim had been baked by the next day's sun, raw shoulders and blistered backs. "I'd kill a Jap for his damned shirt if I could find one my size," a big Marine snarled.

As for Cromwell's feet, what the coral and gritty sand hadn't done, the deck of the sloop and the steel hull of the *Nautilus* accomplished. Now, whenever he could, he crawled rather than attempting to walk upright and put weight on the soles.

No one can say just when during this water-soaked, parboiled nightmare Evans Carlson decided to contact the Japanese commander, offering to surrender.

The word itself was first uttered by an enlisted man. It was full night, and Carlson was prowling the beach, stumbling across individual Marines or small groups and chatting, trying to cheer them, assessing their condition.

"Hiya, boys."

"Hiya, Colonel."

One Marine said, "We're in a spot, ain't we, Colonel?"

"Don't say I didn't warn you, boys. I told you it would be tough in the Raiders."

"Who's complaining?"

Men shared the last of the food—corned beef and chocolate bars.

Down the beach a man—no one identified him—called out.

"Let's surrender, Goddamnit. Just find the Japs and surrender."

Tractor Maghakian put a quick stop to that stuff:

"Shut up!"

When the man continued to shout, hysterically some thought, Tractor moved toward him. There was a sound of slaps and Maghakian's repeated order, "Just shut up."

Somewhere during this process various plans were discussed at officers' call, with Carlson seemingly resolved to await daylight, move to the north end of the island, and get away by outrigger canoes. At another point he summoned Captain Ralph Coyte. It is the captain's account that Carlson sent Coyte to find the Japanese commander and offer to surrender the command if the Marines would be treated honorably as prisoners of war.

Cromwell wasn't in on any of the discussions. Later, men's testimony differed. One version had Carlson considering surrender on grounds he couldn't take responsibility for getting the president's son killed.

"Better to have him paraded around Tokyo as a prisoner?" another officer demanded.

"Why not ask Roosevelt to sit in on this. It concerns him as much as any of us—maybe more."

"I won't put that onus on Major Roosevelt," Carlson declared.

In another version, Carlson, having heard the exchange between Tractor and the out-of-control Marine, recalled that the possibility of surrender had come up in briefings back at Pearl. And that he now went to talk with Jimmy Roosevelt—a conversation that ended in the two agreeing only to try to get some sleep and then resume trying to reach the American subs.

Whatever the actual sitation, it was following those exchanges that Captain Coyte and Private William McCall set out at 3:30 A.M., unarmed and wearing only trousers and shoes, to find the Japanese commander.

It was the Japs who found Captain Coyte. Or, more accurately, one Jap out scrounging cigarettes.

Coyte and McCall were in a hut, talking pidgin to some natives, when the lone Japanese soldier entered the hut, saw Coyte smoking, and went into a tantrum. He'd been shooed off earlier by the natives, who claimed they had no tobacco, and now he rammed his rifle into the Marine's middle. Coyte, so exhausted that it didn't really matter if he got shot, kept pushing the rifle away and demanding to see his commanding officer. The natives now calmed down the irate Japanese by giving him some smokes, at which he allowed Coyte to compose a letter to his commander. The note read:

"Dear Sir, I am a member of the American forces now on Makin. We have suffered severe casualties and wish to make an end of the bloodshed and bombings. There are approximately sixty of us left, and we have all voted to surrender. I would like to see you personally as soon as possible. . . ."

The Japanese soldier set off with Coyte's note, but, moments later, a single shot was heard, and when Coyte ran outside, he encountered two Raiders coming along the road toward him, with one pistol between them, which they had just used to kill an enemy soldier. McCall and Coyte assumed this was their messenger boy, and Coyte returned to the beach and reported his failure to Carlson.

By now, word of the planned surrender had leaked out to mixed dismay, disbelief, and anger. Carlson's cupbearer, Arzt, was muttering to himself. Though Roosevelt was at the center of the debate, no one seemed to blame him.

In the end, the thing became moot: outrigger canoes, sloops, rowboats, the few surviving rafts, and an eight-hour window during which no Jap planes appeared, and the surviving Marine Raiders boarded *Nautilus* and *Argonaut* and sailed for home.

In the confusion, Carlson would not learn until at sea that dead Marines had been left behind, as well as another nine still fighting when the battalion pulled out. An Australian coast-watcher reported the nine were swiftly rounded up by the Japanese and executed. Natives gave him two versions of the execution: one source said they were shot. But maybe, said the Aussie, they had been beheaded. The Japs enjoyed a good beheading of a Westerner, or so the Aussie said. The witnesses spoke only pidgin. And his own pidgin was hardly reliable.

All the Aussie knew for sure, the nine Marines Carlson left behind were dead.

▪ 15 ▪

"YOU'LL NEED CASH. LOCAL MAGISTRATES WON'T TAKE MARINE CHECKS
FOR BAIL."

At Pearl Harbor they declared a holiday. Bands played, flashbulbs popped,
cheering crews manned the rails of moored warships, Admiral Nimitz himself boarded one of the returning subs to welcome back the Marines, and
Major Roosevelt (with his political genes) saw to it that a handsome samurai
sword was handed over to Nimitz by Lieutenant Le François, chosen for
the honor because of his wounds and then spoken to, quite privately, by
Nimitz.

Cromwell wasn't bashful about asking questions. The Jesuits teach the
spirit of inquiry. As do lawyer fathers.

"What did Nimitz say, Frankey?"

"I asked him if he was pleased with what we did. And he said, 'Very
pleased, very pleased. A very successful raid.' "

Le François, too good a Marine and for too long, gave the admiral no
argument. He would then be carted off to hospital, put back together, and
be awarded the Navy Cross.

The men were paid, given six-days' leave, and assigned free quarters in
the Royal Hawaiian Hotel on Waikiki Beach. Arzt didn't think this was a
terribly good idea. "Those boys will get screwed, blewed and tattooed and
then they'll get into trouble," he predicted.

"I'd tell Carlson except he's sensitive these days. That stuff Coyte ped-
dled . . ."

Gunny refused to believe that Carlson, even for a moment, considered
surrender.

"People make up shit like that. They're jealous of Carlson—that he
knows the president, that Jimmy Roosevelt's one of his officers, that he's
got fellows like I on his staff."

And about this ill-advised leave?

"The colonel has only so much patience. So I don't harass the man.
But turning those boys loose on the Royal Hawaiian with a few dollars in
their kicks? Ollie, it's damned foolishness."

That night Arzt, that prudent man who counseled senior officers, went on a modest spree of his own. One that resulted in the partial demolition of one saloon and a bordello and the sending of three sailors, one barkeep, and one Marine (not a Raider) to local hospitals. Carlson, informed of the damage and casualties, summoned Oliver Cromwell to get Gunny Arzt out of the brig.

"You'll need cash. I know these local magistrates. They won't take Marine checks, either for bail or costs. The courts are aware of how easily a stop-payment order can go through. See the Sergeant Major, and if he's short, I'll cash my own check for funds. We'll get it back out of Arzt, garnish his pay if need be. May take a year, but we'll get it, Arzt being an honorable man."

Ollie, deferentially identifying himself to a Honolulu judge as the son of an attorney, and citing several precedents of which the judge was aware, got Arzt off reasonably cheap.

"I couldn't help myself, Ollie," the older man said. "That crap about Evans Carlson running up the white flag. I couldn't listen to that and *not* get drunk."

Cromwell half-believed Captain Coyte. How could Coyte make up lies like that about Carlson? McCall, who was Coyte's man, nearly killed another Raider who called his captain a liar. Ollie loved Arzt and admired Colonel Carlson, but every man had his breaking point. He knew how close he himself had come on Makin with his bloody feet and his platoon scattered, his own youthful confidence shaken. Makin Island, he concluded, might have shaken old Vercingetorix.

Carlson, assessing the raid in tranquility, was, despite his messianic streak, a realist not given to denial, and he concluded that he wasn't nearly as "very pleased" as Chester Nimitz about the operation. He knew the Raiders had been fortunate to get off Makin alive. Knew how he himself despaired, understood now what a disaster capitulation would have been, especially with Jimmy Roosevelt. The raid was trumpeted by the Corps and the Navy as a brilliant success that caught the Japs by surprise, the first land engagement we'd yet won against the Japanese (Coral Sea and Midway being air and naval battles). Eventually the raid would become a motion picture starring Randolph Scott as Carlson. The American press, hungry for a victory—any victory—magnified a minor operation, with a couple hundred men on each side, to epic proportions.

Colonel Carlson knew better, recognized his own blunders and those of his officers and men, the failures of equipment, especially the radios and those rubber landing craft, the hazards of transferring from the deck of a wallowing sub in less-than-pondlike conditions. But at the same time, officers were quietly instructed that their postbattle written reports should make no mention of surrender or supposed letters to the Japanese. Nimitz, it was believed, but never proved, issued these instructions. Later in the war, Japanese propagandist Tokyo Rose somehow got hold of Captain Coyte's letter asking surrender terms and gleefully broadcast it over and over again on wavelengths available to the entire Pacific theater.

Tactically, the raid was bedlam. The result: after Makin, there was less Raider oratory, no more flowery talk of condottieri, of Richard Lionheart challenging Saladin and his hordes. The Raiders' arrogance was shaken. Stoneking, a hard case and not a tactful man, put it this way:

"Makin Island was a fuckup, and everybody knows it was. We just don't say so outside the battalion." That old us-against-them attitude held. It was okay for a Raider to admit they'd screwed up; don't let anyone else say it.

What took the place of that early zealotry was healthy: a solid professionalism founded on the realization that this was going to be a long, hard war that would be won not by exhortation but by tough, well-trained young men and NCOs and officers who knew what they were doing. In future operations there would be better radios, sturdier boats, superior small-boat training. And out of Makin and its embarrassments, there also came this: that a couple of hundred raggedy-assed Marines penetrated eighteen-hundred miles behind enemy lines, surprised an enemy garrison, did substantial damage, and battled on at least equal terms with a more experienced foe, and half of them had gotten away to fight another day.

Much later the Marine Corps would realize the raid on Makin in the Gilbert Islands was also a strategic disaster. What Carlson and the brass had seen as an inexpensive diversion to distract the main Japanese forces from our serious, large-scale landings on Guadalcanal, Tulagi, and the other Solomon Islands had boomeranged.

The Japanese, until then casual about the Gilberts, had been rudely alerted, Makin their wake-up call. An immediate fortification and buildup was ordered at Tarawa Atoll, and especially on its key island element, Betio, barely one mile in length but boasting the atoll's only airfield. It would be those fortifications and a beefed-up defense garrison of some forty-eight-hundred Japanese Imperial Marines, the best troops Japan had, with literally hundreds of massed machine guns dug in just behind the beaches, lashing the shallow lagoon with fire, that would mean appalling losses in the tragic slaughter of the 2nd Marine Division at Tarawa in November of 1943.

War was a learning process. The rapid training, hurried promotion of both NCOs and officers, and accelerated buildup of the Marine Corps from little more than a palace guard prewar to 157,000 officers and men by the Guadalcanal summer of 1942, made foul-ups inevitable. The Marine Raiders weren't the only offenders.

"The Army has paratroopers. So do the Germans. Why can't the Marine Corps have paratroopers?" a Marine general wondered one morning over his bacon and egg. Three or four months later, they did—trained and graduated from the Army's jump school at Fort Benning, with parachute insignia pinned on and all.

Some brainstorms were pretty good. Others ludicrous. Too often, tragic.

The first "sticks" of Marine parachutists floated down in the earliest days at the 'Canal, survived the fall, and fought well. Later, on Bougainville, Major Victor ("Brute") Krulak led seven hundred Marine paratroops on a surprise raid that sent the Japanese reeling in dismay.

But on another drop, a training exercise, the wind was wrong, and several sticks of Marines dropped into the ocean a mile off course, where, weighed down by helmets, boots, and weapons, they drowned almost immediately. It was said that the transport pilots who drove the bus, who dropped the paratroopers, wept as they flew helplessly in circles in the bright blue sky above the dark blue sea and as the last exhausted, flailing Marine sank from view.

And the paratroops, like the Raiders, were among the strongest and toughest of Marines.

Back in Hawaii to refit, even a green officer like Cromwell, who'd just seen his first combat, recognized the time of amateur theatrics was over.

While the 2nd Raider Battalion, Carlson's bunch, was on Maui for rest and recuperation, Merrill ("Red Mike") Edson's 1st Raider Battalion landed on Guadalcanal along with larger elements of the 1st Marine Division and fought a more conventional campaign, a real, grown-up war in the jungle and the hills, months of murderous slogging.

Cromwell and Gunny Arzt had sailed back to Pearl on different submarines, and since the morning Ollie bailed the older man out of a Honolulu city jail, they'd not had the opportunity to talk. Now, on Maui, not far from the beach resort hotel where he first glimpsed Darcy striding up out of the sea, Ollie spoke of the men he'd lost on Makin.

"Did I know the dead guys?" Gunny inquired.

"One of them you did. Ape Lombardi, from Wisconsin." Ollie recalled how Stoneking told him aboard the sub, "I didn't even know we'd lost him. Stoney said Lombardi was stitched by a machine gun. Took him a while to die, and then they couldn't get the body out—not that big a stiff in a rubber boat. That's Stoney's word for them, stiffs."

"It don't bother the dead none, what you call 'em."

"I suppose." Cromwell, still feeling guilty about not having somehow gotten the body back, reminded Arzt just who Ape Lombardi was.

"Yeah, well, maybe I was right about him, Ollie."

"What do you mean?"

"That he was too old, maybe too slow. That'll get you killed in this business."

Arzt understood Ollie's confusion about his first battle and his question, Was it always like this?

"Well, not hardly," he conceded.

"Y' see, champ, we don't usually have Marines in pink silk underwear when they're supposed to be out killing people. I never myself ever seen that before. Colonel Carlson damned near used a bad word over them undies. I know he chewed out Roosevelt."

For Ollie those Raiders in pink silk chasing Japanese infantrymen were an absurd metaphor for the entire Makin fight, etched in memory by the sun glinting off Jimmy Roosevelt's bald pate.

Word began to filter back about the fighting on Guadalcanal from one Marine Raider battalion to the other, refitting on Maui, via bush telegraph and scuttlebutt.

"This here Guadal, it's something," the Raiders sent back: steaming hot jungle, snakes, quicksand, leeches, craggy mountains with waterfalls, sinkholes and rapids, sharks cruising offshore and cannibals and headhunters in the hills.

"Them fellers hate the Japs worseer than us," the Raiders were comforted to learn.

The 'Canal was a hundred times bigger than Makin, with thousands of Japanese instead of a few hundred.

"Can't wait to get there, can you?" Bobby Swing asked pals.

It enthused Arzt enormously to learn that with the first elements on Guadalcanal was one of his personal favorites, the legendary mortarman Lou Diamond.

"What's he like, Gunny?" Ollie inquired.

"About two hundred years old, more or less, with a full gray beard. He can drop a .60-millimeter mortar shell down a chimney at a thousand yards' dead reckoning. All mortarmen are crazy, and their patron saint, ol' Lou, a gentle and ancient soul like that who ought to be dandling the grandkids on his knee, maybe he's craziest of all. Lou's out there at his age in the jungles slaughtering Japs. Mean as a snake, besides."

Arzt shook his head in admiration. He had few heroes, but Lou was one of them. The old sonuvabitch.

Other news arrived through more-traditional means, including tales of great naval battles in the ocean around the Solomons, the infamous "Slot" between Guadalcanal and other, smaller islands, where Japanese and American and Australian warships met in violent collision night after night, the Japs shelling the Marine positions ashore and attempting to land reinforcements— battles that raged so ferociously that the sea beneath the Slot soon became known as Ironbottom Sound.

Guadalcanal was where they were sending Carlson and his 2nd Raiders in November as replacements (what the cynical called "fresh meat") for other U.S. Marines killed or wounded or broken by fever, the jungle, and hard fighting.

Before they broke camp on Maui, in an issue of *Stars and Stripes,* Cromwell came across a familiar name:

"Ben Sweet's gripping, though fictional, account of the fall of France, *Debacle,* has been made a selection of the Book of the Month Club. And is headed for the bestseller lists. In Hollywood, Darryl F. Zanuck is negotiating with Sweet's literary agent over movie rights."

My, my.

A few days later he received a four-month-old letter from Darcy in San Francisco. The Fleet P.O. did wonders if they had a man's name, rank, and serial number. Wherever you were in the Pacific, a letter would eventually find you. But later that week the battalion moved up, and Ollie didn't have the opportunity to reply. No, that wasn't true.

He just didn't know what to say to a rational young woman living in a chic little house in Marin County, doing fashion illustration, going out for cocktails, and returning home to a clean bed and a flush toilet, with no one lying dead on the front lawn. How could he tell her about men who duked it out over a lousy flag, sported silk underwear over their uniforms, beat people to death with axes and shovels, and were now headed to an island of snakes, headhunters, fever, quicksand, and thousands of enemy soldiers? He stowed Darcy's letter, intending to write when he knew what to say.

Maybe he'd find time on the 'Canal, as men now called it. Maybe he wouldn't.

▪ 16 ▪

No longer was Ollie expected to tag along puppylike on the heels of the
salty Frankey or anyone else. Makin Island had done that. He'd been in
the same firefights as Le François, had also lost men, hadn't cracked or run,
had killed enemy soldiers, as coldly efficient as any of them. He'd fought
before in the ring for a trophy or a title. Now he'd fought for his life, and
in the doing he had changed, had grown more sure of himself. It was a
confidence that communicated itself to his men. During a field problem
they ran on Maui, one of his riflemen, Fleurie the hockey player, was sent
on report by the platoon sergeant.

"He gave me a parcel of shit, Lieutenant," Stoneking said.

When Ollie asked why, a sulky Canuck snarled, "I should of stayed in
Canada." Cromwell shrugged it off, but when the Canadian pushed, he
was taken out into the boondocks by his lieutenant and given a boxing
lesson.

The chastened Fleurie, spitting out two of the few front teeth he still
had, afterwards attempted to make his peace with the platoon commander.

"We coulda used you at Camloops on the power play, Mr. Cromwell."

"Can't skate, Canuck."

"Plenty guys can skate, sir. Not all of 'em can fight."

The big Canadian seemed to mean it, and Ollie accepted the gesture
without saying so, just nodding.

When Navy admiral John S. McCain was ordered back to Washington
from the Solomon Islands fight, he wrote to General Vandegrift, the Marine
commander on Guadalcanal whose Marine division was fighting the ground
war under McCain's overall direction:

"What I hate most is the breaking off of my close association with
yourself and the tough eggs under you."

Now, Cromwell would be one of those "tough eggs" fighting under
Vandegrift, along with Canuck Fleurie and Stoneking and the rest of the
refitted 2nd Raider Battalion landing as replacements on the 'Canal.

Vandegrift, delighted to have them, threw in the Raiders to relieve the Marine parachutists, trimmed by battle losses and fever to a mere company masquerading as a battalion. Vandegrift knew even the best troops had their limits. "Lean Marines are better than fat Marines. But they can get too lean to fight."

As Cromwell's platoon and the rest of the Raider battalion hiked inland to take over their share of the main line of resistance (MLR), they passed the paratroops filing out, men bleached by tropical rain and blistered by sun, whittled down by fatigue, hunger, bites, and the crud, huskies reduced to bone, tendon, and ligament, their eyes darkly sunken, teeth wobbly and falling out from illness and the fever, twenty-year-olds moving like old men.

But tough eggs still able to shout, "Better you than us, Bud."

The 2nd Raiders would eventually put their own brand on the Guadalcanal campaign. But Red Mike Edson's 1st Raiders, during their famous and slightly mad "long patrol," got there months earlier than Carlson's bunch. When Merrill Edson (who would be awarded the Medal of Honor) proposed a monthlong combat patrol the entire length of Guadalcanal, most of it Japanese-held territory, senior officers were incredulous.

"You can't travel that light, Edson. Rations for a single day when you're gone for weeks?"

"Yessir, we do travel light—more weapons and ammo, less food."

"But men have to eat, Mike!"

"Yessir, and will, living off the country."

"The country, Edson? That's pure jungle."

"Jungle crawling with Japanese. And where there are Japs, you'll find good, cooked rice. You feed a Marine a little rice every day and plenty of water, that's all he needs. So we'll find the Japs and take their rice bowl away from them. Before, or after, we kill them. That's what this patrol is all about. Killing Japs, sir." At which the brass, reluctantly, gave him the green light.

Red Mike may have lacked Carlson's antic charm and messianic fervor, but he did get off a good line.

Arzt, when he heard of Edson's successful "long Patrol," indignantly rallied to Carlson's side.

"Oh, hell, Ollie. Edson's a good officer. We all know that. But fellows like me and Carlson and this battalion, we can go without home cooking as long as anyone. I don't recall too many meals on Makin Island, and no one got mal-something. What's the word when you're starving?"

"Malnutrition."

"That's it! And nobody perished of it. A few people got shot or drownded but in a war that's the price of admission, ain't it?"

Much of the Raider mystique, from the very start, was hokum, was bravado, recruiting-poster bullshit, but at the heart of it was a pagan ferocity, a willingness, an eagerness, to kill. Nothing synthetic about that. Edson was furious when men broke off an assault to take shelter.

"Every time a Japanese fires a shot, some of these birds stop to dig a hole and move in."

It wasn't just carping. Edson and Carlson, both with plenty of small-unit fighting in the Banana Wars, knew that the quicker advancing troops reached an enemy objective, the fewer dead they left behind. A hesitant, plodding assault lost momentum, lost its shock value. It was on the open ground of the approach that you lost the most men, not in those murderous little brawls in the trenches or the underbrush. Jungle warfare was instinctive, primitive stuff, Neanderthal in its simplicity. It wasn't just Marine craziness; there were commonsensical reasons for what the Raiders preached. You lived like animals, fought like animals; some died like animals.

Carlson's own thirty-day patrol behind enemy lines, "swift, silent, deadly," accounted for five hundred Japanese dead at the cost of thirty-five Marine Raiders killed. They scaled chill mountains, slogged through malarial swamps, drafted local headhunters as guides, and all this on a few rations, supplemented by small game (including rats) and rice captured from the enemy. And despite hunger, the Japs, snakes, leeches, and the headhunters, with crocodiles slithering off the mud banks to stalk Marines wading those jungle rivers, Lieutenant Cromwell was starting to feel at home on the 'Canal.

It was on this "long patrol" that Jimmy Roosevelt, liking his instincts, first tried Ollie as their point man, sending him out with a small detachment scouting ahead of the main party. From the first day Cromwell's men fell on the Japanese with a deadly, efficient ferocity. That assignment led to another. And another. Ollie was learning to kill, doing it swiftly and well. He had that indefinable quality of dash, what the French Army calls élan.

And he proved resourceful. One of Ollie's originals, a geologist named Woody Martin from Houston, who'd worked for the oil company before going off wildcatting on his own, was discovered to have unique skills. Asked why an oil man (they were all assumed to be rich) would be joining the Marines, he responded, "For the dough, Sarge. I'm the frigging king of dry holes." Woody knew the East Texas swamps, the nearby Cajun bayous, and now on the 'Canal he set about teaching Marines to catch and roast small crocodiles. "Nothing better than a young gator roasted over mesquite wood," Martin testified, "and crocs and gators are cousins, ain't they?" After Cromwell's fourth or fifth such mission, James Roosevelt plucked proudly at Carlson's sleeve.

"Yes, yes, Jimmy. The young man knows the game."

It took only a few more patrols for Carlson to realize he might have a prodigy on his hands. Ollie possessed a rare talent for infiltration, a flair for ruse and ambush, the imagination to concoct the unexpected move, the swift, cold instincts to carry it through. In the nightmare of a Japanese-held forest north of the Temaru, with a local as their guide (a headhunter short of fresh material whom they christened Tonto), Cromwell and eight men forded the crocodile-plagued river at midnight and fell suddenly upon a full platoon of Jap infantry, killing them all in perhaps ten minutes. It says something for Cromwell's restraint (the Jesuits and all that) that he permitted their faithful native guide to take only the Japanese officers' heads.

Though some Raiders thought Tonto should have done the lot of them. "For what happened at Makin, y'know."

Carlson beamed to see the increasing maturity of Ollie's work.

"You were right, Jimmy," he told Roosevelt. "We have ourselves a natural."

The major nodded agreement. He knew.

His men knew, too, though it was left to the pugnacious Fleurie to boast of their intimacy, "Don't tell me about Cromwell. He's maybe the best lieutenant the battalion's got."

"Whupped your sorry ass, too, Canuck," Bobby Swing reminded all.

Arzt added his endorsement. "Damned Japs are eating raw fish, and thanks to Ollie, we're feasting on loin o' croc."

When Carlson's men returned to Henderson Field, they drew forty-eight-hours' rest before being sent back into the line. It was then that Major Roosevelt again called up Cromwell. "Colonel wants a reconnaissance patrol out across the Savo Straits for a look-see on Florida Island. I'm sending you with some attached weapons. You're bound to run into Japs."

Being singled out for a job like this was good news/bad news. The brass trusted you to do the work; but the work itself might be nasty. This one sounded very nasty. Since he had no choice in the matter, Ollie took the graceful course. "Thank you, Major."

A salty Australian coast-watcher, Lieutenant Henry Josselyn, and one of Edson's veteran First Battalion men, Robert Neuffer from Dog Company, were brought in to brief the patrol.

To maintain silence they would cross the Savo Straits by canoe, the boats rented from local headhunters on Tulagi and paddled by natives, some of them headhunters as well. There was a naval battle offshore during the night—flashes, booms, explosions of all sort, noisy as hell but nothing to disturb the land-bound Marines. By dawn things had calmed down, and there were four sizable war canoes pulled up on the beach waiting for Cromwell's platoon. The natives had sharply filed teeth and beetlenut orange gums, though Neuffer insisted they gathered Sundays in a thatched-roof church without walls or stained glass to sing full-throated vespers.

"You couldn't find better Christians at a Baptist church supper in South Carolina," the Marine assured them.

"These fellows also dislike the Japs," Josselyn offered. "A good Jap head brings a handsome bounty in the outback villages. And the trip itself should be amusing. Loaded down as you Marines are, there'll be about an inch of freeboard between floating and sinking. You may be using your helmets to bail, Mr. Cromwell." The chief, also rented for the day, thought it was funny to have all these large, heavily armed Marines getting into his boats. Or perhaps he was merely studying their heads, sizing them for market, and calculating bounties.

Lieutenant Josselyn carried a canvas gas-mask bag filled with rope tobacco that he cut into chunks for the paddlers, punctiliously reserving a generous twist for the chief, who didn't deign to paddle but sat there Buddha-like, chewing and spitting. Having fallen silent and in brilliant sunlight, Savo Strait was strangely empty. The natives were accustomed to paddling island to island across the open water but never before so laden with cargo: Marines, weapons including a sixty-millimeter mortar, and their light machine guns. There was considerable jabbering among the headhunters about the weight to be carried, whether they should take passengers at all. More tobacco changed hands, and the war canoes were launched, smoothly at first, and then more precariously, into a rising wind.

"You're sure this is going to be okay?" Cromwell asked Josselyn, who was in the same canoe.

"Right, mate, unless we capsize."

Still well off Florida Island's shores, Cromwell's Raiders were confronted with a sight none of them expected. The surface water between them and the island was boiling, churned by what seemed to be hundreds of sharks feeding on the surface.

"Cortez! You've seen sharks. Will they come at the boats?"

"Lieutenant, I never seen this many schooling up in the Keys. Who the hell knows?"

The closer they came to this deadly armada the more fearsome it was—
"sails" as high as five feet, the dorsal fins, cruising all about. The native
paddlers were almost in panic, and none of the Raiders was very confident.
Even the chief was no longer amused. Ollie certainly wasn't. And worse,
the wind was getting up.

"Lieutenant," a Raider called out, "we going down, sir?"

"Hell, no," Cromwell said, making it up as he went along. "Not with
these boys paddling."

In truth, Ollie admitted to himself, "these boys paddling" didn't look
very cocky themselves. Not with those tall dorsal fins drawing closer. So,
as an afterthought, he shouted out to Stoneking in the next canoe, "Tell
them to bail, Stoney. Use their helmets."

Stoneking, from a Dry state and unused to oceans, thought sure they
were going down, the waves lapping over the gunwales and everyone bailing like madmen.

Then Neuffer said, smart as paint, "If we go down, them sharks is
going to be working at us. Why don't we toss a couple grenades off there
to port. Let the bastards feed on each other and not on decent Christian
fellows like us and our headhunter pards."

"You think so?" Cromwell asked. He was no expert on sharks.

"Fuck, yes." Then, "sir," Neuffer added.

Sure enough, with the first explosions a couple of sharks came up
barreling and rolling and lurching, pouring out blood, and a dozen other
sharks gave up feeding off whatever baits had drawn them and went for
their own kin and brethren, snapping and biting and tearing away big
chunks of shark, with the Raiders bailing even harder, the headhunters
paddling faster. The carnage was terrible, with sharks ripping into other
sharks, the dead and the still alive. As the canoes slid more smoothly into
shallow water, Ollie saw close-up what had drawn the sharks. Bobbing
facedown in the water were the dead from last night's naval battle, Japanese
and Americans both, the bodies of victims, the men blown off warships in
the night. Blood and dying men's struggles had called up the brutes. But
once the war canoes fetched up on Florida Island, all the Marines had to
worry about was Japs. And compared to being in a leaking canoe with
headhunters and among sharks, that was almost plummy.

As Bob Neuffer put it, "Mr. Cromwell, we got our pass."

Maybe so. But the nightmare memory of those five-foot sails cruising
toward them through dead bodies would stay with them for a long time.

▪ 17 ▪

If you read Ben Sweet's bestseller *The Deadly Beaches,* or saw the film, you know something of Ollie's war. Homogenized versions, but still . . .

In ways, Cromwell had been fashioned early as a soldier—shaped in the panicky confusion of Makin Island, bloodily honed on Guadalcanal. He was still only a junior officer. Colonels like Carlson and Edson lay out the operational plans; the generals set strategy, the long-term goals. A company-grade officer like Ollie took his platoon where it was sent, fought the enemy where he found him, and tried to get back.

But while he dreamt uneasily of the big sharks of the Savo Straits, he no longer suffered those early guilts when his men died and he'd survived. How much mourning was a young officer supposed to do? Cold-bloodedly, Cromwell attempted to remember his dead as they had been, vital and alive.

As soldiers do, he grew a protective carapace, accepting death as what Arzt called war's "price of admission," echoing the cynical wisdom of the salty enlisted man about his beloved Corps, invariably called, "this here Crotch."

From the 'Canal to the Russell Islands to Wickham Anchorage to New Georgia and to Bougainville, Paruta Island, the Piva Trail, and the raid on Koiara, Cromwell and his men did their bloody work. Much of it by now, to satisfy the poet among us, "under the Southern Cross."

How many were left in the platoon from the start, from tent city in California?

Not too many.

Ape Lombardi and Gallatin of Princeton, dead on Makin. Inge was gone, Black Cloud. So was Ollie's favorite, Bobby Swing, jumped by the Japs and crucified on a banyan tree, bayonets driven through his hands and feet. He remembered Bobby as he was—swift, lithe, graceful—and not at "the hour of our death, Amen." Fleurie the Canuck lost a leg and one eye. He was back in Canada, trying to pull together a hockey player's one-legged life. Woody Martin was gone, too, sent to OCS at Quantico. Dash was dead. The New York Jew who'd survived Barcelona and who in July of '43 had been caught in the barbed wire at Enogi Inlet, had been machine-gunned to death.

"Good man, Dash," Ollie said, and meant it.

"Yessir," agreed Stoneking, "played a nice guitar." Platoon sergeants measured loss in their own way.

It was early in 1944, the third year of the Pacific war, when Headquarters Marine Corps decided to shut down the Raiders, now swollen to four battalions and eight thousand men. Nobody leveled with them that they were de facto being disbanded.

Oh, maybe Carlson knew. And Red Mike. But if they did, they kept shut about it, fearing a loss of control over their tough eggs, their wild men, if word got out. So, instead of being told the truth, the Raiders were shipped home to Camp Pendleton, where, they were told, they would rest, refit, and be trained on new weapons and in brilliant new tactics.

"Getting us ready to take Japan," men whispered among themselves, rather proud of the distinction, while dourly convinced they were reading their own obituaries. If the Japs fought tenaciously for sand spits or volcanic rocks out there on the far Pacific, how tough would they be when defending their homes, their god figure of an emperor, sacred Mount Fuji, and the Land of the Rising Sun—all that crap they were forever going on about?

"It does give a man pause," even Jimmy Roosevelt, himself now a light colonel, admitted.

Captain Oliver Cromwell, fresh from an Australian hospital, caught up to one of the returning Raider transports at Pearl and reported in to Camp Pendleton with the rest of them.

Bougainville was where Cromwell won his medal.

He had been a first lieutenant leading a daylight recon patrol of a reinforced rifle platoon up a bare-assed little hill called Yoke about twenty-five hundred yards in front of the Marine line when they began receiving heavy small arms, and antitank grenades and thrown grenades as well, tumbling at them down the slope. The Japs were dug in at the crest, and the Marines were out in the open on the hardscrabble slope. Ollie ordered an assault that was beaten back by an entrenched enemy force estimated at company strength. Intense rifle and machine-gun fire and dozens of hand grenades rolling and bouncing along the ground stopped them. When he ordered another attack and it too was stonewalled, they settled into a nice little firefight, sniping on both sides and pretty lively. It was then Sergeant Stoneking spoke up.

"Mister Cromwell, we go up there again, we ain't gonna have enough men left to carry back the wounded, never mind the deads."

He was right. The platoon sergeant had been around, and when he spoke, it carried weight with Ollie. And this was a recon, not a combat patrol, and with fewer and fewer Marines on their feet and plenty of Japs up there, and with night coming on, the hillside was feeling more and more lonely.

"Okay, Sergeant. You're making sense."

"Yessir."

The citation signed by "Sec/Nav," the secretary of the Navy, took it from there—the prose clipped, terse, and official, and for all that the more impressive:

> When it became necessary to withdraw the patrol due to the number of casualties, First Lieutenant Cromwell took command of all able-bodied and walking wounded to evacuate the seriously wounded from the hill. With total disregard for his own personal safety, he exposed himself to an intense barrage of enemy hand grenades and small-arms fire while ensuring the successful evacuation of the Marine casualties.

He was written up for a Silver Star for his "extraordinary heroism in the face of extreme danger," but the Marine Corps being stiff about such matters, the medal was routinely bargained down to a Bronze Star with combat "V" for valor. When the cynical Gunny Arzt heard about it, he dropped Cromwell a congratulatory note:

"Don't be pissed off about not getting the Silver Star, Ollie. The Bronze Star's fine. And, looking at it like the Marine Corps does, you didn't take the frigging hill, did you?"

Cromwell had to admire the pragmatism of both Arzt and the Corps.

In early 1944 Ben Sweet caught up with Ollie at Pendleton, where they were reforming a 4th Marine Regiment. The original 4th ceased to exist after the surrender of the Marine Guard detachment at Peking the day of Pearl Harbor and the rest of the 4th Marines on Luzon in 1942. Those were men who would die in the Bataan Death March.

"*Life* magazine wants me to do a piece on the Marines," Ben explained. "I figured you know as much as anyone."

"Oh, hell, Ben. Go interview some general. I was in the sideshow. The

Raider battalions were colorful, but it was the Corps itself that took the 'Canal and Tarawa and the rest. I missed most of the big battles."

"Then who punched that hole in your hand and shot off half your ear?"

"The hand was a rifle shot. Not my fault. The ear? I did something stupid. Caught a grenade, tossed it back, and began congratulating myself. I was still taking bows when the second one came along."

"Where was that?"

"Last November, back on Makin Island. When the Second Division landed on Tarawa, I was with a short battalion that took Makin. We killed five hundred Japanese; they killed two hundred of us. A small fight but a hard one. They sent me because I'd been there before and qualified as an expert on local flora and fauna."

The Marine Corps knew who Ben was, how influential, and they assigned Ollie to brief the writer, shepherd him around the huge base where young Marines were trained before shipping out to the Pacific as replacements. Ben asked plenty of questions, and having been approved by the brass, Ollie answered most of them. Tossing in a few anecdotes of the Raiders as local color. Ben wrote it down, had already a few wild stories of his own.

"You ever hear, Ollie, that Marines collect Jap ears and skulls? Threaded the ears into necklaces to send home for their girls?"

Ollie looked at him. It was too stupid a question for an intelligent reporter like Sweet to ask. But Ollie tried to answer.

"Don't buy crap like that, Ben. That doesn't say it never happened. After a certain number of landings, so many pals dead, men get brutalized, they go nuts. But wild stories like those could be why Jap civilians living on the islands commit suicide. They heard about Marines collecting ears. Passing on half-assed folktales like that makes trouble. And it demeans you."

Sweet didn't really listen. He made up his mind on things and wouldn't be budged. Like Hemingway knowing more about Miura bulls than the matador. Ollie tried one more time.

"I'll give you a *true* tall tale. You ever hear of a Marine called Johnny the Hard?"

Ben shook his head, intrigued, thinking maybe some usable gore was coming.

"Back in France of 1918 at Soissons there was a Major John Arthur Hughes who wore the Medal of Honor. Won it in Central America, I think. Strictly buttoned-up, ran a very tight ship. His men feared Hughes, but they idolized him. Called him Johnny the Hard. Being hard is okay, Ben. Collecting ears is sick. Marines are better than that. And as a writer, *you're* better than that."

"Sure, Ollie."

Cromwell gave up. He sensed Ben was interested only in "the good stuff," Marines who collected ears. He was glad he hadn't told Ben about the Makin Marines wearing pink silk Jap underwear. He didn't want to see *that* in *Life* magazine.

That night, at the officers' club, where Ollie hosted dinner, men queued up to shake Sweet's hand. Even the base commanding general stopped by. They all wanted to chat with a man who'd won the Pulitzer Prize and married movie stars, and who at this very moment was writing a cover story for *Life*. Ben lived up to his marquee billing, you had to say that. He regaled them with yarns: Madrid under siege, the fall of France, the Stukas strafing the Tommies. Here, his listeners felt, was a witness to history, a man whose work and colorful private life qualified him, as columnist Robert Ruark put it, as "a younger, sober Hemingway."

Men who'd fought on the Temaru, or waded the deadly lagoon at Tarawa, goggled at Sweet's war stories. What of their own stories?

How odd it all seemed to Cromwell, who really knew Ben Sweet. Would this vast Marine base, this club, these officers, even this particular dinner show up in print, in a future book, a Hollywood film?

Ben's cover story about Marines did run in *Life,* a first-person account of war complete with colorful tales of combat-maddened Marines vengefully slicing off ears, and it was immediately snapped up by his book publishers in Manhattan. An expanded hardcover version swiftly made the *New York Times* and *Herald Tribune* bestseller lists. The book, even Cromwell would later admit, was lively reading, a real fire-breather. Critics not only admired Sweet's work, they acknowledged his courage, getting so close to frontline Marines that you wondered how he came through unscathed.

"Ben Sweet," said the *Chicago Tribune*'s book page, "goes with the fighting men into harm's way. And takes the reader thrillingly with him."

Of course, the *Trib* was Ben's first newspaper, and he was a local boy. So treating him respectfully was to be expected. Only trouble was, Ben didn't make clear he'd not really been in any of the actual fighting. Cromwell had earlier had his suspicions about Ben's "eyewitness" war correspondence from a besieged Madrid and then from France.

But Ollie didn't know those wars, hadn't fought in Spain or France. He did know the Pacific, about which Sweet was now writing gripping prose. And as far as Ollie could determine, the most riveting vignettes, the most colorful anecdotes, had, in fact, derived from two days of conversation with Captain James T. Cromwell while the two men jeeped across the dry brown hills of Camp Pendleton and yarned over dinner with other Marine veterans at the officers' club.

Some Marine officers came down hard, not on the imaginative Ben, but on Ollie Cromwell for having promoted the Raiders (and himself) to an important journalist at the expense of the Corps in general. Ollie ignored the unfair criticism but had to take seriously a fitness report that suggested Captain Cromwell be shunted off to a desk job because of a damaged hand. It was a bum rap, some senior officer getting back at him, and Ollie didn't hesitate. He phoned James Roosevelt, now working in Washington as an aide to the president. As the call was going through, Cromwell considered the irony of having become a "user" in the grand tradition of his pal Ben.

"Colonel," Ollie said, "you know a Raider doesn't need a manicure to kill a fellow. They put me behind a desk, I'll take to drink. Ask Arzt, if he's still alive. He'll tell you."

Cromwell in the end beat the fitness report, and orders were cut sending him to "duty beyond the seas," in command of a rifle company in the 1st Marine Division, refitting in Australia. It was a job Cromwell wanted, and Roosevelt knew it.

"Don't screw up now, Ollie. You're a good man, but you have your wiseass moments, and the brass has a long memory. They don't like a self-promoter feeding a college buddy his war stories. They'd prefer to feed Ben Sweet their own war stories . . ."

"Jesus, Colonel, I was ordered to brief Ben. I did it and got screwed. They can't believe . . ."

"Ollie, shut up. This war's into the ninth inning, and you don't want to miss your last turn at bat."

The two old Raiders talked for a few moments about mutual friends—men they'd lost, men who were still serving—and then Roosevelt broke off, laughing. "And I don't want to hear about you cursing out superior officers for being bald."

"Yessir, Colonel."

"The name's Jimmy, as you well know. Come see me after the war. We both live in New York, and my dad will be retired by then, living up the Hudson and writing his memoirs. I'd like you to meet the old man. He makes a grand dry martini. You could tell him about Hitler. . . ."

And from that day, if there was a newspaperman around, Ollie kept his mouth shut. Not even saintly old Ernie Pyle, "the G.I.'s reporter," would get an on-the-record "good morning" out of Captain Cromwell.

■ 18 ■

Cromwell led his rifle company ashore on Saipan June 15, 1944, green youngsters with spirited, untested platoon leaders, but with good sergeants, the kind who kept young officers alive and turned boys into warriors, the essential spine of the Marine Corps. There was a wisecrack about such salty noncoms:

"Give those guys two hundred pounds of steel wool, and they'll knit you a stove."

The Marines fought their way off the beach and up into the hills, capturing Garapan after a tough fight. There were thirty-two thousand Japanese troops on the island, half Imperial army, half Special Naval Landing Force men, just as tough as they sounded, the largest enemy garrison on any Pacific island the Marines would take. Saipan was worth defending since it had flat, open space for the landing strips heavy bombers needed. From Saipan, you could reach Tokyo with a full bomb bay.

Saipan was also the site of *Smith vs. Smith,* pitting Marine general Holland M. ("Howlin' Mad") Smith against an Army general named Ralph Smith whom Howlin' Mad had to relieve to get the Army's sluggish Twenty-seventh Division moving. Ralph Smith, Howlin' Mad was convinced, was squatting there on the Saipan beaches with his finger up his ass. As Marine colonel Joe Alexander wrote:

". . . the thought of a Marine officer relieving an Army officer of his command in the midst of battle proved too much for the Army brass to stomach. Charges were leveled against Holland Smith; [Admiral] Nimitz was besieged by Army generals."

But Ralph Smith was sent home. And the Twenty-seventh Division moved up and out, carving through Jap lines, fighting aggressively, taking its objectives.

Still, said Joe Alexander, "the whole case clouded the otherwise good relations between Leathernecks and GIs on Saipan and led to poisonous senior-level relations between the two services for a generation."

A time span that would include Korea. Where Marine generals would be reporting to an Army general who was a son of a bitch.

Cromwell's people fought their way up into the hills, witnessed close-up the bizarre mass suicide at towering Marpi Point of Japanese troops and civilians, the elderly and children and women. One Jap rifleman fired a final clip of ammo at the Americans before he, too, stepped off into space and smashed onto the seaside rocks below. It was one of those last bullets that broke Ollie's shoulder.

He was evacuated to Australia, to a hospital at Adelaide to be repaired. The surgeon, a Bostonian new to the Pacific, having set bone and patched up torn muscle around the broken shoulder, marveled at Ollie's disfigured hand.

"Before the war, in civilian life, Captain, did your work involved using your hands?"

"Yes, Doc, I was a boxer."

"Oh?"

The nurses were a mix of Americans—U.S. Navy ensigns and lieutenants mostly—and Aussie civilians. One of the latter attached herself to Cromwell, giving his shoulder attention, helping him in and out of his shirt. Ollie could walk fine, that was no problem, and the nurse, a nice-looking kid with freckles, made a positive thing of getting him out into the sun every day. She was the Australia Chamber of Commerce when it came to the benefits of a little sun.

"That's where your freckles come from, I guess," he said.

"Red hair and freckles go together, Captain. Even Yanks must know that."

She was twenty-two years old and on the bounce from losing her one true love, an Aussie "leftenant," fighting the Germans at Monte Cassino. "We grew up together, me a year younger, and we were best mates, surfed and played mixed doubles along with everything else. So that when he got his orders to Europe, we decided, why not? and got married. We had six weeks, and then he shipped out. He's dead four months now—a nice Catholic boy killed trying to capture an old Catholic monastery from Germans who might have been Catholic as well. Doesn't make much sense, does it?"

Her name was Nan Murdoch, related to a local press lord, Sir Keith Murdoch, who'd been knighted in the first war for his war correspondence from Gallipoli, where Brit officers sent wonderful young Australian and New Zealand soldiers to be massacred by the Turks and the local dysentery. Murdoch smuggled out dispatches and, narrowly evading prosecution for breaking the censorship rules, was dubbed Sir Keith. Nan owned a small car but had no rationed petrol, so she took Ollie to the beach on a two-seater bike, riding slowly so as not to risk what he called his "wounded flipper." On the beach, as he enjoyed the sun and read, she swam, body-surfing and going well out, to where the "gentlemen in the gray suit" swam, the big sharks you find cruising off all Australian beaches.

"You're not afraid?"

"No. You see the fin, you catch the next wave and just ride it in. So long as you don't panic and splash a lot, they take little notice. I don't believe we really taste all that good to them."

Cromwell might argue that, remembering the man-eaters of the Savo Straits, but what was the point? When his shoulder was finally healed, he joined her in the ocean, the saltwater on his wounds soothing and healing, but he stayed prudently this side of where the surf broke.

"You *are* afraid, aren't you?" she asked. "Or am I being rude to ask?"

Cromwell shook his head, smiling at her.

"You're not rude. I'm afraid. At Guadalcanal the sharks came following the naval battles. They ate the dead sailors, the living as well. The Japs and us both. No distinctions made; they ate everyone."

"But the battles didn't scare you."

"No. I was trained for that, to fight alongside other men. To fight *against* men. I understand that. But not to go someplace where I'm just bait."

She nodded.

"I see. But you're wrong. Men are far more dangerous than fish."

Nan was still remembering Monte Cassino. And her young husband, her best mate, who didn't worry about sharks and played wonderful tennis, and who was now dead.

He was alone, she was lost, and they were falling for each other, Ollie and Nan Murdoch, both understanding it was the war that hurried such things along. But it didn't entirely deprive them of reasoned thought, so that when, in a spasm of passion and just plain liking this girl, Cromwell blurted out an awkward sort of proposal, Nan smiled and proved herself smarter than he was. She said no.

"I'll sleep with you and happily so, Ollie, but I won't marry you. I've married one decent bloke and sent him off to die, and I shan't do it again. Never!"

Since he protested that he was unkillable and that he had the citations to prove it, Nan made one concession:

"I've no need of citations, and I've seen the scars. Outlive the war, Captain Cromwell, come back to Adelaide, and we'll make more beautiful love and talk about it over a cuppa."

In late 1944, Ollie was now no longer a boy—twenty-nine, nearing thirty, still a young man by most criteria—and with the war surely heading to its conclusion. The Marines invaded the Palaus in September while he was still recuperating from Saipan, and they fought through the month and into October on Peleliu—very hard fighting with terrible casualties on both sides. Never heard of Peleliu? You're not alone. But it was one of the keys to ending the war, only 450 miles from Mindanao and MacArthur's dramatically promised, "I shall return."

The scales had tilted; we really were winning the war. Which didn't mean it was fast. Or cheap.

Captain Cromwell counted his losses, ticked off the dead. Going all the way back to tent city in southern California, each of Ollie's losses a vignette of war, another Goya panel titled, *Los Desastros de La Guerra*. Only Arzt, it seemed, the ultimate survivor, canny and invulnerable, remained whole. Stoneking the platoon sergeant? Oh, hell, platoon leaders get killed, platoon sergeants retire after thirty years, that was the conventional wisdom, and, in Stoneking's case, it might be true. He was somewhere in the States, training new men.

It was then that his father wrote Ollie for the last time:

> You know how proud I was of you in Berlin in '36 when you lost that fight. Well, in different ways, I am just as proud today. I hope your shoulder is coming around. The things you've accomplished are almost beyond my ken. You were just a baby when they put in the draft in 1917 and I missed World War I. At the time, how glad I was. In love with your mother and with a young son and my law career sailing along. Later on, I wasn't so sure. If Shakespeare is correct, and we owe one life, maybe we also owe one war. You're fighting yours, and I never did. I feel, too, that I missed something. That I shortchanged the country, maybe shortchanged myself . . .

Ollie wrote back a day or two later; just a note, but one of reassurance, which began, "Dad, you didn't miss a damned thing." And told him how he loved and admired his old man, and missed him, too.

A month later he got word his father was dead. Cardiac. Ollie was glad he wrote that note.

There were Marines with the blood lust who didn't want the war to end quite yet. The rumor was that when we invaded the big home island of Honshu, all six Marine divisions, 120,000 men, would go ashore first, attacking abreast on the Jap beaches. That, men said, with mingled awe and solemn dread, would be maybe the biggest single battle ever fought by men, and something you didn't want to miss, not if you were a Marine. Sensible men shuddered at the prospect, but there were plenty who wanted to go chest to chest with the Japanese Army on its home field, to kill them and take their country from them. To men who'd done tours at Pearl Harbor and had friends who died in the Bataan Death March or were beheaded on Makin or worked to death in the coal mines of Honshu, this was the only way the war should end. Was Cromwell one of those who thought like that? "A widow-maker"? "Kill-crazy"? Sometimes, he had to admit, yes, maybe so. But cold crazy. Not inflamed with hate, but cold and with calculation. As he was long ago in the ring.

Ordered to North China to help oversee the surrender of a half-million Japanese troops in Manchuria, Mongolia, and China itself, Captain Cromwell found these undefeated Japs arrogant, surly, defiant. He experienced an upsetting, but understandable, fury, tempting him to unleash his men. But you didn't do that, did you? Not against a defeated army. Yet how could he forget his Key West sponge diver Cortez, lying sightless in a naval hospital, or Bobby Swing bayoneted to a banyan tree?

Or forget Gunny Arzt?

By then, he, too, was dead. Remember Arzt on Makin Island, sweaty and happy, a shotgun in his paw, glorying in the fight, shouting out to the young Cromwell, "Meat and drink, Ollie! It's meat and drink!" He'd survived the Banana Wars and all that early fighting against the Japanese on Makin and the 'Canal, and now the indestructible Arzt was dead on Iwo. Not dramatically on Mount Suribachi, glorious symbol of a fight that went on for weeks after the historic flag was raised and Joe Rosenthal took his unforgettable picture. It was at the mouth of one of those anonymous little caves sheltering the defeated Japanese in the last hours of the fighting for Iwo that Gunny Arzt finally got it from a grenade he never saw coming. It had been tossed by a slug-nutty, shell-shocked Jap soldier who then promptly killed himself with his last grenade, having gotten one more American and being pleased about it.

Casualties. The price of admission. And, as far as Cromwell was concerned, you could add one more to the casualty roll: Evans Carlson himself. Oh, he survived all right. They gave him a few more medals he didn't need, eventually promoted him to brigadier. But that was all window dressing. When they broke up the Raider battalions in '44, the flame went out. Carlson still served the Corps, but it wasn't commanding Raiders. He no longer led Marines in a fight.

It was never the same.

▪ 19 ▪

NOW, CARLSON WAS DEAD. SO OLLIE SAT DOWN AND WROTE TO JIMMY
ROOSEVELT.

Nor, once the war had ended, was it the same for Ollie Cromwell.

After the big parades, the bands and the shouting, the kisses and the
"well-dones", peacetime, which most Americans welcomed, was turning
out to be pretty dull, enervating, somewhat empty for a soldier. In a series
of hot, dusty garrison posts in places like Camp Lejeune, North Carolina,
wartime glories gave way to pared-down budgetary restraints, pointless
snapping-in without ammo, to field exercises little more than Boy Scout
hikes, and boredom relieved by hard drink and soft women.

Marines of Ollie's age and rank were being forcibly retired. A Corps
of seventy-five thousand Marines didn't need as many officers as one of
half-a-million men. Like all of us Ollie had his moments of self-doubt, but
they were rare and of brief duration. His natural and vigorous confidence
usually bubbled through. When a woman he was seeing, sensing his rest-
lessness and intent on taking him in hand, pounced, urging Cromwell to
quit the Marine Corps, he was quite ready to defend the position. . . .

"Take the initiative, darling," she said. "Seize the day!"

"I've been seizing things for five years," he responded drily, "*and* taking
initiatives."

An attractive offer came in via a fellow Notre Dame alum who was
doing important things at a big Madison Avenue ad agency and thought
Ollie might be effective at bringing in new business. He saw this for what
it was, a salesman's job, and he was quickly able to say no, but owing the
man the courtesy of a personal response, he flew up to New York to meet
over drinks at the Biltmore Men's Bar and tell a college pal he was staying
in the Marine Corps.

"There's bound to be another war, Johnnie. Too many ornery Russians
and other sons of bitches out there for there not to be."

Occasional ugly incidents sustained his argument and held out the
cheerful, if flickering, promise of new wars: a brush with Tito when two
U.S. fighters were shot down over the Adriatic; the Berlin airlift with its

Stalinist saber rattling; ominous rumblings out of China, where the Reds seemed to be winning.

So Ollie hung on, staying in the Corps, waiting for a new war, occasionally lifting a glass to it with other, like-minded men:

"The next war!"

Then, in late May of 1947, in a local North Carolina paper, he came across a small item, bottom of the front page:

> Marine hero Brigadier General Evans Fordyce Carlson, 51, died yesterday in Enman Hospital, Portland, Oregon. During World War II Carlson created and led the so-called Marine Raider battalions, and, based on his wartime experience in China gave them their slogan, "Gung Ho," or, "Work Together." A successful movie about the Raiders, *Gung Ho,* starred Randolph Scott in the role of then Colonel Carlson.

That was all. Months later Cromwell's orders came through, transferring him to Camp Pendleton, and once he'd gotten squared away, Ollie wrote to Jimmy Roosevelt, wanting to talk to someone about Carlson and intent on asking a question that had eaten at him since 1942.

Like so many veterans the late president's son had settled in California, where he was making a run at a local congressional seat. Jimmy seemed to have inherited FDR's booming cheer.

"Cromwell! Good to see you again. And a major yourself by now!"

They chatted of Pendleton, which for both men held a mystique, the base where Roosevelt and Ollie had become Raiders and from which they'd gone to war. Many Marines, Cromwell among them, even now trailed a clandestine love affair with sprawling Pendleton: the raw, tan landscape; distant mountains; the big barracks of yellow pine freshly sawed and smelling of sawdust and sap; the ocean lapping golden beaches; the tall, tailored palm trees in officers' country; the tall and tailored wives as well. Despite the the hills swarming with rattlers and tarantulas, Pendleton took on a romantic, pioneer sweetness.

The Roosevelt place was elegantly casual; his wife, sleek, blond, very nice, fetched cold drinks as the men sat by the pool to talk. The Roosevelts were old money, old lineage, the family tree making its sinuous way through two distinct American presidencies, fleshing out the genealogy of the country itself. Ollie had no insecurities about his own Park Avenue background, but it was hard not to be impressed by Roosevelts.

He wasn't quite sure how to proceed; only sure that Carlson's death and a postwar unease had triggered this visit.

"Colonel . . ."

"Call me Jimmy; everyone does. Even people I've never met. Tell me what's on your mind."

"Okay, sir. The Makin Raid was five or six years ago. But it stays with me, how freighted those three days were, the impact they had on me as a young officer."

"On all of us, Cromwell."

"Yessir. But what I can't shake is whether in those final hours, did Colonel Carlson have some sort of breakdown? Had the Old Man gone nuts? Or had we failed *him?*"

Roosevelt listened without speaking, and Ollie went on.

"When Carlson died last spring, I thought I could finally ask a few questions and not betray the colonel. Whatever my doubts, I would never do that. Never. I was only a kid lieutenant back then. But you were the battalion exec; you must have *known.*"

Roosevelt looked stricken. Ollie wasn't the only hero-worshiper. Jimmy had assumed this was yet another old Raider eager to yarn about the past, maybe sucking around for a political job if Roosevelt were elected, cashing in on his Raider credentials. But here was Cromwell raising questions about a national American hero and Roosevelt's own personal icon. Seeing the stunned look, Ollie said:

"I'll withdraw the question, sir."

"No, no. It's bothered me as well."

Mrs. Roosevelt came out then with iced tea, and, sensing the men's intensity, she excused herself on some errand. Ollie heard a car pulling out of the graveled drive. Now Roosevelt tugged his chair closer.

"You were only a youngster on Makin but already famous. I knew that, knew about the Olympics, about your fight on the flight deck against that Army gorilla. . . ."

"Wells, Bruiser Wells. He lost, but I went to the hospital."

". . . and I was the son of a *very* famous man. There we were, both of us, among the few Marines privileged to serve under a strange but great man, Evans Carlson." Roosevelt was now as caught up in memory as Cromwell.

"You know, in the thirties, my dad used to have Major Carlson to the White House for a jaw. Obviously, he didn't do that for many junior officers. And due to Carlson's fascination with things Chinese and with the Communists, there was some risk in having a 'pinko' to dinner. You know how Washington talks. And then when we got in the war and I decided to join the Marine Corps, Carlson was helpful cutting the red tape. I had lousy eyesight, and he smoothed the way.

"It was funny. It's 1941, just after Pearl, and the whole country is still reeling, and I decide to join the Marines. My dad shook his head; my mother was appalled. But at the same time FDR was a politician, and it didn't hurt to have one of his kids a Marine. He used to tease me about it, how many votes I was worth. Every time one of my brothers got his name in a gossip column, Dad would ask, being a needler, 'Why can't you be more like Jimmy and get shot at instead of written about?' And then he'd roar that great laugh of his."

"I remember, and with enormous pleasure," Cromwell responded, "how you once invited me to visit after the war when your dad would be writing his memoirs and mixing martinis."

"Very good ones."

"Anyway, I'm sorry the president didn't live to see the war won and to write that book."

Roosevelt nodded, the familiar bald head gleaming in the southern California sun, a half-smile on his face. Then, returning to Carlson:

"I don't have to tell you how screwed-up Makin was. We weren't such hotshots after all, but just cocky gyrenes under fire for the first time and in over our heads. By that third day the only thing organized on Makin was the chaos. Maybe we never would get out; maybe the Japs had us. And, when we most needed his calm, our CO was losing either his mind or his nerve. One minute Carlson walked on water; the next, he didn't seem to know what orders to issue.

"When Carlson briefed Commodore Haines aboard the sub coming home, he never mentioned surrender. It was assumed the colonel would discuss what happened, and why, during his postraid critique back at Camp Catlin in Hawaii. He never did.

"I just walked away from it. Can you imagine the talk if I confronted him? 'FDR's son second-guesses Marine hero Carlson!'

"Remember this, Ollie: after months of Jap wins, America had a colorful little fight we might plausibly claim to have won. The newspapers ate it up. People finally had something to cheer about. Why smear the officer who led the operation and got home with more than half his men? I'm still tending the lamp of Carlson's memory, and I'm not alone in that.

"We left some dead behind and nine Marines still alive. That's how crapped out we were. But you never hear how Carlson got the natives to take care of and bury the dead, bribing them with Raider knives and other gear. Paying them off in junk to bury our sacred dead. While he was agonizing over surrender, he was busy doing that, too. People don't have any idea how screwed-up Makin was, top to bottom. . . ."

Mrs. Roosevelt had returned by now, and Ollie thanked Colonel Roosevelt, who walked with him to where he was parked.

Wanting to change the subject, and genuinely wanting to hear the answer, Ollie asked, "In 1945 we thoght we'd fought the last war. You think we're going to fight the Russians?"

"Might have to, Ollie. Depends on them, I guess."

Cromwell nodded, and then Roosevelt said:

"I'm not sure I answered your real question, Cromwell, because I'm still confused myself. Life isn't a whodunit, and maybe some things are meant to remain mysteries. Whatever Carlson did on Makin, I know what you did, know a little about the rest of your war. I'd be proud to wear your fruit salad myself. Win me a few votes, those Purple Hearts alone. So don't go sour on Evans Carlson, *or* the Marine Corps. You're too good a Marine for that. . . ."

Ollie thanked him. Then he said, "I'm not sour, Colonel. But when you're young and fall in love, as I did with the Raiders, you expect things to be perfect. When they're not, you feel betrayed."

"You know as well as anyone, war's an imperfect business. But when it was over and guys like me got out and went back to making money, you didn't. And you could have, with your brains, your connections. But you stayed in. Can I ask why?"

"Why does a man stay married?"

Roosevelt said, "You tell me."

"Love. Comfortable together. Habit? I dunno. I can't conceive of not being a Marine. Maybe some of us never grow up, still playing cowboys and Indians. So I stay in and get ready for the Russians."

As he drove south toward Pendleton, Ollie glimpsed off to his right the starlit ocean to which Marines seemed inevitably to be drawn, the oddly named Pacific that had been central to his life, to his work. And might be again one day if things went right.

Which in Marine Corps jargon meant, "If things went bad."

BOOK THREE
KOREA

■

▪ 20 ▪

THE BEACH AT DANA POINT, CALIFORNIA, EARLY JUNE 1950.

This was 1950, maybe the best time there'd been or ever would be in America.

By 1950 the Big War, as men who fought it called World War II, had been over nearly five years, and people again had new cars and jobs, and all the soldiers were long home and going to college on the GI Bill, or apprenticing at their trades and buying those neat little seven-thousand-dollar houses that Mr. Levitt was putting up, spanking bright with carpeting and washers and dryers, anywhere there was a bit of green lawn. The Germans and the Japanese were finished, and unless the Russians did something stupid, there would never again be a big war, and the United States, rich, powerful, and untouched, would pretty much run the world.

The best of times. Except maybe for a handful of restless men like James T. Cromwell who had no more wars to fight and realized by now just how much they missed the last one.

Cromwell was still a serving Marine and in the spring of 1950 was a recently promoted lieutenant colonel serving as operations officer, or S-3, of the 5th Marines, a famous infantry regiment stationed at Camp Joseph H. Pendleton, on the lovely rock-cliffed southern California coast between Los Angeles and San Diego. S-3 was a staff position and no job for a light colonel with ambitions, and Ollie Cromwell hoped, and with reason, soon to command one of the three rifle battalions of the 5th Regiment.

Standing in his way, though unspoken, was an uneasiness about Cromwell on the part of the brass. Because he'd been a Marine Raider, one of Carlson's men, more-orthodox Marines regarded Colonel Cromwell with wary and conflicted attitudes. With respect surely, even awe, but also with suspicion. Such men, in a shooting war, had value, being capable of feats of arms. But they were also dangerous—likely to get you into trouble, lead you into temptation, into what theologians called "occasions of sin." A Cromwell could raise hell with the enemy and win a fight for you; he might also lose you your command. Ollie was aware of these reservations about him, tried to ignore them and do his job well, and hoped things could work out so that he would soon be commanding troops once more, eventually one of the great Marine regiments.

In the meanwhile he'd been enjoying this lovely house and serving creditably at Pendleton, and, as even Ollie would have to admit, he was living pretty well.

On the first Sunday of June, Cromwell sat on the red-tiled patio of his oceanfront bungalow, which was set nicely atop one of the low cliffs at Dana Point, about thirty miles north of Camp Pendleton. Sipping freshly squeezed grapefruit juice and a second cup of black coffee, he went from reading the Sunday edition of the *Los Angeles Times* to squinting out at the Pacific Ocean and the slow rollers coming in on a light breeze. He was barefoot and wore faded khaki shorts and a navy wool sweater against the cool morning. Cromwell was now in his mid-thirties, a big, suntanned, very fit, square-headed man with closely cropped brown hair and a battered claw of a right hand. There were other scars, none of them debilitating or to be embarrassed about: they derived from Colonel Carlson's war, plus a comic-opera sword wound suffered up in North China fighting bandits after the war. Cromwell's flat nose owed nothing to combat but to his years as a prizefighter.

During the war Cromwell's father had died, leaving his only son a bit of money, which a broker pal and classmate from Regis High School invested for him, and wisely, and on the strength of which, and certainly not on his Marine Corps pay, he could afford to lease a house like this one, overlooking the water, and with an admiral's widow living on one side and a Hollywood talent agent on the other, Mr. Bone.

"Hi, Major! I mean, hi, Colonel!"

"Hi, Jay Jay."

"That's swell, being a colonel now."

"Only lieutenant colonel. You don't have to salute."

It was the girl next door, agent Bone's daughter, heading down the narrow cliff trail toward the beach with her surfboard, a big twelve-foot board boys used. Cute, rangy kid, potentially a heartbreaker, but also strong, with the long legs and the swimmer's shoulders especially. Jay Jay's father was a power in the movies, and they had a place in Bel Air as well as this beach house at Dana Point. Mr. Bone, when he spoke at all to Cromwell, seemed to be tiptoeing around him, as if Marine officers were menacing or carriers of some exotic disease. The kid attended UCLA, but as far as Ollie could see, she was majoring in surfboards. She didn't tiptoe around him at all and had even gotten him to try her board himself, though he was a beach-runner mostly and only occasionally a swimmer and bodysurfer (prudently close in to the beach). Didn't like sharks. Once, here at Dana Point during a swim, he'd ventured out near the line of breakers, a seal came up under him, gray and sleek and big, and Ollie panicked, thinking it was a shark. Out of pride he didn't share this with his young neighbor as she tried to inculcate the surfer code in him.

The great gaffe in surfing, Jay Jay explained, was "dropping in."

"What's that?" the colonel asked.

"You've caught a wave at the curl, and you're riding it, real nice, and some meat cuts in front of you, underneath. Steals your damned wave, makes you pull up and bail out. That's 'dropping in.' "

"And it's a mortal sin," Cromwell remarked, having been taught by Jesuits.

"Yeah, if you think in religious terms, which I don't much," Jay Jay said, "but when they pull that shit on me, I don't pull up. I drive right through 'em. Pile-drive them right into the goddamned sand."

"You would have done very well in the Marine Corps," he said thoughtfully.

"Why, thanks, Colonel Cromwell."

He meant it, too. But he'd stick to swimming in close to shore and to runs on the beach.

When Jay Jay headed down the cliff, he watched her go, enjoying the view of her legs and her bottom, and then he went back to his *L.A. Times*.

There was nothing much in this edition, and Sunday passed quite pleasantly—a swim, a run, a Red Sox–Yankee game on the radio from Fenway Park—and about six he showered and got into gabardine slacks, black-and-white saddle shoes, and a linen jacket and drove up to Laguna Beach, to a place he liked called the White House, where, before taking a small table for dinner, he had something called a Moscow Mule (vodka and ginger beer) at the bar while the nance of a piano player riffed through his repertory of show tunes. Shrimp cocktail, a steak, a baked potato, and a half bottle of St. Emilion later, Cromwell was back outside waiting for his car, just in time to see the gorgeous southern California day fade as the sun fell toward the Pacific. Way out there, in the line of breakers, he could see the last of the day's surfers, waiting for that final ride, that ninth wave of legend, the ninth wave of a ninth wave that would carry a rider halfway up the dry sand to the cliffs.

Nice, it was all nice here at the beach in southern California.

Cromwell knew there were other great places in the world, for he had been to some of them, but this was pretty good; life was pretty good. He understood that some people thought of him as a loner, perhaps even a lonely man for whom they ought to feel a marginal pity: no wife, no kids, no family.

They were wrong. If you were a Marine, that was one thing you did have. If you were a Marine, you had family.

"Here's your car, Colonel," the attendant called to him, interrupting his reverie.

"Thank you," he said, giving the boy a quarter. The car, too, was pretty nice, a big Buick Roadmaster ragtop, dark blue with a tan canvas top. Ollie got in, turned on the radio and picked up orchestra music he thought might be Artie Shaw, coming from the Mark Hopkins Hotel four hundred miles up the coast in San Francisco, from that big rooftop bar and dining room, the Top of the Mark.

That wasn't bad either, picking up music from the Top, and he hummed along as he drove south fast along Route 101, the loom of hills dark to his left, the Pacific with its last glints of gold and pink in the western sky to his right.

About ten that night, as he sat up in bed reading this new Budd Schulberg novel about Scott Fitzgerald, the phone on his night table rang.

"Cromwell," he said.

"Ollie, it's Lou Tynan." Tynan was the S-1 of the 5th Marines, the adjutant.

"Yes, Lou?"

"Just a heads-up, Ollie. Headquarters Marine Corps will be calling you tomorrow. They need a man for a job overseas. They think you're the guy."

"What job? And where?"

He wanted to stay with the regiment here and get a command. They wouldn't have to go through headquarters to arrange that.

"Don't know the job. But it's in South Korea is what I hear."

When he put down the phone, Ollie got up and went into the den where he kept his books, and he pulled out a big atlas. He didn't know Korea, had never been there, but it wasn't too soon to start learning.

He fixed a primitive outline of the country in his mind, noting North Korea's long border with that of Communist China and the proximity (only 40 or 50 miles) of the Soviet Union's Siberian frontier. Interesting to note that the South Korean capital city of Seoul was no more than 20 or 25 miles south of the country's artificial dividing line, the 38th Parallel. And that Japan was only 100, 150 miles away.

Then, without agonizing over it, Ollie got back into bed with Budd Schulberg and the ghost of Fitzgerald and read himself to sleep. No tossing, no turning, no nightmares. And when he woke just after six Monday morning, he remembered Tynan's call and the atlas. Was something going on in Korea? Had some ill-defined new tension arisen? And was something about to happen along that phony border of theirs that divided the supposedly democratic South from the decidedly Commie North?

Some ten days later Colonel Cromwell was flying west across the Pacific toward Asia and his new job as military attaché to our ambassador at Seoul. A promotion? Hardly that. Though he'd been taken aside and told, "We like to have a good man on the ground in chancy places, Cromwell. Just to keep the Marine Corps in the picture. In case we have to fight."

And was Korea a chancy place? Was a fight coming?

Oh, Headquarters Marine Corps wouldn't go that far, he was told, but it was worth keeping an eye on. And, on that basis, and being a good soldier hoping for another war, Ollie agreed to take the job.

On Sunday June 25 North Korea invaded the South, a new shooting war was on, and Ollie was in the middle of it, not commanding Marines but baby-sitting the American ambassador. Trying like hell not to get him killed or captured on their frantic run south.

▪ 21 ▪

The war was only in its third day, and in the capital despairing people were already saying that it was lost.

Such early hopelessness was not unreasonable. It was based partly on rumor—wild stories you heard repeated and passed along by frightened civilians or by enemy subversives stirring trouble and preying on natural fears. Some of the defeatism was quite real, of course, and undeniable. Those were certainly actual fighter planes, identifiable as Russian Yaks, coming in low over the rooftops and without opposition (the South Koreans didn't seem to believe in antiaircraft guns) and shooting up the place, strafing and bombing targets of opportunity. Schools, railroads, little old ladies with parasols against the sun, bridges, power plants, small boys on a playground's swings, military barracks, a crowded department store, the trolley car or an ox-drawn cart, barges chugging up the river Han, the country's largest airport at Kimpo, fishing trawlers with their trawling nets offshore at Inchon—they were all in play.

And by that first Tuesday of summer, June 27, the onrushing enemy had closed sufficiently that their big .155-millimeter artillery shells were slamming into midtown Seoul; shorter-range .105s were hitting the northern suburbs. Which had the shaken South Korean government and officials of the highest rank planning to get out of town, making it understandable that ordinary people were scared, listening to rumors and saying the war was lost.

More to the point, even "Fat Chae," who weighed three hundred pounds and was the Republic of Korea (ROK) army chief of staff, was saying the war was lost. Wringing his pudgy hands, sweat staining his khakis in the humid heat of early summer, Fat Chae said so.

Didn't take long, did it? Not as fast as the North Korean enemy was coming south. As swiftly as the ROK army was collapsing.

Korea had been a nation only five years. Liberated by the Americans in 1945 after half a century of brutal Japanese occupation dating to the

Russo-Japanese War, Koreans didn't yet know how to *be* a country, never mind defend one. And against their own kinfolk in the North, their own people. Putatively a democracy, actually a minor despotism, South Korea was growing a sort of youthful patriotism, lively but not yet rooted, bursting into enthusiastic choruses of their new anthem, "Arrirang," when President Rhee passed. Now, unknown to them, their president, his Western wife, and their cronies were already packing, readying to abandon the capital, the people, and their freshly minted democratic system.

Early Sunday morning on June 25, first day of the war, Korean president Syngman Rhee called Tokyo to alert Douglas MacArthur at his official proconsular shogunate and to demand air and other U.S. military assistance. At first MacArthur's aides refused to wake the general. But when Rhee began his incredulous screech about leaving Americans in Korea to be killed "one by one while you keep the general asleep in peace," even complacent Tokyo began to stir. And smartly! When MacArthur finally got on the phone, he promised Rhee ten planes and to airlift a few howitzers and some bazookas, but in the end did nothing. Rhee was an old man and often cried wolf. The supreme commander had brought the Japanese to their knees aboard the USS *Missouri,* moored majestically in Tokyo Bay just five years earlier. He was not about to be panicked by an elderly Korean politician. Later on Sunday, approached by an American correspondent about the war situation, General MacArthur sloughed it off as another "border incident." "The Koreans can handle it," he assured the reporter. By Tuesday the 27th, with the North Koreans punching through everywhere and with South Korean troops changing hurriedly into civvies or running, MacArthur (still in Tokyo, managing affairs at a distance) was no longer as jaunty. Much like the pope, he tended to speak infallibly, issuing oracular statements: "If Seoul falls, Korea falls, and the war is lost."

And Seoul was in the process of falling. Even Lieutenant Colonel James T. ("Oliver") Cromwell, U.S. Marine Corps, could see that, and he'd been in town a mere four days. You couldn't walk from his hotel to the U.S. embassy, a ten-minute stroll, without sensing a palpable tension, seeing the fear in peoples' faces. The distant boom of big guns and the first noisy and frightening, if not very deadly, air raids did little to reassure the populace.

Several varieties of hell were already loose in the city, with its million-and-a-half inhabitants. Officials and citizens both were painfully aware they were only twenty-five miles south of the artificial border with North Korea on the 38th Parallel, with no sizable mountains and only one barrier river intervening, the shallow, sluggish Imjin, which, at its "double bend" just north of the city, was eminently fordable. Though plagued with the local leeches.

As the Red Army rolled powerfully south, those leeches may have been the most impressive thing about the defensive line protecting the Republic of South Korea's capital.

On his long flight to Seoul from Camp Pendleton in southern California, Cromwell had time for plenty of reading. He relaxed with an old favorite, a schoolboy's well-thumbed copy in Latin of Caesar's *Gallic Wars,* a wonderful adventure yarn full of wisdom and statesmanship, also excellent on infantry tactics. Julius Caesar aside, and more to the proximate point, the colonel had also done his professional homework, boning up in mid-Pacific on State Department and Marine Corps position papers, a paperback history of Korea (they were forever being invaded and frequently pillaged), an AAA road map and a better one issued by Humble Oil, and a two-week old copy of *Time* magazine with an article by Frank Gibney assessing the ROK army, calling it "the finest for its size" in Asia. Now, after forty-eight hours of combat, that "finest" of small armies was throwing down its weapons and fleeing, trampling the slaughtered bodies of its own officers and NCOs who got in the way. In the army's panicked wake, chaos, confusion, cowardice, looting, and the casual rape; bridges were blown; railroad tracks torn up; fires raged (set by marauding North Korean People's Army units? Or by South Koreans leaving scorched earth behind?).

And where was South Korea's benevolent patron in all this? Where stood the United States? Beyond MacArthur's windy, empty promises of aid he never sent, what was America doing to help out its smallish client state?

Not much. As a lousy 450 American military advisers tried haplessly to buck up the retreating ROKs, Yak fighters screamed overhead, machine-gunning pockets of ROK resistance and panicked refugees both. Big Russian T-34 tanks were reported clanking into the city's northern limits, while execution squads of South Korean battle police rounded up deserters, shoving any man without a weapon or a documented excuse up against the nearest wall to be shot. Adding to the confusion and doing their damaging best were infiltrated NKPA troops in civilian clothes, a few even masquerading as women. When ROK defenders found the first dead armed North Koreans in petticoats, trigger-happy MPs began shooting any fleeing female walking awkwardly in skirts. None of this energized morale or instilled much confidence in the population.

The ROK Air Force, one hundred fighters and thirty-five obsolete bombers, was caught by surprise, still lined up wingtip to wingtip on South Korean tarmacs hours after the invasion began. It was destroyed on the ground. Douglas MacArthur, who privately expressed doubts that any Korean, North or South, was capable of even flying a warplane, considered this a small loss. Kaesong, a provincial city on the border between the two Koreas, fell almost farcically in the early hours of Sunday when a fifteen-car freight train chugged routinely into the center of town without even a cursory by-your-leave. And when the frieght-car doors were abruptly slid open, a thousand NKPA shock troops jumped out and began shooting people. The ROKs weren't just outgunned; they were stupefied. MacArthur's "border incident" was swiftly becoming a near-Biblical "slaughter of the innocents."

Cromwell had arrived on Friday of the previous week and presented himself and his credentials that afternoon to the American ambassador, John J. Muccio, Naples-born and a sophisticated veteran of other Asian and Chinaside postings. Courtly, meticulous, he questioned the new arrival.

"Where have you previously served as attaché, Colonel?"

"Never have, sir."

"Know Korea pretty well?"

"My first trip, sir."

"Yes, well." The ambassador, inured to the strange ways of Foggy Bottom, didn't even bother to roll his eyes or issue protest. He'd asked the pertinent questions; answers were what was lacking. Muccio shrugged, accustomed to having a backwater like Seoul treated shabbily.

All but the smallest U.S. embassies rated a naval or military attaché or both to advise the ambassador, effect liaison with the host country's defense establishment, and gather whatever conveniently useful intelligence scraps might fall from the diplomatic dinner table or be dropped over cocktails. The job was half glad-hander, half spy, and senior diplomats like Muccio tended to regard an attaché as nothing more than a handy appurtenance, an extra man for the embassy social whirl. A weekend loomed, and Ambassador Muccio, well mannered and dapper, with something of a reputation as a gallant, seemed anxious to be away. A dinner party beckoned. But he paused sufficiently for a few polite, perfunctory remarks about the country, the amiable Korean people, their leader, that great patriot Syngman Rhee, and their crack armed forces, "our valiant and most reliable allies in this part of the world."

"I see, sir. Yes."

Cromwell knew when he was being fobbed off.

"So why don't we get together Monday, Colonel, and I'll introduce you around the office, give you a rundown on what's happening in Seoul, get you included on the cocktail-party invitation roster, and we can talk about your job, how you can be of help. I'll assign a car and driver so you can get out to see a bit of the country on Saturday if it doesn't rain. The Marine outside will arrange things."

"That'll be fine, Mr. Ambassador."

"Call me John, Colonel."

"Yes, Mr. Ambassador."

Cromwell tarried long enough at the embassy to change some money, to get a hotel recommendation and the address of the officers' club, and to inquire if this were the rainy season or just a wet day. The exchange rate was favorable, the hotel fine, and the club lively, but then it was Friday, wasn't it? Almost all the men were in uniform, Army mostly, a few Air Force, many of them with pretty Korean girls. The few, mostly drab American women, Army wives on a rare night out, he supposed, raising the kids and making do on a meager budget, looked narrowly at the slim young Korean women. The scene was an unwitting paradigm of military garrison life at its peacetime dullest. Ollie asked for a table, was told it would be thirty minutes or so, and grabbed a piece of bar and a vodka and tonic with lime.

"Hi, Colonel," said an Army officer, a young captain. "We don't get many Marines here, sir."

"Ollie Cromwell. I'm new."

The captain's name was Podesta, one of the Americans assigned to KMAG, the Korean Military Adviser Group, and he was talkative. Chatty, even. Well, maybe listening was part of what being an attaché was all about. Let the man talk.

Podesta did. Mostly about himself, airing his theories. They had a drink, and when Cromwell's table was ready, the young Army man accepted his invitation to dinner.

"Great steak. Jap. They're known for fattening their beef on Asahi beer. Whether they actually do, it works."

Captain Podesta was an expert on just about everything. He was an artilleryman and had been in Korea a year training ROK troops.

"They any good?" Cromwell asked.

"Not much. For starters, they have no artillery. So I teach them a little range-finding and fire control, which without any guns is sort of a joke. Not many tanks, and those are light stuff, just tarted-up armored cars. Local roads and bridges won't carry the heavies. These ROKs are more like state troopers than a real army. They enjoy a nice parade, though; keep in step with the music."

"No artillery, mmm . . ."

"They don't shoot too well, either. Fat Chae likes a nice uniform but doesn't waste dough on ammo, tries to stay within budget, so they don't spend much time on the rifle range. They snap-in but don't do any actual shooting. Cartridges cost money."

"Snapping-in" meant dry firing without bullets, what American recruits do in their first days at Fort Dix or Parris Island boot camp.

"Fat Chae's their top soldier?"

"That's the one, Colonel—the size of Vermont. Enjoys a meal."

Ollie asked if Podesta had read that *Time* magazine story about the ROK Army.

"Fat Chae must have taken that boy to dinner. Or the reporter saw them march. They march pretty."

"Oh?"

"That's about it. You can't even get these boys to run a field problem up in the hills or camp out overnight. It might rain. One of their officers told me they got a slogan in English. Gave a toothy grin and recited it for me:

" 'If it rains, we don't train.'

"He wasn't embarrassed, not one damn bit. Seemed pretty pleased how clever they were. ROKs would rather do close-order drill on the parade-ground pavement, showing off for the girls. Crawling around and getting dirty? You gotta pay overtime. And it's their own crappy little country they're supposed to be defending."

You couldn't miss the contempt in the American officer's words, in the tone. About one thing, Podesta wasn't at all contemptuous. That was "the visiting team," as he called them, the Red Army on the far, unfriendly side of the Parallel.

"Y'know, Colonel, there's a firefight somewhere along the line between our ROKs and the North Koreans just about every day. They've been fighting an undeclared war along that Thirty-eighth Parallel long before I ever got here. Barbed wire and land mines up the giggy on both sides. Small-arms fire, snipers, mortar, the occasional .105 shell. We don't even write up reports anymore on firefights. No one in Washington reads 'em anyway."

"The North Koreans, tell me about them."

Podesta whistled low, no mocking superiority now.

"Not bad, sir. Pretty good, in fact."

"Why's that? They're the same people, except for politics and the Parallel."

"Well, the Reds, they got the guns. Plenty of .105s, a few .155s—American guns and good ones. The Russkis supply 'em out of Lend Lease we gave them in the Big War. Or Mao Tse-tung captured 'em from Chiang Kai-shek last year and sent them gift wrapped.

"But more than guns, it's their officers and NCOs. Most of them either fought in the war for the Soviet Army or for Mao and his Chinese Commies. Lot of the rank and file did, too."

"But Japan occupied Korea," Cromwell protested. "They were drafting Koreans. Had a lot of them fighting us in the Pacific. Most Japanese Imperial Marines were Koreans. Big guys."

"Yessir, the Japs ran the place, but young fellows fed up with them got out, sneaked across borders. That was when the Russkis and the Communist Chinese welcomed those boys with open arms. Handed them their first pair of store-bought shoes, a uniform, and a hat with a Red star on it. Taught them their trade, sold them the usual Commie indoctrination—hooray for Lenin and all that. They're motivated and pretty well trained, and they got the guns and them big Russian tanks, the T-34s."

"It's that bad?"

"Colonel, Rhee's a hundred years old, their army stinks, and the place runs on influence peddling and corruption. Makes the Truman administration look good. Up north, they got their own dictator, their own little Mussolini. Kim Il Sung. He's not just a Commie; during the Big War he commanded a Korean battalion in the Soviet Red Army fighting the Nazis. A hard boy, Kim. You gotta respect men that fought the Germans outside Moscow or downstream at Stalingrad.

"Our local heroes got four hundred people like me teaching them to salute and how to dig a latrine. War comes along, you figure who's favored in the betting."

Cromwell wasn't even expected to answer. So Podesta went ahead.

"Colonel, put the rent money on it. Old Kim by six lengths."

Ollie was aware of the line between a soldier's gripes and objective judgment. He bought dinner and got change back from a ten, permitting Podesta to buy him a Johnny Walker Black nightcap at the bar and turning down the invitation of an Army major and an Air Force pilot to join their table for a card game. Ollie didn't play poker with strangers, so he just stood there at the mahogany, nursing the scotch, watching sinuous, graceful local girls dance with clean-cut American boys in uniform and listening to a nice little eight-piece dance band play songs that had been hits six months ago in the States, the dinner-jacketed musicians all Koreans and not bad.

It wasn't El Morocco or the Top of the Mark or even the Pump Room in Chicago, but it was okay. What Winter would have thought, what critical scrutiny she might have brought to bear, was something else again, given the standards she set for such places, set for life itself. Winter? Hadn't thought of her for a time.

Winter was a girl Ollie knew in the States. That was her last name, but also what everyone called her, what she called herself. Winter. Just Winter. Even her phone calls opened that way: "Winter here!" She was a New York girl who worked on a fashion magazine, *Harper's Bazaar,* very sleek—the magazine and the girl both.

Cromwell was tall and tough and didn't particularly care what people thought of him, wreathed as he was in the aura of being "one of Carlson's men, y'know. One of the Raiders." Within the Corps there were Marines who feared him, others who pulled strings to serve with or under him. But that was the Marines, where they knew his record as a fighter in and out of the ring, knew about his war. Winter was different.

Ollie had been stationed at Quantico, Virginia, teaching small-unit tactics at the Marine Corps schools and just promoted to major, and he met Winter at a cocktail in Manhattan that a pal got him invited to on an autumn week-end. She was ambivalent about the Marine Corps, intrigued by him, by his wounds and his medals, admiring his uniform and the public glances it drew to them both. The uniform and the medals, that is. The wounds she learned about privately as they went along. But, she sometimes badgered him, musing aloud, mightn't a man as well educated and intelligent as Ollie "improve himself," do "something better"? More "significant"?

Feeling a bit stagy about having to discuss it, Ollie decided quite firmly against telling her of boyhood dreams of soldiering, of the Jesuits at Regis who introduced him to Caesar. And to his idol, Vercingetorix.

"I might make more money elsewhere," he conceded, "but I do, on occasion, fight for my country. Some think of that as significant."

"Oh, darling," she said, running the two words together, and topping him as she usually did in repartee, their rapid table-tennis exchanges of dialogue, "What is it they call patriotism, 'the last refuge of scoundrels'?"

Wiseass cracks like that said something about her acuity, also about her guts. Winter didn't intimidate or shy away; give her that. She and Ollie were such opposites that, for a time, it worked, the elctricity not only pleasant but damned exciting. He was spending weekends in New York, her apartment on Central Park South, or she came down to Washington. He took her to Warrenton the following spring for the point-to-point races (Winter rode, and well, and enjoyed watching the jumpers), the Virginia Gold Cup, to dinner at the Fairfax's Jockey Club on Mass Avenue, to parties along Embassy Row, the diplomatic cocktail circuit. (Youngish, single officers were invariably asked. And who could say no to girls who looked like Winter?)

He got tickets to the year's big Broadway hit, *South Pacific,* and together they thrilled to the soaring music, Pinza and Mary Martin, the sweet love story playing out against an offstage and bloodless war, the handsome, doomed young Marine officer Joe Cable, those perky nurses and jolly tars. "So that's how one spent the war," she said, teasing.

He smiled, wishing that it had been.

"No, Winter, not really. What we saw tonight was the musical comedy version, courtesy of Mr. Rodgers and Mr. Hammerstein. The original was somewhat different."

Winter thought he might go on, tell her more. He didn't.

That December they tried an entire week together, The Breakers in Palm Beach. It was there he made the mistake of grousing about the Corps, momentarily annoyed by some small irritant. She picked up on it.

"My point exactly, darling. They're petty tyrants, unworthy of you, dismissing good men because of budgets. And don't mention how badly they underpay."

"I get along."

"Because you've got a private income."

"Look," he said, knowing she deserved some sort of answer, recognizing her arguments carried weight, "there's an enormous appeal to what I do, to what I am. The Corps, the men, responsibility coupled with authority, the spirit, the adventure, the constantly changing landscape of your life . . ."

When she shook her head, he continued: "How can I possibly explain it? You've never been to war, never known the satisfaction of having fought and won, the camararderie and sheer exhilaration of men at war, the bonding, even the insane, boyish fun of playing soldier. . . ."

"No, I don't understand." In all fairness, few civilians did.

More gently, he gave it a shot. "Look, here's what it's like. You're young and strong, a bunch of healthy young guys in nifty uniforms running around, yelling and shouting, firing guns and blowing things up, diving over barbed-wire fences or out windows, rolling around in the mud, driving fast, speeding around in boats, throwing grenades, riding in planes, fording rivers, scaling cliffs, shooting people before they can shoot you, dodging and snooping and crawling around, giving orders and seeing them carried out, and just plain having themselves a hell of a time with no one to tell you, 'No, you can't!'

"And getting paid to do all this stuff on government time, you see?"

"No. You make war sound like a big ballgame, the World Series or the Kentucky Derby or show-jumping for the blue. . . ."

"Except for the killing, in ways, it is."

"No, it's not. Killing makes it different."

"Well, yeah."

"Ollie, I think you're all crazy."

"You're right, you know," he said, a sappy grin on his face. "We are, a little. All good soldiers are a bit nuts."

She was stubborn, but he was worse, and there was no budging him, and she changed the subject to real-estate futures.

"This mightn't be bad, y'know, a place in Palm Beach for Christmas and New Year's, sunny and warm and where we'd never have to wear any clothes at all. And the flat on Central Park South the rest of the time. You might grow rather fond of it. And of me."

"I'm already fond of you." Which didn't mean she'd closed the sale. As he said:

"Except that I'd forever be off commanding troops at Lejeune or Camp Pendleton. I can't quite see you in government quarters in rural North Carolina. Or I'd be fighting banana wars or confronting the big bad Russians somewhere . . ."

Winter screwed up her beautiful face. "But you're *so* much better than that, Ollie."

"Am I?" he asked rhetorically, for he knew the answer.

"Oh, yes, darling," she said, with considerable passion but giving the entirely wrong answer.

Their relationship sort of piddled away over time, but that was the night, sweet as it was, when Cromwell knew it was over. And maybe, in some instinctive, feline way, Winter knew it as well.

A few months later he was transferred, and that tore it permanently.

Now they were ten thousand miles apart, and she was seeing a banker, a man who did "significant" things (if you believed the columns, and Ollie did), and he was in a hotel room in Seoul, alone and in bed by eleven. Before he slept, Ollie again scrutinized a map of Korea, trying to make sense of its topography and its roadwork and where the railroad tracks ran, fixing the major cities and the larger rivers, setting them in his mind, and making out the heights given for the mountains. Some of the high ground was impressive, places up north as high as nine thousand feet. If you were, like Oliver Cromwell, a professional soldier stationed in a strange country where you might someday have to fight, you liked to know where things were. How you might get there, how you might get away.

Then he reread *Time*, checking reporter Gibney's enthusiasms against what Captain Podesta told him over drinks. Being a skeptical fellow (it went with the work), Ollie took both *Time* and Podesta's disillusioned whine (as well as Muccio's diplomatic blandishments) with a grain of salt.

To Colonel Cromwell, Korea looked like a dull, second-rate posting in a minor, nothing country with its little problems, an assignment that would do nothing to advance a career, specifically his hopes of again commanding Marines in combat, an infantry battalion, perhaps one day a full regiment. But Marine officers go where they're sent. Friday, June 23, was his first day in Korea. Saturday he shook off the time changes, spent the morning sightseeing from the backseat of an embassy chevvy with a bright young, college-educated Korean driver who showed him the splendors of downtown and then drove across the Han River into Yongdungpo, an industrial suburb of Seoul rather as Long Island City is to Manhattan. Cromwell had already seen Kimpo airfield, having landed there, so the driver, and proudly so, showed off the Yellow Sea (which on this particular day looked distinctly gray) as seen from a breakwater protecting the anchorage at Inchon, the port that served Seoul, pointing out the famous seawall, the British consulate, the salt-evaporating plant, and the few heights of land, from which, the driver testified, the ocean views were admirably scenic. He was back in time for lunch at the embassy mess and spent a wasted afternoon haunting the building, looking into rooms and hoping to find someone who knew, really knew, what was going on here.

No one was around. Sleepy sort of place. He wrote a few postcards and dropped into a movie theater where a John Wayne western was playing in English; it had subtitles in a language he did not recognize but assumed to be Korean, and it roused his fellow theatergoers to mingled cheering and cries of alarm as the drama and its climactic bloody showdown played itself out on the dusty streets of a Texas cowtown of the last century.

The Korean War began Sunday morning at 4:00 A.M.

▪ 22 ▪

FOR THE FIRST TIME THE MARINE COLONEL WORE A HOLSTERED
REVOLVER.

By Tuesday morning Ambassador Muccio was burning his papers and trying to get either Tokyo or Washington on the phone and not doing very
well at either. Had the lines already been cut? The Rhee government, to
which he was credentialed, had skipped town. Its pragmatic president, an
exile much of his life and grown sly, was intent on living to fight another
day. He and his Austrian wife, his cronies, a palace guard, and the national
treasury, much of it in gold bars, had taken off in two special trains for the
South. Windblown, trigger-happy riflemen sitting on the roofs of the railroad cars fired at the occasional Yak fighter whizzing overhead. The Yaks
didn't have much to worry about.

To President Rhee's rear, still sitting in the National Assembly in Seoul,
opposition politicians denounced the government for abandoning the capital, vowing to remain in session so as to greet the invaders with a calm
dignity and to inform them the Assembly now constituted the legitimate
government with whom the North Koreans simply must appreciate they
would have to deal. The possibility enemy infantrymen would drive Assembly members at bayonet point from the building and into the courtyard
and shoot them all had not yet occurred to the legislators.

It would, shortly. As they were lined up to be shot.

Outside Muccio's residence a lone, but apparently unflappable, Marine
guard, helmeted and legginged and wearing the three stripes of a buck
sergeant, stood his post with a Thompson submachine gun and holstered
.45-caliber automatic, shooing off petitioners and frightened, confused
members of the embassy staff. Several visitors were passed through, one of
them the ambassador's brand-new military attaché, Colonel Cromwell.

"Come in, come in!" Muccio shouted down cheerfully from an upstairs
bedroom. "You're Cantwell, right?"

"Cromwell, sir."

"Come up, come up."

Muccio was cramming shirts and underwear and several framed, signed pictures of attractive women into a couple of matching soft-leather suit-cases, a .45 of his own stuffed into the waistband of his pin-striped trousers. Cromwell stifled the understandable temptation to ask if the diplomat knew how it worked.

"The maids didn't show yesterday, and the other staff and houseboy ran away last night. Figured it was time to cut their losses, I guess. I sent my number two and most of the staff ahead to establish an embassy wherever Rhee is. You'd better get out too, Colonel."

"Yessir, I guess I will."

Muccio noted for the first time that the Marine colonel had changed into field uniform, including leggings, cartridge belt, and holstered revolver. All he needed now was a helmet, and Ollie was working on that. The small Marine detachment, except for the sentry outside, had also pulled out for the South under orders to find quarters and set up radio and/or phone links wherever the Rhee government dropped anchor. Muccio speculated on that as he continued packing.

"They say the old boy wanted to go all the way to Pusan, three hundred miles away at the southeast tip of the country. But they talked him out of it. Said it would look as if he were giving up. My money's on Suwon, fifty miles from here. Or, if he's really spooked, at Taejon another fifty miles south. That's where Old Rhee will make his stand."

Oliver Cromwell, four days in the country, had a vague idea where these places were, and he knew Old Rhee was president. But just what was Rhee going to "make his stand" with?

"And you'll be joining him, sir?" the colonel asked, not knowing exactly how these things worked and, as a professional, wanting to find out.

"That's what ambassadors do, Cromwell. When a country is falling apart, you accompany the rightful government as best you can to represent properly our own national interests."

That, at least, made sense. Just then another Yak came in low and firing. Was the U.S. embassy a target or simply in the way? There came the sound of window glass shattering and people yelling as bullets whistled through the embassy walls, smashing up the fixtures and fittings, and to hell with diplomatic immunity. To the Marine such sounds were familiar coin, but Muccio flinched, crouching slightly.

Most people do. Crouching under fire was rational and didn't diminish Muccio in Cromwell's eyes.

But it convinced him of one thing: he was assigned to this man as his military attaché and adviser, and he'd better start advising. Cromwell didn't

know the country or the politics or the niceties of the diplomatic trade.
But he knew about war.

"Sir, I think we've got to get you out of here, and now. They're paying
me to be your military aide, and I'm not earning much standing around
here while they shoot up the place."

Muccio, an intelligent sort, didn't argue or pull rank. "Glad to have
you on the job, Colonel. Tell me what we ought to do."

Ollie began by recruiting the salty sergeant outside the door, the Marine
and his submachine gun both. "Sergeant Will Buggy, sir," he introduced
himself.

"Fine, Buggy," Cromwell said. "You're working for me now."

Muccio finished packing. The sergeant had already rounded up a Marine, PFC McGraw, who seemed lost ("I was on leave, Sarge. Where is
everybody?"), and he immediately nicknamed him Lonesome and put him
to work loading Muccio's gear into the embassy Buick and humping Cromwell's Valpak up from bachelor officers' quarters. Good thing his footlocker
was following by ship and hadn't gotten here yet. That footlocker must
weigh a hundred pounds.

"Local roads any good, Buggy?"

"Okay in town, Colonel, but outside, pretty shitty."

That's when Cromwell sent the sergeant to requisition a jeep. In case
the Buick sedan got hung up, they'd want a fallback vehicle. He wished
they had a couple more Marines, and, without saying so, he concluded the
ambassador's decision to send the others south ahead of him had been at
least foolhardy, at worst dangerous.

Ollie looked out through the embassy gates to what they faced on
leaving. The streets were clogged, some soldiers marching but mostly pe-
destrian traffic, some bicycles, a few pickup trucks, and some packed city
buses, carrying people standing on the rear bumper and hanging on, with
even a few on the roof. Most of the civilians plodded along on foot under
the burden of their goods—men, women, and children, not moving very
fast until they heard shots or a Yak screamed overhead or a shell landed
nearby. That was when even the oldsters and the smaller children broke
into pitiful, lurching runs, struggling to keep up and sometimes falling to
be trampled upon and tripped over by the people coming up behind. Hell
of a thing.

War went better without civilians, Ollie told himself, nostalgic for the
broad, empty space of the South Pacific. Just then Muccio reappeared, coming out of the embassy, double-breasted pin-striped suit jacket on now,

Burberry raincoat slung over a shoulder, a panama hat dipping rakishly toward one eye. He glanced right and left at the thronged streets, inhaled deeply, and bathed all there assembled in the warmth of a winning smile. Ollie wondered if this was the usual diplomatic sangfroid or if Muccio had not yet appreciated their situation.

Dorothy and Toto hadn't set out on the Yellow Brick Road as gaily.

As the Marines and Muccio pulled out slowly through the gate into the crowd milling just outside, forcing the mob of refugees to eddy around them as flowing water does around a boulder or submerged rocks, a big shell, maybe a .155, came shuttling in noisily to hit a building on the opposite side of the broad downtown street and bring a sizable concrete cornice smashing down onto sidewalk and gutter, the explosion and the fallen cornice burying perhaps a dozen of the fleeing people. When Muccio's party regained their feet, the ambassador, still quite cool, said, "Why don't I drive, Cromwell? Seeing that it's my auto and I know the roads."

"Fine, sir." Cromwell was starting to learn a few things about Muccio: he might flinch, but he didn't scare.

Fully loaded, off they went, the kid driving their jeep with Sergeant Buggy riding shotgun, the Thompson gun handy, and Muccio and Cromwell (Buggy had found him a helmet) following close on their rear bumper, signaling the turns with hand and arm gestures from the big black sedan with its small, but brightly brave, American flag fluttering from the antenna.

It takes a long time for a million-and-a-half people to leave town, any town, and no one, certainly not Cromwell, had any idea where the tragic, shambling march of refugees began or ended. This big-city stuff, combat in built-up areas as the Marine Corps manuals termed it, was something they hadn't faced in the Pacific except on Okinawa, and Ollie had missed that fight, pulled out with the rest of the former Raider battalion men to prepare for the landings in Japan proper, landings on hostile beaches with which they were to be gifted. Or, as old Raiders themselves said sourly at the time, "Holy shit, ain't we the fortunate ones!"

Muccio certainly knew the town. "We'll try some back streets, narrow, but not likely to be as jammed."

"Fine," Cromwell said. Sergeant Buggy had gotten him a second submachine gun, and Ollie had it next to him on the front seat, this one an M-3, what they called a grease gun, cheap but efficient at short range, firing a .45-caliber bullet. Not as sophisticated as the Thompson, but no one was counting.

Before they got off onto the side streets, they were held up by an execution.

"Look, Colonel," said Muccio excitedly. ROK MPs had waded into the mob to haul out a uniformed South Korean soldier. He was hardly the first deserter they had seen shuffling along with the civilians trying to get out. But he was the first they saw shot.

The MPs had him by both arms, and, shouting at people to get out of their way, they hustled him onto the sidewalk, and smashed him bodily against the wall of a building so that, when they shoved him to his knees, there was blood running down his face. There were no words, no charges leveled, no last wishes. One of the MPs pulled a handgun, a .45, put it to the back of the deserter's head, and fired one shot. When the prisoner crumpled to the pavement, the other MP fired two more shots carelessly into the dead body, not really aiming so much as just getting into the act.

"Well, that's something," Muccio said. "I've never actually seen a man executed before."

"Yeah," Ollie said reasonably, "but with a deserter, what else are you going to do? You shoot a few of them, the others may stay around to fight instead of skipping out."

"Yes, yes," said the ambassador, impressed by the colonel's pragmatism but still a bit uncertain. Also nervy from having seen the execution. Then Cromwell said, "We'd better get rolling again, sir. Not making a profit here."

"Of course," Muccio said, hitting the horn to get the jeep moving and pushing the Buick ahead as fast as traffic allowed.

An hour later they were still in town, with the Han bridges but a distant hope. "Can't be more than two miles, but at this rate . . . ," Muccio apologized.

"Any other shortcuts?"

"Maybe. Let's turn hard left at this corner and see what happens."

The left wasn't clogged, but maybe that meant it was taking them back into the city and not toward the river. Cromwell had to rely on the ambassador's local knowledge, having none himself.

It was then that he saw the tank.

"John! That's a tank coming straight at us!"

"My God, it is."

It was the first time Cromwell had called the ambassador by his first name, but they didn't bother to chat about it. Some Korean civilians were on this same side street between the Americans and the oncoming tank, and they began to sprint away from the tank and toward the jeep and the Buick, scared and looking back over their shoulders.

You couldn't blame them. Even though neither they nor the Americans were yet sure if this was enemy armor and not just a wandering and forlorn ROK tank. Ollie knew it wasn't one of the big Russian T-34s, but maybe the Reds had mediums as well.

It was then that Muccio, almost apologetically, said, "I can get off this street just beyond that warehouse, Cromwell. There's an alley that'll take a Buick but maybe not a tank."

"Yessir, that's *just* what we ought to do."

Muccio was delighted with his new aide. He'd known any number of attachés, none of them nearly as sensible as this fellow Cromwell. Maybe it came with being a Marine? Or that he was a colonel, which made him senior to most attachés. Muccio, being fifty, thought a lot about seniority. Worried about it, too. Younger women began to appraise you more skeptically. Even a man like himself who took care with his appearance, stayed fit. He wished he were Cromwell's age.

How old *was* Cromwell? he wondered. Funny how quickly you forget a tank once you've given it the slip and how you start to worry about other things.

They had one more scare before they got to the Han bridges.

This time, it was a fight. And, afterwards, John J. Muccio didn't really fret about how old Cromwell was.

"Let's play switch," Ollie said. "This end of town's pretty empty, and I've got a feeling we might run into something. Sergeant, let's you and me ride the jeep up ahead. Lonesome can go in style in the Buick with His Excellency."

"Yessir."

Ollie's hunch paid out. They'd just rounded a broken-down city bus abandoned in the middle of the narrow street Muccio assured them led to the river when Sergeant Buggy hit the brakes.

"Geezus!"

Not fifty yards ahead three uniformed men were busily emplacing some sort of machine gun, using heavy rice bags to steady the weapon's legs, and they saw the American jeep a second later than Buggy saw them.

A fatal second.

Cromwell was on his feet on the passenger side with his grease gun firing before the first of the enemy soldiers could start threading the ammo belt, never mind firing the damned thing. And Buggy wasn't far behind with the Thompson. All three machine gunners were down. They hadn't gotten off a shot.

"Okay, Buggy, let's get moving," Oliver Cromwell said coldly. "Like cockroaches in the kitchen. You see one, you know there's plenty more around."

"Aye aye, sir." Sergeants don't question colonels about cockroaches.

As they drove past the bodies, they looked carefully for signs of life. Nothing. For a moment there, Cromwell worried they might have been ROKs setting up in defense, but the South Koreans he'd seen wore GI hand-me-downs.

"They're Commies all right, Colonel," Buggy said. As quick as the firefight began and ended, he'd had the same initial doubts. "I seen them quilted cotton soldier suits before."

"Good," Cromwell said without great enthusiasm.

The Colonel don't really give a shit who they was, our side or theirs, Sergeant Buggy concluded, *just that they was in his way.*

Behind them, tailgating the jeep, the Buick rolled slowly past the bodies. Ambassador Muccio pointedly looked away. He'd seen one execution already that day, and one was sufficient for him.

At last and without further incident, they reached the ramps leading to the Han bridge, with its three vehicle lanes and two sets of railroad tracks in parallel. Which didn't mean it would be an easy crossing. Not with the milling crowds of Koreans jammed up on the approaches and the span itself.

"My God," Muccio groaned, "there's a million of them."

Well, hardly a million. But there were plenty. And beyond a single Yak that thought it might be fun to strafe a bridge, there was no hostile action. Yet it still took three hours to cross the mile-wide Han, during which time the sun died and night fell and a sliver of moon began to rise and people continued slowly to push ahead in a mournful, exhausted stagger. When the two American vehicles finally reached the other, south bank of the river, Cromwell pulled off the road to the bare brown earthen shoulder.

"Piss call, Mr. Ambassador. Do it now or grit your teeth."

Buggy snorted amusement. Around the old embassy, no one talked to Muccio like that. Maybe this Cromwell would turn out okay. He'd heard things about him, things from the war. But you know how Marines jaw. . . .

The sergeant was less intent on slop-chute gossip about Colonel Cromwell and more concerned about catching up with the rest of the Marine guard detachment south of here, to become proper soldiers again and not just guys in a traffic jam. Maybe . . .

Buggy never finished the thought.

It was precisely then that a South Korean engineer colonel, fearful that the advancing Reds were coming too fast, faster than anyone, even General Chae, had anticipated, and worried that the enemy might reach and take the northern end of the bridge before it could be blown, cutting off and destroying what was left of the ROK army and leaving the entire rest of the country open to invasion, decided to beat the North Koreans to the punch.

And to blow the bridge.

That perhaps ten thousand of his own people and from five-to-eight-hundred ROK troops were at that instant crossing the bridge did not seem to occur to the engineer colonel.

THERE WAS AN UNEASY EDGE TO THE SERGEANT'S VOICE. "WE HEARD
ABOUT YOU, SIR."

To Ambassador Muccio and his three Marines, safely on the distant shore, it seemed the world itself had shattered, blown apart and falling to pieces, dizzying and staggering them off their feet. The blast, surely the most impressive ROK gesture so far in this lost cause of a war, set Muccio's Buick to jolting sideways and flipped over their jeep with poor Lonesome lazing there at the wheel. It lasted only seconds and then rained rock and steel fragments and splintered lumber and earth and river water on them. And it moved the ground sufficiently on this side of the Han to drop a thousand yards of steel bridge into the river, temporarily blocking the powerful, brown downstream flow and causing the water to flood out sideways on both banks hundreds of yards inland. The bridge, which now sat on the bottom of Korea's greatest river, had been densely packed with men, women, children, troops, deserters, and even a few overeager North Korean infiltrators, and every material thing any of them owned or had pilfered and could tug or roll or carry along with them.

The night passed slowly, not helped along at all by the cries of the hurt and the drowning—cries that after a time diminished and fell silent. As false dawn broke, Muccio's little task force, brushed off and pulled together unhurt but for a few bruises, stared out at the dead. And the rare survivor still drowning, the thousands of Korean bodies littering the roiled and for the moment blocked and sluggish surface of the Han River, the broad stream slowly carrying corpses to the sea, the bodies just part of the debris, the flotsam and jetsam of war.

At first, Cromwell tried to clear his mind, tried to think back. And failed.

Nothing he could recall from his four years of war, the big one against the Japanese, had prepared him for this. He'd seen plenty of dead, us and them, but never this many in one place at one time, not with women and babies and old people, most of them civilians.

Although Ollie could not yet know it, this catastrophe of the Han bridge would be the single deadliest moment of the entire war.

He turned away, giving his back to the river, not being ghoulish or addicted to mortuaries.

Sergeant Buggy turned as well, this time looking into Cromwell's face in the glow of the colonel's first cigarette of the dawn.

"Begging the colonel's pardon, sir . . ."

"Yes?"

Buggy, still in shock from the blast, had been thinking about this for two days, and now, reticence blown, he just went ahead and asked.

"You're Colonel Cromwell, ain't you?"

Ollie didn't answer. Why did it matter to a sergeant *what* a damned colonel's name was?

"I know who you are, Colonel. You're 'Raider' Cromwell; you're the fighter."

What the hell.

Buggy knew he had said too much already. But he couldn't get it out of his mind what men said, the old-timers, regulars. What they said about Colonel Cromwell.

"Nothing, sir. Guess I'm shook up. Sorry. Didn't mean to be impertinent."

"You weren't, Sergeant. Now just drop it, and let's get this outfit squared away."

"Aye aye, sir," Buggy said. He was feeling better now, less shaky, and glad to drop the subject. Except that he remembered just what it was men said of Cromwell.

How death followed him around.

Muccio, who had a healthy ego and was a personage himself, only half-heard all this and was slightly miffed not to be in on a private joke, whatever it was, and he demanded:

"What's this fellow talking about, Cromwell?"

Was this newly arrived officer some sort of celebrity?

"Nothing, Mr. Ambassador. Just a Marine running his mouth."

At least it stopped Muccio's blathering about the tragedy of the bridge, the shame of what had happened, the innocent dead, all that worthy crap. Ollie gave Buggy a look and unfolded his Humble Oil road map of Korea. Not a bad map. Clever, those Houston petroleum people. Ignoring Muccio's annoyance and Buggy's impertinence, he turned to the job at hand:

protecting the diplomat and catching up with a fugitive government. And not getting caught himself.

"There's a railroad bridge west of us a few miles and another bridge five or six miles east. If they're not blown yet, the Reds will be crossing them, coming after us with tanks. The infantry may be already crossing in boats. We better shag ass, Mr. Ambassador."

Without waiting for a reply he turned back to the sergeant and his PFC. Lonesome was back on his feet and recovered from having a jeep fall on him, but his mouth still hung open.

"Shape up, Lonesome. And Buggy, get these engines turning over. We've got to get Ambassador Muccio to Suwon, wherever that is, and to hook up with the South Korean government and maybe our Marines."

Muccio tried once more.

"But if we could be of some help to these people . . ."

Cromwell looked at him.

"These people are dead, sir, and we can't do a damned thing for the poor bastards. You're what's left of the American government here in Korea. We can't risk getting you captured."

"No, no, I understand."

Muccio was said to cut something of a figure in Seoul's diplomatic community, especially among embassy wives, but no one ever said he didn't have balls. And even now, in full retreat under fire, rumpled, a bit soiled and dusty, he sported the panama. His bow tie was neatly in place; his eyeglasses were squared on the bridge of his nose; a half inch of French cuff showed nicely at the wrist.

The view was wasted on Cromwell, who was scanning the sky and the far bank of the Han River, looking for the enemy. Overhead, in the high blue June sky, the only planes were Yaks; the only vehicle movement he could see on the other shore was T-34 tanks. Even at a mile or more distance, they were so damned big you couldn't miss the silhouettes, and he knew that their long guns easily had this bank of the Han within range. He made the point to Muccio.

"Right, Cromwell," the ambassador threw in agreeably. "At Suwon we'll find the government, catch up with Rhee. And, just maybe, the first U.S. troops come to help us. Suwon, that could be the turning point. . . ."

"Yessir," Cromwell said, less optimistic, knowing the only American troops within five thousand miles were the GIs of the Army of Occupation in Japan—garrison soldiers drinking beer, getting laid, smoking dope, and not precisely sure how you field-strip a weapon or, Lord help us, actually fight a battle. You might as well turn over the war to the Church of Latter-Day Saints.

Colonel Cromwell had signed on a long time ago to fight for his country, and for nearly four years he'd done so against the Japanese.

But he'd never before seen anything like this, the whole business falling apart around him. This was First Bull Run, the last stand on Bataan, the French throwing down their rifles in the spring of 1940. . . .

How did a respectable Marine officer get himself into a mess like this? Getting no answer, he spit to insure that his mouth hadn't yet gone dry and he said quietly:

"If your calculations are correct, Mr. Ambassador, it's fifty miles to Suwon." Then, to encourage them all and slightly louder, he added, "Fifty miles to safety!"

As he spoke, a volley of three shells whistled in and exploded, one, two, three, perhaps 150 yards beyond them, bracketing the road south and sending hundreds of Koreans civilians scuttling and scattering in renewed panic.

"Getting close, Colonel."

"Yes, Ambassador, they are."

"Then it's 'Hi ho! for Suwon!'" Muccio said cheerfully, perhaps a little bravado for effect.

Lonesome and Buggy were having trouble starting the jeep, and as they lifted the hood and pored over its working parts, Ollie thought, *Hope you're right, Muccio*. He knew Suwon could be this bad or worse. But why dampen the man's perfectly healthy enthusiasms?

As for the diplomat, he was thinking "big-picture thoughts": had the UN convened? Would the world respond to Rhee's call for international help? Would a Soviet veto screw things up? Were American GIs on the way? And would Douglas MacArthur come marching home again, hurrah, hurrah . . . ?

Ollie was thinking ahead, too. Basic, foot-soldier stuff, looking not into tomorrow or next week or fretting about Soviet vetoes but peering a few hundred yards ahead, looking for North Korean infantrymen he would try to kill, looking for big Russian tanks from which he would run. Korea wasn't yet a proper war; for a professional soldier, it was more a midsummer's nightmare: no troops to command, no strong point to defend, no enemy position to assault. The bastards were coming, and he had nothing to fight them with.

Korea so far was only retreat, fear, and flight; tired, hungry, tattered, dirty, and frightened people trudging south. "And us with them," he reminded himself. A trio of ill-matched Marines with a striped-pantsed diplomatic dandy to nurture and protect. Two weeks ago Ollie was at Camp Pendleton dreaming of the crack Marine infantry battalion he was soon to command. And now . . . ?

The jeep engine turned over, and Ollie said, "Let's go, Ambassador. The North Koreans will be coming, sir."

"Yes, yes, Colonel."

Ollie was thirty-five years old and thought there were no surprises left. He'd been a Marine since he was twenty-one and fresh out of college had been on the Olympic team, and one afternoon in Berlin had actually seen Hitler.

And now? And now . . . ?

▪ 24 ▪

THE AIRSTRIP AT SUWON AND A BRIEF, INSPIRING GLIMPSE OF DOUGLAS
MACARTHUR.

Suwon, fifty miles south of Seoul, didn't look like much; worse, it stank
of defeat.

Nothing but a couple hundred dispirited ROK soldiers, most of them
sleeping where they lay, their rifles and other weapons strewn about in the
mud puddles. There was a dirt airstrip, turned to slop following the rains,
surrounded by paddies, but with a couple of low hills squeezed in just close
enough that a plane didn't have much leeway landing or taking off. Suwon
was pretty thoroughly screwed-up all by itself, never mind being regularly
bombed and strafed by Yaks. To add to the confusion, the town was unaware it was about to be taken over as the site of an ad hoc summit con-
ference, with all manner of generals, the press, and possibly a president on
hand.

When Ambassador Muccio's doughty little band arrived as refugees
from the North, a KMAG colonel named Sterling Wright seemed to be in
charge at the airstrip, but the way things were changing—not for the
better—how long was that going to last? Wright had only gotten into town
himself and wasn't quite sure about anything. Ambassador Muccio slipped
and fell getting out of his own Buick, and his mud-caked pinstripes could
have used a dry-cleaning. Nor had the ambassador been overly cheerful
even before his tumble.

"I'd hoped President Rhee would be here and setting up some sort of
functioning government."

"Well, sir, he's not," said the American, Wright. "He and the Missus
and their two special trains didn't even stop for the buffet lunch. They got
as far south as Taegu before anyone took attendance. Then it occurred to
President Rhee, after he telephoned back to Seoul, that he'd already run
too far too fast and was facing accusations of cowardice. So they doubled
back north by train fifty miles or so to Taejon. That's where your boy
Drumwright showed the old gentleman a wire intended for me that said,
'Be of good cheer,' signed, 'MacArthur.' So Rhee bucked up a bit on that."

"Drumwright's my deputy," Muccio explained to Colonel Cromwell.

"That's fine, sir," Ollie said. Wright and Drumwright, great; they could go out as a vaudeville act, maybe appear on *The Ed Sullivan show.*

But what else was happening here at Suwon beyond ROK soldiers asleep in the rain, express trains running through, Yaks raising hob, and President Syngman Rhee on the list of missing persons? Cromwell left Muccio to his own devices (the ambassador had a change of clothes that badly needed getting into and was looking for a place to shave) and spent his time pestering Colonel Wright and other American officers. Unlike Muccio, Ollie had the enemy on his mind—where they were, how fast they might be coming. The Marine Corps didn't like it when Marine colonels got themselves captured.

So he posed questions, looking for intelligence, information that could help them reach the South, might enable them to avoid getting taken, might keep them from getting killed.

Did the KMAG people think the North Koreans were yet across the Han anywhere in force? Were the ROKs digging in north of here and slowing them? Were the ROK forces fighting at all? Or were the South Koreans just running?

"Running's the word for it, Cromwell. Look at the sorry bunch we got here. They won't even dig foxholes, never mind set up a perimeter defense. And half their officers changed into civvies and went home."

And these KMAG officers were the American military advisers to the ROKs. If anyone knew them, they did.

One of the Yanks asked Ollie if he knew about any GIs being committed.

"I don't know. The ambassador's in the dark, too."

" 'Cause this bunch of ours isn't doing much fighting on their own."

Ollie wondered why the KMAG Americans didn't try kicking a little butt. But he'd been in the country less than a week, and what did he know? The Army resented Marines anyway, and you don't want to be a wiseass. Sergeant Buggy reported that the rest of the small Marine embassy detachment was fifty miles south of here at Taejon, where Rhee had set up shop.

It was then that Fat Chae appeared at Suwon. A couple of ROK Jeeps with sirens and a truck full of troops rolled out onto the tarmac toward the scatter of corrugated steel buildings, where Cromwell and the KMAG officers talked and where Muccio was tidying up.

"Attention!" someone called out, and they all snapped to.

With some difficulty, General Chae, commander in chief of the South

Korean Army, clambered out of the front seat of the leading jeep—all three hundred pounds of him, helped upright by huskies tugging at each arm. Colonel Wright went over to salute and welcome the general. From what Ollie could hear the two were speaking Korean. He glanced around, curious to see whether this unexpected apparition of their commander in chief might rouse the South Korean troops from torpor. One or two turned to see the excitement but remained lounging about. Most didn't even bother to stare. The only saluting was done by Americans. *Great army,* Ollie thought. He signaled Buggy over.

"Hang around, Sergeant, and tell me if they say anything in Korean you understand that I ought to know."

"Aye aye, sir."

As Wright and Fat Chae strolled together, in apparently affable conversation, another of Muccio's embassy aides, Harold Noble, appeared from a small, warehouselike building, with a full-blown U.S. Army general in tow. Suddenly general officers were popping up everywhere.

Cromwell and the other officers saluted again. It was all becoming very Kiplingesque, indeed. Ollie thought of Cary Grant complimenting the regimental "beastie," Gunga Din.

This latest general was John Church, a frail, elderly gent with arthritis who'd never before set foot in Korea but had been sent over from Japan as a troubleshooter by MacArthur to assess the situation. The Church mission, as details gradually leaked out, resembled a Marx Brothers movie. He'd left Haneda Airport outside Tokyo with a command of thirteen officers and two enlisted men. Instead of flying directly to Korea, they flew to a USAF air base in northern Japan, where Church announced he wanted breakfast. Staff cars were called for, and the party was whisked off to what is described as a "posh officers' club." When Church phoned Tokyo for an update, he was told the planned landing in Kimpo, Korea, might be scrubbed since the North Koreans had already captured the place. Church was then flown back to Tokyo over the pilot's objections. This plane was supposed to drop off General Church and then bring back American refugees stranded by the Communist advance. So far, a hell of a troubleshooter!

On yet another flight, old General Church, in brand-new combat fatigues accessorized by his World War II ribbons, finally got to Suwon. An Army antiaircraft battalion was readied to follow, to protect the Suwon airstrip, but it hadn't appeared. Meanwhile, KMAG colonel Wright and a diplomat or two were meeting in a schoolhouse with Fat Chae, demanding to know where he would establish a defense line. General Chae gestured vaguely south. For some reason, Generals Church and Chae never bothered to talk or even shake hands, but held separate meetings on the little airstrip with the same U.S. officers.

Now came word MacArthur himself was headed this way! You'd think Moses had just parted the Red Sea by the reaction to *that* item of news. While yet another thunderstorm swept wetly across the airfield.

Just before MacArthur's C-54 *Bataan* and its Mustang fighter escort arrived, six Yak fighter-bombers screamed in low, bombing and strafing.

It was then that President Rhee manifested himself, dropped off by one of his special trains and driven by truck to the airstrip, afraid to miss the chance to consult with his patron, MacArthur.

At this chaotic moment, less than a full minute after the latest Yak had strafed the field, *Bataan* touched down and splashed to a perfect landing. The general, accompanied by four American reporters, climbed down the ladder to the mud, and, taking the salute, he began shaking hands, the familiar corncob pipe unlit, but clenched in his teeth.

Nearly everyone, including Rhee, with Muccio dancing attendance at his side, and the correspondents, went into a little schoolhouse to talk.

Cromwell, being only a lieutenant colonel, and the ill-starred Fat Chae were among those left outside standing in the rain. Sergeant Will Buggy looked at Cromwell. No one had thought to throw out a perimeter screen of troops to secure the area, and it was raining harder.

"We could sit in the ambassador's Buick, sir, and stay dry."

"Not a bad idea, Buggy." So they and Lonesome, all three of them armed and watching alertly through the car windows, waited. At some point, one of the reporters inquired of General Church what he thought so far of his South Korean allies.

Harold Noble, Ambassador Muccio's man, reported that General Church blurted out he'd "rather have one hundred New York City policemen than the whole Korean Army."

Inside the schoolhouse, Church, who didn't know Korea, presided, using a pointer and a map tacked up on the wall. Fat Chae, commander in chief of the ROK Army, was still cooling his heels until Noble got Muccio to insist that the South Korean general at least be asked indoors out of the rain.

Fat Chae entered the schoolhouse, but that was about it. No one asked for his views, which, since he spoke little English, may have been just as well.

Cromwell, Buggy, and Lonesome didn't have long to wait. After no more than twenty minutes, MacArthur emerged, followed by Rhee and the others. MacArthur grabbed Church by a frail arm and beckoned the four war correspondents:

"Boys, we're going to the front," the generalissimo announced airily.

One of the KMAG brass, bolder than the rest, spoke up:

"General, just north of here the ground is crawling with gooks."

"Good," said MacArthur enthusiastically, "I want to see what our enemy looks like."

The press boys looked less enthusiastic. Now, almost surrealistically, MacArthur got into a battered old Dodge and with two jeeps as escorts instructed his driver to drive north to the Han River. He wanted to see if the North Koreans were truly across. President Rhee and Muccio were pointedly left behind. Though not the war correspondents. Oliver Cromwell pulled Muccio aside.

"Sir, I don't know how the State Department operates, but unless you have orders to the contrary, I suggest we get the hell out of here."

Suppose MacArthur were killed or captured. This sinkhole would be seething with Commies *and* the press. Which neither Ambassador Muccio nor the Marine Corps needed more of right now, thank you very much.

"Ambassador?" Ollie prompted. Had Muccio frozen?

"Yes, yes, Colonel. We'll get going."

Which was what President Rhee was doing: not bothering to invite Muccio along, he headed back to his train. Cromwell, recalling his history, was beginning to think of Rhee as a latter-day Lenin, transported in a sealed railroad car across Europe to the Finland Station so he could start the Russian Revolution.

"They're all nuts," one of the KMAG Americans muttered. And how could you argue with him? There was something bizarre and even disorienting about the speed and totality of the South Korean collapse. About MacArthur's flamboyant drive to the Han River. About the coterie of reporters he shepherded about so they could dance attendance. And about poor Church himself. As foolish and woebegone as he now appeared and as dottering, the man had been a gallant and decorated officer in an infinitely larger and more complex and serious war. But this? This wasn't war; it was anarchy, with MacArthur, mad as Lear, in capering command on a windswept, muddy airstrip a mile or several from nowhere.

He'd seen screw-ups in the Pacific during the war, but Cromwell shuddered in disbelief at what he'd seen so far in a week of Korea.

▪

As soon as MacArthur was back in Tokyo, his intelligence chief, General Willoughby, functioning as the supremo's press agent, got the publicity mills grinding. Descriptions were issued, totally concocted and imaginary, of the retreat MacArthur had "witnessed." According to Willoughby, South Korean ambulances carried the casualties south to safety (there were no ambulances). Retreating ROK troops waved flags and cheered and vowed they would soon turn and counterattack. There were no flags, no cheers, and most ROK troops seemed happy just to be out of the fight. Willoughby described the ROK troops as saluting smartly, cheering the general, and demanding to be turned loose to slaughter those North Korean bastards. Even the bedraggled and pitiful refugees, said Willoughby, squared their shoulders to break into spontaneous applause and traditional native chants when MacArthur appeared.

None of this happened.

What was not concocted, and really a better yarn, was that on his return to Suwon in the battered old Dodge, another flight of Yaks appeared, and everyone in the car jumped out to dash for the ditches, leaving General Douglas MacArthur alone in the backseat, where he stayed, calmly puffing his pipe, until the strafing was over, the only one of them who hadn't panicked. . . .

The rain ended again, and, in the first real heat of summer, steam rose from the puddles as the sun came out.

"How hot does it get?" Ollie asked Sergeant Buggy.

Seoul fell to the North Koreans on Wednesday, June 28. On that same day Harry Truman ordered American planes and warships to the defense of South Korea.

The first American ground troops would not see action until July 5. On July 9 Truman named General MacArthur (who'd been doing the job without portfolio) supreme commander in Korea. But as early as June 30, MacArthur had already ordered the U.S. Army's Twenty-fourth Division (Major General William F. Dean, commanding) to board ship for transport to South Korea—the first American division to enter the war. The Twenty-fourth Division to the rescue? The Twenty-fourth had, according to a report dated May 30, "the lowest combat effectiveness of any of the Occupation forces in Japan."

But how would Douglas MacArthur know this? The great man, pride of West Point, the ultimate professional officer, had visited his American Army of Occupation divisions in Japan in the field only twice in five years.

And the staff sychophants surrounding him were too awed to tell the Old Man an unpleasant truth.

In his book about MacArthur, Stanley Weintraub would later write of the "understrength, inexperienced, and poorly equipped 24th division . . . five troublemaker enlistees, court-martialed for everything from VD to fighting, disobeying orders to showing up late, going AWOL to drinking too much . . . ," who had been shipped to a stockade in Yokohama. Except that, as Lieutenant Philip Day would report, "Someone up there decided that C Company could not do without these five thugs and they were shipped back to us."

Thugs and all, the Twenty-fourth Division set out for the front to save South Korea from the Commies.

■ 25 ■

YOU DON'T CREATE AN ARMY IN A FEW WEEKS. NOT ONE THAT CAN
FIGHT.

Muccio washed up and came back to the car. Except for the panama hat,
the worse for wear from his sleeping rough and from the rain, he looked
pretty good.

"Taejon, that's where we'll catch up to the ROK government. And to
the rest of your Marines, Colonel."

"Yessir," said Cromwell. He liked that part about joining up with some
other Marines. This freelancing amid diplomats and the U.S. Army got
tired pretty fast.

"You've kept dry, then."

"Took shelter in the Buick."

"Smart. Did you get to meet MacArthur?"

"Nossir."

"Mmmmm . . ." Muccio said, leaving it at that. State discouraged its
people from criticizing other departments. Even if everyone did enjoy a
good gossip.

Their stopover in Suwon accomplished something. It gave Cromwell a
good feel for Sergeant Buggy.

You know how an officer measures a new man. While they sheltered
from the rain and waited for the ambassador, Ollie questioned the sergeant.

"Tell me about yourself, Buggy."

"Yessir. Well, I joined the Marine Corps in San Antone July 1942 outa
Texas A and M, where I did freshman year. I was sent to boot camp at
Dago, sir, and my first duty station was . . ."

"Spare me the service personnel jacket, Sergeant. I can read that for
myself. What are you good at, really good? I know you palaver some Korean."

"Yessir, Colonel. I got me what they talk about in the Bible. I got the
gift of tongues."

You rarely got a line like that out of a noncom, and Cromwell was impressed, even if the sergeant spoke in a commonplace tone, with no whiff of boasting.

"Go on," he said.

"Yessir. It ain't nothing special, but it comes in handy. It began back home where most of the cowboys on the ranches around there was vaqueros. So I grew up speaking Mex fluent, and in high school I took French and found that pretty easy. Took German at A and M, and lazing around Seoul for a year or two, and not being much of a drinker or hell-raiser, I studied up on Korean. Got me some Jap as well. I can't explain just why, but it got so I can say, 'Blow it out your ass!' and get understood almost everywhere."

Ollie nodded. "Okay, Sergeant, stick close to me. We may have to talk a lot more Korean before we get out of this mess."

"Yessir," Buggy said, relieved that despite all the Raider scare stories, maybe this Cromwell would turn out okay.

Along with retreating ROKs, and just missing MacArthur, a somewhat bedraggled press contingent (not the well-groomed bunch flown in from Tokyo) had now drifted into Suwon, including Marguerite Higgins of the *New York Herald Tribune,* who, with three other American reporters, crossed the Han River on rafts after the bridges were blown. With them were about sixty more American military advisers who had bullied or bought their way aboard small boats.

Cromwell nudged the ambassador, who was still playing laggard. "Sir, they all tell the same story. The Reds are heading this way. If we expect to get to Taejon, we'd better . . ."

"Absolutely. Next stop, Taejon," he said jauntily. It was amazing what clean clothes and a shave did for a man's spirits. Cromwell commandeered a truck, and Muccio and his handful of dips piled aboard.

No more than a pit stop later, the correspondents and the KMAG advisers were off again to the South as the first North Korean patrols were sighted just north of Suwon and the ROKs were pulling out; the airstrip was closed down. The enemy was coming south, and Suwon was finished. But it was near Suwon that American troops just arrived from Japan would join the war.

The first American unit to meet the North Koreans in combat was called, somewhat grandly, Task Force Smith—only four hundred officers and men of the first battalion, Twenty-first Infantry Regiment, part of the Twenty-fourth Division. The task force was commanded by a Lieutenant Colonel Smith and possessed no artillery or serious antitank weapons (they had the pathetic World War II bazookas but not the bigger 3.5 rockets). Yet Smith was assured the mere presence of American ground troops was sure to intimidate the North Koreans and encourage the fleeing ROKs to turn and do a little fighting themselves.

Smith, a West Pointer who had fought against the Japanese, may have taken all this with a grain of salt, but as a good soldier he led his command north out of the port of Pusan, looking for North Koreans to fight. They found them at Osan, about eight miles south of Suwon, the morning of July 5, when thirty big Russian T-34 tanks clanked into view. By now Colonel Smith had picked up a field artillery unit, and his command totaled five hundred men. The artillerymen, somewhat abashed, reported that they had only six antitank shells. Six shells with thirty Russian tanks coming.

And the North Korean infantry, not at all intimidated by the Americans, was coming on along with the tanks. A couple of U.S. soldiers let the first few tanks pass and then jumped atop them to pry open turrets and drop grenades inside. In so doing the first American ground soldier of the war was killed. And as the remaining Russian tanks rolled up, Smith's men fired and fell back. Soon, the outgunned GIs were running, the dead, the wounded, and some of their weapons abandoned.

American soldiers were now behaving much like the ROKs they derided.

■

A few other Americans were also fighting, only not against the Reds but occasionally against their staunch allies, the ROKs. At a nothing crossroads along the Suwon-Taejon road, Sergeant Buggy signaled a halt.

"Don't like the look of this bunch, Colonel."

"Nor do I, Buggy. Can you talk to them?"

It wasn't North Koreans coming south. Not this time. This time it was a mob of ROK troops who weren't going anywhere. "Mob" being the operative word. Maybe forty or fifty of them, lazing about, some of the men clearly drunk. They had a few bedraggled Korean women with them, too; the young girls among them looked pretty bad, dresses filthy and torn, the girls' eyes glazed, their faces bruised.

Buggy called out for the commanding officer to present himself. A couple of ROKs with rifles looked over the little convoy, taking Cromwell's measure. Behind him, the diplomats smiled. That was what dips did, winning over people's hearts and minds. Finally an ROK came forward, a "captain," he said.

"We need transport," he told Sergeant Buggy without preamble. "Those vehicles. NK coming fast. We'll use your truck."

Buggy gave Ollie an instant transcript, blow by blow.

"The hell they will."

"That's what I figured you'd say, Colonel. So I didn't encourage him none."

"What happened to those women?"

Buggy asked, the ROK answered.

"He says they're saving them women from the Reds. The Reds will rape the girls, he says."

"And his men beat them to it."

"Looks that way, Colonel."

"He really a captain?"

"Don't believe so, sir. Looks like just another shitbird to me, sir."

"Fine. We take care of shitbirds, Sergeant.

There was another declaration from the "captain."

"What did he say?"

"He says he's got more soldiers than we do, and he ought to be asking the questions, and you ought to be answering."

"Get ready, Buggy. We're going to have to kill this fellow."

"Yessir, I figure."

Muccio came up then.

"Are these troops being of any help, Colonel?"

"I don't think they are, Mr. Ambassador. Will you please step back to your vehicle, sir. You and the other dips."

"Oh?"

"Yessir. We're going to have to shoot a few of these people."

Cromwell said it so calmly—no drama about it in either his words or the tone of voice—that Muccio didn't grasp what he said. The ambassador was, in fact, still smiling as he said, brightly:

"They're ROKs, Cromwell. Our Allies in the host country. Not enemy troops. We're on the same side, remember?" Muccio might have been lecturing a class.

"Yessir. But they intend to steal our wheels, including your car. They're armed, and they're drunk, and they've been looting, and they've raped these women. Or so it looks to us. The women are South Koreans, too."

Muccio blinked.

"So, if you could just return to your Buick . . ."

"Of course, Colonel, of course," Muccio said, backing away.

The winning, diplomatic smile had vanished. He really did catch on once you explained things to him.

There was more palaver, and, as a few more of the ROKs, the drunken ones, picked up their weapons and began to swagger, Cromwell called out.

"Ready on the right, ready on the left, all ready on the firing line. On my command shoot this fellow we're talking to and anyone else holding a weapon. Careful of the women."

"All ready, Colonel," Buggy growled.

"Okay, Sergeant. On three, fire."

The Koreans shuffled around, not understanding the words, but a few of them getting the message. The girls, too, sensed something and began to edge away.

"One, two . . . three!"

The Marines took out the ROK "captain" and maybe six or seven others with the first burst. As for the rest, they ran. The girls ran, too, which seemed sensible.

"Anyone hit?" Ollie asked, meaning among the Americans. The Marines, the three of them, were okay.

"Nossir. Though we'll take a head count, make it official. Lonesome, check 'em out."

"Aye aye, Sar'n't," the PFC said agreeably. "But there's just me, and I ain't been shot, not even once."

A couple of the South Korean soldiers were still rolling around on the ground, with one of them screaming. Gut-shot, probably. Gut-shots always yelled. The others were a hundred or more yards away, out across the paddy. Heading to the horizon. Funny how even drunks run fast if they are going to be shot.

"Put down in the report they were deserters and mutineers, Buggy, raping women and abducting children." Cromwell ordered. "I don't want complications with the Rhee government. You sign off on all that, Ambassador?"

"Yes, yes. Surely. Mutineers and rapists. Though I'm not sure I saw any children."

"Thank you, sir," Colonel Cromwell said. "I'm told children mature early in these climes."

"I daresay, sir."

Buggy then passed the hat.

"These gals, sir. They ain't got much."

"Well-done, Sergeant." Ollie tossed in two twenty-dollar bills. Then turned to Muccio. "Mr. Ambassador?"

"Absolutely, Colonel. Will this do?"

He put in some money, too. Even Lonesome threw in. A dollar.

"You'll retire rich, McGraw," Buggy said.

"You think so, Sar'nt? That's great."

They had their truck, the jeep, and the Buick rolling south very shortly. Along the side of the road, the freed women waved, still slack and shocked and stunned-looking, but they did summon up a wave. One or two even smiled. What would happen to them, where they might go from here, no one knew. But they'd be living high. A little dough went a long way during wars. Muccio had occasionally, as a dip, overseen foreign aid to various troubled places. And now, out of his wallet, he was contributing a little foreign aid on his own.

Except for one Yak pilot who, surly about lacking a better target, shot them up, the trek south went smoothly all the way to Taejon. As Muccio told himself, any day when Colonel Cromwell didn't have to shoot some-one was a day well spent.

In Taejon, the reality of the larger, strategic situation, the so-called big picture, was magnified by rumor, exaggeration, and panic. President Rhee and his government planned to pull out yet again. Muccio went off to attend conferences, while Ollie waited, wanting to know what was hap-pening. After an hour or two, he collared Harold Noble, a Muccio aide.

"Harold, this place is finished, you know."

"Yes, Colonel, I'm sure. The ambassador will be coming along pres-ently."

Harold didn't pressure easy.

"Can you make 'presently' come along a little quicker, Harold? I don't know what's going on. There are no, repeat no, functioning ROK troops that I know of north of here. Only some drunks and rapists and deserters. The Commies can just drive into town and round us all up. You and Ambassador Muccio have diplomatic immunity, and you'll get swapped home pretty soon. Not me. Not my Marines, Sergeant Buggy and Lone-some . . ."

"Lonesome?"

"We call him that because we're fond of him. But I don't want Buggy or Lonesome and most of all myself getting shot or captured; you get my drift."

"I'm sure the ambassador shares your concern."

Ollie resolved never again to join the State Department. Polite was one thing. Letting the enemy catch up and bite you in the ass was something quite else.

They got away finally after spending nearly a week at Taejon while Rhee left for the South and then returned and then left again. Why the damned Reds didn't just roll into town and grab the lot of them no one could explain. As Muccio urged, "Disport yourselves, Colonel. These things take time. One doesn't rush heads of state."

"No, sir. I guess."

By now the Yaks no longer had a monopoly on shooting up the place. There were U.S. planes in the air, P–51 Mustangs, which did very well among the Yaks. There were also the first Australian pilots and planes, and how did they get here so soon? Trouble was, very early on, the Aussies shot up one of the first columns of American troops being trucked north.

"You'd think they could figure it out. The fellows going north are on our side. The fellows coming south are the bad guys."

"Well, they *are* Australians."

▪ 26 ▪

The Task Force Smith debacle had no sooner been digested than new calamities loomed.

Except for the distinction of having the U.S. ambassador along for the ride, Cromwell's convoy of little lost sheep gone astray was a mere footnote to retreat that first summer of the war. Ollie found it depressing to be part of the debacle and yet somehow comforting to realize there were bigger and better foul-ups in the works all around him. There was consolation in the fact that his detachment wasn't alone, that the whole damned army was confused, muddled, going to pieces, and pulling back. So they had company in their misery. It was mere days since the first war correspondents and nicely tailored staff officers arrived in Korea fresh from HQ at Tokyo— confident, brimming with assurances everything would change, and for the better, once the GIs got here. Ollie half-expected them to burst into song, a few rousing choruses of George M. Cohan:

> *The Yanks are coming,*
> *The Yanks are coming,*
> *They're drum drum drumming everywhere!*

Well, the first Yanks had come. And some of them had gone. Several regiments and at least one entire U.S. Army division were falling apart under North Korean hammering. And they were running away, every bit as shameless as our Allies the ROKs. Prominent among these was the less-than-glorious performance of the Twenty-fourth Infantry Regiment, an all-black unit with mostly white officers and lousy morale. No one was anxious even to talk about the disaster of the Twenty-fourth, wary of being, or being labeled, racist.

But there was a hell of a stink about the Twenty-fourth Regiment. Cromwell's little band heard the stories at almost every pit stop or watering

hole or airstrip at which they paused on the retreat south. A clearly embarrassed West Point regular, a major, briefed Cromwell on the Twenty-
fourth at a rural bridge where they'd both stopped to water their vehicles.

"You hear about shit like this, Colonel, you want to tear off your
damned uniform and burn it."

At first Ollie and Muccio discounted much of the talk. Or tried to.
Told the enlisted Marines to shut up about it. Race relations were touchy,
and regardless of race, you didn't want to believe this stuff, not if you were
a serving American officer or the senior American diplomat on the ground.

Truman had only two years earlier mandated immediate integration of
the Armed Forces. But in the military, as in life, issuing an order and having
it carried out were two different things. Ollie remembered that even at
postwar Quantico, Virginia, an American military base thirty-five miles
from the White House, black Marines and their families still sat in the
balcony at the base movie house. Add to racism incompetence, stupidity,
poor leadership, and lack of training. Did anyone mention drugs?

Trouble began before the Twenty-fourth ever left Japan. Historian Stanley Weintraub delved into the sorry tale for his MacArthur biography: the
highest-ranking black officer, a lieutenant colonel, refused to go to Korea
with his troops. Instead of being court-martialed, or shot, this creep was
fobbed off with a cushy rear-echelon job. Just before the regiment shipped,
a black chaplain was reported to have told black troops they ought not be
sent to fight other "people of color." As the troops boarded trains for the
seaport, their Japanese girlfriends handed up gift packages, some of which
were found to contain drugs.

With the big port of Sasebo doing a rush-hour business of ships coming
and going, the Twenty-fourth Regiment was diverted to another, smaller
Japanese port for decidedly second-rate treatment: they were loaded aboard
a motley collection of tubs, colliers, tugs, ferries, even haulers of manure.
While the flotilla was being assembled, the troops rioted, shooting up the
town. Disorders continued aboard ship during the twelve-hour voyage to
Pusan.

Arriving in Korea, the regiment found the longshoremen on strike. The
troops strolled ashore but without their heavy weapons and equipment.
When eventually they were off-loaded, the regiment's field kitchens were
missing, either lost or stolen. Despite foul-ups, the men boarded trains for
Pohang and the front, 110 miles away. At this critical moment, the Twenty-
fourth's executive officer, a white lieutenant colonel, was evacuated for

medical reasons. The rumor spread that he'd faked a heart attack. Not irrationally, some blacks believed they were being sent into combat by shirking white officers.

While both white and black officers of the Twenty-fourth panicked under fire and ran, it was a black lieutenant, Leon A. Gilbert, who flat out refused to go into action at all. When given the opportunity to change his mind, Gilbert continued to refuse and was tried, convicted, and sentenced to death, the sentence later commuted by Truman to twenty years.

Another white officer, a battalion commander, never moved closer than two miles of the front line. A brief firefight anywhere north of their lines sent the Twenty-fourth's soldiers running, leaving behind both trucks and artillery. Yet the only officer arrested for dereliction was a black lieutenant.

By the time the regiment was in action, a new word had been coined and a song composed. The word was "bug-out," meaning retreat. And the song, composed by the men of the Twenty-fourth and sung without embarrassment, was quickly notorious:

> When the Commie mortars start to chug,
> The ol' Deuce Four begin to bug.
> When you hear the pitter-patter of little feet,
> It's the ol' Deuce Four in full retreat.

No one could remember an American military unit, in any war, this loudly celebrating its own cowardice and retreats.

Ed Murrow of CBS was by now in Korea and did several generally favorable broadcasts about the Twenty-fourth Infantry. American newspapers breathlessly announced, "Negro Troops Score Victory" when the Twenty-fourth temporarily occupied a small Korean village the North Koreans hadn't even defended.

The press agentry was so blatant, so patronizing, men cringed who were on the scene and knew what actually happened.

Bowing to the inevitable, on August 1 the Twenty-fourth Infantry was pulled off the line and placed in reserve, and never again was there put into the field a segregated American Army unit. For better, for worse, the Army from that day on would be integrated.

By July 20 Washington realized Taejon could not be held, and MacArthur began preparations to move both government and HQ further south. There were rumors General Dean, a division commander, had vanished, perhaps been captured. Reports of Dean's disappearance, the failures of Task Force Smith, the "bug-outs" of the infamous Deuce Four trickled back. To Muccio and the Marines accompanying Rhee, such reports dashed any hope that American troops would automatically turn the war's tide. For Cromwell, embarrassed by how badly Americans were doing in this little sideshow of a war, the only cheering news was a report that the famed 5th Marines, his old outfit, was at sea and heading for South Korea, formed up as the 1st Marine Provisional Brigade.

If that was true, Ollie might be getting out of the diplomatic business and going home. Not to the States but to his real home, the Marine Corps. Meanwhile, panicky and disorganized, the retreat went on, both ROKs and Americans defeated, outmarched, outfought, and outgeneraled, heading south, tossing away their weapons, their helmets, and brushing aside the odd officer trying to stem the flood. Not all the GIs sang about it as did the Deuce Four. That didn't mean they were any less beaten, only less cynical. They ran just as fast.

Career officers like Cromwell shook their heads and wondered what had happened to the American military in the five years since it defeated both the Nazis and the Empire of Japan. General Dean, also a professional officer, did more than shake his head and wonder. He went out lugging a rifle and had gotten himself captured.

"Have we ever had an American two-star general captured by the enemy?" That was the initial reaction. Then a man who took the long view suggested:

"MacArthur will shit bricks. You know why? Because the last American general taken prisoner was MacArthur's second-in-command on Corregidor, Skinny Wainwright. And it was MacArthur who ordered him to surrender. That was eight years ago, and we ought never to forget it."

"Amen to that, sir," someone said.

Cromwell, being the only Marine officer at Taejon, kept shut. There are times you just don't say anything.

Marines enjoyed putting down the dogfaces and having a laugh at their expense. But this went beyond laughter, beyond intramural rivalry. This was shameful. Marines knew it was the Army that won wars, that fielded hundreds of divisions, millions of men. You couldn't beat the Germans with a Marine Corps of six divisions, couldn't handle the Japs. Maybe you couldn't even take on North Korea. Not with Marines alone. No one took pleasure in situations like this, with GIs running away, officers refusing to fight, and two-star generals captured.

This wasn't an army MacArthur had yet, just some pieces thrown at the puzzle and not fitting. The material they had to work with that terrible summer of 1950 were the dregs, drunks, criminals, druggies, white officers contemptuous of black soldiers, furious or sullen blacks angered by racism, old-timers like General Church too feeble for the field, and amateurs who didn't know war.

You don't create an army in a couple of weeks.

■

When Cromwell heard U.S. officers gossiping about General Bill Dean's capture, he kept his mouth shut about that, too. He didn't even tell Ambassador Muccio; who yet knew the diplomat's tolerance for bad news?

Dean was one of the few ranking American officers who actually knew Korea, having served there during the U.S. occupation and before the 1950 invasion. Which should have given him an edge. But didn't.

His tragedy began just after dawn on July 20 when his Twenty-fourth Division, badly beaten by two very good Red divisions, was no longer functioning as a division or even as a collection of battalions. To Dean, to most of them, it was obvious Taejon, linchpin of the South's defense, could not be held. Watching the demoralized, defeated Yanks retreating through the town, most without rifles, one hapless trooper shoeless, Dean drew conclusions.

A brave man, but a defeated general, saying, "There was no longer a general's duty to be done," Dean with an aide and an interpreter, commandeered a truck mounting a seventy-five-millimeter recoilless rifle to "go tank-hunting."

They were a flop even at that. Firing at two North Korean tanks stalled on the road, they missed. Later, finding a lone bazookaman with a single round remaining, Dean had the man fire a shot at one hundred yards' range at an NK tank. Nervous in the presence of a general, the gunner missed. Exasperated, Dean stood up, and as the tank closed to twenty yards, he fired shot after shot at its armor with his .45-caliber pistol. By late afternoon Dean, now in a jeep, caught up with fleeing Thirty-fourth Regiment soldiers and a couple of light tanks heading south. No wonder the Thirty-fourth was running. Their commanding colonel, Robert R. Martin, the only man in the regiment who knew how to load and fire a bazooka, took on a Red tank with an enlisted man loading for him, and as he fired the small bazooka, he was literally cut in two by the Russian's big gun. Dean fell in behind the small column as its rear guard.

By now the general was serving as a rifleman, swapping shots with North Korean snipers with an M-1 until he lost his jeep in an ambush.

When a retreating half-track crammed with beaten American troops came along, Dean boarded it, hanging on with his fingertips. As night fell, the Reds snapped another ambush, and Dean and a few others headed for the Kum River. If they could ford the Kum in the dark, they just might be able to walk their way into friendly lines down south.

Dean fell, breaking his shoulder, gashing his head, and reopening an incision from an abdominal operation. Fainting, the general was abandoned by his companions, and when he regained consciousness, he hid from enemy patrols scouting the ground. At dawn he and another straggler hid in a South Korean peasant's hut, giving the family a million won (just over a hundred bucks). The grateful peasants sent for a North Korean patrol that just missed bagging the two Yanks.

Bill Dean, incredibly, wandered, hurt and hungry, for thirty-five days through rough country, then once more trusted South Koreans—two men who promptly sold the general to the enemy for a bounty split between the two of them, a generous bribe that amounted to about five dollars.

Men were pretty bitter about it, about what happened to Dean. What an inspiring place this was, and what a truly noble people South Koreans turned out to be. Sullen mountains, stinking paddies, and civilians who sold you for less than thirty pieces of silver. No wonder our soldiers grew cynical, asking why we fought wars in places like this, for people like these, just why the hell we were there. Even asking, was this going to be the first war the United States ever lost?

Getting our asses kicked in a two-bit little fight like this one?

▪ 27 ▪

"AMERICAN BOYS SHOT THROUGH THE HEAD WITH NOBODY DOING
ANYTHING ABOUT IT."

The first seven murdered American prisoners of war in South Korea were found July 7, wrists tied with communications wire, face down in the dirt, each of them shot once through the back of the head. Task Force Smith guys.

"A shitty way to die, your face in the dirt, dirt in your damned mouth," Buggy said.

"Know any nice ways, Sergeant?"

"Nossir." Jesus, Cromwell jumped you over nothing.

How the dead men were taken and just when weren't quite clear. Not even who killed them. But when a wandering patrol of ROK troops found them, they were surely dead.

"Good thing, in a way," Ollie remarked.

"Oh?" said Buggy.

"Yeah, American soldiers from now on might be a little less eager to surrender. Maybe fight it out instead of quitting, you know."

Sergeant Buggy nodded.

It made sense, what Cromwell said. It was just you didn't often hear officers laying it out that blunt.

While Task Force Smith was being steamrollered and poor Bill Dean was on the lam, Muccio and his truckload of dips, bouncing and jolting along rutted rural roads, tried to keep up with the South Korean government's special trains.

Cromwell knew why he was in Korea. He was a professional, a career Marine, ordered here by Headquarters Marine Corps to do a job—a job he was doing as best he could with the slim means at his command. But he understood why other men doubted and groused and lapsed into despair. Young Americans were not used to losing. At games, in business, in combat.

He pondered these and other matters from the front seat of a jeep on the sorry road south out of Taejon. Their little caravan—the jeep, the ambassador's Buick—was now augmented by a second six-by truckful of minor American diplomats, their consular paperwork, and a couple of keepers, two more embassy Marine guards. Ollie recognized that these were legitimate questions for men to ask when their country sends them to war. He'd asked such questions himself.

One of the great enduring strengths of the Marine Corps is that you always have someone to go to when you have to talk out and analyze a problem or a weakness. There was no one in Korea Ollie could go to. No Carlson, no Gunny Arzt, no bald-headed Jimmy Roosevelt. The enlisted men, the dips, Muccio himself—they looked to him. So, as serious people do when they're in trouble, as he was now, on the run in hostile territory, Cromwell reached back into himself, drawing on past battles fought, objectives taken, wounds survived. He'd done it before; now he had to do it again.

The landscape and cast of characters remained much the same: President Rhee, his wife the Austrian, two trains, the gold, a successor commanding general (the unfortunate Fat Chae had somehow gotten himself killed), a clergyman in a Roman collar (Rhee was a Christian), a claque of pet journalists from the Seoul papers, the usual courtiers and sychophants, a medical staff (at Rhee's age, who knew?), and a detachment of nattily turned-out troops, what was left of the palace guard, men sworn to lay down their lives for Syngman Rhee. But who had run like hell when the first Reds arrived in town.

"Honor guards?" Buggy remarked sourly. "From what I seen, Mrs. Rhee better keep up the old man's life insurance."

Their army defeated, their tinpot little country half-lost, the South Korean president and his first lady snobbishly maintained protocol. They chatted easily with the American ambassador, ignored pointedly his staff and military escort. In one of their unscripted conversations (at which Ollie stood listening but unasked to join in), Muccio courteously mentioned having caught a concert at the Hollywood Bowl of Madame Rhee's fellow Austrians, the Trapp Family Singers.

"I was enormously fond of the captain, Baron von Trapp," said Rhee's wife complacently, as her husband, the president, smiled tight-lipped approval of a world-traveled consort with such connections.

"Though that was when the *real* baroness was still alive, and the baron hadn't yet married the nanny."

"But wonderful voices," Muccio said pleasantly.

"*Ja,* Maria sings well, but she's really quite common."

As the fugitive Rhee party meandered still further south and east, hugging closely their gold, snubbing lower-caste mortals, dodging the marauding Yaks, and, as reports came in of predatory North Koreans, changing course, throwing switches, and flitting from railhead to railhead, from airstrip to airstrip, and doubling back and then back again, mirabile dictu, there out of the blue-gray skies his flagship *Bataan* would again bounce heavily to a landing, bearing MacArthur and his viceregal retinue from Tokyo. With P-51 fighters circling overhead for cover, MacArthur would amble across the open field to a hangar or small warehouse, even a local school or grocery store, shake a few hands, gesticulate with his corncob, and hold court.

And very much with him was the press. One of his favorites among them, Marguerite Higgins of the *New York Herald Tribune,* a Republican paper MacArthur enjoyed. As he also enjoyed, though from a courtly distance, Miss Higgins, very much aware as they all were of what rival reporters, male (and jealous?), said of Maggie: ". . . using her little-girl voice and her big-girl body" to get a story.

Inexplicably, none of his "house" press ever thought to ask the Great Man why his personal plane was named not for one of his famous victories, but for his most bitter defeat.

Muccio and his aides mingled with the Correspondents and various MacArthur flunkies of rank.

Miss Higgins, that rare wartime commodity, an attractive woman, was the focus, chatting easily with the general and swapping yarns with the others, especially anecdotes about her newspaper's colorful history and about hard-drinking colleagues, buccaneering competitors, powerful and colorful bosses she had served or competed against:

"Today's press lords are businessmen. Our original owner at the *New York Herald* was the celebrated James Gordon Bennett. He sent Stanley to Africa to find a Livingstone who wasn't lost, and he enjoyed riding about Paris in open carriages after midnight, drinking vintage wines and stark naked.

"You don't see Henry Luce or Jock Whitney cavorting like that, now do you!"

Other correspondents, loathe to have Maggie hold center stage with her one-woman show, offered their own yarns, trotted out their own accounts of wild, tormented colleagues, talented men run desperately amok, of city-room despots, of historic scoops and memorable headlines.

Sergeant Buggy, who had sea stories of his own, but was unaccustomed to New York women, ignored the other reporters to knit his brow over Miss Higgins.

"You ever hear such stuff, Colonel?"

"Not often, Buggy."

"I mean, riding naked around Paris? And I seen that movie about Stanley and Livingstone, with Spencer Tracy. Seemed to me Dr. Livingstone was pretty friggin' lost until ol' Spencer came along. Didn't it look that way to you, sir?"

Cromwell promised to question Maggie Higgins more closely on the matter.

Except that he then spied Ben Sweet and never got to ask Miss Higgins anything.

"Well, if it isn't the War Correspondent. What happened, Ben, Hemingway couldn't attend?"

Ollie made no effort to mask the sarcasm, still sore at Ben for pumping him at Pendleton and getting Ollie in bad with the brass.

Ben just smiled his winning smile and looked cocky, ignoring the dig and pleased Cromwell recognized he was in Korea and Hemingway wasn't.

"He's fifty years old, Ollie. War's a young man's game."

"This one's not much of a game, Ben. But you certainly look splendid."

He did, too, and knew it, togged out in a vaguely safari costume military uniform with a "war correspondent" shoulder patch and lots of pockets, and sporting highly polished paratrooper jump boots.

"Thanks, Ollie. How goes it?"

"Okay, now that you and MacArthur have dropped in."

His newspaper syndicate was to blame for getting him to Korea, Ben explained defensively, as if this war wasn't sufficiently important to deserve him.

"When the story broke about those seven murdered POWs, they got me on a plane the next day. 'Tell America about its heroes, Ben.' In Tokyo they pulled strings, and I was invited to fly over on *Bataan*. The general's a big favorite of the *Trib*."

"So I take it."

Ben introduced several of the officers he was traveling with, and Cromwell introduced Sergeant Will Buggy. Ollie enjoyed seeing Army colonels and generals having to shake hands with a Marine noncom. "If the ambassador breaks free, do you want to meet him, Ben?"

Sweet shook his head. "Diplomats aren't the story, Ollie. Not when

American boys have been shot through the head and no one's doing anything about it."

"What is there to do, Ben? Those guys are dead."

"It's why MacArthur's here. They won't go unavenged."

Not liking being orated to and irritated by Sweet's editorial-page lingo, he said, "Ben, I never heard such crap. Come on, let's get some coffee."

Ben just shrugged, calculating it wasn't worth his trouble to debate, and the two old college mates strolled across the tarmac to where a sort of mess kitchen had been set up. For once it wasn't raining, and you could see the steam, smell the coffee.

It was Army coffee but pretty good, Cromwell admitted.

"What can you tell me about those poor kids, Ollie?"

"What kids? The guys the North Koreans shot?"

Ben had his notebook out, the spiral wire glistening in the thin sun.

"They're why I'm here."

Ollie sipped the coffee, calculating what to tell a man he didn't really trust.

"I don't know much, Ben. Some of these Army connections of yours might know something. It's a pretty confused sort of war so far."

"Ollie, seven American heroes have been murdered. The public is asking questions. So is General MacArthur."

"You're tossing around the word 'heroes' a lot, Ben. The GIs we've seen aren't exactly fighting to the last man. One outfit has a song about it, 'The Bug-out Blues.' "

"I don't believe that, Ollie."

Cromwell didn't argue the case, just looked at him, half-smiling.

"And, besides, you really don't think MacArthur flew here from Japan to pray over a few GIs?"

"Among other things, yes."

"Ben, this war's falling apart on him, and he's commander in chief, a man who speaks directly to God. If his army doesn't start fighting pretty soon, MacArthur's going to be chased clear out of the damned country. Which would annoy God *and* the Republicans."

Sweet looked sternly at Cromwell.

"You find it corny that a reporter can sell newspapers and be patriotic at the same time?"

"Ben, I'm talking about phony heroics. That isn't war correspondence. It's cheerleading."

"And newspapermen are supposed to be the cynics. . . ."

"Forget it, Ben. Just a dumb Marine mouthing off."

To change the subject he asked:

"Tell me about MacArthur. What's he really like, up close?"

Ben responded with the sort of boyish enthusiasm he once reserved for Ernest Hemingway.

"He could be my next book. He's sure going to be in there. How can you write about war and omit Douglas MacArthur? He's focused, so totally focused, Ollie. Sees the war in global terms, able to shut out the incidental stuff to zero in on the objective. Like Ahab's obsession with Moby-Dick, determined to kill the beast that maimed him, 'a-thirst for human blood' . . ."

"And who's MacArthur's whale?"

"Don't know yet. Maybe the White House. I'm not sure. Most of all, to be counted among the great captains of history: Alexander, Wellington, Bonaparte until Moscow, Julius Caesar, your namesake Cromwell."

"Which means he's slightly nuts?" Ollie asked, teasing but with a laugh.

Ben Sweet had clearly studied the matter, perhaps anticipated the question.

"Aren't all great men?" he said agreeably.

The MacArthur-Rhee-Muccio talks having ended, the Supremo seemed in no hurry to get back to Tokyo. Maybe the fact not a single Yak had strafed him on this visit and no rain fell encouraged the general to work the crowd, sign autographs, pose for pictures. Which was what got Cromwell into trouble. As Ollie and Ben strolled back from their coffee break, a one-star general called out to the writer.

"That a Marine you've got in tow, Sweet? Bring him over."

So it happened that Cromwell was actually spoken to by the Great Man. Not that MacArthur was really interested in him; Ollie just happened to be the only Marine they had.

MacArthur stood there chatting easily, the corncob pipe punctuating his eloquence. As he waited, Cromwell kept his eyes on the general, noticing the thickening belly, the marginally slimming pleated trousers, and the hair cunningly combed over the bald spots. The brigadier now got MacArthur's ear.

"Yes, yes, of course," MacArthur could be heard to say. What he saw was a young Marine officer standing there casually with the celebrated Ben Sweet, as if they were old friends.

Ben and Ollie were beckoned forward, and the Marine introduced.

MacArthur returned Ollie's snapped-off salute, and, grinning flat mouthed, he said:

"You must be the first Marine in Korea, Colonel Cromwell. I hope now that you've landed, you have the situation well in hand."

Cromwell started to explain that he'd been here for weeks as Muccio's attaché, and then thought, *What the hell.*

"Yessir, or we will have. Once the brigade gets here."

"That's what I want to hear," MacArthur said enthusiastically. "Too much negative talk so far. Couple of minor local setbacks blown out of proportion. You don't win wars wringing your hands."

"Nossir," Ollie said. He'd never spoken to a five-star general and saw no need to be rude.

"Seen much of the North Koreans yet?" MacArthur inquired.

"A few of their advance patrols, sir."

"And?"

"They look like very good light infantry to me, General. They'll march twenty miles by day and fight that night. And those big T-34 tanks of theirs are something. You need more than a bazooka with them."

"We've got bigger stuff coming in, Colonel. Once the fellows stabilize this line of ours and buy a little time, you'll see." Then:

"Seen any of our American Army units in action, Cromwell?"

"A few, along the road."

"Well?"

Ollie had hoped it wouldn't come to this. Standing a few paces away, he could sense Ben Sweet tense, waiting for his pal Ollie to speak up. After all, Ben had introduced him to the supreme commander.

"General MacArthur wants straight talk, Colonel," a brigadier prompted. "Don't tap-dance."

"I've seen only the replacement drafts over from Japan, General. Not proper units as such. They looked like what they are—Army of Occupation soldiers, sir. Not the way you want good troops to look."

There was an uneasy silence. Then MacArthur said, "I appreciate your candor, Colonel Cromwell. Men like that need a little seasoning. First time under fire, I don't have to tell you. But you've seen some of our GIs fight, haven't you?"

"A few, sir. Mostly I've seen them retreating."

The general looked bleak. Ollie should have packed it in then. Instead, restive under Sweet's flag-waving and patronized by MacArthur, he went one sentence too far.

"They have a song about it."

"A song about retreating?" MacArthur asked, the corncob more tightly clenched between his teeth.

"Yessir, 'The Bug-out Blues.' "

MacArthur, stern faced, gave a brief, dismissive nod and wheeled, calling for his party and a return to *Bataan* and the flight home.

While Keyes Beech, the veteran war correspondent for the *Chicago Daily News,* scribbled hastily, taking down the exchange—MacArthur's question and the Marine colonel's answer both. The story ran the next day on the front page of Beech's newspaper as well as in other papers that took the Field Syndicate. . . .

Muccio, all affability and tact, was tugging at Colonel Cromwell's arm, trying to lead Ollie away before charges were leveled and the MPs whistled up.

The other Chicago paper, a day or two later, also had a front-page story from Korea, this one bylined, "by Pulitzer Prize–winning journalist Ben Sweet," recounting the glorious (though imaginary) heroics performed by seven gallant American GIs before being forced by overwhelming numbers to surrender, only to be murdered in cold blood. Sweet's dispatch reported on General MacArthur's deeply felt outrage as he flew to the scene to pay tribute to the "heroes," to the young "martyrs."

Ben's story was considerably more moving and eloquent than that of Keyes Beech.

And it carried no reference to American troops' "bugging-out." Or singing about it . . .

■ 28 ■

The retreat, though not officially recognized as one by either MacArthur or Ben Sweet, dragged on, mirthless and despairing.

By now the Muccio party consisted of the diplomats and a dozen Marines, the full complement of embassy Marines having finally been gathered up by Muccio, including a staff sergeant named Haire (who outranked Buggy but whom Cromwell bypassed, since he had seen Will Buggy under fire and didn't know this bird at all), two trucks with radios and other gear, Muccio's Buick, and several jeeps. Just beyond another half-assed village, Buggy in the lead jeep signaled a halt.

Cromwell, jumping out of his own jeep and carrying an M-1 picked up en route, joined the sergeant.

"Look at what we got here, Colonel."

Maybe twenty American soldiers slouched or lay, some of them full asleep, in the shade of a faded wooden barn of sorts. Ben Sweet ought to see this bunch. He could do a little cheerleading, issue appeals to patriotism.

"What's your unit, pal?" Buggy asked a fellow with corporal's stripes.

"Thirty-fourth Regiment, First Battalion, Charlie Company, Sarge."

"You wounded?"

"Some of us. The others are just beat. You can't believe what we been through."

Cromwell was leaving it to Buggy to handle this. Now he stepped up.

"Get on your feet, Corporal. We can take your wounded, some of them at least. Just hand 'em up into the trucks. My Marines will give you a hand."

"Yessir."

"Then the rest of you can walk out. Get them up if they're not wounded. And let's get some weapons in their hands. Chon-Ju's twenty miles southwest of here. You ought to catch up to your outfit there if not before. North Koreans aren't far behind us, so you'd better get started."

The corporal looked around.

"I think we'll just wait 'em out, sir. At least the Commies'll have docs and morphine and maybe some food. These men of mine can't walk twenty miles. Not no more after what we been through. And most ain't got weapons. Lost 'em along the road."

"You mean threw them away."

"Well, maybe so. A man gets tired lugging."

Buggy realized this wasn't precisely the tack to take with Raider Cromwell; looked into the corporal's slack face.

"Fall your men in, corporal, and be quick about it. I mean *now!*"

"Sarge, we can't go twenty miles. These boys ain't got a mile more in 'em, I swear to Christ."

Cromwell gave them one more chance. How do you win wars with men like this? Some heroes they were. Well, maybe he could scare them.

"Last week seven troopers from Task Force Smith surrendered a bit north of here. Near Sinanju. The Commies tied their hands with com wire, shoved them facedown so they were eating dirt, and shot them through the back of the head. Uniformed American soldiers taken prisoners of war, and they murdered them."

The corporal was sullen. He wasn't a damned Marine, didn't need their gung ho crap.

"You always hear stories like that, sir," he lectured the Marine officer. "We'll take our chances."

"Okay, Corporal," Buggy said, egged on by Cromwell, "have it your way. We'll shoot you here and now for desertion. Save the Commies the trouble. Your boys see their corporal getting shot for desertion in the face of the enemy, I figure they'll pull themselves together. Be able to go a mile. Maybe twenty miles even. Maybe even find a weapon. Maybe fight a goddamned battle. You get me?"

The corporal made a mistake. He appealed over Sergeant Buggy to Cromwell.

"Colonel, you can't let this crazy man shoot another American, sir. Not in front of an officer, sir."

Cromwell ignored the plea. Looking instead at Buggy, he said, "Sergeant, I don't want to see it in case there's a court of inquiry. But you take this coward around back of the barn and shoot him."

"Aye aye, sir," Buggy said, snapping off a salute and then prodding the corporal along with his rifle.

Cromwell hoped to hell Buggy had seen his wink. Otherwise, they really were going to be one corporal short.

The rest of the Thirty-fourth Regiment soldiers looked to each other, eyes wide, mouths hung open. Muccio's dips, gathered around and curious, were also staring, somewhat stunned. And when the unseen Buggy fired a single shot into the earth behind the barn, the slacking American soldiers, even the wounded, jumped to their feet. The Marine staff sergeant Haire, by now eager to impress this wild man Cromwell by doing something, anything, fell them in with a shout and had them count off. Which was when Buggy reappeared with a shaken, but unshot, Army corporal.

"He okay, Buggy?"

"Yessir. Shit his pants is all."

The Marines loaded the wounded into trucks and took them along when the little convoy pulled away as the remaining soldiers, momentarily shaken, shouldered their weapons—the handful of them still armed—and began to shuffle off south.

"Can they get to Chon-Ju, do you think?" Muccio asked, appalled at threats of execution, but impressed by Cromwell's decisiveness.

"They can, sir. But I don't think they will. They'll wait 'til we're out of sight, and they'll crap out again on the side of the road and wait to be captured. Those boys have quit; you can see it in their eyes. They're whipped. If they're lucky, the Reds won't shoot them."

"Oh."

That afternoon what they were now jocularly calling Task Force Muccio fought its first actual firefight.

Cromwell, expecting it, if not here then somewhere down the line, had already laid out the rules of engagement.

"If they've got tanks, we run. Run like hell. Step on the gas, dodge and evade, but go! Go like hell. If it's infantry, or trucks, we hit 'em hard and right away. Fight it out. And then head south again after we've finished them."

The Marines, all of them regulars, understood. Ollie was less certain about the diplomatic corps.

"You understand what I'm telling your people, Ambassador? It's our one chance of getting through alive and in one piece, to hook up with Rhee wherever it is the ROK government digs in. We may have to fight every mile of the way. Red patrols and advance parties are all over the landscape. It's rough country just made for ambush. But it's also got some hidey-holes we can use. And your folks have to be alert and do exactly what I or Sergeants Buggy or Haire tell them."

After ten days with Cromwell, Muccio was sufficiently savvy not to cite diplomatic immunity, assuming the Marine would enlighten him about the North Koreans not being particular about such things. So, he said:

"Good of you, Colonel. My staff will follow your orders."

"Thank you, Mr. Ambassador. The State Department would never forgive me if I get one of their diplomats shot."

Ollie was thinking about what the Navy brass called Marines on Guadalcanal—"tough eggs."

For a long time now, Cromwell concluded, he had been himself a very tough egg. And didn't much give a damn who knew it and whether they liked it or not.

The firefight was pretty good. And the Marines got the best of it. Only a dozen North Koreans in a Russian jeep and a commandeered GM truck, and they came around the corner, and there were the Marines waiting.

The North Koreans, all of whom died gallantly, never had a chance.

Muccio shook his head in admiration. Addressing Buggy, whom he knew well as one of his embassy guards, he said:

"Sergeant, that was . . . magnificent. No other word for it."

"Thank you, sir. We took 'em by surprise. If you can do that with automatic weapons, it ain't hardly fair."

On July 25 Task Force Muccio reached Taegu, an ancient Korean town not improved by war, with a dirt landing strip bulldozed out of raw earth, a woebegone place with a mere corporal's guard of American soldiers and airmen and the usual ROK troops asleep or scrounging food. But for lack of a better, Taegu had been chosen as HQ, pro tem, by Lieutenant General Walton Walker, U.S. Army, commanding officer of forces now on the ground in South Korea.

As the fatigue-clad Marines and their diplomatic party, the latter understandably rumpled, pulled up in front of a scatter of small buildings that seemed to be functioning as a command post, a couple of beefy Army MPs blocked the way in their white-painted helmets, their spiffy white web belts and holsters, plus their MP armbands. They actually looked like soldiers, and they didn't much like Marines.

"Go around back. No entry here."

Cromwell got out of the second jeep.

"Please inform your duty officer that United States Ambassador John Muccio is here to see the commanding officer. And it might be wise to turn out the guard. And smartly."

"Yeah, yeah, but tell 'em that out back. You don't come in here."

Will Buggy whipped a slung Thompson gun off his shoulder and jabbed it into the big MP's doughy middle, doubling him over. The man's cry of mingled pain and rage brought a U.S. Army captain running.

"What's this? What's this?"

Muccio, by now standing shoulder to shoulder with Ollie, identified himself, and he and the Marines were quickly invited inside.

Walker, who had good manners, came as soon as he was told about the ambassador.

"What can we do for you, sir?"

Muccio asked first for someplace to wash up and some food, and Walker sent men hopping. Then, looking at Cromwell's globe-and-anchor insignia, he asked:

"You from General Craig, Colonel?"

"Nossir, I'm military attaché to the ambassador."

"Well, you may see your general Ed Craig pretty soon. He and an advance party of the Marine brigade are flying over from Japan."

"That's good news, sir. Will they be landing here?"

"Depends. I may be out of Taegu myself by tomorrow. As fluid a front as this, you can't say. We'll try to keep Craig informed. Don't want to lose our first Marines to the Commies."

He grinned when he said it, and Cromwell appreciated that. Unlike his MPs, Walker seemed okay.

"On behalf of the United States Marine Corps, sir, you have our appreciation."

They washed up and were fed, and after Muccio spent an hour with several senior officers, he and Cromwell and their party drew a couple of abandoned Korean homes for the night, sleeping on the floor and out of the nightly rain, and being woken only once by distant artillery and then again at daybreak by a strafing Yak on the dawn patrol.

A major in a helmet and sporting a nice shoulder holster came to brief them.

"We're not pulling out yet, but Taegu's not a long-term bet. When we go, it'll probably be as far as Masan. General Craig will fly in here to be briefed and then go south to Pusan to welcome his brigade. General Walker will be leaving by plane after he briefs Craig, and the rest of us by truck and jeep. I wouldn't hang around here after that if I were you."

"North Koreans coming?" Ollie asked.

"A few advance patrols only sixteen miles north of here. We can hold our own against patrols but not their heavy units, Colonel."

"Thanks, Major."

The Marine turned to Muccio. "Mr. Ambassador, it's your call. Can we stay in Taegu until General Craig gets here so I can see him?"

"Right, Oliver. I understand. But my place is wherever Rhee is, and I can't get there without you and your Marines taking us there."

"Yessir," Cromwell said, keeping reluctance out of his voice. If there was anything he disliked in a serving officer, it was an "aye aye" with a whine. Besides, Pusan, or so they'd been told, was where Craig was headed after he met here with Walker. And Pusan was where the Marine brigade would come ashore. He saluted Ambassador Muccio smartly and called out to Buggy, "You and Sergeant Haire get the men squared away. We'll be moving out within the hour. Setting a course for Pusan and the brigade."

As Muccio and his Marines drove south out of Taegu, they could hear the first few explosions to their rear, could see a little smoke rising, as Walker's rear guards started blowing up whatever useful material they wouldn't be able to carry along when Walton Walker and his staff pulled out. That day's trek by Task Force Muccio was simple, steady but slow, the muddy roads clogged by civilian refugees heading south. There were plenty of ROK soldiers, but most of them were without weapons, shambling along with the farmers and peasants and women and old men, refugees as well, the only difference being that the soldiers wore uniforms.

Buggy looked at them.

"No more ROK execution squads, Colonel. Not like up north."

"Maybe the MPs quit, too."

Sure looked that way.

From what Cromwell and his Marines could see, except for a temporarily stablized wide place in the road like Taegu, everyone was going south, and that included the Yanks. Withdrawal having become retreat, retreat a rout, the rout disintegrating now into scared-as-hell, flat-out flight for the ROKs and the U.S. troops sent over to bail them out.

Ollie was driving for a time with Muccio. "Five years ago," he said, "this was the American army that destroyed Nazi Germany and the Empire of Japan."

Muccio nodded. Whatever he might not know about fighting a war, he knew his history.

"And you're wondering how it all fell apart this way?"

"I am, sir," said Cromwell.

"Because we didn't just disarm and cut back. We sent men home by the millions, junked the planes, scrapped the big guns, scuttled the ships.

You couldn't get Americans to pay for an army that size. And, in all fairness, in 1945 did you think we'd ever fight another war, Colonel?"

"Not a big one. Unless it was nuclear. But small wars like this one, sure. Small, brushfire wars shouldn't be a surprise. There are always going to be wars. It's why we have standing armies."

The diplomat considered debating that conclusion but thought better of it. After all, wasn't war the failure of diplomacy?

Perhaps he and the colonel could discuss the matter over drinks sometime.

But first, they came to Kosong.

Kosong was a market town that would later achieve a certain celebrity where Marine Corsairs off the carriers just massacred the North Koreans. "The Kosong Turkey Shoot" they'd call it. Even though the turkeys would fight back and knock down a couple of the Corsairs, one Marine Captain drowning in a rice paddy. But that was in the future.

Right now Kosong was just a place screwed-up because two retreating columns of American and ROK soldiers, meeting at a rural crossroads, had been squeezed into a narrow place in the road where a Yak fighter found and strafed them.

Sergeant Buggy and two other Marines jogged ahead, weapons at high port, to see to the delay, and they were back in minutes.

"Well?" Cromwell asked.

"Yak caught 'em, Colonel. Some deads, lots of woundeds. Worse than that, couple of Army trucks burnt out and blocking the damned road." No one knew just how many dead, how many wounded; the U.S. Army wasn't keeping score anymore. The Twenty-fourth and the Twenty-fifth Divisions were mixed up here, both scattered and on the run, and no one knew who was in charge.

"Some army," Cromwell told himself. West Point wouldn't be putting up plaques memorializing glorious feats of arms at places like Kosong.

The roadblock and the strafing had occurred maybe an hour before the Marines got there.

"Can we flank the traffic jam and cut across the fields?" Ollie asked.

"We'd bog down, sir," Buggy said. "No way the Buick will make it. Those are all irrigated paddies out there to the right. Foot of water atop a foot of mud."

To the left, granite mountains rose sheer, right out of the shoulder of the road. So they weren't going there, either.

"We're screwed," someone said.

No one had bothered to haul the dead American soldiers off the road at Kosong, and an hour later, when Cromwell and Muccio and their vehicles passed along, the dead men were flattened like squirrels or deer on a rural road back home, just roadkill. The blood wasn't even crimson anymore, but dried rust color. The blood didn't look like blood; the men no longer resembled men.

"Oh, hell," one of the Marines said, looking down at them as they drove past.

"Better them than us," another Marine said, but not really getting any wit into the crack.

It was pretty bad. It said something about how the Army had fallen apart that no one, officer or noncom or enlisted, thought of dragging the dead GIs off the road, tipping them over the edge into the paddies. At least in the paddies vehicles wouldn't be rolling over them and squashing the corpses flat.

The men still alive in the trucks looked bad, but the men on foot worse. Most seemed to have thrown away their helmets, some their packs. Only a few still carried rifles, and those were slung carelessly. These were beaten troops, the officers as hangdog as their men. There was no water except in the flooded paddies, and men knelt to drink straight from the water or to fill canteens. Since the paddies were fertilized with human waste, you knew what that was going to do to men already worn down. Twenty-year-old Americans stood around or slogged along, stiff-jointed some of them, moving like people in the old folks' home. Other men were strangely sloven, their trousers flapping loose and hung low. Cromwell supposed those were soldiers who'd sweated off the beer bellies and the soft life of Japanese occupation in the baking heat and humidity of Korea.

"They look like bums, sir," Buggy said.

And they did. Like men in the hobo jungles of the Depression thirties, that's how they looked. Not like soldiers at all.

And then it got worse. Until now it had been tough North Korean foot soldiers dogging the GIs, with the huge Russian T-34 tanks thrown in, scaring hell out of people and rolling right over the odd pocket of resistance. That was bad enough. But now the enemy was coming on so fast, and the road-bound Americans were retreating so slowly, they were within range of the field artillery. So that from Tonsong south, UN troops and refugees were under shell fire from Communist guns, the wonderfully reliable and accurate .105 guns, American-made—an irony U.S. soldiers were too tired or scared even to remark. And the shells kept falling, blowing hell out of men and machines on the long road south. The GIs seemed to lack the will, or the strength, to turn and fight back. They just wanted out.

Oh, there were exceptions: an outfit coming along that seemed open for business, a few men under an officer or a grizzled NCO, men packing weapons and helmeted and, despite fatigue and the heat, still with the heft and bearing of a military unit. The Marines, appreciative of professionalism, snapped off salutes as they passed. Except for those few still properly soldiering, this was the sad, beaten look of the U.S. Army in South Korea that summer of 1950.

It was hard, mountainous country they were passing through now, with a spine of mountains running north and south three or four thousand feet high, and steep, steep as hell—so steep Cromwell thought armed men with field packs couldn't scale such slopes, except on hands and knees. Under fire it would be worse than tough. But you couldn't just bypass the hills; you would have to take them. You always had to take the high ground. Ollie was already thinking ahead, scoping out the terrain, not as an attaché wet-nursing a bunch of diplomats, but as an infantry officer who would soon be commanding Marines in combat. Not retreating, as he'd been doing ever since he arrived in the damned country, but attacking, coming north through these same hills and knocking the North Koreans back. Knocking them on their ass.

Task Force Muccio camped out that night in fields unfertilized by human excrement and thought themselves fortunate. For the first time all week, they didn't have rain. And the Marine brigade was coming. That knowledge alone buoyed Cromwell and set Buggy and Haire to chivying their men, ordering them to shave and beat some of the caked mud and the foul dust off their boots and uniforms. They didn't have to say anything about their weapons. They were Marines; they saw to their weapons.

Ambassador Muccio, who was falling in love with his Marines, liked the way they tidied themselves up—"getting squared away," as they called it.

The ambassador wished there were some way *he* could get squared away. He regarded his panama sadly, wondering if there might be a hat shop in Pusan.

"I want a smart-looking outfit when we come into Pusan," Haire went on, looking to Buggy for his approval, "and even smarter-looking when the brigade comes ashore." Buggy knew his cue:

"You listen up now to Sergeant Haire, you people. He's got it right about us looking smart. General Craig'll expect it of us veterans to set those new boys an example."

It wasn't until they were south of the Naktong River, a considerable water barrier, that Cromwell's Marines began seeing the first signs of an organized American army, with artillery dug in, barbed-wire and machine-gun strong points, scouts with field glasses on the high ground scanning north, truckloads of troops heading toward the enemy and not fleeing south.

In fairness, Cromwell realized, not all the Army units had cut and run. A few had stood, held, and died. Marines had no monopoly on courage; their discipline just didn't let them discourage as easily.

At the Naktong, staring out at the broad, brown river from its far bank, Muccio asked, "Can we stop them here?"

"I don't know, Mr. Ambassador," Ollie replied honestly. "But we better hold somewhere, or that Marine brigade of ours won't be marching down gangways at Pusan Harbor with bands playing; they'll be coming ashore through the surf and shooting."

Pusan was bloody chaos.

The embassy Marine guard came down out of the hills clean-shaven and squared-away and drove into town on a rainy morning that last week of July just as a flight of Yaks flew over, heading back home after doing a job on the city docks. The port's thousands of stevedores were again on strike, and this when American troop reinforcements and matériel—arms and ammo, food and fuel—were arriving and not being unloaded. The Yanks were coming, all right, but in this sad excuse for a country, or a war, labor negotiations had priority. Unless it was hefted and carried ashore by hand and the sheer muscle of American GIs forced into labor as longshoremen by the strike, the cargo stayed aboard. If defeatism simmered up there in the hills and the paddies north of Pusan, it was here as well. With a dollop of local opportunism, black-marketeering, and North Korean sabotage cleverly thrown in.

Pusan was a big port city at the little country's utmost southeast tip, part Galveston, part Brooklyn, with most of its activity centered on the wharves and dry docks and warehouses of the waterfront, and now, in the fifth week of war, its normally clogged and crowded streets and its skeletal municipal facilities were overwhelmed by strangers and events. Not to mention North Korean bombs. All this on top of the peacetime insufficiency of hotels and inns, hospitals and shops, and a primitive infrastructure. The cops and firemen seemed to be on hiatus; the town seethed with frightened refugees: the homeless and hungry from the newly captive North; urban tradespeople and bespectacled clerks in Western togs; illiterate, white-robed people from the country—rural peasants, distraught parents searching for lost children, lost children seeking parents; émigré politicians and bureaucrats who'd gotten out of Seoul without being shot; monks telling their prayer beads; smalltime criminals working their scams and petty thefts; despairing women abandoned by husbands who had been conscripted into the Army or had run away, dodging the draft. Refugees with money bribed their way into shared homes with profiteering locals; penniless peasants slept hungry and thirsty on sidewalks or in fields and villages just outside town, drenched by the heavy rain, baked by the July sun. In the city itself almost nothing worked, with power intermittently down and electric lights weak and flickering, the water reduced to a trickle and fouled, stinking of something (you hoped it was chemicals introduced as purifiers!), the streetcars rolling from time to time, no cabs, the few gas stations closed for lack of product, bicycles at a premium, trucks reserved for what still functioned of the Army. Summer rain puddled and mosquitoes hatched. Fat cockroaches swarmed, and the first rats had moved in, scurrying busily through uncollected trash and nosing about food shops and storehouses that offered promise. And not a pied piper in town to be offered employment. No one seemed in charge, with the Rhee government, such as it was, frozen into inactivity, fretting about its own prospects and gloomy with pessimism.

The Americans already here, with thousands more rumored to be coming, just over the horizon, were awaited by the hopeful as saviors. And by the cynical as fresh victims to be plundered. That, briefly, was the port of Pusan in summer 1950 when Cromwell, Muccio, and their party rolled into town.

The MPs here were less hostile, and Muccio was quickly, and almost accurately, directed toward where President Rhee had set up for business.

Further north they'd seen plenty of bodies, wrecked and burnt-out villages, ravaged farms, and the blackened carcasses of trucks and South Korean light tanks hit by enemy air or artillery and the T-34 heavies. Here at Pusan, forty or fifty miles from the nearest Communist advance units, there wasn't much damage at all except down in the dock area, and that from the enemy air. It was the ROKs themselves—the military, the politicians, and civilian looters—who did most of the damage, making trouble and doing mischief. Though with the occasional assist from literal-minded U.S. Army bureaucrats.

When Muccio, also tidied up and with his horn-rimmed glasses polished clean of road dust, sent Harold Noble to Rhee headquarters to inform him the American ambassador had arrived and was opening a downtown office, Noble came back with a laundry list of ROK government complaints. Some were just the usual whine. A few were justifiable and some downright outrageous. Since the U.S. military was now in effect not only defending the country but running it, the only long-distance communications had to go through Army radios or land lines, even those from President Rhee to other countries with which South Korea had diplomatic relations. When Harold Noble complained to the Army communications people about Rhee's lack of communications access, he was rudely dismissed.

"Let the gooks set up their own phone company."

Muccio, a veteran at dealing with difficult people, sent Noble back. "Tell their two-star general or whoever's in charge over there that you're a forty-eight-star general, because you represent the United States of America and our ally President Syngman Rhee needs a clear phone line or a radio frequency, and he needs it now! And the government of the United States intends to see to it that he has it."

"Well said, sir," said Cromwell, impressed. Sometimes, civilians got it right.

And, by God, when Noble returned two hours later, Rhee was starting to send and receive messages. Even Muccio seemed surprised his bleat, conveyed by Noble, actually worked.

And, even better than the restored phone service, the first handful of Marines were in town.

Cromwell found a major he knew from Pendleton, now on Craig's staff, just back from Taegu, where Craig and his advance party had huddled with an affable Walton Walker before going off to reconnoiter. They'd traveled first-class, courtesy of General Walker's own plane, and accompanied by his G-3, the operations officer.

Ollie pumped his pal for a quick boil-down of what Craig, and the brigade, were up to.

"I've been flying blind for five weeks. Cut off from the Marine Corps and straight dope. Give me a break."

"It's my ass if you blabber, Ollie," the major said. Then told his fellow Marine everything he knew, what had gone on as the Marines paid their respects to the Army:

"Well, General Craig?" Walker had asked when they landed back at Taegu.

"Thanks to you, sir, I got a pretty good look. And the Commies are coming fast, General," responded Craig.

"They are, sir," Walker agreed. And now he and his G-2, the intelligence officer, gave Craig and his staff the latest bad news. Chinju had fallen to the Reds, and they were pushing hard toward Masan.

"Masan? Chinju?" The Marine brigade commander, not yet up on Korean geography, asked how significant that was. Walker's G-2 responded:

"Sir, Masan is forty miles from downtown Pusan. And we don't have any substantial forces to commit there."

What Walker told the Marine about the importance of Masan undercut any hope Craig had of gradually committing his Marine brigade to the fight and choosing the ground for his opening offensive. His operational plans were being overtaken by events. They had to stabilize the front before launching an attack. And the front wouldn't stabilize unless they patched the fresh Marines into the line to stiffen the defense.

In other words, the brigade was screwed.

That was all Ollie's source knew. What Cromwell would learn or pick up over the next few days filled in the blanks.

Ed Craig was fifty-four years old, slender, erect, and white-haired, with a chiseled face, and he looked like a Marine. And had been since commissioning as a second lieutenant in 1917. In fighting on Bougainville and Guam, he was awarded the Navy Cross and Bronze Star for gallantry. Ollie had met Craig at Camp Pendleton, where he was aide-de-camp to the commanding general of the 1st Marine Division, Erskine B. Graves, but he didn't really know the man. And when Cromwell pried himself free of Muccio their first day at Pusan and called at Craig's temporary command post in the headquarters building of General Garvin's base command, he was refused an audience.

Ollie needed a job, and Craig was the man who could give it to him. But he couldn't get to Craig.

"Old Man's busy as hell, Ollie," Cromwell was told. "He's getting ready to bring Ray Murray—" (commanding the 5th Marines and a man with his own Navy Cross, two Silver Stars, and a Purple Heart) "—up to speed as soon as Murray's regiment lands. Craig used up two days huddling with Walton Walker, and he's inside now, plotting and planning. The brigade's due tomorrow or day after, and there's a shitload of stuff still to do. Like getting those damned longshoremen back to work. And deciding whether we go north on the attack or due west on the defensive. Nuttiest preparatory situation you've ever seen. We don't even know if we move by rail or by road."

"Can I lend a hand?" Cromwell asked.

The staff man gave him a look.

"Ollie, we've got staff people up the ass. If I were you, I'd come back once the brigade lands. You know Ray Murray. Try to get to see Ray."

Ollie had been a Marine for a long time, and he understood. So he cruised around the base command, buttonholing any Marine officer he came across, hoping one might turn out to be an old *compadre*. Just before he got back to the quarters Muccio had found for them, Ollie's jeep, driven by Lonesome, was turned back by some ROK MPs.

"What's up?" Lonesome asked a lounging GI, who pulled himself together sufficiently to crank off a vague salute in Cromwell's direction.

"Nothing much. They're shooting a fellow down that alleyway. They think he's a Commie or something."

Cromwell nodded.

They "think" he might be a Commie. He heard a volley of shots. Then a single shot following, the coup de grace.

Sergeant Buggy, sitting behind Cromwell with a submachine gun on his lap, said, "Let's move it, Lonesome. You can do your sightseeing next leave."

"Aye aye, Sar'nt."

To Ed Craig's dismay, with the 266 officers and more than 4,000 men of his brigade still at sea but closing fast, the gossip in U.S. Army circles at Pusan had gone bleak, despairing, even defeatist. No longer did men speak of a powerful Marine offensive or even of defending the city. With the Allied left flank collapsing, the talk was of getting the hell out, a humiliating evacuation by sea. A new Dunkirk! That was how bad the fight was going.

On their side, the enemy could taste victory.

On July 28, as North Korean major general Pang ordered the advance on Chinju to commence, he sent a message to his victorious Red troops, congratulatory and ripe with Party rhetoric:

"Comrades," General Pang wrote, "the enemy is demoralized. The task given to us is the liberation of Masan and Chinju and the annihilation of the remnants of the enemy . . . to cut off his windpipe. Comrades, this glorious task has fallen to our division! Men of the Sixth Division, let us annihilate the enemy and distinguish ourselves!"

And it wasn't all rhetoric. These were good troops Pang commanded. In hard fighting against the American Twenty-fourth Division, the North Korean Sixth and an attached unit, the Eighty-third Motorcycle Regiment, fought their way into Chinju on July 30.

On our side, Craig had his first good news. The 1st Marine Air Wing planes were by now all in Japan and ready to start flying combat missions in support of the brigade. The problem: a paucity of landing strips on Korean soil. Japanese airports weren't that far away, but, especially for fighters, distance limited their operating range. The carriers were heading this way, and that would help, but the farther south the Commies advanced, the fewer airstrips the Allies had. Also in the air, B-29 "Superforts" based in Japan had walloped the North Korean capital of Pyongyang for the first time and were hitting military targets as far north as the Yalu River, Korea's border with China.

Surely, Generals Walker and Craig and the others thought (or maybe just hoped), the North Koreans would eventually outrun their supply lines and have to slow down. If not, there wouldn't be a Pusan Perimeter to defend. Which was where talk of another Dunkirk began, of possibly having to evacuate U.S. ground forces through the port of Pusan and off the beaches, under cover of naval gunfire and air support, and leaving the damned South Koreans, who weren't doing much fighting anyway, to fend for themselves.

An Army light colonel who'd been helpful to Muccio, a man with a gallows sense of humor, asked Ollie:

"You notice the USO hasn't arrived yet? No Bob Hope show scheduled. There hasn't been an American theatre of war since 1941 that Bob Hope hasn't been to. Not until now. That doesn't imbue me with optimism, Cromwell."

Muccio, who had access to the top people, was less amusing but just as gloomy.

"Even Rhee knows his troops haven't put up much of a fight. I don't think he really expected that they would. What frightens him is that we Americans haven't done much better. Rhee expected the North Koreans would pull back the first time they encountered U.S. troops. Instead, they ran right over them. The people around Rhee are already checking the Greyhound Bus schedules out of town."

"Only there isn't any 'out of town' if we lose Pusan," Cromwell said.

"That's the problem," the diplomat agreed.

On the morning of August 2, the first Marine transport, a barely seaworthy hulk called *Henrico,* sighted the gray hills of Korea as it passed through the Tsushima Straits, the same narrow passage between Japan and Korea where the Japs sank the czar's fleet in a couple of hours in 1904. As she came closer, *Henrico*'s Marines could see that the hills were actually pretty forbidding-looking peaks that began not all that far inland. To men hardened by the hills of Camp Pendleton, the sight was not a welcome one.

It wasn't until five that afternoon that the first of the Marine ships nosed up to its berth in Pusan Harbor. American Army troops hooted derisive catcalls and insults as a South Korean band played a tinny rendition of the "Marines' Hymn" and General Craig himself shouted up at officers aboard the first ship, the *Clymer,* as she was being moored, asking, "Which battalion is the advance guard?"

Men cupped hands to their ears and shrugged. No one seemed to know. Organizational orders Craig thought had been passed along had not been.

It was just the start of things. As the official Marine Corps history puts it:

"It is not surprising that the Pusan waterfront turned into a bedlam." And as Colonel Ray Murray of "the 1st Marine Provisional Brigade" could tell you, the trouble didn't start dockside at Pusan but two weeks earlier and nearly ten thousand miles away at the Naval Supply Depot, Oakland, where the ill-fated transport *Henrico* loaded its Marines, sailed west under the Golden Gate for the Orient, had to return to Oakland for repairs, sailed beneath the great bridge a second time, had to turn back once more for additional work, and, on a third and final try, sailed south to San Diego and then west to the war. While on July 13 in mid-ocean worse things were happening aboard the LSD (landing ship dock) Fort Marion, where the well deck suddenly flooded, inundating with corroding seawater the brigade's fourteen brand-new M-26 tanks to a depth of five feet. And those were the tanks Craig was relying on to fight on equal terms with the Russian T-34s. On July 14, more angst aboard *Henrico,* which carried Ray Murray, his regimental staff, and the entire 1st Battalion Landing Team: mechanical failure had the ship temporarily declared "unseaworthy," and Murray and his HQ staff were transferred by small boat to another transport, the *Pickaway; Henrico* returned yet again to Oakland, where Marines, forbidden from going ashore, worked out and sat forlorn on deck, staring at the lights of San Francisco.

And all of this after the Commandant of the Marine Corps, General Clifton B. Cates himself, had come down to the docks at San Diego to see the brigade off. Cates, a very cool gent who brandished a cigarette holder and could mesmerize a Washington audience with his eloquence, spoke to the embarking Marines in their language:

"You boys clean this up in a couple of months," Cates warned, "or I'll be over to see you."

▪ 30 ▪

Now, in the first week of August, the brigade's Marines would finally be going ashore in Korea, ready to fight, to "clean this up." Or would they?

Darkness fell over the Perimeter as thousands of Marines, many of them young men who'd never before been out of the States, poured off the transports and onto the docks. Cranes and working parties unloaded supplies, vehicles, and gear under searchlights, while Marines mustered on piers and city streets and inside buildings, with cardboard boxes of C-rations, grenades, and machine-gun belts in their arms and cloth bandoliers of ammo clips slung. Men shuffled back and forth all night long, few of them able to sleep with the noise and shouted orders and general clamor, and those few slept on the street or on the floors of buildings. One basic snarl: back in the States the ships had been loaded operationally, not combat-loaded. Because the brigade was supposed to land first at Japan, rearrange things, and only then ship out for a landing in Korea, the tanks and big guns and trucks were now coming off last, while cases of rations, rolls of barbed wire, tentage, toilet paper, field kitchens, and the like came off first.

As the sun came up, the tired troops clambered back aboard ship for a hot meal and a trip to the head. But these were simply the usual logistical screw-ups and snafus. More vital: a basic disagreement over just where and how the Marines, the best soldiers General Walton Walker had, would be used.

Even Ed Craig still didn't know for sure. And Craig commanded them.

At nine that night in the wardroom of *Clymer,* he and his staff had gathered to hear another pessimistic assessment of the battlefront from an Army officer. Craig, in his turn, reminded everyone that he'd been assured the Marines would be going over to the offensive, not patched into the line at its weak points like the little Dutch boy at the dike. The Army told the Marines that fifty trucks and a number of railroad trains would be available at 6:00 A.M. to carry the Marine brigade to the war. Still not quite clear: which war? Would they be transported due north to attack? Or to the west to defend Masan and Changwon, where the Reds were attacking and the Allied lines were caving?

At dawn on August 3 Lieutenant Colonel George Newton's 1st Battalion boarded Marine and Army trucks for the forty-mile drive to Changwon in the West, arriving there at two in the afternoon. The decision had been made: the Marines first had to shore up the UN left flank, or there wouldn't be an offensive.

By now the Pusan Perimeter had shrunk to roughly ninety miles long by sixty wide. And, especially at its southwest corner, it was fast coming unhinged. American soldiers—seasoned men, not the slack garrison troops from Tokyo—asked themselves, Do we get the hell out of here, board ship, and just quit? Or do we somehow pull ourselves together and fight back, to beat the shit out of the enemy, start killing people, and try to win the damned war? To good troops, it was that simple; it was that complicated.

Men with an historic bent, aware that other wars had begun badly, wondered how Washington felt when he heard Gentleman Johnny Burgoyne was heading from Canada down the Champlain Valley with his redcoats and hired Hessians to crush the rebels and cut the colonies in half— New England and New York from Virginia and the Carolinas.

Well, the optimists remembered what happened at Saratoga, how Benedict Arnold and his boys whipped Gentleman Johnny and kept the Revolution going.

Between 6:30 and 7:00 A.M. of August 3, the rest of the brigade boarded trucks and trains, the M-26 tanks loaded on flatcars to save their treads and conserve fuel. By 4:00 in the afternoon the entire brigade, minus one tank platoon and logistical elements left at base in Pusan to oversee the supply line, was united at Changwon.

All three of Murray's rifle battalions took up positions on high ground—the hills and ridgelines on three sides of Changwon—without enemy opposition or coming under fire. That night, men who'd barely slept the night before, edgy and exhausted, were just getting to sleep in shifts when at 10:00 P.M. a single rifle shot was accidently squeezed off. To the many young Marines who'd never seen combat, that was sufficient. For the rest of the night, men were firing at rocks and scrub growth, seeing, in imagination, North Korean infantrymen crawling uphill toward them in the dark. At midnight, two Marine machine guns joined in the sport.

Craig, furious at the lack of fire discipline and having lost two men to friendly fire, reamed out a few fresh anuses at dawn among his junior officers. Not an auspicious beginning. Saltier Marines looked at each other and shook their heads, muttering. "You'd think we were sojers, for God's sake."

But it was also on August 3 that the first eight Marine Corsairs were in the air over enemy lines at Chinju and the village of Sinban-ni, strafing and bombing enemy supply routes. The next day, Corsairs flew twenty-one sorties. Even jumpy young Marine infantry, raised on tales of Pappy Boyington and his Black Sheep Squadron, took heart at looking up and seeing only Corsairs. The marauding Yaks were scoured from the blue Korean skies.

On August 5 Craig and Colonel Stewart flew to Masan to meet again with the Eighth Army's Walker. Walker sketched out the latest position, said he wanted the Marines to jump off on the offensive at Hill 342 near Chindong-ni. But that in the meanwhile all American and Allied units, in order to preserve the integrity of the swiftly vanishing Perimeter, would "stand to the death." Eighth Army could afford to lose no more ground, no more equipment.

"The trading of ground for time is ended," General Walker ordered.

Arrival of the Marine brigade, less than five thousand men, seemed to have stiffened Walker, and, to an extent, it revitalized his entire command. And the Marines hadn't yet fired a shot in anger.

Only a few nervous shots in the dark.

But at least they were going on the offensive at Hill 342. Left behind, and useless, in Pusan, Ollie Cromwell met again with Ambassador Muccio and attempted, without much success, to resign from the Foreign Service. Muccio was having little of it.

"Ollie, now more than ever, with a war being waged all about us, I need a military attaché." At least Muccio succeeded in getting his embassy Marines, including Ollie, suitable quarters on the campus of Pusan University, a site chosen by Ed Craig for his HQ, there being no classes on account of summer. And, oh yes, the war. Cromwell kept laying for Craig, but, with the brigade about to go into action in the hills to the southwest, there was little opportunity. It was the university campus that inspired the first even marginally memorable Korean War song since "The Bug-out Blues":

Old Pusan U.,
Old Pusan U.
I asked her what her school was.
She said, "Oh, Pusan you."

Cromwell had again failed to see General Craig. Ray Murray, commanding the 5th Marines, was more encouraging.

"Ollie, I've got battalion commanders. What I need more than another light colonel is one more rifle company. All our battalions are down to two companies instead of three, and, as far as riflemen go, we're on short rations. In a rifleman's war.

"I'd be proud to have you back in the regiment. But Marine lieutenant colonels who steal attachés away from the State Department don't grow up to become full colonels. You get Muccio to release you, and we'll talk business, salary, fringe benefits—the works. I've got three fine battalion commanders, and I can assure you, if any of them are seriously damaged, you'll be on a shortlist."

Cromwell made sure he saw all three battalion commanders in order to pass on Ray Murray's lugubrious pledge.

"Gee, Ollie, I never knew you cared."

"Listen, I'm just repeating what Ray said. In case you run into a little bad luck up there."

"Cromwell," a battalion commander said laughing, "like all you damned Raiders, you're a snake."

"I am that," he agreed. "I am."

The fight on Hill 342 began unexpectedly toward midnight when Taplett's 3rd Battalion was ordered by Army colonel Mike Michaelis to send a reinforced rifle platoon to Hill 342 to relieve an Army company "being slowly eaten away in a private little war of attrition" with the North Koreans. Taplett dispatched a Lieutenant Cahill and his First Platoon of G Company, reinforced by a machine-gun squad and an SCR-300 radio operator. But as they moved up in the dark toward 342, two of Cahill's men were shot and badly wounded. When dawn broke, it was realized it was 2nd Battalion Marines who'd shot Cahill's men, thinking they were being infiltrated.

By midday, due to enemy fire, small arms and mortars, and hundred-degree heat, Cahill had lost both his platoon sergeant and platoon guide, the first dead and the second dying, and by the time his men reached the summit of the hill, 52 Marines had been whittled down to 37. At the summit the Marines were nearly overwhelmed by panicking soldiers hurrying to get off the hill now that their relief had arrived. A cool young Army lieutenant stopped the rout, and from then on Marines and soldiers fought effectively side by side on Hill 342. But before dark, Cahill had 11 more men down from heat stroke or exhaustion, all in varying degrees of unconsciousness. Lieutenant Cahill had never before been in combat. And now this? On his first day at war he'd lost 26 out of 52 Marines.

Senior officers assumed the enemy, hardened by six weeks of combat, would be tough; no one expected heat to be such a factor.

That night the North Koreans wormed their way uphill toward the summit. Hand-to-hand fighting featured grenades and bayonet duels. By morning on the 8th Cahill's platoon and the remaining soldiers had been so badly hurt that an entire Marine rifle company, Dog Company, under Captain Finn, was sent to their relief.

Finn ran into North Korean fire so heavy that two of his three rifle platoon leaders were killed and the third suffered a bad head wound. Then Finn himself was shot in the shoulder and the head, and, half-blind and covered in blood, he crawled downhill to friendly lines.

That night a Marine forward observer, Lieutenant Leroy Wirth, not an infantryman at all, took command of the surviving Marines left on Hill 342, and with the guidance of Dog Company's gunnery sergeant, a thirty-year man named Reeves, they held the hill until eventually relieved by Easy Company.

Lieutenant Cahill, who survived, estimated that between 500 and 600 enemy infantrymen had fought on Hill 342 and that their losses added up to more than 150. And these were men of General Pang's Sixth Division, which had been ordered to cut the enemy's windpipe and finish him off.

The experienced Marine officers, Craig and Ray Murray among them, men who'd helped defeat the Empire of Japan, looked at each other and nodded silent agreement. They were again in a real war.

This was hard country, with its heat and its hills, and the North Koreans were tough, resourceful, and courageous soldiers. Even though Hill 342 was just another nothing, steep, but featureless hill not much more than a thousand feet high and way out in the boondocks, the enemy fought day and night to hang onto it, not just against American soldiers, but also against two companies of U.S. Marine regulars, and they hadn't given or asked quarter.

The Marine brigade had been blooded.

▪ 31 ▪

They won't quit. They're like the Japs. You have to kill them."

Up on the line that's what they were saying, Marines who'd fought in the Pacific. The ultimate compliment Marines could offer a tough foe. And, largely, it was the cauldron of little Hill 342 and its gritty North Korean defenders that inspired such praise.

"Commie bastards!"

Forty miles from the ridgelines and hills of the Naktong River line, through the day and into night, the olive-drab Ford and GM trucks rolled past Ollie's ground-floor office at the temporary embassy, carting Marine replacements out of Pusan to the war.

Fresh meat.

The look and cadence of marching troops, the grinding low-gear sound of weighted trucks, the aching awareness they were headed to the front—all this ate at Cromwell. Helplessly he watched them pass, knowing he should be with them, might justifiably be leading them. Even more bitter were the sight and sound of traffic coming down off the line, the trucks piled with the dead and wounded rolling into Pusan and through the town down to the port and the hospital ship and to where they had a tented morgue with barely enough ice to keep the corpses. They ran those trucks with the tailgates down to afford more room for the bodies stacked neat as cordwood, and Ollie could see the the booted feet sticking out the back, see the yellow canvas leggings of dead Marines. And here he was snared in red tape, consigned, perhaps forever, to the duties of a rear-echelon pogue.

The Marines were fighting now on the Naktong—fighting North Korean regulars, fighting the heat, fighting the monsoon rains. And back into Pusan, past Old Pusan U. and our temporary embassy, came men bearing news of hard fighting; back from the front came the trucks with their dead, their wounded (ambulances being insufficient for the job), rolling into Pusan past where Colonel Cromwell briefed the ambassador, ran errands, and shuffled paper.

Sensible folk, civilians mostly, yearn for peace, a life of placid calm; they abhor violence. A professional soldier such as Cromwell is tolerant, understanding such instincts; but he thirsts for war. It is his calling, his craft, his route to higher rank, his passion. Fully to appreciate the angst felt by Cromwell, beached here in the rear, you must understand that all Marine officers, even pilots or engineers or seagoing bellhops, from the day of commissioning, are infantry officers, rifle platoon leaders. So if you were one of them, an infantryman and serious about it, trapped in a drab little office at Pusan University while the trucks and the tanks splashed by, it gave you a new aspect on things. You saw the war passing you by.

Cromwell might as well be parceling out Red Cross donuts and coffee to the troops or playing war correspondent like Sweet or Maggie Higgins, seeing the war but not fighting it. To an aggressive Marine officer with his combat experience, the situation was intolerable. He'd not been this bitter since they accused him of dirty play in wrecking Jack Ballard's knee. Then he was only a boy and not a grown man who knew how he was being wasted, a military leper who bore the mark of Cain, some malevolent ID card singling him out as one of Carlson's men, as a Raider, a Marine gone wrong.

Then came a message from General Craig. Would Colonel Cromwell come by his HQ next morning, August 17. Craig, not a great one for the niceties, was standing behind a battered desk in fatigues and with a shoulder-holstered .45 strapped on. He kept Ollie standing, too.

"I have a job for you, Cromwell. A temp job that could lead to something bigger. But it'll be General O. P. Smith's call, and nothing's certain—no guarantees.

"Aye aye, sir," Cromwell said, unsure of where this was leading but buoyed nonetheless. He knew that his rank and his record qualified him to command. But serving as an ambassador's attaché while men he knew fought and died up on the Naktong . . .

Whatever Craig ordered him to do, Ollie was ready. What options had he?

"It's not the rifle battalion command job you want. I'm assigning you to Operations as assistant-3. I know, I know—that's a major's billet and not a light colonel's. But I want you to get the feel of the ground by going up there with the rifle companies, and yet keep you handy enough that I can pull you back here when General Smith sends the word. You game?"

"Yessir, I am, General." He didn't entirely like the sound of it, but with Ed Craig you didn't enter into lengthy discussions.

Which was how Ollie got himself into the war, up on a height of ground called Obong-ni Ridge, where Captain Ike Fenton and his rifle company were fighting a battle against North Korean regulars along the Naktong River.

But first, in Pusan, a courtesy farewell call was made on Ambassador Muccio at the very pro tem U.S. embassy.

"You got me out of Seoul and over that bridge, Cromwell. If they ever assign me another attaché, I'll insist on a Marine."

"It was my privilege, sir."

"Call me John. And after the war, when I'm an ambassador somewhere else, drop in. I'll see to it you get on the right cocktail party lists."

"I will, sir. And thanks."

Will Buggy arranged a jeep and had Lonesome and himself officially detached from the embassy guard, and they drove north out of town that following morning in a warm sun, pleasant after all the rain. The roads were mud, of course, splashing as they drove, even the few paved roads broken up by the tanks and the big trucks. Cromwell rode up front next to Lonesome while Buggy lounged behind, checking out the weapons as they rolled north. "Get me a clean M-1," Ollie told him. He liked the M-1, had used it plenty in the war. He had his Smith and Wesson .38, of course, but up on the line you wanted a rifle. The carbine they issued to company-grade officers was a joke—unreliable, inaccurate, almost as bad and not as fast as the old Riesing, and with little stopping power. Ollie thought he might get himself one of these Russian burp guns if he could. Marines who'd been in the Perimeter fighting spoke highly of the burp guns, cheap, quick, reliable.

It was comforting to be thinking again about weapons; it was nice to be back in the war. It had started to rain again by the time—two hours later—that they caught up with Baker Company and Captain Fenton.

Ike Fenton, Captain Francis I. Fenton Jr. to be formal about it, was "Old Corps." He'd just taken command of Baker Company when its commanding officer, Captain John L. Tobin, was machine-gunned while looking over the ground from Observation Hill with his company exec. Fenton, the exec, saw to Tobin's evacuation, and then, without fuss, he took command. It was the work Fenton had been preparing for all his adult life. In this, Ike was a lot like Cromwell.

He was a regular, of course, the son of a famous Marine general, and his brother was also a Marine officer. Ike—and no one ever called him anything but Ike—was a lean, spare, rather elegant man. Though not when

Cromwell finally met him after three days of fighting day and night, most of the time in the rain. When Ollie met him, Ike Fenton looked exhausted, half-drowned. David Douglas Duncan, a Marine during the Big War and now a photographer for *Life,* wrote about Ike in a dispatch for his magazine:

> Captain Ike Fenton stood close behind the firing line, shouting his orders above the noise of the rain and rifles and other men. Observers up on the lip of the hill signaled back that the Communists were launching waves of attacking men from the top of No-Name Ridge, that already they were racing across the valley below, scaling the frontal slopes of the hill and starting to take the crest. Enemy machine gunners and mortarmen were pouring fire everywhere ahead of their attacking troops. Other Red riflemen were supporting the gunners, and from somewhere to the left they opened fire with a high-velocity, self-propelled gun which sent its shells screaming and ricocheting along the spine of the hill. Fenton brushed aside the useless radio (shorted out by the rain) and—with carbine ready—shouted the command to the arc of crouched, momentarily rigid Marines . . . "Attack!"

That kind of fighting had gone on for three days on the Naktong ridgelines by the time Ollie joined Fenton.

Ever see a guy out on his feet, drained, sappy, nearly dead, yet still moving forward? The sunken eyes, mouth agape, lungs never getting enough air; mud-caked pants soaked and pissed in; filthy, unshaven, all but gone and yet going on? That was Ike Fenton by August 20 of 1950 in the heat and monsoon rains, fighting on the Naktong River, alternately holding the line against swarming enemy charges and jumping off on the attack, advancing with his company of zombies, none of them much better off than their leader, as the two armies grappled and swayed, winning the advantage, then losing it, then striving to win it again. Cromwell, seeing Fenton's men, how bad they looked, was tempted to say, "Lie down, you poor bastards. Quit, die, and get it over with. . . ."

He didn't say that, of course. Couldn't. Not to Marines who still had their yellow canvas leggings properly fastened. There were some shortcuts no Marine would take.

And then, surprising Ike, probably surprising themselves, the Baker Company Marines again moved ahead, shuffled another foot forward, hunched and firing as they went, pushing back the enemy, not in some glorious, gallant charge, but in an exhausted inching north.

That night, sitting with Fenton under shelter-halves draped against the rain, both men with M-1s cradled ready in their laps, Cromwell listened as the company commander talked.

"I don't know what keeps them going, Colonel. Don't know what keeps me going. Yesterday—maybe it was yesterday; I'm not sure—we were just about out of ammo. If the Reds came up against us one more time, we were down to bayonets and rifle butts. But they never came. I still don't know why. We were finished. We might not have stopped them. This foul little hill we're hanging on to—Craig says it's the key. We lose this, and they'll come through, and that's the end of the offensive. That's the beginning of the end for the Perimeter. Maybe for the war . . ."

"Take it easy, Captain. Try to get some sleep. I've just come from a clean bed in town, so let me stand a watch or two for you. I'll sit up with your sergeant here. We'll wake you if anything's happening."

"Yessir, some sleep. I could use a little sleep."

Fenton was snoring before a minute passed.

There was no more fighting that night, and in the morning Cromwell roamed the position, the weight and heft of the M-1 familiar, even comforting, in his fist. With Buggy and Lonesome in tow, he checked out the men, not hustling or harassing them, talking to a few of them, handing out dry cigarettes while he still had a few packs. The South Korean ammo carriers, porters really, had been turned into litter bearers, carrying wounded men down the reverse slope, carrying the dead. A Marine with a shattered knee cried out when a bearer tripped and nearly fell. Fenton, still looking awful but up and about, kept trying his radio. Nothing. Some of the wounded—you could tell them by the bloody bandages—hadn't been evacuated and were still manning the line.

"We need 'em," Fenton said. "Too thin to spare them. If a man can fight, he stays here."

"You're right, Captain," Ollie agreed. He remembered Le François on Makin, shot through but fighting three days after that, and getting out to the subs. Man can do a lot of things not even he could believe possible. Frankey sure did.

Then, squinting up, Ike asked, slightly confused and not at all sure, "Does that look like the sun to you, Colonel?"

"Could be, Ike. Looks like it."

"Thank God if it's sun. If it's sun, the Corsairs can fly. They haven't been up for three days now, and we need that close air support. This company's a different quantity with a little air supporting us. You'll see. These are good men Tobin had. Fine men. Don't want you to go back thinking otherwise just because of how bad we look. My men now, not Tobin's anymore. Got to live up to these men and not fail them. Can't fail them, can't fail the regiment and Craig . . ."

"You're not failing anyone, Ike. You're doing fine."

Fenton looked into Cromwell's face, wanting to see something there which meant the colonel wasn't just blowing smoke. Senior officers do that, sometimes. Blow smoke just to buck up a man. Fenton's dad knew that they did; taught Ike and his brother how to tell if it was smoke they were blowing. Or the truth.

Finally, the words tugged out, Fenton said:

"Thanks, Colonel. Means a lot, coming from a Raider . . ."

So he knew, too. That was the Marine Corps: so small, really, that there were few secrets, no unknown men.

Within the hour Corsairs were crisscrossing the ridgelines, coming in low, strafing, firing their cannon, dropping the napalm tanks. It was the turn of the North Koreans to catch a little hell. A few of the Marines with energy to spare cheered the planes on, shouting and waving their arms. Fenton, hearing the shouts, seeing them wave, and watching the Corsairs attack the enemy ridgelines over and over, actually looked a little better, the rainwater no longer running down his face, his eyes still sunken but crinkling at the corners.

A runner came up.

"Captain, message from battalion. They said they can't reach you on the radio."

"Give it here."

"Aye aye, sir."

Fenton read the penciled sheet of notepaper, half-smiled, and then nodded to Cromwell.

"Battalion says once the Corsairs finish up, artillery will be shelling No-Name Ridge for ten minutes."

"And . . . ?" Ollie asked, seeing the look on Ike's face.

"Then Baker Company jumps off again against No-Name Ridge. This'll be the third time we've gone against it. 'You've got them on the run, Ike.' That's what the colonel says."

"Well," Ollie said, "you do, y'know."

Fenton tried to smile. Almost succeeded. He was still remembering those two earlier assaults that failed.

"I guess," he said. Then, to the gunnery sergeant: "I want the platoon leaders up here. Now!"

"Aye aye, sir," the gunny said as he got to his feet and started off along the line, looking for the rifle platoon leaders of Baker Company.

Fenton looked at his wristwatch, fastened not around his wrist but threaded by the strap through a buttonhole in the lapel of his fatigue shirt.

"Still morning. Not quite noon. I thought it was at least mid-afternoon."

"Combat winds its own clock," Ollie said.

Fenton was a bit uneasy about having the brass looking over his shoulder. An officer doesn't like being second-guessed. "Will you be observing from here, Colonel?" he inquired politely.

"No, Captain, I'll be coming with you and your men. Don't worry, you're in charge."

It was what Ike Fenton wanted to hear.

By three that afternoon Fenton's men had moved, slowly, heavily, and taking losses, up the next ridgeline when the sound of firing slackened. Cromwell had stayed with the captain, following the two leading platoons as they worked their bloody way uphill. It was five years since Ollie had been in a real firefight, those skirmishes south from Seoul not qualifying, and he felt pretty good about it.

Fenton turned to him and shouted above the battlefield din.

"They're running, sir. Damned Reds are running."

And they were. The Fourth Division of the North Korean Peoples' Army, a good division that had been fighting and successfully so for seven weeks over more than 350 miles, had not only been stopped, they were falling back.

"By God, Colonel, we did it."

"*You* did, Captain. Good job . . ."

It wasn't over, not quite. The Fourth Division's commander, seeing his men break and run, angrily called up and sent in the last four T-34 tanks he had at hand, sent rolling toward the advancing Marine infantry without infantry support of their own. Big mistake. There had been Red infantry, but the marauding Corsairs had broken them up. Now, approaching the brigade's main supply route at about 8:00 P.M., still daylight but fading fast, the four Russian tanks rumbled ahead. Waiting for the T-34s were two U.S. M-26 Pershings, with their slightly larger .90-millimeter guns, a rocket section of the antitank assault platoon dug in on Hill 125, the recoilless rifle platoon on Observation Hill, and, coming in fast from the west, out of the falling sun still topping the mountain peaks, another flight of six Corsairs. Within five minutes all four T-34s had been destroyed, the vehicles smashed, their crews incinerated, without American loss. That did it for the Fourth NKPA Division on the Naktong Line. Cromwell, remembering those early weeks of the invasion when nothing the Allied side had could stand up to the T-34s, looked at Fenton.

"Lot of men died buying the time to get those big Pershings and Corsairs into the war, Ike."

Ollie realized Fenton wasn't really listening, was still too much into his own and his company's problems. *Well,* Cromwell thought, *can you blame the bastard?*

After the tank battle the North Korean retreat became a rout. The Marine artillery and the Corsairs would get into it first thing next morning, turning an even fight into a turkey shoot. Some of the Fourth Division got away in the dark but not those caught by the dawn. Men who saw the river said you couldn't count the dead bodies floating in the Naktong, NK regulars trying to get back across as their bridgehead on the south shore was gradually compressed and then wiped out. To Cromwell, who until now in this war had seen only defeat, desertion, retreat, and rout of his side, it was a reminder of how swiftly the fortunes of war changed. On the river Han it was our dead who floated on the stream facedown; on the Naktong it was Reds.

Ollie stayed with Fenton and his men for a second night. A better night, with only distant firing of the big guns, nothing up close, and Cromwell again taking a midnight-to-four watch for the exhausted Ike, trooping the line, checking on the men, back in small ways to being a Marine officer again.

The radios were still functioning badly, if at all, and it was yet another runner who arrived early that next morning at Fenton's HQ. "Colonel Cromwell?"

"No," a revivified Fenton replied cheerfully, pleased to be taken for a field-grade officer. "That's the colonel over there."

A note was handed over.

"Report to General O. P. Smith in Pusan immediately."

■ 32 ■

THE MARINES PROPPED UP THE DEAD SOLDIER AND STUCK A CAMEL
BETWEEN HIS TEETH.

Before he was entirely sure just what and where Inchon was, Douglas Mac-Arthur was considering its invasion.

As early as the Fourth of July in Tokyo, before the first American infantryman had died in Korea, MacArthur told senior aides it was not his intention to defeat the North Koreans and get back to Seoul by slugging it out with the enemy mile by mile, mountain by mountain, rice paddy by paddy, all the way up the Korean Peninsula. Such a ground campaign would be costly in time and men, and MacArthur was short of both.

His plan? An end run by sea around the enemy's flank and a landing somewhere along the coastline of South Korea as far north as was feasible, with the Marine brigade about to sail from San Diego as the spearhead of the operation. The U.S.-based Marines would, in fact, not land in Korea but in Japan, there to plan, prepare, and even rehearse a landing on hostile shores somewhere on the Korean coast. Those were the plans. The collapse of the South Koreans and the incompetence of the first Americans in the fight would scrub them.

The first Marines even to hear about MacArthur's plan were relatively low-level officers attending a Fourth of July party hosted in Tokyo by the American colony in the Japanese capital. Brigadier William S. Fellers, in charge of troop training, and Colonel Edward Forney, both with a reputation in amphibious warfare, were called away from the festivities to meet with Army and Air Force officers at Far East Command headquarters, where they were briefed by MacArthur's chief of staff, a thoroughly nasty major general, Ned Almond. MacArthur, the assembled officers were told, was considering an amphibious landing as early as September somewhere behind enemy lines to attack the North Koreans, cut their supply lines, and pin them between the Allied landing force and a frontal attack by the troops, who would by then be in substantial numbers in the South, probably based on Pusan and fighting north of there to stem the enemy advance. These troops would be the U.S. Army's Twenty-fourth and Twenty-fifth Divisions (both of which would turn out to be flops). Inchon, on the west coast, was only one of a number of possible landing sites. A Marine regimental combat team would spearhead the landings supported by U.S. Army regulars. The project was code-named Operation Bluehearts.

Even men who despised or were jealous of MacArthur were stunned by the scope and boldness of the general's thinking, as described to them by his stooge Almond. At this stage of the Korean War, only a single battalion of American troops, and those not very good, had been sent to the aid of the shattered ROK forces. The two Army divisions had not yet left Japan. The Marines were in California.

By the time—a few days later—that Marine general Lemuel C. Shepherd, just named to command the Marine Corps in the Pacific, arrived in Tokyo, planning was well underway. Lem Shepherd and Douglas MacArthur met in Tokyo on July 10. The Great Man had turned pessimistic. The ROKs had fallen apart, the North Koreans were proving formidable, and who knew if Red China or the Soviet Union might pitch in? Three days before the session with Shepherd, Truman had named MacArthur supreme commander of all UN forces. But what forces did he have?

He and the Marine got on well at their first meeting, Shepherd reminding the general that he'd been assistant division commander of the 1st Marine Division that served under MacArthur seven years earlier in the fight for Japanese-held New Britain. And when MacArthur spoke of his admiration and even affection for the Marines, Shepherd suggested the supreme commander ask Washington for an entire Marine division, with appropriate air support. MacArthur said he would, and by the time their meeting ended, MacArthur was sounding "enthusiastic" about having a Marine division in the offing and feeling better about things generally.

Over the next three weeks, Operation Bluehearts took shape and came haltingly to life. While back in the States, Marine and other reservists were mobilized, and the 1st Provisional Marine brigade began to form at Camp Pendleton. Orders were cut for the first Marines to ship out, to land in Japan before mounting the assault at Inchon.

At least that was the plan. By late July, early August, MacArthur himself realized that, in this worst of all possible wars, even the best of all possible plans might have to be scrapped:

The Marine brigade was desperately needed, not in training camps in Japan, but in South Korea to beef up the Pusan Perimeter before the Allies were driven into the sea. If they lost the Perimeter, their only foothold, an amphibious landing would be moot.

If only the Perimeter could hold, MacArthur intended to fight the South Pacific campaign all over again, bypassing Japanese strong points like Rabaul and Port Moresby and island-hopping his way toward the Philippines and, eventually, to the Japanese home islands to end the war.

Now he put his brain trust to work on choosing the right place in Korea to go ashore. No one is quite sure what genius first suggested Inchon. But there were plenty ready to argue *against* it as a landing site. For one thing, Inchon had vicious tides—some of the highest and swiftest tides anywhere in the world. And wasn't it too far north, too close to the North Korean border, vulnerable to Russian-supplied air and to massive enemy reinforcements?

As the strategic planning began and the tactical details of time and tide and phases of the moon were worked out, it became clear that MacArthur was working and waging war according to a timetable all his own. Short-term, he wanted to reverse the early defeats and to liberate Seoul by September 25. And why was September 25th significant? Because it would be three months precisely since the North Korean invasion on June 25.

But there was an even more significant, longer-range schedule.

General MacArthur, buoyed and encouraged by the cheerleading of the Hearst newspapers and by Colonel Robert R. McCormick of *The Chicago Tribune,* was thinking ahead to the summer of 1952. That was when the Republican party in convention assembled, would nominate a presidential candidate to defeat the Democrats and recapture the White House from Harry Truman. There were already the usual politicians vying for the GOP nomination: globalist and liberal Harold Stassen; dour, dull Robert Taft; Tom Dewey, who'd already had two unsuccessful shots in '44 and '48; colorless, if worthy, Senator Vandenburg; and most absurd of all, the popular, but naive, Eisenhower. Ike, of course, was MacArthur's most galling rival, being a junior officer and one who, despite his high rank, had never smelled gunsmoke, never actually fought. Whatever you thought of MacArthur, the man was a fighter. And having been Army chief of staff when Ike was a mere major working as his aide, the general was given, cruelly, to dismissing Eisenhower as "the best secretary I ever had."

Sure, Ike had triumphed in Europe, defeating the Germans with the enormous help of the Soviet Union and the Brits and all the money and weapons he needed. MacArthur, fighting an even more ferocious enemy and over thousands of miles of ocean and island, and doing so on a shoe-string, couldn't tolerate even the idea of Eisenhower as president. That, to MacArthur, would be a tragedy for the nation, putting its future in the hands of a chamber of commerce booster, a glad-hander and a backslapper. MacArthur, serious, austere, a great orator and original thinker, the son of a famous general, was revolted by the notion of a door-to-door salesman (like Ike) in the White House.

Douglas MacArthur had defeated the Empire of Japan, rebuilt the country and its economy, established its democracy, and he was now fighting another Asian war on behalf his country and of the UN and the free world.

Which, if he could win it quickly, might provide just the springboard required for a presidential nomination two years from now in the summer of '52.

■

"So you're Cromwell," said General O. P. Smith, commander of the 1st Marine Division, which was supplanting the provisional brigade. They had turned over a classroom at Pusan U. to Smith and a few staffers. The general sat behind what seemed the professor's desk. Cromwell stood.

"Yessir."

"Ray Murray vouches for you. I know you had a good record in the war. Did some fighting. And that you know Korea pretty well. I can use a man like that."

Marines are supposed to tell tall tales—essential part of the mystique. But you don't lie to superior officers about important matters. Ollie swiftly corrected the general.

"Sir, I've been in the country only since June 23. As the new military attaché to Ambassador Muccio, I spent a few days in Seoul. Then I drove south with the ambassador and a couple of embassy guards all the way to Pusan over about four weeks. Seen something of the country. A little of the fighting. But I'm no expert on Korea."

"You've seen more than I have. Or Ray Murray has. We're the new boys in town. So we'll let it go at that. We need a good man to do some recon work along the coast."

"If I can help, I'm your man, sir."

No one had mentioned Inchon until now.

"You were with Carlson, weren't you?"

"Yessir."

"I admired Evans Carlson. Lot of us didn't."

"I know." Cromwell had carried the baggage, the Carlson legacy, had felt the enmity.

General Smith got back en point.

"Been to Inchon?"

"Yessir, a sightseeing tour the Saturday before the war began. I saw the place from a car. All anyone talked about was the famous tides, something fierce."

"Yeah."

While Inchon was the only site seriously being considered for an American landing behind enemy lines, reconnaissance patrols were landing at a half-dozen other sites along the South Korean coast. Part of this was just good sense, seeking alternatives just in case; much of it was smoke and mirrors. Some of these operations were actual recons; others were raids, demolitions, and the like. Don't tip your hand to the North Koreans. Keep them confused as to where we might be going and what we might be doing there.

While General O. P. Smith had flown to Korea from the States via Tokyo, his key scouts had arrived by ship at Pusan. These were elements of the 1st Mar Div's own recon company and U.S. Navy UDT (underwater demolition team) men. Between August 12 and 16 these troops had landed at several places along the west coast (being sure to stay away from Inchon) to raid enemy communications and ratchet up uncertainty and panic. Two railroad bridges and three tunnels were blown. General Smith and his boss, Lem Shepherd, and four admirals, Sherman, Turner Joy, Radford, and Doyle, met in Tokyo and decided to send in additional reconnaissance landings on other sites in the Posung-Myon area during the period August 22–25.

As a result of these operations, an alternative pitch was made to Mac-Arthur, suggesting he drop Inchon and choose another landing area. Mac-Arthur slapped that down. "I know all about the damned tides, and I have more faith in the Navy and its ability to land the invasion force than the Navy has in itself," he announced.

Whatever reservations men had about the supreme commander, and among the Marines there were plenty, you had to admit MacArthur didn't double-talk.

It was then that O. P. Smith, also a plain speaker, again told Admiral Doyle, designated commander of the task force that would land the Marines and Army at Inchon, that Inchon "was a terrible place to land." Now Cromwell was sent for and ordered by O. P. Smith to join this final, and crucial, recon patrol of Inchon and to report back to him, Smith, immediately afterward. Ollie wasn't quite sure if Smith hoped to be told the place was impossible. Or that Inchon just might fly.

"I'd like to accompany the colonel, sir," Sergeant Buggy said.

"Can you swim? Ever wear scuba gear?"

"Nossir, not in Texas. But I speak the lingo and . . ."

The man had a point. "Okay, Buggy, but I don't want lawsuits if you drown."

"Nossir." A destroyer rushed Cromwell, Sergeant Buggy, two young Marine officers, a Navy lieutenant, and a dozen enlisted recon company Marines north that next day, arriving off Inchon just after dark and two hours short of that night's highest tide. Cromwell stripped off dog tags and anything else identifying him as a field-grade officer. The North Koreans weren't stupid; they knew that recon and demolition teams were manned by younger officers and men, not by colonels. A colonel, dead or alive, would tip them off something special was afoot. But Cromwell was important to the recon boys, he and Buggy being the only ones who'd ever been here.

The destroyer lay a few miles offshore on the moonless night without much of a sea running, and launched in darkness three Zodiacs, motorized rafts that drew eighteen inches of water, less when they tilted up the outboard and paddled. Shades of Makin Island. Ollie hoped this was going to go smoother than Makin. The landing was to be in an area they'd already code-named Red Beach, just north of Wolmi-do, a small island linked to Inchon by a causeway. How many NKPA guns were emplaced at Red Beach, at Green Beach on Wolmi-do itself? And what caliber, what fields of fire? Were they dug in or open to naval gunfire or air? The guns of Wolmi-do would be in position to take the American landing craft with flanking fire and massacre the first few waves. Was there wire, and was it concertina hoops or barbed wire strung between steel posts? A man could fling himself atop concertina to flatten it while other men crossed the barrier treading on his back. As Marines given the assignment cracked, "It only hurts the first hundred men across." Were there mines? Underwater obstacles to overturn landing craft?

Ollie had been checked out on scuba gear two years ago at Pendleton and had done more than a few small boat exercises over the years, but this would be his first landing on a hostile shore since 1945. Compared to the men in his Zodiac, he must have seemed an old man. *Well, that's fine,* he thought. O. P. Smith sent him on this show, and to hell with what anyone else thinks. Aboard the tin can on the trip north, he didn't say much, and his having been a Marine Raider never came up. Why should it? Navy UDT teams and Marine recon companies were themselves elite units.

They clambered down cargo nets to the boats in darkness, and, as always, someone's hand was stepped on, a weapon clanked against the hull, a man cursed, not quite under his breath. Ollie supposed that in the third interplanetary war of the year 2100, such things would still be happening, and he didn't sweat it. In fact, it relaxed Ollie, reminding him of Makin Island and the mess the Raiders made out of simply getting off a submarine.

These new boys, he quickly realized, were pretty good.

"Your orders:" the division operations officer told them, "are to avoid combat. We want reconnaissance information. There'll be plenty of time later to kill North Koreans. I need to know where and what guns they have on Red Beach, at the northern base of the island."

"Wolmi-do." Had a nice sound, like an island ought to sound. Like Bali-Hai, or Pago Pago. Ollie wished he knew some Korean like Buggy. Musical sort of lingo, wasn't it?

The ride to shore was pretty smooth. And quiet, even the outboards. He remembered how noisy they used to be, and how unreliable, always flooding out. This silent cruising forcibly reminded him of something else, the war canoes they rented from the headhunters of Tulagi and how little freeboard they had, and how peacefully they'd been paddling across Savo Straits when the sharks came. No sharks like that this far north, thank God. Or at least Ollie hoped not. He could still see those five-foot dorsal sails.

But the canoes got them to the beach, safe and unhurt, the Marines and headhunters both, sliding smoothly into shallow water, through and past what had drawn the sharks. Bobbing facedown in the water, the bodies of the men who'd died the night before off the ships, the enemy ships and ours, had been bobbing there all night and into the dawn like chum, calling to the predators, all those men in the water, bloating from the heat and swelling, young Americans much like himself, off ships like his *Juneau,* the bodies floating out there just off the pleasant, golden, sloping beaches of Florida Island, dead sailors being eaten and having nothing to say about it. Lots of Japs, too, who died during the night. But mostly it was us and the Australians, though the sharks didn't distinguish. They ate whoever was closest or trailing the best blood. Brutes!

The imagery of the big, feeding fish stayed with him. For a Marine Raider long ocean swims came routinely with the job. No longer. For Ollie a long ocean swim would never again be routine. Not with the memory of those five-foot dorsals.

"Auughh!"

"Sir?" a polite Buggy asked.

"Nothing. Clearing the phlegm." He must have said something aloud. But Buggy didn't press him, and none of the recon men or the others seemed to have heard. And now they were nearly there, closing on the beaches of Florida Island, their canoes sliding up swiftly onto the sand where . . .

Cromwell shook himself roughly, shoving back the past, reminding himself this wasn't the Savo Straits, but Korea.

The recon Zodiacs rode the high tide to Red Beach and a stone seawall, stark and steep, twenty feet above high tide, not a surprise because it was on all the maps, and the men, Cromwell among them, tossed up grappling irons and scrambled up the sheer wall, losing a little skin and some blood to barnacles on stretches of the barrier that the tides reached. Two men— one on watch, the other fending off and controlling the boat—stayed behind in each Zodiac while the others, once over the top of the wall, trotted quietly inland, left and right. And, this time, they really were quiet, Marines and swabbies both. Ollie could hear his own heart and his breath laboring. But that was it. No metallic clangs, no cursing. Now, to count the guns, count 'em and assess how vulnerable they were and would be. Amazingly, there seemed to be no North Korean sentries out. The gun emplacements, and there were plenty of the bastards, weren't manned. Not at this hour they weren't. Cromwell wondered if they had court-martials in this comrade's army. If so, they ought to run someone up for that! Big guns, too, a few of them eight-inchers. The rest, .155s, with machine guns filling in the gaps between gun emplacements, and a few sizable trench mortars as well. Ollie didn't see any rockets. Or flamethrower setups. But there might have been some that he missed in the dark. Plenty of barbed wire though. But no mines. At least they hadn't stumbled over any. They scribbled notes, plotted locations.

"Colonel," someone hissed at him. "The tide—not much time now."

Whoever it was, he was right. At high tide, deep water sloshed against the seawall; at low tide, stinking mudflats stretched half a mile or more from the wall out to sea, and the Zodiacs would be beached, the men forced to slog helplessly, exhaustingly, through deep mud to get back to open water. Or they could bog down, to be found there at first light by the North Koreans, who could amuse themselves picking the Marines off, one by one, with rifle fire.

Fun for them; not much fun for the bogged Americans.

"Okay," Ollie said, "not much longer."

He was still taking notes, still counting guns, asking himself, could they find some lightweight ladders somewhere? A good ladder would be a hell of a lot better than grappling irons and ropes.

What they found out tonight or a week from now, might save a thousand Marine lives. It was worth taking the time, taking care.

It was then that the one North Korean soldier on Wolmi-do who was actually on the job stumbled across the Americans.

Cromwell heard the scuffle, heard the dull thuds of rifle butts and gun barrels hitting flesh. No shooting; they knew enough for that.

"We got him, Colonel. He's out."

"Just one of them? See any more?"

"Just this bird. And he's croaked. We hit him pretty hard."

"Bring him along."

"I think he's croaked."

"Bring him with us."

"We can just slide him over the wall into the water."

"I don't want bodies floating up on the tide," Ollie said.

A Navy diver said, "Won't they miss him at breakfast? They'll notice he's gone."

"Bring him along," Cromwell ordered. "No one ever went over the hill from the People's Army? They'll think he has a girl in town."

"Aye aye, sir."

In the Zodiac, heading back to the waiting destroyer, a couple of the Marines propped up the North Korean soldier against the side of the craft, and one stuck an unlighted Camel between his lips.

"Looks more at home like that," the Marine said.

These boys would have made pretty good Raiders, Ollie thought. Until now, he'd felt a little isolated from these men, not knowing them and being a few years older.

Now, in their midst, having done a good operation, having easily handled the only enemy they'd come across, Colonel Cromwell didn't feel like an outsider anymore.

Especially when a big first lieutenant gave him a grin and in a wonderfully flat Midwestern twang told him.

"You know, Colonel, when it works out, this shit is fun."

Other recon patrols, landed by destroyer that same night, went ashore south of Wolmi-do on the Inchon mainland and on the little island itself. They were fortunate as well. It was as if all those phony raids farther south had disarmed and lulled the North Koreans. Or no one on the enemy side could believe anyone would be dumb enough to land at Inchon and challenge its awful tides. God really did smile on Douglas MacArthur, didn't He?

▪ 33 ▪

THE NIGHT BEFORE YOU LAND ON A HOSTILE BEACH, YOU DON'T MAKE
ENEMIES.

Aboard the invasion command vessel *Mount McKinley,* the brass had little
time for a mere lieutenant colonel. War correspondents, the press—that was
something else again. Such people wrote tomorrow's front-page headlines;
they made, or broke, reputations, careers. That Colonel Cromwell would
be one of those in the first wave and—even more rare—had already been
ashore on the hostile beaches signified little. That Ollie actually knew Ben
Sweet, a famous man—that made the difference, got him invited above
stairs.

"You've got pull, Ben. I'm impressed."

Sweet was cocky, very sure of himself, so much so he could afford to
poke fun at his access to the icon, the demigod commander.

"I trot along in MacArthur's shadow. Wherever the great man goes,
there I am. No one stops to ask my bona fides. Try it sometime, Ollie."

Same old Ben Sweet, but stepping up in class. Now he was using Mac-
Arthur.

The original plan was to carry the supreme commander to Inchon
aboard Admiral Struble's flagship, USS *Rochester,* a cruiser. But with Mac-
Arthur's party including seven general officers, plus all those aides and the
press, the roomier *Mount McKinley* was chosen. Warped into Sasebo harbor
in Japan by two tugs, the MacArthur party was taken aboard the evening
of September 12. General Lem Shepherd, the senior Marine officer in the
Pacific, had earlier been assigned to his staff by MacArthur personally to
serve as his amphibious-warfare expert and to handle liaison with the 1st
Marine Division under Oliver Smith. Accompanying Shepherd was the G-3
(Operations), Colonel Victor Krulak, and Shepherd's aide, Major Ord. Typhoon Jane had blown itself out harmlessly, and now the concern centered
on another storm, Typhoon Kezia, with winds of 125 miles per hour at
top speed. Kezia was the storm that could push back the invasion deadline
of September 15 beyond reach, and it had everyone worried—except Mac-
Arthur, who for unfathomable reasons predicted it too would wash itself

out on the other side of the peninsula. It did. Here, in the Yellow Sea steaming north, they had squalls, big swells, and seasickness, but tolerable wind. There was an officers' mess, an enlarged wardwoom, and Ben Sweet was able to talk to Ollie inside. MacArthur, they said, was on the bridge.

"He and God speak every hour on the hour. No one is quite sure who talks, who listens. But there are suspicions."

Everyone knew who Ben Sweet was: bestselling author, war correspondent, pal of Hemingway. Professional soldiers and sailors, bored with routine and eager to have the shooting start, liked having a celebrity among them, hearing about places some of them had never been. There'd recently been a photo in *Life* of Ben with a mannequin who worked for Dior, a slender, long-legged lovely with a raven's cap of black hair and a gamine's face, the two of them at Longchamps for the races, Ben in his Savile Row tweeds and cap, field glasses hung, the girl leaning slimly against his side. She was auditioning, the gossip columns said, to be "the celebrated author Sweet's wife number three."

Ben never discussed his women aloud. He did go on, however, colorfully and at length, about Paris. Dinners with Sartre and Simone de Beauvoir. Drinks with Picasso. Hanging out with Camus, with Jacques Fath and Maggy Rouff, and meeting Coco Chanel. "A collaborationist during the war," he might concede with an insider's license, "but then, who wasn't?" Handicapping the horses at Auteuil with Georges, Hemingway's old bartender at the Ritz.

"You go to the track together?" Ollie asked, not able to resist. "You and Papa handicapping the horses?"

Ben looked stiffly at his old college chum.

"Last time I saw Hemingway in Paris it was at the Travelers Club. He was drinking and a man barely under control. Sad. We haven't that many great writers we can afford to lose one. Just think what Fitzgerald might have written."

None of them thought to mention *Gatsby*.

They crowded in closer, officers and correspondents, impressed by being let in on all this lit'ry inside stuff. Ben took their interest as a sort of homage. They were assaulting a hostile beach in the morning, quite possibly some of them would be killed, and here was Sweet providing diversion.

By now Ben was talking about Jean Prouvost, whose *Paris Match* was just as good as, maybe better than, Luce's *Life,* and who had just paid Sweet an enormous fee for first serial rights to his Korean reportage.

"He doesn't hire journalists. He finds ex-Resistance boys from the Maquis, paras from Indo-China—the toughest guy in the best bistro with the prettiest girl. Prouvost gives them his card. 'Come see me at the office. I might have a job for you.'

"They jump from planes onto yachts, seduce actresses, punch out rich men's bodyguards, and get the story. Some old hack in the office does the rewrite, and *Paris Match* sells out that week."

"Monsieur Prouvost hire any Americans, Mr. Sweet?"

"He might do, Admiral. The French don't win many wars, but they surely know how to enjoy the peace."

He was clearly the hit of the officers' mess.

Ollie held the wisecracks. The night before you land on a hostile beach, you don't make more enemies.

He and Ben later chatted briefly, on deck by the rail under a clearing sky, low cloud scudding, the sea still up but not as bad now. Plenty of others, officers and enlisted, were restless too, up and about, roaming the decks, unable to sleep, or staving off mal de mer. Only hours to Inchon. Thanks to Ollie Cromwell's recon and a half-dozen others, MacArthur, Almond, and Oliver Smith had a pretty good appreciation of enemy strength in the landing areas: they reckoned there were 2,500 NKPA troops at the most, 400 to 500 of them on Wolmi-do, 500 defending Kimpo airfield, the balance stationed in and around the city of Inchon.

Before MacArthur slept, he sent for his cronies, a few pets, Ben among them. Maggie Higgins, too. Ned Almond. Admiral Doyle. No Marines. MacArthur was affable on the night before battle, but not *that* affable.

"I recall a night like this in Leyte Gulf, the night before I returned to the Philippines. Warmer there, of course, but dark then, too, and men wondering, as men always do before battle, just what the morrow would bring . . ."

He was still the spellbinder, the deep, resonant voice dramatically rising and falling, the diction spot-on, the words precise, aptly chosen. Even Ben shut up. Men who feared MacArthur, men who disliked him, and the paid skeptics of the press corps found themselves leaning forward with eyes locked on his craggy face, unable not to, so as not to miss the imagery, a word, a thought, a gesture. The general went on:

". . . and I had this odd sense of being able to picture what it would be like. Which was strange. I'd lived a long time in the Philippines, but I'd been away three years. Even the weather was unsure, like this typhoon of ours. Would the Japanese be expecting us? Would the landing go well? Was the beach properly selected, or might there be reefs? or mines? In war, there are so many variables. And yet I knew all would go well. That our cause was just, and our arms powerful . . ."

Maggie Higgins piped up.

"You were right then, General. Can you picture what tomorrow might bring?"

"Marguerite," he said, the formality intended, "if I could tell you that, then after this war is done I would set up in Wall Street and make my fortune. Soldiers' pay, soldiers' pay, I need not tell you all about soldiers' pay. . . ."

As his voice fell away, there was an impressed silence, the only sound in this oversized wardroom the familiar creaking and squeaking of a ship at sea in heavy weather.

It was left to MacArthur to break the stillness.

"I'm to the bridge," he announced, even the choice of words arch and posturing, sending messages, cutting off follow-up questions. "And in the morning we shall see what we shall see: a great adventure, a great feat of arms, the defeat of enemies, the rescue of a small and gallant nation that relied on our sacred word. . . ."

More than one of his captive listeners had to struggle with himself not to applaud. This was a man who made history, who indeed *was* history, and they were privileged to be in his company the night before battle.

Cromwell and Ben Sweet bade farewell on deck.

"I'm off, Ben. Early call. Take care of yourself tomorrow. It's not a game, and you want to watch out."

"You, too, Ollie. And don't worry about me. Not the first war I've seen. I ought to be able to handle myself."

"I'm sure you will, Ben. Sure you will."

The *Mount McKinley* reached its staging point off Inchon at three that morning, the weather cooperating. And whatever gods to whom MacArthur spoke.

More tangibly, Navy and Marine aviation and the Air Force had been walloping Wolmi-do and adjacent targets for three days, with Marine aviators leading each day's first raid by dropping napalm as markers so that subsequent flights just headed for the columns of rising black smoke and followed them in to the target.

The bad news? An ROK patrol craft that same morning came across a North Korean boat laying mines on the approaches.

The aerial attacks had continued through September 13. Then it became the turn of Admiral Higgins and his flotilla of destroyers. Higgins was always described as "a bold leader," and he now began living up to the billing. Rather than risking collision or grounding in a night approach to the Korean coast, he decided to forego the surprise advantages of a night attack and go in instead in broad daylight. And far from avoiding enemy fire, providing a target in order to sucker enemy shore installations into revealing their gun positions to our air and heavy guns. One nightmare gnawed at the edges of Higgins's mind: no one had issued the historic "prepare to repel boarders" order in perhaps a century. And here were Higgins's dozen destroyers steaming so close to shore and the vast Inchon mudflats, he had a vision of enemy infantry swarming out from shore across the flats to attack a disabled and grounded American destroyer. No pikes or cutlasses being available, the admiral ordered his crews to be issued side-arms, grenades, and tommy guns.

Standing farther out to sea, four Allied cruisers were by September 13 also on station: the American *Rochester* and *Toledo* and the British warships *Kenya* and *Jamaica*. And some twenty miles out, the battlewagons with their sixteen-inch guns. No fear of boarders there!

▪ 34 ▪

No one, from Douglas MacArthur to the lowliest naval rating or jaded wire-service correspondent, had seen anything like this since World War II.

The great fleet was everywhere you looked out across the Yellow Sea. Overhead, the constant roaring shuttle of high-altitude bombers and noisy, low-flying fighters and attack planes, the biggest of the naval guns heard but not seen, invisible beyond the far horizon, the smaller, yet powerful, guns of cruisers and destroyers, all targeting the shore, igniting flickers of flame in the fading night, smoke rising, the reek of cremating napalm, the constant din a noise to wake the world. Aboard ship, perhaps the only ones maintaining a sort of silence, the thousands of assault troops, edgy, impatient, waiting the word, clustered at the rail of the troopships, ready and overready, eager to hit the cargo nets, to scramble down the ships' sides to the waiting boats, their ungainly landing craft buglike, circling aimlessly as they waited the word to board and set their course for pummeled, punished Inchon, smoking and aflame, beaten almost to its knees. But waiting, too.

In the predawn gloom of September 15, at 5:45 A.M. the six- and eight-inch guns of the cruisers opened up, and explosions rocked the city of Inchon. To General MacArthur, who had orchestrated the show and was watching from the bridge as the opening-act curtain rose, the grand scene jogged memory. The planes roaring in overhead, the broadsides slamming into the enemy shore, the swift destroyers maneuvering, the cruisers firing and making smoke, the big battlewagons further out and firing sixteen-inch guns at a twenty-mile range, "the rockets' red glare" of the barges, the explosions echoing back from the beaches over water to the bombarding ships all recalled for MacArthur the Japanese war, especially and most moving, that last day aboard *Missouri* in Tokyo Harbor, with the Allies victorious and the enemy defeated and coming in striped trousers and formal cutaways to beg terms. That had been a glorious day choreographed in every detail by the general, very much as had been this morning at Inchon. Never before, and maybe never again, would American power be so dramatically, impressively, and nakedly arrayed. If this reprise at Inchon was to be Mac-Arthur's "last post," it was one worthy of the man and his legacy.

"You set, Buggy?" Cromwell asked.

"Yessir, locked and loaded. Lonesome, too."

"Good."

As assistant G-2, a division intelligence officer, Ollie rode one of the first-wave landing craft heading for Green Beach. He was the only man on board who'd already been ashore at Inchon, so that both the coxswain and the Marine lieutenant commanding a rifle platoon of 5th Marines looked to the colonel for local guidance, leaving Ollie somewhat amused. He understood their nerves, knew the feeling. But they had jobs to do, and he wasn't about to start babying them.

"Welcome to the Spanish Armada, gentlemen. I was here once for about four hours in the dead of night and didn't see very much. You'd better keep checking your maps."

The invading force had a far better source of intelligence than Cromwell, and he was aware of it. On September 1 a British frigate linking up with a South Korean patrol boat had put ashore a young naval lieutenant on MacArthur's staff, Eugene F. Clark, who was still hiding out behind enemy lines and sending out radio reports as late as September 14, recruiting local scouts, fighting and winning one firefight with an enemy sampan, testing the mudflats personally at low tide (sinking up to his waist), and ready at any time to kill himself with a grenade he carried, intent on not being taken prisoner. As the invasion armada approached the night of the 14th, Lieutenant Clark set out a beacon light to guide in the fleet.

Not until then did the young officer agree to let himself be taken off the beach by Zodiac and carried to safety.

Clark's reports, generally accurate, overstated Red defenses at Wolmi-do. Once the fighter-bombers left off and the cruiser fire abated, a couple of clumsy rocket-firing scows were maneuvered in close to finish off the gun emplacements and observation posts of the little island. So that by the time the first landing craft nosed up onto the sand and the first wave of Marine infantry scrambled ashore, firing as they ran, the only surprise was how easy it all was.

Damn, but this is going well, Cromwell told himself. He hadn't yet seen a single Marine go down, and he and Buggy and Lonesome, sprinting inland with the rifle platoon, were already halfway to one of the first-wave objectives, Radio Hill.

Ollie felt pretty good: relaxed, cool even, his mind crisp, his head clear.

As he was accustomed to do in combat, he lugged an M-1 rifle with the usual .38 revolver on his hip, a couple of canteens of water, one day's rations, the map issued aboard ship, toilet paper, a small flashlight, cigarette lighter, cigars, a notebook and pencil stub, a shelter-half against rain if it came, and the old Raider knife he carried mostly out of sentiment and in case he had to sharpen the pencil, crop a shoelace, or open a can.

Colonels don't cut many throats.

By 6:55 the platoon guide, Alvin E. Smith of the 3rd Platoon, had secured a small American flag to a shell-shattered tree trunk atop the hill.

On board *Mount McKinley*, overseeing the operation from the ship's bridge, MacArthur wore his leather Air Force jacket and the familiar (from newsreels and newspaper photos) "old Bataan cap with its tarnished gold braid." On hearing of the flag-raising on Radio Hill, the general got out of his swivel chair and said, "That's it. Let's get a cup of coffee."

It wasn't over yet, not hardly, but by now the Marines had ten tanks ashore, six M-26s (big enough to outslug a T-34), one flamethrower, two bulldozer models, and a tank retriever. And the only North Koreans Cromwell had seen were dead or coming toward him with their hands up surrendering. An hour later, a rifle platoon landed in the fourth wave and was surprised by a shower of grenades tossed into their midst from cleverly concealed enemy hidey-holes in a cliff earlier waves had bypassed, and a lively firefight ensued.

By an hour after the first wave landed, the 3rd Battalion, 5th Marines, estimated that half the island had been secured. By 8:00 A.M. Radio Hill was completely taken, and forty-five prisoners rounded up. Wolmi-do itself, and with it Inchon Harbor, were now in Allied hands or under Allied control. From *Mount McKinley* a delighted MacArthur dispatched this message:

"The Navy and Marines have never shone more brightly than on this morning."

By now the Marines were prodding prisoners in front of them and turning the dry swimming pool at a now-abandoned, but once posh, North Point beach resort into a POW holding pen. With the fight winding down, the entire battalion hadn't suffered a single death and had only seventeen wounded.

Cromwell hadn't yet fired a shot. Was that a first for an assault on a hostile beach? By noon even the mopping up on Wolmi-do and its smaller sister island in the harbor had been completed. But also by now the tide was running out fast, exposing the sodden mudflats so that the Marines, though triumphant, would by evening be in effect marooned until the next high tide.

Maggie Higgins and other reporters came ashore in the fifth wave, landing on Red Beach after rounding Wolmi-do. Lugging her portable, she would write that the enemy island, now under Marine control, "looked like a giant forest fire had swept over it." After she'd toured the beach, interviewing a couple of chatty Marines and getting chewed out by a captain she failed to charm (enlisted men and the brass sought out reporters; lieutenants and captains were too busy or were wary of them), Miss Higgins hitched a ride on a returning assault boat so that she could send her story to New York. When they reached the *Mount McKinley,* a deck officer shouted, "We don't want any more correspondents." Maggie and the other correspondents clambered up the rope ladders anyway and were soon luxuriating in the warmth of MacArthur's wardroom, described by her as "the last word." The publicity-savvy MacArthur, with a great story to tell, a victory to be savored, wasn't going to allow deck officers to chase off the press. You could ban reporters when an operation flopped.

Maggie's dispatch got out and ran next morning on the front page of the *Herald Tribune.*

By afternoon, the tides falling, the other two battalions of the 5th Marines had begun their assaults on Inchon proper. Seeing no enemy forces barring his way, the 3rd battalion CO, Lieutenant Colonel Robert D. Taplett, suggested to the command ship that he and his men might as well drive down the causeway from Wolmi-do and attack the mainland as well. A swift "negative" came whistling back. Too risky. Hold your ground. With no way to get reinforcements to Taplett until the next morning, the brass didn't want him taking heavy casualties in a new assault and not being able to replace them.

Cromwell and his scouts stuck close to Taplett, enjoying the man and his command and their obvious competence.

Taplett, who knew a little about Ollie's Raider roots and that he'd actually reconnoitered this ground a week before, proved good mine host. The two colonels shared a smoke, Ollie coming up with a Havana cigar and the other man puffing a Chesterfield.

"Nice if all landings went this well, Cromwell."

"You said it." Ollie was thinking back to the retreat from Seoul when nothing went well.

Had MacArthur's hunch about Inchon paid off? Or was Wolmi-do a fluke? The NKPA troops he'd seen here so far had nothing in common with those tough boys rolling south from Seoul and smashing the GIs fresh from the gin mills and whorehouses of occupied Japan. And try telling the Marine brigade or Ike Fenton down there on the Perimeter that the North Koreans weren't good soldiers. Try telling that to *any* of the 5th Marines. Ollie looked at Taplett.

"You fought them down south at the Perimeter. These fellows don't seem like they're in the same army. They just caved in."

"Quite all right with me, Cromwell. I don't look gift horses in the mouth. And since we're pretty much stranded until the next high tide, I hope they all stack arms."

Neither man thought the war was over. All very well for MacArthur to send singing telegrams congratulating people. Honest, hardworking field-grade officers didn't have that luxury. Having been up all night and with more fighting to come on the mainland, Ollie went back to where Buggy and Lonesome had set up in a shallow ditch and were lunching on C rations. He wolfed down a can of ham and lima beans and some crackers with grape jelly and a half-canteen of metallic-tasting water.

"One o'clock, Buggy. I'm going take a crap and roll up and get some sleep. Wake me at three. Or sooner if anything happens. Okay?"

"Yessir. Me and Lonesome getting along fine. They want any translating done?"

"I forgot to ask, Sergeant."

"Okay with me, Colonel. I slept pretty good last night aboard ship. Maybe Lonesome can grab some sack time after you."

Taking off his helmet and leaving on his field shoes and leggings and his gun belt, Cromwell stretched out on the dirt, pulled a shelter-half over him in case of rain, and was quickly asleep.

It would be tougher on beaches where the tides were less of a factor. Plenty tougher at the seawall. And the occasional squalls lashing the assault craft and cutting visibility weren't much help. As Marine fighter-bombers screamed over, providing close air support, and the Marine battalion on Wolmi-do pitched in with covering fire on the flanks of the enemy defenders behind the seawall, the first landing craft of the other two Marine battalions nosed up onto the narrow beach to butt against the actual seawall itself.

Alerted by earlier recons to the sheer height of the wall, the first assault elements were equipped with aluminum scaling ladders, and when the riflemen scrambled out of the boats to slap ladders up against the wall, before the point men went up the rungs, assault troops lobbed hand grenades over the wall at an as-yet-unseen enemy defender. Behind the Marines the LCVPs bobbed and bumped, with boat number one broken down and drifting helplessly and unable to reach the beach. Onshore, under the the weight of Marines, the rickety ladders swayed and slipped, and three or four of the first Marines up were cut down immediately, shot through the face and falling backward, clattering as they fell with their weapons and accoutrements, their bodies brusquely fended off by men on the lower rungs unwilling to be dislodged or delayed by the dead, and eager to take their places at the top. Below them, from the shingle, sergeants cursed and shouted, hurrying their fire teams on. "Move it! Move it! Move it!"

Others made it untouched off the ladders and over the wall but were quickly pinned down by heavy fire. They hadn't been able to see the North Koreans from the boats, but they were there at the seawall all right. Platoon guide Charles D. Allen from boat number two got over the wall only to be fired on by submachine guns from a North Korean bunker. Boat-number-three Marines confronted a machine-gun emplacement. Naval gunfire was slamming into the beachhead, and fighter-plane strafing fire ripped up the ground not fifty yards ahead of the Marines who sheltered in a shallow trench. Two Marines wriggled close enough to the bunker to toss grenades, and after an explosion, six bloody North Koreans staggered out, hands high, to surrender.

Aft of the seawall loomed the ominously named Cemetery Hill, with, on its seaward side, a nearly vertical bluff cliff facing the Marines. Not wanting to be pinched between beach and high ground, Second Lieutenant Francis W. Muetzel led his number-three boat infantrymen toward their objective, the Asahi Brewery, without waiting for a tardy second wave. Abeam Cemetery Hill Muetzel found himself unopposed as his men entered the city of Inchon itself and headed for the brewery, passing padlocked and flaming buildings.

Along the beach to their left, the fighting was heavier, the Marine casualties as well. Lieutenant Baldomer Lopez, shot down as he prepared to lob a grenade, was killed when he rolled over atop the grenade to smother its explosion and shield the men around him. Two Marines attacking with flamethrowers were both killed.

With Cemetery Hill bypassed and still in enemy hands, Lieutenant Muetzel, without loss, had reached the brewery, where he was called and told of Lopez's death and of pinned-down Marines on Red Beach. The nimble Muetzel about-faced, and from the rear he found a path up Cemetery Hill and headed for the summit, flushing out a dozen NK troops en route—men who put up no fight at all and surrendered. The Marines drove ahead toward the summit, where the crest crawled with North Korean mortarmen and infantry. But instead of running into a brisk firefight, the Marines were surprised to find Red soldiers, dazed and demoralized from their pounding by air and naval gunfire, meekly hoisting both arms in surrender. Seizure of the high ground enabled the other two Marine platoons to break out of their narrow bridgehead and drive inland into the city.

By five minutes to six the fight was pretty much over on that sector of Red Beach. In a half hour, Able Company of the 5th Marines had lost eight dead and twenty-eight wounded.

Fighting continued on several of the beaches, but by that evening, the 16th, Marine spearheads were already six miles inland. If the foot soldiers were moving that fast, what would the armored and mechanized units do when they were all ashore? On the morning of the 17th, two hundred NK infantry with six Russian T-34 tanks headed from Ascom City to stop the invaders. But the Americans ambushed the force with their own, more powerful tanks and big new rocket launchers, wiping out the counterattackers. Only one Marine was wounded.

With more heavy equipment being off-loaded from LSTs grounded on the mudflats, MacArthur was sufficiently buoyed to tell General Almond, "You will be in Seoul in five days, Ned."

"No, but I will have the city within two weeks."

Almond thought his response would please the boss. It didn't.

MacArthur wanted Seoul within a week. By September 25.

▪ 35 ▪

MACARTHUR'S AN OLD MAN AND CRAZY. HE'S ALSO ONE HELL OF A
SOLDIER.

In New York at 7:45 Eastern time, Edward R. Murrow of CBS was one
of the few to sound a cautionary note on the evening of the Inchon landings on Friday, September 15. After broadcasting an eyewitness report by
Ensign Jack Siegal aboard the flagship, describing the power and accuracy
of the covering bombardment and the Marine assault, Ed Murrow warned:

> It will probably be a couple of days before we can mea-
> sure the success of the Inchon landing. It involves a cal-
> culated risk, and it brings nearer the time when the
> Chinese Communists and the Russians must make a fate-
> ful decision. The dark cloud of Chinese Communist di-
> visions to the North hangs over the entire operation. The
> question of whether the Russians and the Chinese will
> permit the defeat of the North Koreans may well become
> urgent. It is our purpose to cut off and then cut up the
> North Korean forces. They may disintegrate, as has been
> predicted, but that hasn't happened yet. It would prob-
> ably be a mistake to assume that the North Korean army
> will turn into a rabble because a landing has been made
> in their rear. This is Ed Murrow.

On the bloody ground of Korea, on the Inchon beaches and in the
South, the war went on.

And now, unexpected and unwelcome, came new orders from on high.

"Cromwell, you've been here before, and most of us haven't; you
know the ground, you've had plenty of combat, and I'm assigning you to
General MacArthur's staff as his Marine liaison."

This was not a mere suggestion from General Lemuel C. Shepherd that
they might discuss over an after-dinner brandy. This was an order.

It had taken Ollie six weeks to get out of the State Department and back to the Corps, where he belonged, and now he was joining the damned Army.

But first, he'd had a final few jolly hours amid Marines.

Cromwell crossed the Wolmi-do causeway to the mainland on the 16th, saw some of the seawall fighting from a distance, and had been in the close-range firefights that comprised the mopping up. Had even run into Ike Fenton, looking considerably perkier, no longer the drained, exhausted man with haunted eyes driving his men uphill in the rain of a Korean wet season. Ollie asked how it was going.

Ike said he was actually enjoying Inchon.

"This morning, with a North Korean foxhole handy, I stepped up to the edge and began urinating." When, to Fenton's astonishment, "up jumped a North Korean bowing and scraping and chin-chinning to me." Ike had been scared out of his wits. But he had his first prisoner.

"You ever get to take your leak, Captain?"

"Yessir, I did."

Major Edwin Simmons reported encountering more difficulty just finding the right beach than he did once he and his Marines were ashore. "Wave guides" with bullhorns directed the landing craft, not always on the proper course, and the smoke and haze cut visibility. Ed Simmons was tough to please: he didn't appreciate sloppy work by anyone, wanted better navigation aids, appreciated a first-class enemy—practically insisted on it. As he later summed up, "If those beaches had been defended by Germans or Japanese of World War II caliber, we would not have gotten ashore. But they were defended by second-rate troops."

Nor was enemy air much of a threat. At dawn on September 17 one Yak and one Stormovik attacked the invasion fleet but scored only near misses on Struble's flagship, the cruiser *Rochester*. The bridge of a British cruiser, HMS *Jamaica,* was strafed, killing one sailor before the Stormovik itself was shot down by the ship's antiaircraft guns.

With MacArthur in great form, issuing congratulations in every direction, and with the Marine generals all ashore and out from under foot, he and his right hand, Ned Almond, and task-force commander Rear Admiral James Doyle dined together aboard *McKinley*. MacArthur used the occasion to award Almond a second Silver Star for his leadership of the amphibious assault. Almond had not yet set foot ashore. Once the ground troops broke through out of their shallow beachhead, ground command was to pass to Almond, a man cordially despised by Marine officers. Never mind,

MacArthur had famously assured Ned, "You will be in Seoul in five days."

The Great Man was in a hurry—no one yet knew quite why. And his impatience led him to do things Lem Shepherd and Oliver Smith, the two senior Marine generals, thought foolish and downright dangerous.

They knew the man was an egomaniac. They also knew that for all his posing and posturing, MacArthur was absolutely fearless. It was this that bothered them. Suppose, by some fluke, the kind of thing that happened in the confusion of battle, the most famous general of our time were killed while trooping the Marine lines or inspecting battlefields with Marine officers.

My God! the Marine brass figured, West Point and the Army establishment hate us already. And were MacArthur, a canonized West Point saint, a former cadet, a former superintendant, the icon and idol of the Army, to be martyred while campaigning, not among his devoted own, but among Marines, where would the blame reside? Never again would senior Marine and Army generals be able to conduct a joint campaign. Or even more desperate, play another friendly round of golf.

So Lieutenant Colonel Ollie Cromwell was ordered up. His qualifications?

A former Raider, with State Department references (baby-sitting Ambassador Muccio), an Olympian who'd pal-ed around with Hitler. Who else at Inchon could boast of *that?*

Lem Shepherd, commanding officer of the Fleet Marine Force Pacific, a Virginian with their good manners and sense of history, made the case, briefing Cromwell.

Their meeting was in the ground-floor lobby of a small Inchon bank a trifle the worse for wear, the place having been both bombed and shelled and then assaulted by Marine infantrymen. Two NK bodies, attended by buzzing flies, lay untidily behind the tellers' cages. Shepherd, seated and wearing a fatigue cap, slung binoculars, and a shoulder-holstered .45, was sipping from a canteen cup what seemed to be hot coffee, and he motioned Ollie to pull up a pew as well.

Neither Marine paid any attention to the dead North Koreans. In a fight, these things happened.

"Now, look, Cromwell, you won't like this assignment, nor would I. And I know you're politicking hard for a command, and I won't say you don't rate it. But this job comes first, you understand?"

"Yessir."

When Shepherd spoke, young officers perked up and took notes. He would eventually become commandant of the Marine Corps but was famous early, graduating from VMI ahead of schedule to join the Marines and sail to France and the Western Front. Wounded twice at Belleau Wood and a third time in the Argonne, he was awarded the croix de guerre, the Navy Cross, and the Army equivalent, their Distinguished Service Cross, and later he served as an aide to President Harding and a Marine division commander against the Japanese.

MacArthur, a snob, knew Shepherd and respected the man.

Now, with Ollie, General Shepherd had the floor.

"MacArthur's a great officer who's going down in the history books when most of us are forgotten. But he's an old man now and crazy. He was reckless even young. And lofty? Ever since France in 1918 he's talked of commanding the Rainbow Division, a job he didn't get until twelve hours before the Armistice. And when any of us called him on it, MacArthur got very grand. 'It was my destiny to command.'

"They talk about George Patton being pushy? Patton was 'Little Miss Muffet, eating her curds and whey' compared to Douglas MacArthur. I'm telling you this because I'm giving you the job of keeping the egomaniac alive. But if you ever repeat it, I'll run you up so fast you'll wish you stayed in Berlin with the Nazis."

"Yessir, General, I understand."

"You ever *really* meet him, Cromwell?"

They chatted about Hitler briefly, and then Shepherd returned to the subject at hand, General of the Army Douglas MacArthur.

"So when I say MacArthur's crazy, he is. But he's also one hell of a soldier. I don't know another general officer, Marine *or* Army, would have come up with this Inchon stunt and pulled it off. The Joint Chiefs didn't believe in it, I didn't believe in it, the United States Navy didn't believe in it, and I don't believe MacArthur's own staff liked the idea. And usually those boys are toadying and shouting, 'Amen!' if the Old Man so much as clears his throat.

"But now that there's cameras in view and bows to be taken, MacArthur insists on going ashore. Not just posing for pictures on the beach like a sensible fellow, but riding up to where the forward units are and passing out Purple Hearts and Silver Stars. Oliver Smith and I have been trying to talk him out of it and can't. So you get yourself a Jeep and a couple of tough boys and just tag along with the generalissimo so long as he's on USMC property. Get yourself killed if you have to. But save MacArthur!

"I won't have Mr. Truman blaming the Marine Corps for what happens. You get MacArthur killed, Cromwell, and the Corps won't ever get another appropriation out of Congress, and I'll go down in the books alongside John Wilkes Booth."

Trouble was, said a major assigned to brief Ollie in detail, MacArthur attracted danger as a magnet draws iron filings; the man courted risk.

"Just yesterday, before dawn, MacArthur was in a motor launch with Admiral Struble heading for the seawall when someone called out through the gloom, 'Get the hell out of there! We're going to blow up the wall!' Later that morning MacArthur wanted to see some T-34 tanks the Marines shot up and hopped in a jeep with Almond and General Shepherd, and they rode up to where the smoke was still rising, and there was sniper fire. What did MacArthur do? He went strolling about lecturing Shepherd about Marine 'luck' and how the North Koreans we beat were only second-rate. 'You damned Marines! Always in the right place at the right time.' Worse, General Shepherd told him, 'I know you want to talk to the front-line troops, but they worry about your safety when you expose yourself.' And MacArthur said:

" 'Anywhere my men are I will go.' "

An exasperated Ollie demanded, "If he won't listen to Lem Shepherd, what makes anyone think he'll listen to me?"

"You got me, Colonel," the major agreed.

Before the day was over, Cromwell had his own MacArthur story to tell. When he reported as the new Marine liaison officer, they passed him along the chain of command to where a brigadier took over.

"Just stay handy, Colonel," he said, "in case General MacArthur asks for you. What's your name again?"

"Cromwell." Ollie hoped MacArthur had forgotten their earlier meeting.

Within the hour he found out.

"Oh, yes, it's you. The fellow who thinks the Army can't fight."

"Yessir," Cromwell said, his face stone. MacArthur wheeled and got into a jeep, which drove off, spinning tires and throwing up grit.

Some start this was.

"Come on, Buggy, let's roll."

"Aye aye, sir."

It was a job just keeping up with MacArthur, never mind protecting him.

Lonesome carried a BAR; Buggy a submachine gun; Ollie had his revolver and the M-1. MacArthur already had a couple of jeeps with four soldiers in each of them. Cromwell's vehicle trailed the lot.

"We're sucking hind tit, Colonel," Buggy complained. Cromwell, who knew they were, said nothing.

But when the Marines' jeep bumped over a humpbacked bridge as they headed back into the harbor area, two Korean civilians, one a teenaged boy, ran out into the road, waving them down, not yet realizing it was Mac-Arthur up ahead who had just passed.

"Buggy!" Ollie snapped. The sergeant rattled off some Korean, and the boy, apparently brighter than the man, responded just as rapidly. Buggy, startled, wheeled:

"Sir! There's North Koreans under that bridge."

Cromwell and Lonesome were quickly out of the Jeep, weapons at the ready, approaching the culvert as Buggy shouted down instructions. At which seven Red soldiers emerged, looking sheepish, hands over their heads. Didn't take long for MacArthur's bodyguards to notice the disturbance to their rear and come running.

"Just think how famous one of them would have been if he'd lobbed a hand grenade onto the road a few minutes before. . . ." PFC Doug Koch is quoted by MacArthur biographer Stanley Weintraub.

Neither the general nor anyone else bothered to thank Cromwell or multilingual Sergeant Buggy. But from then on, the Marine jeep was permitted to ride closer up in the little motorcade.

By the 18th, the invasion's fourth day, Kimpo airfield, the largest in the country, had been secured. Bottlenecks at the beachhead, ebb tide–caused, made Kimpo essential for resupply—everything from fuel to ammo to rations to men. General MacArthur made another royal command appearance there as the first transport and cargo planes touched down with reinforcements and supplies.

Clearly enjoying the moment, the general strolled the tarmac shaking hands, followed by a half-dozen correspondents and cameramen.

No one took a shot at the supremo, but the Marines hung close. Orders were orders, especially when they came from Lem Shepherd.

"By the Christ!" an impatient Buggy cried aloud, "will he ever go back to Tokyo and the missus?"

"Sergeant, we're still working for G-2, and you're the boy with the gift of tongues. Chat up some of these characters wandering around. Find out what they know, if anything."

"Aye aye, sir," said Will Buggy, a bit sulky. Cromwell didn't blame him;

it was a stupid assignment, and this wasn't even Marine turf. The Marines had captured the airfield, but there was now some sort of jurisdictional dispute over who owned it. Army or Air Force? He wasn't sure.

Lonesome, product of a small town, was thrilled to be here and in on the act, writing home about it. This was even better than ambassadors— guarding generals and hanging out with Douglas MacArthur himself!

"I'd write home too," Buggy said sourly, "if I lived in East Overshoe, Tennessee. What else they got to talk about in a burg like that."

"East Marion," Lonesome corrected the sergeant, earning a scowl. Shrugging off his own irritations, Cromwell focused on the general, trying to be sure no one got close who didn't belong. That was the job he'd been given; that was the job he'd do. Let staff officers and journalists wonder why a light colonel of Marines was lugging an infantryman's rifle. For all the glad-handing, there were firefights still breaking out at the fringes of the vast field and so many Koreans wandering about, uniformed and civilian both, and who knew North from South? Any one of these people could bump off MacArthur. This was Indian Territory, and Cromwell kept Will Buggy hopping.

"Ask that character his business, Sergeant. Let's see if he gets nervous."

"Aye aye, sir."

MacArthur, unconcerned, kept right on touring the area, posing, greeting the troops. Shots were fired; tanks and trucks full of soldiers, armed jeeps sped here and there. Engineers searched and prodded for mines in the earth bordering the paved tarmac, and communications men strung wire and counted into field telephones and tuned big radios mounted in the rear seats of stripped-down jeeps. Men shouted orders; fighter planes came in bouncing to a landing on the shot-up, pitted surfaces to rearm. As ground crews threaded the belts of fresh machine-gun ammo and fed the aerial cannon, slamming home the big clips of .20-millimeter cannon shells, the fighters refueled and took off. Cargo planes landed and disgorged their loads. Even big guns, the usual field artillery, the .105s, and out of the maw of the larger planes came a few .155s and what Ollie took to be an eight-inch howitzer. Big stuff. Well, they'd need it to take Seoul, he guessed. Inchon hadn't turned out to be much, but with a city the size of Seoul— you could lose a whole division in the streets and byways and industrial zones of a place that big. Seoul could be a hell of a fight.

MacArthur never stopped talking. He had a great, rolling, eloquent, and powerful voice, and he loved hearing it. And the reporters never stopped taking notes; where else did you get such copy? All of it on the record, and to hell with his instructions from Washington! A rain squall swept across the field; the sun came back out; steam rose from the tarmac. Through it all, the newsreel cameras rolled; the Nikons and Canons of the press clicked over and over, catching the MacArthur image and his familiar props: the battered, jaunty cap, the stressed-leather Air Force jacket, the rumpled khaki trousers, the sunglasses, the corncob pipe. More planes landed and took off, firefights erupted and ended, a mortar round came arcing in to explode. Didn't hit anyone; scared some gooks. A combat patrol trotted heavily this way or that, weapons at high port, seeking out infiltrators, looking for a scrap. And the general continued his orations for the cameras.

Tomorrow. Or after tomorrow. Or after, *after* tomorrow, those images, over and over, would impress themselves on the American consciousness while, even swifter, the Great Man's words, eloquent and thrilling, were conveyed to the States from the portable typewriters of Keyes Beech, David Douglas Duncan (a photographer who could write!), Marguerite Higgins, Bill Lawrence and William White of the *Times,* and the anonymous, but competent, professionals of the AP, the UP, the INS, Reuter, and Agence France Presse.

Everyone was there but Tass.

For three or four days Ned Almond had been politicking for his own Army troops to start coming ashore. Didn't pay with so many correspondents to have the Marines getting all the ink. MacArthur, strangely, didn't seem offended. These Marines in the assault waves, they, too, were "my boys."

But they weren't Ned Almond's "boys," and finally Admiral Doyle gave in, and on September 18, the same day the Marines took Kimpo, the Thirty-second Infantry Regiment of the Army Seventh Division meandered ashore.

Trouble was, to flesh out the regiment and bring it up to fighting strength, eighteen-hundred poorly trained Korean draftees had been added to the thirty-two hundred American GIs, most of whom were themselves new to combat. These flaws would cost the Seventh Division later.

It was then that Ben Sweet drove up.

"Ollie! I came in on Blue Beach. Bodies all over the place. Commies mostly, I guess. You okay?"

Blue Beach had been secured two days ago. Ben hadn't been at great risk.

"Fine, Ben. Welcome to the war."

Sweet blathered on at a great rate about how MacArthur gave him the run of the battlefield, total access.

"He's read my books, Ollie."

Ben could swash and buckle with the best, but despite the swagger, when Sweet was with Ollie there was still a puppy-dog eargerness to please. They chatted easily, and then Sweet dropped a tidbit that caught at Cromwell's attention. Something about a deadline for the liberation of Seoul.

"MacArthur wants to take the city by the twenty-fifth. Three months to the day since the North Korean invasion. Told Almond he wants it done."

"Oh?"

"Yeah, he likes the symmetry of it: losing, and then recapturing, the capital city in exactly ninety days."

"You can't always fight battles on a railroad timetable, Ben. Things happen: you get hung up; it rains and the bridge washes out; someone misreads the map. Napoleon had piles at Waterloo, and Wellington didn't."

"I know, I know, Ollie. This isn't my first war."

"Sorry." Cromwell bit off a wise rejoinder.

Ben Sweet was as self-absorbed as anyone Cromwell knew, but it was hard to dislike him. He grew up wanting to be tough and wasn't, grew older aping Hemingway, and now that he was famous, he made a positive thing of going to the wars, yet had never fought.

Ollie started to think, *Poor Ben . . . ,* but thought better of it.

He'd led the life he wanted to live—travel, adventure, cosseted and moneyed, writing for a living and a good one, achieving a certain celebrity, had met and married gorgeous women.

Could Ollie Cromwell claim anything like Ben's achievements?

▪ 36 ▪

THE TWO KOREAN PRISONERS BROKE FOR IT AND WERE SHOT DOWN
RIGHT AWAY.

Then came the moment about which Lemuel Shepherd had worried and for which he'd prepared. Someone got close to MacArthur.

As usual, there was rain, and the little caravan with MacArthur, his outrider jeeps, and the Marines trying to keep up, splashed into the village of Tongdok, in the shadow of a minor mountain by that name, where the Great Man was responding to a call of nature. Lonesome was driving their jeep.

"Follow the general up closer, Lonesome."

"Sir, the general's going to take a leak. How close do I go?"

"You've got a point. Buggy. Let's you and I get out and take one ourselves."

The general might object to a jeepful of Marines tagging along when he made a piss call, but no one could reasonably complain if a few men on foot joined him in relieving themselves.

It was then that the North Korean rifleman, hearing the engines and hoping it might be his people, but fearful it wasn't, came out of one of the village huts, where he'd been sheltering from the rain, his burp gun held steady in both hands with the sling over his shoulder. Startled by the sight of a half-dozen Americans strolling toward him, he threw down on the first of them, the older man in khakis and leather jacket with the fancy cap.

It was Buggy who saw the Red soldier first and who called out, "General!"

And it was Oliver Cromwell's M-1 that fired even before a curious MacArthur could turn to see who'd called, and that nailed the Korean in the chest with the three quick .30-caliber rounds that killed him.

Before the dead man stopped kicking, American soldiers and officers were all over the place, screening the general and protectively pushing Buggy and Cromwell back from where MacArthur stood observing the scene and figuring out what happened.

Cromwell let himself be pushed, understanding the soldiers were only reacting out of shock, frightened by such a near thing, and he wasn't even annoyed at them but just glad Buggy had been on the stick and he himself had been quick.

General MacArthur was first to speak. Calmly, too, with only a dry resentment at being interrupted. You had to admire the cool son of a bitch.

"Nice job," the general said, "whoever did the shooting. And now, if no one objects, I've got a leak to take."

Any hopes of a new assignment were dashed. "Forget it, Cromwell," the Marine G-2 told him. "They've had a scare, and you shot straight. MacArthur's your baby. And will be until he flies home to Japan."

Worse, Ollie was falling under the MacArthur spell, the legend and the reality (how he took the shooting at Tongdok, for example). Ben Sweet was clearly in thrall. Colonel Cromwell was a tougher sell; his admiration came grudgingly; he was reluctant to hero-worship anyone since his disillusionment with Evans Carlson over a single flawed moment. Yet, MacArthur drew him, and despite the frustrations of a baby-sitting job, Ollie's fascination with the man grew.

The Supremo, despite his age, was again on the prowl. The three Marine regiments—the 1st Marines under Chesty Puller, the 5th under Ray Murray, and the newly arrived 7th Marines commanded by Homer Litzenberg—were to bridge or ford the Han River, last serious topographic barrier between the advancing armies and the captive capital of Seoul. And Douglas MacArthur wanted to be there on the riverbank to see them cross. Meanwhile, in the South, back at the Pusan Perimeter, the other half of his two-pronged drive to defeat the enemy and end the war was being launched. Eighth Army had jumped off all along the line on September 16, hoping the Inchon landings would force the North Korean generals to shift troops north and weaken their lines in the South. This was MacArthur's strategy. His Eighth Army was the hammer, and his newly formed X Corps up north the anvil. Between the two, the Communist forces would be smashed. But so far, in hard fighting on the Naktong River, the lines had barely moved.

In the North the Marines smashed sixteen miles ahead on September 18; in the South, at the Perimeter, gains were in yards. Finally, the next day, against four North Korean divisions, the UN forced a crossing of the Naktong River, led by the U.S. First Cavalry, the ROK First, the rehabilitated U.S. Twenty-fourth Infantry Division, and a British brigade. By that day's end, NK units were retreating all across the line. The Inchon left hook had done its job; the enemy was starting to fold.

The Han River was to be forced on September 20. MacArthur and his entourage in their Jeeps, Cromwell among them, were on the shore to watch the Marines cross. This was the sixth day of the Inchon invasion, and MacArthur was still trooping the line, frequently under fire. By now, and despite himself, Cromwell found it difficult to look away, except when distracted by a burst of fire or when a potential risk to the general was about to materialize.

Energized by action, by victory, by having yet again been called on by his country, and by living in the open air and not in the stale offices of the Dai Ichi Building in Japan, MacArthur no longer required his afternoon naps, a daily routine in Tokyo. His belly thickening, one hand palsied (the Parkinson's concealed by jamming his fist into a trouser pocket), his hair dyed black and combed cunningly across the bald scalp, he needed prescription glasses to see and pretended the tinted glasses were simply shades against the sun. He was past seventy and had grown sentimental: when he visited the battleship *Missouri* offshore and was shown a plaque commemorating the Japanese surrender to him on her decks September 2, 1945, Douglas MacArthur wept openly.

None of his poses and subterfuges really fooled those close to him. But neither did they erode their respect for the man. Even in Cromwell, no courtier, respect grew.

MacArthur was old and mad, but he belonged to this country's history and carried himself as captains and the kings ought. Men aped his histrionics and made private sport, but even the lowliest of shifty-eyed enlisted men, who hated the Army and being in it, took pleasure from being able to tell the folks at home or brag when with drinking pals that he had served with (pointedly not *under*) the great MacArthur. Most of this was harmless sycophancy, sheer adulation, or not-too-subtle sucking-up. Some of it was pernicious, such as the faulty intelligence fed MacArthur by G-2 General Willoughby, a poisonous figure, who back in Tokyo told the boss only what Willoughby thought he wanted to hear, and as a result consistently underestimated enemy strength, and who before the year was out would very nearly lose MacArthur his armies to the Communist Chinese in the winter mountains of the Chosin Reservoir.

But that was in an unforeseeable future.

In the wake of a brilliant Inchon, no one wanted to cross MacArthur.

And it wasn't just subordinates who feared him. Even his superiors, Joint Chiefs chairman Omar Bradley among them, were wary of the man. Truman hated but did not fear him. Nor could he afford the political coin it would cost to sack him.

These were hardly Ollie's concerns. His measure of MacArthur was subjective, short-range, emotional rather than rational. He'd been witness to the Old Gentleman's stiff-legged strolls through the small-arms fire here on the the beachhead, to his fearlessness under fire earlier that summer of retreat, when he ignored the strafing Yaks as others ran. He felt a tug. Wasn't this the breed of man you wanted in command, the sort of officer a good soldier could cheerfully serve?

And yet, and yet . . .

The reporters hustled up, wanting to be there when the Marines forced the river Han, wanting to be there with MacArthur as he watched their crossing. Marguerite Higgins was among them, arriving with Jimmy Cannon of the *New York Post,* who groused, "Sharing a jeep with Maggie is like being the jockey on Lady Godiva's horse."

Fighting continued in their rear between the sea and the river, on either side of sprawling Kimpo air base, in the hills and isolated pockets of resistance bypassed by fast-moving tanks and light Marine units hitching rides on trucks or double-timing to keep up. But the focus (of the press as well as the brass) was on the Han. Chesty Puller, for one, had an additional concern. Before he even got to the riverbank in order to cross, he would have to fight his way through the big industrial suburb of Yongdungpo, already half-obscured by smoke and in flames from air and artillery bombardment.

On September 19 Ray Murray's 5th Marines' CP, in a basement room lighted by Coleman lanterns, was so overrun by war correspondents, he had to shout to make himself heard by his own officers. So he had the reporters thrown out. Or, as the Marine Corps official operations report tactfully notes, "Finally it became necessary to request the gentlemen of the press to leave, so that the battalion and company commanders could be summoned for briefing and orders."

Murray was to cross the river (about four hundred yards wide at this point) aboard amphibious tractors (amtraks) at the old ferry crossing to Haengju on the far shore, and, on landing, he was to attack and take Hill 125, the local high ground. Attached to his 5th Marine Regiment were a battalion of KMCs (Korean Marine Corps), very good troops; the 1st

Division's recon company; a tank company; and a company of Army amtraks.

Murray had other worries besides the press.

His own S-2, Major William Esterline, confessed there was only scanty intelligence about the north (far) bank of the river, where the enemy was.

"Well," said Ray Murray, thinking the problem through as Marine officers were paid to do, "if you don't know how many folks Sitting Bull has on t'other side of the river, you have someone swim across and find out. Custer never bothered to ask at the Little Bighorn, did he?"

So they found a Captain Kenneth Houghton.

After dark the night of September 19, a team of swimmers from Houghton's recon company would be sent across. If the far shore was free of Red troops, the rest of the company would follow in LVTs (landing vehicle tanks) to establish a bridgehead which was to be held until the regiment itself crossed at dawn. Tanks would be ferried on fifty-ton floating bridge sections and the sections then bolted together to create bridges. Plans like this didn't come down from MacArthur; they were cobbled up on an ad hoc basis by regimental officers and carried through. It was a flexibility typical of the Marines and not always of the American Army.

Trouble was, it didn't work. "Best-laid plans . . . ?"

The swimmers entered the water (described by the official USMC ops report as "tepid," the Corps being punctilious about such things) shortly after 8:00 P.M.—fourteen or fifteen men, including several U.S. Navy officers and an interpreter, the men all stripped to their skivvies and towing behind them two small rubber boats laden with weapons, uniforms, canteens, field shoes, and the like. Houghton shrugged off a shortage of swim fins. They weren't out for speed but for silence, and using an easy, quiet breaststroke, who needed swim fins? The recon company swimmers got across without incident, and, on landing, they overpowered two Koreans who claimed they'd "escaped" from Seoul. It was assumed the men were lying.

Captain Houghton radioed back the traditional signal, about situations being well in hand. As they were for the moment. But when the signal had been passed along, the night's still was shattered by the noisy firing up of the amtraks, alerting North Korean units that came swarming down to the water's edge, where Houghton's swimmers waited. In the excitement, the two Korean prisoners broke for it and were shot down by the Marines. With stronger enemy forces approaching, the Marines dove back into the

Han to swim across it once again and make for friendlier shores. Only to run into short rounds from Marine 4.2 heavy mortars firing in their support but falling into the river and injuring Houghton with concussion and slightly wounding two others. Several of the LTVs had gotten nearly across, but, on a falling tide, they hung up on the mud. Mudflats at Inchon, riverine mud here. Houghton, dazed, was pulled aboard one of the stranded LVTs. Back at the command post, Murray shrugged off the reports as early reverses. In war, few things went according to plan. But as assistant division commander Ed Craig put it, "It would have looked bad for the Marines, of all people, to reach a river and not be able to cross."

By now some of the 5th Marines were across, and a patrol had already scaled Hill 125 to report, "No enemy encountered."

Except that on the way down, the patrol was hit from behind by concealed guns. One man fell dead. Down on the beachhead and out on the river, there was very heavy enemy fire, especially on the LVTs hung up on sandbars and unable to move either toward the enemy or out of range. Hill 125 had sprung to life and was now pouring fire on the Marines, with the first wave of amtraks estimating they took more than a hundred hits from .145-millimeter antitank weapons, small-caliber explosive shells, and the usual machine-gun fire. Fortunately the lightly armored swimming vehicles provided good protection for the infantry they carried, and the only casualties were among the amtrak crews. When four Corsairs roared in low to hit Hill 125, the .50-caliber machine guns of the amtraks also took up the cause, and Item Company mounted an assault on 125, taking such heavy casualties in the first minutes that the 3rd Platoon had to fall back and reform. A reserve platoon passed through the 3rd and resumed the attack, eventually winning to the top of the small plateau and bringing fire on the hill's crest. By 9:40 that morning, Hill 125 was secured. The balance sheet: forty-five Marine casualties and an estimated two hundred NK killed.

An exiled Ollie Cromwell heard bits and pieces of what was happening there at the old Haengju ferry crossing.

Damn! Damn! Damn!

It was only yesterday, well, a few years ago, that a young officer named Cromwell was leading such raids, swimming lagoons, capturing prisoners, getting himself blown up and knocked silly, and doing all these things with a cheerful competence.

Now? Now he was nursemaiding Douglas MacArthur, a legendary, but crazy, old man intent on a timetable that might kill a lot of Marines. No, let's be fair. Don't blame MacArthur; instead, blame the passage of years.

Cromwell was thirty-five; this fellow Houghton might be twenty-six or twenty-seven. A day cometh, and it passeth away. We all have our shot.

Oh, hell, Cromwell thought. *Another few days and MacArthur will be out of here; they'll give me another chance, and I can stop feeling sorry for myself.* Coming to this conclusion, he roared an unexpected laugh and punched the air. Startled, his sergeant looked up.

"Buggy! Wind up the jeep. I want to get up there to the Han River before General MacArthur misses us. Looks around and says, 'Why, where's Sergeant Buggy and friends? They ought to be here, shouldn't they?' "

"Yessir, whenever the colonel gives the order, sir," Buggy said. What he thought, was:

Damned officers. All nuts! Worse than women at the wrong time of the month.

They were soon rolling toward the Han in the predawn darkness, the occasional artillery shell whistling overhead and exploding off in the distance, the only noise beyond the jeep's passage and the sound of birds waking in the predawn and calling for the day to begin.

Buggy got them to the riverbank before MacArthur arrived. Which for obvious security reasons was the idea.

▪ 37 ▪

The imperturbable MacArthur, accompanied by Lemuel Shepherd (who
gave Ollie a knowing nod as they passed) and Admiral Struble, witnessed
the 5th Marine crossing of the Han from a vantage point on the south
bank, where they had a good view of the fight for Hill 125. When the hill
seemed to be secured, and he was satisfied that the Han, final water barrier
to Seoul, had been bridged, MacArthur set off for a final tour. He was due
to return to Tokyo that afternoon, something no one had yet bothered to
tell Colonel Cromwell.

And since the commander in chief was still on Marine turf, Cromwell
and his two Marines fell in line as the convoy sped off toward the zone of
Chesty Puller's 1st Marines, where the fight for Yongdungpo was going full
blast. Again, MacArthur got out of his Jeep to stroll on foot through rice
paddies where Puller's people were still flushing out snipers. It was now
that Cromwell, Buggy, and Lonesome shouldered more senior staff out of
the way to splash closer to MacArthur. Just in case . . .

Oliver Smith would have the same thing on his mind until MacArthur
passed into the adjacent zone of the Army's Seventh Infantry Division and
their General David G. Barr took on responsibility for "the boss."

That afternoon, September 21, General Smith would take one last trip
with his commanding officer, to Kimpo to say good-bye before MacArthur
took off for Tokyo. Cromwell, too, would be there on the tarmac.

MacArthur had been ashore and visiting the frontline troops every day
since D-plus One, and this was D-plus Seven. As Smith saw off the generalissimo, he thought the Old Man had never worn his famous cap with
more verve, as if he had shed years with this return, perhaps for the last
time, to an actual battlefield in a shooting war. Was it just the old warhorse
in MacArthur? Or an irresistible opportunity to rub Eisenhower's nose in
it?

Marine general Smith recalled, vividly, how they'd all viewed Inchon
with deep mistrust. All except MacArthur, who, as recently as two weeks

ago, was still having to reassure the joint chiefs that a landing could be made:

"I and all of my commanders and staff officers, without exception, are enthusiastic and confident of the success of the enveloping operation."

This was not true, the Marine generals and several admirals having expressed their doubts. But the Old Man had played his cards and swept up the pot and could now, on the tarmac at Kimpo, be forgiven for preening, for jutting the celebrated MacArthur chin, as he decorated General Oliver P. Smith, USMC, pinning a Silver Star on his chest:

"To the gallant commander of a gallant division!" said the general by way of citation.

Sergeant Buggy, who had received no medals and was not a very romantic fellow, shed no tears as the supreme commander's plane rose into the summer sky. As he told Lonesome out of earshot of Colonel Cromwell.

"I thought there for a goddamned minute we was going to have to go with the old fart, nursemaiding all the way to Tokyo."

"That wouldn't of been too bad, Sarge. I ain't never been there, have you?"

Buggy, with his gift of tongues, didn't bother to reply in any of them.

■

The Marines, Smith and Lem Shepherd, didn't need MacArthur's regal nod to know precisely what role they'd played in the victory at Inchon. No other infantry division in the world, they firmly believed, could have come ashore on a hostile beach with those tides and done it with so few casualties. But this was no time for celebrations. The general would be in Toyko in an hour; they had a war to fight against an intact and veteran army that was free to maneuver and choose the ground on which to do battle. And there was still a great city to take. Seoul was roughly forty miles from Inchon an hour's drive in peacetime. But this was not peacetime. And from now on not Smith but X Corps would determine the pace.

Was there really a serious timetable for Seoul? Had Almond promised to have the city by September 25? Had MacArthur ordered him to take it by then? That was Ben Sweet's story and as good an explanation as any. But only MacArthur could tell them. And he was back in Tokyo. These were among the things unsettling the armies as they prepared the attack on Seoul.

Other events of great moment occurred that day, September 21. The 7th Marines, commanded by Litzenberg, arrived in Korea and joined the other two infantry regiments, the 1st and 5th, bringing the Marine brigade fully up to divisional strength. And command of the entire area, including the 1st Marine Division, now passed to Army major general Ned Almond, a man most Marines disliked and some despised. Oliver Smith had one additional item on his agenda: vague promises made to Lieutenant Colonel James T. Cromwell about giving him a combat command. Preoccupied and rushed, Smith saw Cromwell, briefly. Ollie had one pitch to make, and he kept it short; eloquence took time.

"General, I've got to get back in the game. You understand that, sir."

Smith, touched by the plaintive simplicity of his appeal, said he'd do what he could.

The general was as good as his word. No more. The division personnel officer, the adjutant, was a full colonel with a jolly red face who knew how fortunate he was no longer to be humping his considerable heft up and down the hills of which this entire misbegotten country seemed to be composed. He had a nicely laid-out tent with a smart clerk typist with four stripes and a couple of runners, two typewriters that worked and a filing cabinet. He also wore a Silver Star and a Purple Heart that indicated he hadn't always been fat, hadn't spent his entire career in the help-wanted trade.

Prompted by Oliver Smith, Cromwell gave the adjutant his tale of woe.

"Detached duty? You don't have to tell me, Cromwell. You've found a sympathetic ear, sir. It's a curse, the bane of every officer's existence. Like being seconded to the Coast Guard, sent to Cayenne with your epaulets torn away and marched off like poor Captain Dreyfus, or having to join the Foreign Legion."

"Colonel, after six weeks with the State Department and then bodyguarding MacArthur, the Foreign Legion's an attractive option. I'd serve under Colour-Sergeant Lejaune at Fort Zinderneuf. . . ."

The adjutant leaped to his feet.

"Dammit! We'll find something suitable for you, Cromwell. Any man who knows his *Beau Geste* deserves nothing less from the Marine Corps and a grateful nation."

At that, the colonel pulled out a fifth of Johnny Walker Black Label and poured the two of them a stiff one, straight up, in surprisingly clean Old Fashioned glasses.

"My clerk typist is a fetishist when it comes to neatness and setting a decent table. Also handles a very nice tommy gun when the need arises. Sorry there's no ice."

"Haven't had scotch for a time, sir." *Especially not at ten in the morning,*

Ollie thought of adding, but restrained himself. The adjutant was gracious and a fellow devotee of Percival Christopher Wren's great stories for boys, but you don't push full colonels too far.

The adjutant bathed Cromwell in a smile.

"Nice to have good things appreciated, Cromwell. Now, as to your next assignment, I regret to inform you all of the division's infantry battalion commanders seem to be in excellent health. No openings there. Shame you're not still a captain. . . ."

"A shame? I spent fifteen years making light colonel."

"I know, I know, no offence intended. But with Captain Houghton still seeing double from his concussion, there's a billet open as recon company commander. Your Raider background would do very nicely there, sir."

"No interest in my forming a new Raider battalion, I suppose."

The adjutant shook his head. Regular officers his age recalled only too well the disbanding in early '44 of the original Raider battalions.

In the end, after a second scotch, the adjutant proposed that Ollie return to intelligence duty as an assistant S-2 for one of the three infantry regiments.

"Give you the chance to do some scouting and recon work and gather enemy intelligence. Like being a Raider again without benefit of clergy." When he saw the look of disillusionment on Cromwell's face, the G-1 added hurriedly, and encouragingly, "And, sooner or later, a better job's bound to open up. Cheer up, Cromwell; someone's sure to get killed."

"No guarantees, though," Ollie said wryly, aware that he shouldn't.

"No, sir!," the adjutant said grinning. "That's a monstrous suggestion and unworthy of you. I simply refer you to the actuarial tables."

Cromwell declined another scotch and said he'd better take the intelligence job if that's all there was, pleading the press of business and the need to report in to the division's G-2 and rejoin the intelligence section.

When the G-2 looked dubious about assigning a man of Cromwell's rank to a major's billet, Ollie went into his sales pitch. Until then he wasn't sure this was really the job he wanted. The G-2's reluctance changed all that, being just the goad he needed.

"You know my record, sir. But perhaps you don't know my sergeant Will Buggy served a couple of years in Seoul and speaks fluent Korean. My driver also served in the city, knows the highways, the byways, the trolley-car schedules."

"And you know the capital yourself, Cromwell?"

"Yessir. I was military attaché to Ambassador Muccio at the embassy, sir. Knew some of the KMAG officers and actually met President Rhee."

God forgive me for tarting up the old résumé, Ollie thought. But what were they going to do, subpoena Muccio? Phone Rhee to check out his references?

He got the assignment. Not much of a job, he admitted, but it was with the 5th Marines, his old regiment!

▪ 38 ▪

THE THIRD PLATOON OPENED UP AND JUST CUT THE FORMATION TO
RIBBONS.

While all this big-picture stuff was going on, Chesty Puller's 1st Marines were fighting not for Seoul, but for the warehouses and factories of Yong-dungpo City, which guarded the approaches to the capital and were proving a tough nut.

And why not? As the North Korean leadership itself said, "If Yong-dungpo falls, Seoul also will fall," and they promptly dispatched a regiment of the Eighteenth Division of the North Korean People's Army to reinforce the town. Coining vigorous slogans was one thing (it cheered up the troops, sounded good, and didn't cost much), but using valuable reserves to back up slogans was something else. Not a brilliant move. For one thing, Yong-dungpo was bound to fall eventually. Seoul, ringed by steep hills, was much more defensible than suburban Yongdungpo, set at the confluence of two rivers and surrounded by sandy flats and no high ground to speak of.

Puller continued to batter at the city. But as early as September 19, his 1st Marines and Murray's 5th had moved so swiftly inland that they had outrun their own naval gunfire support from our destroyers and cruisers just offshore. The battleship *Missouri* was still out there, with its longer-range sixteen-inch guns, but even those couldn't reach Seoul and so would be of assistance for only a few more miles. Meanwhile, Chesty had Marine aviation support plus his own regimental field artillery, mortars, and a battery of big 4.5-inch rockets.

While, stunning just about everyone, the NKPA mounted a surprise counterattack in the Marine rear on Kimpo airfield, which the Allied command had believed to be secure. It took a battalion of Korean Marines with naval gunfire support from the cruisers *Rochester* and *Toledo*, firing five hundred eight-inch shells at extreme range, to break up the enemy assault, with a loss of forty NK dead and 150 prisoners. This would be the last significant NK offensive south and west of the Han.

In fighting for three low hills situated halfway between Kimpo and

Yongdungpo, the 5th Marines took all three, one captured without casualties by Ike Fenton's company.

By now, of course, as the Marine regiments marched, maneuvered, and fought, and as the first American Army divisions moved into the X Corps line, Ned Almond, sniffing his third star, that of a lieutenant general, focused on taking Seoul by the 25th.

War is rarely simple. And now even an officer as powerful as Almond found this so. He had two tasks: take Seoul by September 25 and link up with the Eighth Army, which was rushing up the peninsula from the south. Could he do both? Could he do either? Could he fail at either and survive, his career intact?

To insure that his objectives were attained, Almond rose each morning by four and was soon off in a jeep, often driving it himself; left behind the creature comforts of his posh command trailer (fitted out with hot and cold running water, a fridge, china dinnerware, flush toilet, and shower), over which he had earlier thrown a tantrum (Admiral Doyle refused to land it out of turn, ahead of the tanks). At a distance, Ned Almond seemed a modest-enough fellow, wearing a simple fatigue jacket and a leather belt snugged tight, and carrying a leather-holstered .38, a leather map case, and a small leather notebook at his side, two cloth stars sewn into his epaulets. There was no chichi about Almond, just the garb of an honest soldier of the line. Unless you knew about his trailer and his tantrums.

Of more concern was Almond's schedule: Seoul by the 25th, no matter the cost (in dead men). Cromwell, an officer finally back in the womb of the Corps, lived with the rifle companies spearheading the advance. When an army is on the move, it is with the rifle companies that you learn about the enemy. Colonel Murray, commanding the regiment, understood this as well as Cromwell and bestowed his blessings.

"I'll take any intelligence edge I can get, Ollie."

Murray had been through all that hot weather fighting down south at the Pusan Perimeter, and Cromwell would do anything Ray Murray wanted. Without elaboration he said:

"Yessir, you'll have whatever we find and quickly. And unless there's an unbroken defense line ringing the city, I may be able to slip into town somehow. My sergeant Buggy and our driver really know Seoul. Better, maybe, than the North Koreans do. If we get in there, you'll have the best intelligence there is. Get me a good radioman, Ray. That's one thing I need. A good radio and a man to operate it."

"You'll have them, Ollie. But remember one thing. The 5th Marines date back to Belleau Wood and the Argonne. You're a grown-up now, an intelligence officer with colonel's eagles in the offing. No Raider insanity, please. This isn't the 2nd Raider Battalion, and I'm not Evans Carlson. Play it cool, Ollie. Play it professionally. One day you may command this regiment. Until then, respect its battle record. Don't go freelancing and winning wars by yourself."

Ollie expected Ray's blessing, not the lecture. Well, that was the baggage a Raider carried. He knew the false stories: Cromwell had been trouble in college, playing dirty. Later on, as a boxer, he'd killed a man in the ring. As a Raider officer he'd taken casualties through rash actions and faulty judgment. You name it . . . Oliver Cromwell probably did it.

Ray Murray, who liked Ollie and respected his skills, his daring, dismissed such tales. But he still kept what sailors call a "weather eye" on Cromwell, lest he and his regiment be blindsided by Ollie, running them into squalls, onto rocks and shoals.

Men who *didn't* like Cromwell went further. He took risks, cut corners, promoted himself (hadn't his chum Ben Sweet put him in a book?), couldn't be trusted.

"Do I have *that* bad a rep, Ray?" Ollie now asked, one man to the other, straight out and eye to eye.

"No," Murray responded to the question. "You're a good Marine, a fine officer. Just cool it is all I'm saying, Ollie. Field-grade officers, distinguished fellows like you and me, we don't take the point on patrol. We send a smart young corporal with quick feet. I don't want to lose you liberating some crappy rice paddy, okay?"

"Whatever you say, Ray."

Murray looked Ollie in the face. What he saw there, Bruiser Wells had seen—a look that Syd Ketchel had recognized, that Colonel Carlson liked,

The killer instinct.

Murray didn't say more. With men like Cromwell, at some point, counsel went unheard, and you were beating dead horses. Ollie would be Ollie.

So now he wished Cromwell luck, wheeled, and went back to his battalion commanders to map their assault on the Korean capital.

■

Murray's fellow regimental commander, Puller of the 1st Marines, didn't know Cromwell and didn't waste time or energy fretting over crazy Marines; he'd known too many of them. His regiment and Murray's were to drive into Seoul while Litzenberger's 7th Marines swung wide around the city through the hills to flank it and cut off a major enemy retreat. But before Puller got to town, there remained Yongdungpo, burning and battered but still heavily defended. Students of war, and Chesty was certainly one, knew the vast absorbing capacity of a wrecked city to hurt an attacking enemy. He'd read the chronicles of Stalingrad, where von Paulus lost the German Sixth Army.

In the evening of September 19, one of Puller's battalions stormed and captured Lookout Hill, the dominant high ground on the approach to Yongdungpo, at a loss of 2 Marines killed and 15 wounded. Another battalion, advancing along the Inchon-Seoul highway, also made gains until its tanks encountered the first mines sown since Inchon, their leading M-26 losing a track to a primitive wooden box mine our metallic mine detectors missed. And when the following tanks pulled off to the shoulders to bypass the mined road, they, too, found mines and tried, unsuccessfully, to detonate them with machine-gun fire. Meanwhile, enemy small arms took Fox Company under fire from Hill 72 on the right front. With three Marine rifle companies now involved, with Marine air and artillery weighing in, quite a lively firefight was going on when First Lieutenant George A. Rabe's engineers came up to remove the antitank mines. To get the armor back in the fight, Rabe ignored the shoulders and told the tanks to stay to the now-cleared highway. Several Jeeps and trucks coming along later, and not getting the word, were blown up. When an enemy roadblock of rice bags and tree trunks blocked the road, a bulldozer cleared the way. There were other mines and plenty of North Korean infantrymen, but with a full battalion of Marine riflemen and a company of tanks heading their way, the Koreans began to retreat.

The "Bug-out Blues" were being played now by another orchestra. The extraordinary thing was that in a daylong advance of three miles against determined resistence, the U.S. losses were 4 killed and 18 wounded; the North Koreans lost 350 dead and wounded and 5 captured.

But the fight wasn't over. The Marine right flank was extended and had not yet occupied the flanking hills, and before dawn on September 20, the North Koreans took advantage of the vacuum to attack, quickly grabbing Hills 80 and 85, while a larger NK force, estimated at a battalion, marched out of smoky Yongdungpo and headed toward the Marines down the highway. Leading the advance, five T-34 Russian tanks and a truck crammed with ammo. A booby trap?

All day long (the 20th) the fighting raged, with Marine planes and guns dueling with North Korean artillery inside Yongdungpo. When the Marine

4.5 rockets rolled up, ready to lend a hand, the story is that Puller enthusiastically ordered the officer commanding the rockets:

"Level Yongdungpo!"

Great story. And it sounded like Chesty. The only trouble, Colonel Puller's dramatic order so unnerved the rocket battery commander that he forgot to arm the rockets before sending them off, and when they landed inside the beleaguered city, only brown dust arose—not a single detonation!

Others said the rockets hadn't been supplied with the proper fuses and it was no one's fault, just flawed combat logistics at work.

Which did not prevent Marines from deriving entertainment value from the situation. They all loved Chesty; but to imagine his cries of rage—how could any usually awed Marine not secretly delight?

Puller's explosion was just about the only laughter there was on the slogging road to Seoul. Chesty's Dog and Fox rifle companies spent the night along the highway, dug into the flanking low hills, with Easy Company straddling the road itself. Standing watch above the highway, the Marines heard the clanking armor and racing engines of the enemy convoy headed by the ammo truck but in the darkness (it wasn't quite 4:00 A.M.) weren't sure who was moving down there below their positions as the vehicles passed them at about 4:30. It was left to an Easy Company Marine, Private Oliver O'Neil Jr., to step out onto the highway to challenge the lead truck, well out ahead of the Red tanks and trucks jammed with North Korean troops. Response to O'Neil's gutsy challenge was swift. He was cut down by automatic-weapons fire as pandemonium instantly broke out on the highway and the higher ground on either flank.

The operations report told what happened:

> Two T-34s stopped short of Easy Company's front and opened up wildly. Companies D and F in turn exploded with machine guns, small arms, grenades, and mortars against the flank of the enemy column, while E fought to deny further passage along the road. Under the hail of fire from above, the Red soldiers milled about in panic and were slaughtered. Some flung themselves into roadside ditches, where the crowding only increased the odds of destruction. Others sought escape by scrambling up the slopes—into the very muzzles of Dog and Fox Company weapons.

As the Red tanks lurched back and forth "like trapped animals . . . the ammunition truck exploded in a brilliant spectacle of pyrotechnics."

A lone Marine armed with a 3.5-inch rocket launcher, PFC Monegan, stepped out onto the road, given covering fire by his mates, and he fired at the first T-34, wrecking it with a single projectile, then reloaded, approached the second tank, took aim, and knocked it out, the blackened hulk turning into a furnace. Monegan, after reloading again, was taking aim at another tank as it pivoted to retreat when he was hit and killed by enemy machine-gun fire.

When dawn broke, the NK convoy had been destroyed, and three hundred of their men were heaped in piles along the road, in ditches, and on the hillsides. They were all dead.

Later that day (the 20th) the Marines turned to recapturing Hills 80 and 85 and to wiping out bypassed enemy units concealed in thickets along the riverbank, from which they ambushed and killed Marine communications men laying wire and a truck carrying four Marine engineers. While these small fights and ambushes played out, the first two U.S. Army regiments, the Thirty-second and Thirty-first Infantry, were moving up into the line on the 1st Marines' right flank. Coming under fire from a ridge "a-buzz with North Korean activity" that was technically on Thirty-second Regiment turf, marine lieutenant colonel Allan Sutter contacted Army colonel Charles M. Mount, asking permission to bring fire to bear on the enemy ridgeline in Mount's area. At 1:00 P.M. Mount gave the okay, but it took seven hours for the necessary clearance to filter through the Seventh Army Division, X Corps, and the 1st Marine Division and eventually reach the Marine artillery regiment, the 11th Marines, before the first shells hurtled out toward the Red position. And by then, darkness had fallen and the forward observers were unable to adjust and direct fire more accurately on the NK strong points.

It was the first, but would not be the last, such failure of the Army and the Marines to coordinate swiftly.

Allied artillery boomed out all night, hitting the already-riddled city of Yongdungpo, but there was no infantry action the night of September 20–21. Both sides were readying themselves for the dawn and the heavy fighting they knew was coming. Strongly defended dikes and entrenched earthworks waited for the Marines, and when they came, except at several places to the west that were left undefended so that a single Marine rifle company burst through, the advance was measured in inches and was accompanied by heavy casualties.

The few officers who'd heard of MacArthur's target date of September 25 for the capture of Seoul shook their heads. Here it was the 21st, and they were still fighting like hell even to enter, never mind capture, Yong-dungpo. Seoul, a few miles away, must have shimmered like some unattainable emerald city to the hard-fighting assault troops. By 3:30 the 2nd Battalion had lost eleven killed and seventy-four wounded, and Puller ordered the 3rd Battalion to move through and take on their front while the 2nd caught its breath. To the south there was good news. The Army Thirty-second Regiment had advanced nine miles in one day in mountainous terrain against light resistance.

But as night fell, there was concern on Puller's staff as to the whereabouts of Captain Barrow's Able Company, missing since morning. After some hard fighting early, the six-foot-four Barrow advanced, against no resistance, into a swampy area, one platoon sinking to its knees and barely able to move. Barrow feared if they bogged down, at any moment the entire company would be easy prey for enemy troops on either flank. But none appeared. Several levees loomed ahead, and once again the Marines expected at any moment to be engaged in a firefight. Again, nothing. After the levees were passed, to the Marines' amazement, they found themselves approaching the first of the city's buildings, again, not defended. But as they now hurried into the town up one street and down another, the Marines saw their first North Koreans since morning, a large detachment trotting down the highway toward them, "chanting a spirited military air," and completely unaware the Marines had come to town.

"The Third platoon opened up and cut the formation to ribbons."

Two other NK units, astonished to find Marines in their midst, just ran. Able Company pushed ahead now, coming across a huge ammo dump defended by a small group of Red troops. During the ensuing firefight, a Marine grenade ignited the dump, which exploded with a tremendous roar, shaking the ground and sending up a plume of smoke that for the first time told the 1st Regiment the whereabouts of their missing company. Running short of ammo but finding a stock of captured U.S. blood plasma they could use, the Marines got out one brief message of their condition and situation before the SCR radio battery died, and prepared to last out the night behind enemy lines.

That night, September 21–22, Barrow's men dug in, and deeply, behind a dike straddling the Inchon-Seoul highway inside the city of Yongdungpo, where they withstood the shelling of five T-34 tanks that rolled up and down past the dike, firing but doing little damage, and eventually tiring and withdrawing. Incredibly, with tanks firing cannon at pistol range, only one Marine had been injured, suffering concussion. At 9:00 P.M. the first enemy infantry counterattack hit. By midnight, Barrow's company had beaten off five more attacks. After which a captured Red officer broke away from Marine custody and ran toward his own people, shouting, as Barrow's ROK interpreter translated, "Don't attack anymore! They're too strong for you!"

At dawn Able Company counted 275 enemy dead in front of their positions, fifty automatic weapons, and four T–34 tanks, abandoned.

The rest of the 1st Marines now rushed into and then surged through the town, chasing or wiping out the last of the defenders until they came out the other side. For Puller and his men, the road to Seoul lay open.

■ 39 ■

Now it was the turn of Ray Murray's 5th Marines, including assistant regimental intelligence officer Colonel James T. Cromwell and his scouts.

The curtain-raising could have been more propitious. During the night of September 21–22, an enemy shell smashed through the roof of the native house serving as command post of the 5th Marines outside Seoul, wounding the executive officer, Lieutenant Colonel Lawrence C. Hays Jr., so severely that he had to be evacuated. Murray, the regimental commander, escaped with a slight cut and ordered the CP moved to a cave on the reverse slope of a nearby hill. The opposition Murray and his regiment now faced would be the fiercest since D-day at Inchon. Some measure of the regimental losses can be grasped if you realize that by the time Seoul was taken, 17 of 18 5th Regiment rifle platoon commanders had been killed or wounded and 5 of the 6 rifle company commanders.

The 5th Marines were scheduled to jump off northwest of Seoul at 7:00 A.M., September 22. Two newly arrived NKPA units would have much to do considering the sudden stiffening of enemy resistance. The first was the Seventy-eighth Independent Regiment commanded by Colonel Pak Han Lin and numbering about two thousand men. The second, and larger, was the Twenty-fifth Brigade of four to five thousand men, commanded by a major general called Wol Ki Chan.

The enemy troops now going up against the Marines included a giant North Korean officer whose stature and bulk, plus his European complexion, suggested to the Marines that he might be a Russian adviser, and whose courage, daring, and apparent unkillability caused How Company to nickname him Fireproof Phil. He was fearless, lucky, or a combination of the two; machine-gun bullets and mortar shells seemed to bounce off the man. Finally the regimental tanks did Fireproof Phil the signal honor of targeting him with ninety-millimeter shells.

Not even those could extinguish Fireproof.

But that fight had not yet begun. On the eve of the offensive, there was first the incident of Sergeant Higgins's steam engine.

This bizarre touch involved a stolen enemy steam locomotive driven through Marine lines and braked to a loud and showy halt just outside of Colonel Murray's command post. Marines are renowned for their ability to scrounge and scavenge, but not even the saltiest of the 5th Marines had ever before heard of a purloined locomotive.

There, now, on Ray Murray's doorstep, the huge machine rested, panting aloud, snorting and chugging, black smoke and sparks belching from its chimney, while Sergeant James I. Higgins and a lone accomplice accepted congratulations and fielded coarse insults from idle Marines, among them Cromwell's driver Lonesome, that were shouted up at Higgins, lounging smugly in the cab.

The first inquiries dealt with just where and how an American Marine in enemy territory came across an unattended steam engine and simply drove it away. On those matters, possibly because he was supposed to have been on other duties at the time, the sergeant was understandably vague.

"How many miles on her, Sarge?"

"Still under warranty, five years or fifty thousand miles, whichever comes first."

"What'll you take for it, Higgins?"

"Cash money?"

"Hell, no, Sarge."

"Kick the wheels and make me your best offer."

There was much laughing and harumphing from both Sergeant Higgins and his swiftly assembled audience. It was Lonesome who asked the pertinent question: "Where'd you learn to drive a locomotive, Sergeant?"

Higgins, clearly enjoying his celebrity, but not a braggart, admitted he knew nothing of locomotives, nor did his partner in crime.

"So we started by firing up and opening throttles and depressing levers until the gauges hit the halfway mark. From there we gradually raised or lowered the power, and off we went. Slow and noisy as billy-be-damned but, by God, moving. And since it's on tracks, you don't have to steer worth shit."

A supply officer, sent out to examine the engine and see if it could be put to use, spoiled the fun.

What with dense smoke rising from the smokestack and into the Korean sky, the locomotive might well be providing enemy artillery with a target marker visible for miles, not only within a few yards of Colonel Murray's headquarters but adjacent to a staging depot stacked with ammunition and high explosives stockpiled for the offensive.

Higgins and his copilot "were invited to keep rolling until they reached the rear."

Locomotives and freelancing sergeants weren't the only headache. Not for the first time, local maps turned out to be confusing, even inaccurate. As a consequence, there were misunderstandings as to routes and unit boundaries, and disagreements about place names and heights of ridgelines and hills. In the 5th Marines' area alone, there were three distinct Hills 105, each one of which was assigned as an objective to one of Murray's infantry battalions. By now, such niggling, but potentially costly, problems had become a concern of Ollie Cromwell. It was the S-3, the operations section, that had to plan the attack; it was the S-2, intelligence section, that supplied the S-3 with updated and accurate information on enemy displacements, strength, morale, and intentions.

The operations officer solved the business of three distinct hills with the same name, offhandedly titling them 105-N (for north), 105-C (for center), 105-S (for south). Easy enough; you just corrected and altered the maps. But it was the 2-section, intelligence, that sent out the reconnaissance patrols, including Ollie's, into no-man's land and beyond to sniff out what the North Korean enemy was up to, what resources of men and weapons they had, how densely they were dug in, and just what the Reds planned to do next. It was hard, exhausting, and risky work, carried out by night, and it demanded a certain dedication. Some men, born warriors, thrived on it; others shied away and sought more-routine service. Cromwell, the trained Marine Raider, swiftly became a nightmare to the North Koreans but vexing to his boss, the regimental intelligence officer, and to Murray.

"Sending out a recon patrol doesn't always mean going yourself, Ollie. There are enough lieutenants and staff NCOs capable of doing the job. As well as you can, maybe even better. Murray says you send the patrol, you don't lead it."

"Sure, sure," Cromwell responded, as Evans Carlson might have done, and not meaning a word of it. And at two the next morning, Ollie and his recon patrol, guided by compass and stars, were padding silently along a narrow footpath bordered on either side by cultivated and as-yet-unharvested rice paddies when Lonesome, taking the point, hissed back, "People coming, sir." Alerted by hand-and-arm signals barely visible in the faint starlight, the Marines were waved off into the thigh-deep water, where they crouched still lower and waited. The North Koreans, half-a-dozen of them, trotted blind, right into the Americans.

Cromwell, seeing the glint of metal on the point man's epaulets and going by guess and instinct (the Korean sported eyeglasses), threw himself at the supposed officer, knocking him bodily off his feet and into the murky, reeking water, where Ollie was quickly on top of him, holding the slender, much smaller man underwater by the throat, choking and driving him deeper into the muck. The rest of the Marines took the others, using knives and gun butts. In the Raider lexicon, the best kind of firefight. Not a shot fired by either side and with even the splashing ended inside of a minute. Getting to his feet, Cromwell easily hauled the half-drowned little Korean, coughing and retching, out of the water. Alive and well if not precisely taking nourishment. The Marine yanked the man's handgun and tossed it off to splash into the dark, then knocked off his spectacles as well. Keep a prisoner confused, disoriented; don't let him get comfortable with you.

"Up here, Buggy. Talk to this gent and let me know who he is and what he says. Quick. Daylight's coming, and I don't want to get caught out here."

Two more Reds were alive, dazed and bloody, and being kept separate from the officer. You don't let them cook up a story. The others were dead, floating facedown in the paddy or already sunken to the bottom of the darkly bloody water. Blood kept bubbling up through the murk.

"I ain't gonna order no rice pudding tonight," someone said. There was a low laugh, which Buggy cut off with a snarl. Then, to Cromwell:

"He's an officer, sir. Says he's a major." He gave Ollie the division and regiment numbers.

"Good, let's take him home. And in one piece."

Cromwell was still thinking about the one prisoner they'd taken during the rubber boat recon at Inchon, the one they killed without meaning to; they then jammed a butt into his gaping mouth. That was a waste. He didn't intend wasting this boy; he wasn't going to lose a North Korean major. Prisoners were the best intelligence there was; officers were the cream. A prisoner here, a prisoner there, interrogated and cross-checked against their buddies, that's what Ray Murray needed on the long and winding road ahead. It was on the basis of good intelligence that regiments advanced or bogged down, lost their lead rifle company in a violent ambush, or burst through enemy lines almost unscathed.

At dawn and within four hundred yards of the Marine line, they stumbled across another Korean whom Ollie shot dead, taking him through the head when he leveled his burp gun, and impressing Buggy.

"Very nice shot, sir."

And their major? He turned out to be solid coin, talkative and reasonably well-informed, earning Ollie a "Well-done!" As well as a mild chewing out: "With all those huskies on the job, you had to jump the guy yourself?"

As for the North Koreans, all they knew was that a Major Park, with a six-man escort, had vanished on an inspection near the front, and without a shot being heard. You lost men in combat; that was understood. They didn't usually go this quietly.

Here on the approach to Seoul in the hills and along the marshy riverbanks, Ollie had no edge, no local knowledge or advantage. Which was why Murray tried to keep him on a leash. Why get Cromwell killed out here where he didn't know much more than the next fellow? Not when in a few days they would really need Ollie and his embassy Marines as the 5th Regiment battled its way into the capital's city limits. A sprawling city of a million and a half people peacetime was where they would be calling on Cromwell the pathfinder to pilot Murray's battalions onto their assigned objectives in the battered maze of a great city aflame and smoking. In Seoul, every street corner, apartment building, retail store, warehouse, train station, factory, or park could mask an ambush or funnel the infantry into a killing zone swept by enemy machine guns, and toward fields of fire cleared for antitank weapons to kill the Marine tanks.

Even Murray had fallen for the myth of Ollie's street smarts. "Inside the city limits, that's where we can use Cromwell. Knows the town, served there as the ambassador's attaché."

Ollie had repeatedly knocked down that story, but no one ever listened. So he'd stopped trying.

"What the hell!" Buggy had lived and worked in Seoul, and Lonesome knew his way around. Ollie had them, and he had his Humble Oil Company map, more accurate than USMC operations sheets based on the work of Japanese Army cartographers dating back to the thirties.

So Ollie and his "boys," Lonesome and Sergeant Buggy, did their early scouting freelance, no charge. Regiment's plan was to keep Colonel Cromwell alive until they got to town. And then put him to profitable use. Give the man a proper squad of intelligence scouts, more vehicles, better radios, and the latest maps and turn their Raider loose on an innocent North Korean People's Army, just waiting to be plucked.

▪ 40 ▪

There was precious little plucking to be done until the Marines got into Seoul. And they weren't there yet.

The grappling for the approaches to the city began in what the regimental history calls "deadly earnest" at 7:00 A.M. on the morning of September 22, three days before MacArthur's deadline to secure the capital. Ray Murray's plan was pretty straightforward. So was the savage enemy defense.

The 1st KMC (Korean Marine Corps) battalion jumped off in the center from Hill 104, immediately meeting heavy resistance. In fact, though Hill 104 had been secured the day before, in the night NKPA detachments infiltrated the Marine lines and scaled the hill, pouring heavy fire on the KMCs from the flanks and rear. The Korean Marines were already taking a pounding from Red artillery and mortars and were soon stalled.

On the left Murray's 3rd Battalion jumped off from Hill 216, moving quickly ahead, with How Company declaring the first objective, Hill 296, secured at 9:45. It was not yet realized 296 was a key Communist defensive position, with several ridgeline spurs still strongly held on either flank of How Company. An enemy counterattack in company strength was repulsed with heavy Red loss, including 40 prisoners. But the North Koreans didn't discourage easily, and another counterattack was launched. The other two Marine rifle companies were also soon engaged on the flanking spurs. In a fight for a hillside village, 2 Marines were killed and 11 wounded. At dusk the fighting broke off, with Hill 296 occupied in part by Marines but far from secured.

The 1st Battalion's objective, Hill 105-S, lay two thousand yards from the jump-off line, but it took until 5:20 that evening to secure the hill with the aid of intense air, mortar, and artillery support. In taking Hill 105-S, 12 Marines were dead and 31 wounded.

At 7:00 the next morning, September 23, the KMCs were ordered to resume their stalled attack and straighten the regimental line, while the 1st and 3rd Battalions remained in position, assisting the Korean Marines with fire but not attacking. The 2nd Battalion was still held back in reserve.

At noon Homer Litzenberg's 7th Marine Regiment joined the 1st and 5th Marines for the first time, under orders to cross the Han River and fall in behind the 5th Marines. After seven weeks of fighting, the 1st Marine Division was formed, all three infantry regiments in action and heading for Seoul, not on MacArthur's timetable, but on their own.

The North Koreans, naturally, would have something to say about it. And what happened on the 23rd at a nearly imperceptible height of ground called Hill 56 proved what appalling things occurred when advancing troops didn't know the ground. Oliver Cromwell, who spent the day observing from just aft of the advance, had not scouted this ground. Nor, apparently, had anyone else. And that was the problem.

The KMCs, suffering heavy casualties, were ordered to drop back from the forward slopes of Hill 56 and to hold there, while Murray got Colonel Roise's 2nd Battalion up from reserve to pass through the battered KMCs and capture the hill. If they had time, Murray would have sent Roise around the flank to take the hill from the rear. But it was already mid-afternoon, and if they were going to take the hill before dark, it was going to have to be by direct assault. Neither Murray nor Roise nor anyone else had yet realized that Hill 56, small as it was—a mere pimple of ground less than two hundred feet high—formed the heart of the North Korean defense line.

Now just about everything began to go wrong.

Murray believed some artillery and a platoon of tanks would be sufficient support for Roise's assault, with Dog and Fox companies attacking and Easy Company supplying overhead fire. But with a thousand yards of rice paddy to be crossed by the tanks, the leading M-26 quickly bogged down in a wide ditch, stalling the advance of the other tanks. A mortar section was ordered forward to support the two rifle companies, but there was a foul-up, and the order didn't go through. Nonetheless, Dog Company moved uphill against "negligible opposition."

No one seemed to know that a railroad tunnel pierced the hill, a tunnel full of North Korean infantry, who now burst out firing and yelling slogans. The shock counterattack caught one of the Marine platoons by surprise, killing its platoon leader, Lieutenant Heck. Heck's senior NCO then went down with a shattered leg. Still unaware of the tunnel, the 2nd Battalion troops were unable to figure out where all these enemy soldiers were coming from on so small a hill. At one point, Lieutenant Anderson's platoon of 27 Marines was slugging it out with an entire NK rifle company. Darkness fell. Why didn't the North Koreans press their advantage and continue to counterattack through the night? An air strike at last light and then artillery support throughout the night might have intimidated them.

By dawn two badly hurt Marine rifle companies of the 2nd Battalion were still hanging on, "by their eyelashes," to the scarred slopes of Hill 56. Fox Company, which would end the fight down to 90 effectives, had all three of its rifle platoon leaders wounded but still commanding their men. Now it was Dog Company's turn. A dozen Marines, including their squad leader, Sergeant Robert Smith, were ordered to execute a wide end sweep around the enemy but collided with a strong force of NK regulars. Smith and 8 of his men were killed. Only 3 survived, all wounded.

When Lieutenant George Grimes's mortars ran out of ammo, the section fought as riflemen. Colonel Roise was wounded by mortar fragments, had the wound dressed, and returned to his CP. Corsairs came in low, strafing and bombing Hill 56 and drenching it with flaming napalm. Battalion mortars, the big .81-millimeter tubes, were called on. Lieutenant H. J. Smith, commanding Dog Company, was down to 44 able-bodied men (a rifle company normally numbers more than 200 Marines) when he was ordered at mid-morning to resume the attack.

These men had been fighting since Pusan, almost two months now, but as they worked their way up the blackened slopes of Hill 56, even they were stunned by the scene: more dead and dying North Koreans than the Americans had yet seen anywhere in Korea. The hill, honeycombed with trenches, bunkers, foxholes, and the railroad tunnel itself, had become the graves of the Red soldiers, men who'd died at their posts, so crowded together that every bomb, every shell, every rocket took its terrible toll. Smith, reaching the summit, formed his surviving Marines in a skirmish line to clear the remainder of the ridge. But as the Marines bounded ahead, sure now of their hard-earned victory, Lieutenant Smith was hit, dying at the head of his men. Only 26 men of Dog Company were standing at the finish.

Hill 56 wasn't a firefight; it was a field of corpses.

As the Marines mopped up, they were startled to see three NK officers on their feet, urging their men to retreat down the reverse slopes of 56. No orders had to be given; the surviving Marines began firing, enjoying another "turkey shoot."

In the end, by late September 23, only one Dog Company officer remained on his feet—Lieutenent Karle Seydel. On the other side of the ledger, 1,500 enemy bodies were found on Hill 56. Another 1,750 dead NK soldiers were found on neighboring Hill 296.

The carnage not quite over, Ray Murray looked around at his staff. Without apportioning blame, without singling out anyone, certainly not Cromwell, the regimental commander talked about the failures of intelligence, the need for accurate, skeptically scrutinized information before sending thousands of trained men into deadly combat. How could a railroad tunnel exist unknown on ground as infinitesmal as Hill 56? Didn't a single map alert us to its existence? How could thousands of North Korean regulars remain hidden in a few holes and caves for so long, only to emerge and do such damage to Marine ranks? Murray shrugged, conveying the notion that he, too, was culpable in all this.

"It's never perfect. Never will be. They don't write a script and then pass it around before the curtain rises. Nice if they did, but they don't. In war there are no dress rehearsals. It isn't pretty, it hurts like hell, but they pay us to win these fights. Good intelligence makes it easier. But it's never really easy, is it?"

The question was clearly rhetorical, not begging answers. Colonel Murray's staff, hard men who loved him, loved this regiment, understood that.

The battle for Seoul would begin on September 24. It was now that Cromwell was given instructions and turned loose. He wasn't the only one, of course. There were other reconnaissance specialists. And on that morning Chesty Puller's 1st Marines began crossing the last river between the division and the capital city that they were about to assault and that they were expected quickly to capture.

But could they do it within the parameters of MacArthur's timetable? Ned Almond paid Marine headquarters one final visit early on the 24th. The Corps commander jeeped into sight and sought out the division's CO, Oliver Smith, who assumed Almond had come up to the front to wish the Marines Godspeed. Instead, perhaps egged on from Tokyo by MacArthur, General Almond threw another tantrum.

If the Marines, and especially the 5th Regiment, fighting steadily since the Inchon landings, didn't get a move on and make real progress in the next twenty-four hours, the Army general would relieve them and order the Army's Seventh Division to spearhead the drive into Seoul.

Smith bit off a retort. No Marine regiment to his knowledge had ever been relieved by the Army. But in his diary, he noted Almond's "complete ignorance" of the fighting qualities of his Marines. As for Almond's naked threat to replace the Marines and his reference to "the next twenty-four hours," Smith drew conclusions. This wasn't Ned talking; this was "his master's voice."

"The next twenty-four hours" would bring them up to September 25, the date MacArthur had set for the liberation of Seoul long before the fight even began.

While on stubborn, deadly little Hill 56, now bypassed and fallen silent, rats scurried across the bodies, and the first dogs, peacetime household pets abandoned by their fleeing owners and gone feral, hungrily nosed the dead, Koreans and Americans both.

▪ 41 ▪

Two days before the Seoul battle ever began, the Allies broke through hundreds of miles to the south. Since June 25, three months ago, the North Koreans had been driving the bus; theirs had been the victories, the towns captured South Korean. Now, at the old Pusan Perimeter, four People's Army divisions crumpled as the ROKs and U.S. troops smashed ahead in an offensive that by September 23 had covered seventy miles. At Masan, also in the south, the U.S. Second and Twenty-fifth Divisions drove a deep salient into the soft midriff of five NK divisions and covered thirty-five miles in three days. On the central front, the British brigade, the ROKs, and the American First Cavalry and Twenty-fourth Division led the parade.

Now, at last, came the turn of Seoul.

At seven o'clock in the morning of September 25, the 1st Marine division jumped off. Twenty thousand men—an entire air wing, three veteran infantry regiments, a regiment of artillery, plus some Korean Marines—were to break the enemy and take the city. And do it in twenty-four hours or be replaced by Almond!

Colonel Puller's 1st Marines were assigned a zone of action a mile wide through the heart of the city, with South Mountain on their right and Ducksoo Palace on the left. The KMCs would follow and mop up. The 5th Marines, with the division recon company and another battalion of KMCs attached, would advance partly through open country and partly within city streets, concentrating on the northwest neighborhoods and Government Palace. Again, the KMCs would mop up. The 7th Regiment (Litzenberg) would skirt the city on the left flank and seize Objective Charlie, the high ground six miles northwest of the city center astride the Seoul-Kaesong road, in order to block enemy flight.

Cromwell was to range ahead of the reconnaissance boys to sniff out the best routes into the heart of the city and the best approaches to Government Palace.

"Report back directly to us, Ollie, not to recon," the regimental intelligence officer told him. "Use your radio to let me know what's going on, what's up there ahead of us, so I can tell Murray. If your radio's broke, send a man back. Best man you've got. If he gets killed, send another. Murray's still down about Hill 56, and he's intent on not getting our troops that badly hurt again. If there's a railroad tunnel waiting to kill Marines, he sure as Christ wants to know about it, y'hear."

"We find a tunnel, you'll know about it. Maybe we'll blow it up first, but you'll sure know where it is and who's inside."

"I know, I know, Ollie, you don't need to be told. But we're all jumpy after yesterday, and with Almond pressuring O. P. Smith, I just want to be sure. Sorry."

"No reason to be, Major." The S-2 was junior to Ollie, but, mindful of Ray Murray's strictures and wanting to keep his nose clean, Cromwell was deferential. Deference didn't cost anything. "We'll give you good intelligence. Ray Murray's been square with me. I won't let him down."

A staff meeting followed.

Suddenly, all around Ollie, men got to their feet, snapping off highballs. General O. P. Smith had just jumped out of his jeep and strode into the small circle of officers, returning the salutes.

"Tell Colonel Murray I'm here. If he has the time, I'd be much obliged if he could join us."

That was Smith, a courteous man.

"That you, Cromwell?"

"Yessir, General."

"You've been out ranging, I hear. Brought in a live one the other night. An NK major?"

"Yessir. Once we kicked his butt and explained the situation, he was anxious to come along."

"Find a few more like that, Cromwell. Seoul isn't going to be a walk-over, and we can use quality intelligence."

Smith turned from Ollie to make a little welcoming motion, and the dozen or so officers closed in a respectful arc around him. The General went on:

"The fact is, the division is hung up, right across the line of advance in half-a-dozen places. General MacArthur's on his tail, which means General Almond's raising hell with me. Tokyo's issuing bulletins to announce the enemy is defeated. Only no one thought to inform the North Koreans. We know the enemy is unbroken and still resisting, and Almond is threatening to relieve this division. You gentlemen know what that means? Passing an Army outfit through the 1st Marine Division to achieve an objective? Something that's never happened before."

Smith didn't have to explain. They all knew it wasn't Marine incompotence or cowardice that was at fault. It was a tough, hard-fighting enemy, the terrible absorbing power of a great city that was swallowing the Marine advance units, sapping their energies and their drive, using up their ammo and their manpower. And with so many radios malfunctioning, the 1st Marine Division was experiencing a general's nightmare, a breakdown in intelligence. . . .

Ray Murray came in quickly then, saluted, and shook Smith's hand, and the two Marine commanders huddled as the others were dismissed.

Cromwell, exiting with the rest of the staff, didn't have to be told more. Find a soft spot somewhere along the front, a weakness the Marines could punch through in order to break out the other side and exploit their gains, to grab this city by the throat and shake it, as Ollie had done back in the rice paddies to that poor little Commie son of a bitch with eyeglasses. And he knew that, as it does in most wars, it would come down to the men—the foot soldiers; to patrols, scribbled messages, and that old reliable, the company runner. And scouts with a little local knowledge like his embassy Marines.

One hole, somewhere along the enemy line, just scout out that one hole. That was the job, finding a weak spot; that was all they needed. One punch, and the rifle battalions would go pouring through. Given a little good dope, the division could take Seoul and screw Ned Almond, too!

The recon company didn't wait around for 7:00 A.M. to get started. They were moving by midnight the night before. Ollie and his embassy Marines, plus a half-dozen Marine scouts, with radios (an extra for backup) were two hours ahead of them, crossing a local stream in rubber boats, and doing it quiet, doing it smooth.

The battle was still shaping up but was generating attention in faraway places. In Moscow the day before, *Pravda* sketched the scene that awaited the Americans in Seoul, melodramatically comparing the Korean capital to the Stalingrad of 1943:

"Cement, streetcar rails, beams and stones are being used to build barricades in the streets, and workers are joining soldiers in the defense. Pillboxes and tank traps dot the scene. Every home a fortress, firing behind every rock. When a soldier is killed, his gun continues to fire, picked up by a worker, a tradesman, an office worker. . . ."

Much of that was the usual party boilerplate—heroic workers springing

to arms! But the North Korean roadblocks were accurately described, except for ignoring the big, heavy, almost impermeable earth-filled burlap rice
sacks derricked into almost every street.

From the first hours of the advance, Marine Corsairs zoomed in low
over the city, providing close air support but suffering their own losses: 3
squadron leaders, all 3 lieutenant colonels, shot down by antiaircraft fire
within two hours, 2 of them getting off with minor injuries, but Lieutenant
Colonel Walter E. Lischeid killed.

From every available road leading into town came not only the infantry
but the Marine tanks, firing high explosives or flame as they came. The
foot soldiers were taking heavy casualties, but here and there across the
front, some North Koreans were quitting. On Hill 105-S, thought to have
been secured two days earlier, a Marine tank rolled up, preparing to fire
into an otherwise-unnoticed cave, when 8 or 10 Reds came out, hands in
the air. When they were not shot down but permitted to surrender unhar-
med, another 120 prisoners emerged, astonishing the Marines. In the end
there were so many of them, the POWs were simply marched to the rear,
escorted by two M-26 tanks. There were also 150 enemy bodies strewn
about 105-South from the earlier fighting. Few of those had faces, the rats
having been busy.

At noon Puller's 1st Marines had taken a city intersection where railroad
tracks intersected with the rails of the Seoul streetcar company. Ollie Cromwell, a mile or two away, had come across a trolley line of his own. Which
by some fluke or miracle, was running, the electricity uncut by either side
or by bomb damage.

"I used to take this line, Colonel," Lonesome reported. "I had a girl
the other end of it." He seemed pleased to have had a girl.

"Good. Now where does it take us if we follow it, where do we end
up?"

Lonesome gave him a reasonably accurate description of the neighborhoods ahead. What he couldn't say was how strongly they were being defended. So far that morning, deftly bypassing enemy strong points and
dodging firefights, Cromwell's people radioed back precise map coordinates
for the artillery gunners and air support. As well as for Murray's S-2 and
the regimental CO himself. Ollie had always been pretty good at maps, and
Buggy was there to question the few civilians not cowering in cellars, to
cross-reference exact locations if the maps were vague or confused. They
also picked up a North Korean deserter, who, once he realized they weren't
going to shoot him, proved gratefully voluble, providing name, rank, serial

number, and lots more. The prisoner's name was Park, and Ollie named him "Central" on the spot.

"We been lucky," Buggy said. And Ollie knew how right he was. It was already early afternoon; their recon patrol had been inside the capital for more than twelve hours, and they hadn't lost a man. And it wasn't only the People's Army they were ducking but incoming UN artillery and the strafing runs of their own air wing Corsairs. Talk about unfriendly fire.

At some point, the luck always changed. It had on Makin and in plenty of fights since. No reason Seoul would be different.

"Keep an eye on Central, Buggy. We can use this boy, and I don't want to lose him."

"Aye aye, sir."

In Tokyo MacArthur read the reports coming in, spoke once with Ned Almond, discussed the fight over a map table with General Willoughby, his G-2 and cheerleader in charge.

On the basis of what he'd been told by Willoughby, much of it errorneous, blended with his own wishful thinking, the general now called in an aide and dictated this communiqué, to be held until sometime tomorrow, September 26, and then released:

"Three months to the day after the North Koreans launched their surprise attack, the combat troops of X Corps recaptured the capital city of Seoul. By 1400 hours (2:00 P.M.) 25 September, the military defenses of Seoul were broken. The enemy is fleeing the city to the northeast."

When Marine general Smith and the 1st Mar Div eventually saw and read the self-congratulatory MacArthur message, they noted it contained no mention of just which "combat troops" "liberated" the city.

"The Coldstream Guards?" one of his division staff wondered mischievously.

An oversight? MacArthur was a calculating man not known for oversights. If he hadn't mentioned the Marines, the omission was intended.

At two that afternoon, September 25, when Seoul was supposed to have been secured, three Marine infantry regiments were still attacking, nearly twenty thousand men grappling within the city in deadly close-range battle with thousands of North Korean regulars fighting to throw back these heavily armed, canvas-legginged Americans with their flame-throwing tanks and air strikes. Street by street, building by building, the advancing Marines slogged ahead, leaving their dead behind them at the barricades and on the pavements of almost every bloody intersection.

Later that afternoon Cromwell was ordered home.

"Ray wants to see you, Ollie. Wants to pick your alleged brains. Where we go next."

"We'll be there."

Regiment supplied the map coordinates so Cromwell would know where to meet Murray, how to make his way back.

"You think maybe the Reds are quitting, Colonel?" one of the two radiomen asked.

"Don't know. Doesn't sound like it to me."

Nor did it. The crackle of small-arms fire and the heavier cough of field artillery continued without slackening, punctuated by the even-heavier thuds of bombs. It was a hot day, and the dust from the fighting hung in the heavy air so that men squinted.

They ran into only one enemy patrol on their way in, and the four NK men, even more surprised than the Marines, were quickly gunned down. Three were dead, one shot through the shoulder, and they hustled him along with them, rigging a primitive sling and tourniquet while taking care to stuff a bandanna into the wounded man's mouth and knot it around his throat as a gag.

Prisoners. Best intelligence there was. Nothing much had changed about that since Caesar's *Gallic Wars*. Never would change, Ollie supposed.

"Keep tabs on that statesman, Buggy. And Central, too. I want to turn those boys over to regiment."

"Aye aye, sir."

The Cromwell patrol was back inside 5th Marine lines before dusk. Ollie turned over his prisoners and was debriefed by the intelligence officer and, for part of the time, by Ray Murray.

"General Smith says we're going to take Seoul tomorrow or the day after, Cromwell. Not because it's MacArthur's schedule but because the longer a fight goes on, the more Marines we lose. I want Seoul but don't want to lose a thousand Marines doing it. We'll be jumping off again at dawn. Try to get a few hours' sleep if you can. Just crap out on the sidewalk or in a doorway if you find one unoccupied. That's what we're all doing. I want you and your scouts out there even earlier. Your patrol and the recon company gave us pretty good stuff today. I want more of it. Knowing what we're going up against will help us win, save Marine lives. You understand?"

"I do, sir."

"Okay, you and the S-2 work out your program for tomorrow morning. Good luck, and don't get yourself killed."

"No, sir."

"Good. Evans Carlson did some crazy things, Ollie. But he outlived the war and died in bed. Keep that in mind."

"Yes, sir."

So it was all settled. Except that it wasn't. No one was going to get much sleep. On sidewalks or anywhere else.

At 2009 that evening, nine minutes after 8:00 P.M., the sun near down and a late summer's darkness already falling over the city and its battlefront, an urgent message came down to Oliver Smith at 1st Marine Division headquarters in a textile factory. Outside the building, Marines littered the streets and sidewalks—exhausted men who'd been fighting for weeks and, on this particular day, since dawn. They were gobbling a meal out of cans, unheated, and then curling up or stretching out in doorways, in the gutters. It was a 50 percent watch. Half the men stayed awake, weapons at the ready. The other half tried to sleep, helmets used as pillows, field shoes and leggings on and snugly tight, rifles clutched and ready. Every so often a man got up, awkwardly, cautiously, to vanish down an alleyway or around a corner and move his bowels on the pavement or urinate against the nearest wall. The men were tired and sweaty, and they stank.

And in the morning they would try to pitchfork out of here the men who captured the city three months ago. Drive them out or kill them.

Except that a message came down from X Corps.

It was addressed to General O. P. Smith, who had been chewed out and told that unless his Marines got moving, an Army division would do the job for them. Here was the message that reached a tired man leading a tired command:

". . . enemy fleeing city of Seoul on road north of Uijongbu. . . . He [Tac Air] is conducting heavy air attack and will continue same. You will push attack now to the limit of your objectives in order to insure maximum destruction of enemy forces. Signed Almond."

The message, at this hour and in this form, was so absurd, Smith's G-3 immediately called Corps for corroboration. Had someone up there gone nuts? Could our pilots at this hour determine if the people streaming out of town were refugees or retreating enemy troops? The Marine ops officer was told that, yes, X Corps wanted the Marine attack to be "executed without delay."

O. P. Smith was still incredulous. He called the X Corps chief of staff for confirmation, pointing out "the inadvisability of attacking at night in an unfamiliar Oriental city of the size and complexity of Seoul, particularly as there was no indication of the enemy fleeing from the division front."

General Ruffner told the Marine commander, "General Almond himself dictated the message, and it was to be executed without delay."

Smith issued the attack order to Puller and Murray, directing them to coordinate efforts and confine them to avenues of advance through the streets and the city's neighborhoods, which could be identified by night. As he issued the orders, he was haunted by the specter of the two regiments straying in the dark, wandering into the other's zone, and getting into a firefight with fellow Marines.

By now an enemy counterattack had hit the 3rd Battalion of Murray's 5th Marines. Far from fleeing the city as Almond claimed, the North Koreans were attacking.

At five minutes after 10:00 P.M. the 1st Marines had their orders from Smith, and ten minutes later the 5th Marines received theirs. By now, many of the exhausted troops were asleep, no matter the hour or the discomfort. A tired man can sleep standing up, like a horse, and it was the sergeants who went from man to man, waking troops who'd expected to sleep until dawn; not only waking them but telling them to check their weapons and ammo, since they were about to go on the offensive.

Most men were too stupefied even to bitch. Like herded cattle they got to their feet to shuffle into squad and platoon formations while the NCOs called the roll and counted off. A runner came for Cromwell, who had just gone to sleep.

"Colonel wants you, sir. We're jumping off."

Ollie looked at the just-visible dial of his watch.

"Ten-thirty, Buggy. That what you've got?"

"Just about, Colonel."

Buggy woke Lonesome, and the two of them roused the other scouts. Now, in the dark, Cromwell, dashing water from a canteen into cupped palms and then scrubbing his face wetly into wakefulness, was more alert, thinking that in the dark the 5th Marines would be more reliant than ever on a PFC named Lonesome and on Sergeant Will Buggy and their familiarity with the city, its people, and its ways.

Around him men filled canteens from a water trailer towed behind a six-by truck. You could fight on an empty stomach, but you couldn't fight thirsty. A few men opened cans of C-rations anyway and ate them cold, standing or sitting on street curbs. Men used flashlights or the light from burning buildings to study maps. The lights made it difficult to maintain good night vision. And night vision was one thing a scout needed while prowling through a ghostly city in the dark.

The attack was scheduled to begin at 1:45 A.M. of September 26, following fifteen minutes of Marine artillery fire in preparation. Then, at 1:38, judging the preparations were inadequate, Puller ordered the assault battalions to stand fast and preparatory fire to be repeated. A new jump-off time of 2:00 A.M. was set, but then came a flash from Puller's 1st Battalion. Lieutenant Colonel Ridge reported that as his Marines were preparing to attack, a very heavy force of the enemy, supported by tanks and self-propelled guns, was moving toward him down the main avenue from the center of the city to the southwest in the zone of the 1st Marines.

Almond had ordered a night attack because the enemy was in flight and he wanted to catch and destroy them. But here on the ground, where men dealt in reality and not in a cuckoo-land concocted to please Tokyo, the North Koreans weren't retreating but mounting their own nighttime attack in force. Ten hours before all this, hundreds of miles away, General MacArthur had dictated and would shortly issue to the world an entirely phony communiqué announcing Seoul had fallen.

Before the Marine attack was postponed, before word came down of an enemy counterattack, Ollie Cromwell and his scouts and the division recon company were already out in front of the Marine lines under orders to scout ahead of the infantry and to radio back enemy displacements, strength, and intentions. Fortunately, they were not the only Marines out there and taking notes. The 3rd Battalion of Puller's 1st Regiment had sent a patrol of eight Marines and three Koreans under Corporal Charles E. Collins to find and make contact with a similar patrol from the 5th Marines. But at 1:30 A.M. the Collins patrol was scuttling back into friendly lines following a firefight just four hundred yards out, and reporting to Major Ed Simmons that Collins was missing. They'd seen two enemy tanks approaching a George Company roadblock defended by heavy machine guns, 3.5-inch rocket launchers, and .75-millimeter recoilless guns. As the tanks rolled up, one was immediately destroyed, and the other was hit and fell back.

Now, on his own and without reference to the appalling Almond, General O. P. Smith postponed the division attack, with all Marine artillery ordered to fire at will on the advancing North Koreans. By 3:00 A.M. the Marine fire on the advancing NK forces was so intense that his own artillery officer warned Chesty Puller against burning out their howitzer tubes. During the lull between then and break of day, enemy infantry attacks had petered out, but the Russian tanks continued to roll up firing at the Marine lines until, at 6:30, the last two T-34s were knocked out.

It was then that Corporal Collins, missing and presumed dead, reappeared. Working his way home through enemy, and friendly, fire, he was now (inexplicably) wearing Korean civvies as camouflage. During this fight in the heart of the city, the North Koreans lost between 475 and 500 infantrymen of the Twenty-fifth Brigade, and another 83 had been taken prisoner.

Marine casualties were light.

Elsewhere on the front, as the inner-city fight tapered down, a battalion of North Koreans hit the Army's Thirty-second Infantry on South Mountain and overran the Army positions. At 7:00 A.M. a spirited counterattack drove the enemy back, leaving behind them on the Army front 394 dead and 174 North Korean prisoners. To the Marines, it looked as if maybe some of these dogfaces could fight after all. They weren't *all* like Ned Almond.

At daybreak the first few Korean civilians edged out tentatively into their own streets, and then, wanting to be sure, they waited a time before smiling and waving at the Americans. What kind of city capture was this? No looting, no rapes, no men shoved against stone walls and shot? For political reasons, so that UN forces would be seen not as aggressors but simply as taking back for the Koreans their own capital city, an ROK regiment was supposed to be heroically there in the front lines. The ROKs seemed to be a bit late. In all fairness, at some strong points the NK fought harder than at others. The ROKs might not be to blame for falling behind schedule.

Smith and the 1st Marine Division weren't concerned about the political rationale. But on purely military grounds they realized any claims that the city had fallen were, at the very least, premature. The Marines still stood where they had the night before. And to the north, just outside the city, the 7th Marines, in their flanking movement to cut off retreat and seal in Seoul against reinforcement, were fighting desperately to relieve Dog Company, trapped behind enemy lines and in danger of being wiped out.

▪ 42 ▪

With half the city taken, much of it on fire, the battered capital dome continued to fly the North Korean flag. Did that mean the enemy still held the building, or simply that nobody had thought of hauling down the flag and running up a South Korean banner? Not important. In chaotic fighting in built-up areas, the opposing sides might occupy different floors of the same building, rolling grenades downstairs or lobbing them up through open windows, firing blind through floors and ceilings. Troops might enter a building by leaping from adjacent roofs, blowing open skylights, and dropping into attics to flush out the enemy floor by floor on the way down. Or squirming through basement windows and then working their way through dusty crawl spaces and up staircases, floor by bloody floor. Outside, in the streets, the fighting was much like that as well: street by street, intersection by intersection. Men dropped down into sewers to make their way a block north or south, a block east or west, and then they popped up to take an enemy barricade from the rear with automatic weapons, blasting their way. And sometimes being blasted themselves by enemy soldiers who also knew the sewer trick and were waiting. While above the battle of NK regulars and the U.S. Marines, artillery dueled and low-flying planes strafed and bombed and scared hell out of both sides.

"Give me a stinking rice paddy, a lousy coral beach anytime." A Marine veteran might breathe a prayer, never having previously fought in and for a big city.

Cromwell's patrol had been fortunate. It was the rifle companies of the 5th Regiment (and of Puller's 1st Marines) that did the house-by-house fighting. On a recon patrol like this, you ducked a fight if you could. You slipped through and came out the other side whole and radioed back what you'd seen or heard or even suspected.

"Got that, got that?" Ollie would shout into the radio handset as someone at regiment took down coordinates and jotted notes and recorded the time. And then, to be sure, they read them back to their scout Cromwell.

"Buggy! What's next? What do we have coming up after we get past this factory?"

"A school, sir. Least I think it's a school. What street is this, Lonesome?"

"Sign's been shot to hell, Sarge. Damned if I know. I don't remember no school around here. Never did hang around schoolyards."

So Ollie sent a two-man scout team sprinting and then crawling and then wriggling on their bellies through the littered streets to the next turning, peeking around corners and taking notes, and then wriggling, crawling, and sprinting back with a breathless report.

"It's a goddamned church, Colonel," the scout reported blasphemously. "Hell of a big cross on top. No school I can see."

A cross? That made sense. Wasn't Old Man Rhee a Baptist? Or was he Presbyterian?

"Hell!"

"Any gooks?" Buggy asked, getting to the point.

"Didn't see none. Church looks bombed out, but it ain't on fire."

"Okay, let's move out," Cromwell ordered. And they did.

And then, two blocks further on, they repeated the drill. On some streets, every two or three hundred yards, rice-bag barriers eight feet tall and thick had been set up, to be fiercely defended by Red infantry. As the reconnaissance patrols called back the locations of such barriers, an M-26 tank might be summoned and sent in with its accompanying Marine riflemen. At one barricade a lone North Korean lugging a huge satchel charge suddenly dashed out from behind his rice bags and tossed the satchel atop the tank, where it went off, damaging the tank and hurling the NK attacker through the air to bounce off a brick wall. Surprising the onlooking Marines, the man scrambled quickly to his feet, seemingly unhurt, and raced around a corner and out of sight, while from the disabled tank its shaken, somewhat woozy crewmen crawled out and staggered away to shelter from shots coming their way from the rice bags. The tankers looked worse off than the guy who blew them up. A lot worse, blood running from their ears.

Toward ten o'clock in the morning, while they worked their way through the warehouses and factories of an industrial area, Cromwell's radio operator shoved the handset at him.

"They want you, Colonel."

"Cromwell here."

It was an ops major.

"Ollie, got your map?"

"Yeah."

The major gave him a set of coordinates.

"One of our rifle platoons is hung up just north of a railroad round-house. Got any roundhouses on your map?"

"Doesn't show any. But I've got the coordinates. Want me to go up there?"

"Yeah, our people lost their lieutenant and are stalled under very heavy fire. Before we call in air or an artillery strike, I'd like some more precise info. Don't want to wipe out a Marine rifle platoon by mistake."

"I got you. We'll call back when we find the roundhouse. Buggy! Get over here. You know any roundhouses in this neck of the woods?"

Lonesome might.

"There're railroad tracks behind the warehouse. They got to lead some-where. A roundhouse sounds about right to me."

"Okay, let's move."

There was a roundhouse, and it was already occupied by one decrepit steam locomotive and a handful of Marines using small windows on the second floor under the eaves to fire down at the rice-bag barricades that had their rifle platoon stopped. A corporal got up from where he was kneeling when he saw Cromwell.

"Yessir, can I help the colonel?"

That's what we like, Ollie thought, *polite young NCOs who don't let a little firefight fluster them.*

"Yeah, Corporal. Where's your platoon leader?"

"He got hit. We dragged him down the street out of the way. Platoon sergeant's down there trying to figure out how we get past these boys without all of us getting kilt. There's a shit pot full of Reds behind them bags, sir. And a big Russki tank backing 'em up. We ain't getting nowhere with those boys."

"You got a mortar?"

"No, sir. Wisht I did."

Cromwell called up the radioman. "Get regiment, the ops major. Tell him we're inside the roundhouse."

After a moment or two the radioman shook his head.

"Can't get through, Colonel."

"Keep cranking it. He wants a report from us. I've got to tell him about that tank."

Lonesome tugged at Buggy's sleeve, and the two spoke for a bit. "What is it?" Ollie asked impatiently. He didn't like a couple of his men whispering while he just stood there. Buggy answered, looking sheepish.

"There's tracks leading out of this place up the street to them rice bags, sir. Lonesome says maybe we could drive this steam engine out of here loaded up with Marines and crash right through that there barricade."

"Lonesome said that?"

"Yes, he did, sir." Buggy clearly didn't want this crackpot idea blamed on him.

Ollie looked at his PFC.

"Not a bad idea, Lonesome. If we knew how to operate a roundtable and then if we had someone to drive the locomotive."

"Yessir, but I was thinking, if Higgins could do it, why not us?"

"Higgins? Who's Higgins?"

"That Higgins which stole the steam engine a couple days ago and drove it right up to Colonel Murray's CP and got chewed out for it. That Higgins."

"Oh, that Higgins."

The radio still wasn't working, and Cromwell ducked out a back door and then crawled over the littered and pockmarked street to where the pinned-down rifle platoon was deployed. A staff sergeant crawled back to meet him.

"Name of Mueller, sir. Platoon sergeant. Our lieutenant's down, and I'm commanding."

Ollie asked a few questions, and the sergeant explained the position.

"We been pinned down here more than an hour, Colonel. Without mortars or calling in an air strike, I don't see no way twenty riflemen gonna make it up the street to them rice bags and—if we get there—get over 'em without us all getting killed."

"I don't either, Sergeant. Maybe get up on the rooftops and try to work your way parallel to the street and fire down on them?"

"I sent one fire team up there already, Colonel. Lost three men. The one who got back says the Reds got people on the rooftops too and they seen our boys coming."

"I'll call in an air strike if I can get through. Oh, yeah, you got a Marine used to work on the railroads?"

Ollie expected a "no, sir" or a weird look. Instead: "Yessir, I got Peachy what claims he used to be a brakeman on the Union Pacific or Southern Pacific or both. But he got hisself shot."

"Dead?"

"No, he's walking wounded. You want him?"

"Hell, yes, Sergeant. And quick! And give me a runner so I can send back word about air support."

"Yessir."

Back at the roundhouse, still no radio contact. But now they had Peachy, who came limping in and cursing.

"What's wrong with you?" Buggy demanded, intolerant of wounded who could still walk.

"For one thing, I got shot. For the other, this got to be the crappiest roundhouse ever. Look at this place! They canned people at Southern Pacific for a lot less."

"That's fine, Peachy," Ollie said crisply. "Maybe we'll get it properly policed up after the war. Meanwhile, you know how to turn on the roundtable? Move that steam engine?"

"There ain't no power, Colonel."

Ollie slumped. Power, of course they'd need power.

"But maybe we can override it manually. Put a few huskies on the winches, we can probably move it. But first of all, start getting steam up on that engine. Steam engines run on steam. Send a boy up there to shovel in the coal. I'll shout up to him what to do next."

"The hell you will, Peachy. I'm promoting you to chief engineer! Buggy! Lift Ol' Peachy up there on his good leg. And detail a couple of men to help him out. Do whatever he says. We've got ourselves a railroad man."

"A brakeman, colonel. I don't claim no more than honest brakeman. Apprenticed out proper and got promoted brakeman."

"No time for modesty, Peachy. You get that steam up and tell my people how to get this roundtable moving, and we can get on with the war. 'Peachy for Congress!' by damn. Make you chief engineer besides."

Buggy stared at Colonel Cromwell. This was a playful side of the man he hadn't seen before. All this fighting seemed to have cheered him up.

Buggy was right. The Ollie Cromwell barking orders now about locomotives and flattering Marines named Peachy was a Cromwell who dated back to 1942 and to a crazy man named Carlson who could see around corners, walk on water, and march his Marines fifty miles in a day.

This was Marine Raider Cromwell enjoying himself and fighting another unorthodox war. Your radio's gone dead, and you can't call up the fly boys? Remember Makin Island and improvise! That was Carlson's mantra: meditate, calculate, improvise—and forget the training manuals. The rubber boats swamp? You bribe the chief and hire war canoes from the headhunters, and you paddle your way to Australia.

Except that this time, you "borrow" someone's locomotive and drive it out the front door of a roundhouse at flank speed with a short platoon of Marines hanging from the sides, firing their weapons and tossing grenades, knocking over some rice bags and running down North Korean regulars as you go, and the other side of the rice bags, you smash the sonuvabitch into the muzzle of a Russki tank before it gets a chance to shoot at you.

Pretty good plan if I do say so m'self, Ollie thought, cheerfully plagiarizing Lonesome.

Not fifteen minutes had passed, with enemy small-arms fire still coming in through the smashed windows and ricocheting off the roundhouse walls, when an impatient Cromwell called up to the locomotive's cab.

"Can't you hurry it up?"

"Doing my best, Colonel," said Peachy. "These old 214 Class engines, they're good. But they don't prime easy."

Next to the wounded railroader two Marines shoveled steadily, one stripped to the waist, both heaving and sweating, the smaller of the two cursing steadily and imaginatively without ever repeating an oath.

"If I wanted to shovel frigging coal for a living, I coulda stayed in West Virginia."

"Well, just hurry it."

By now the enemy T-34 tank had moved up closer to an aperture in the barricade of rice bags. The North Korean officer commanding, whoever he was, wasn't stupid. He knew the damned Americans were up to something. All this coming and going at the old roundhouse.

"Radio?" Ollie called out.

"Nothing, sir. She's still dead."

If only regiment could get the word and send up a couple of M-26 tanks. They wouldn't even need an air strike. Just one tank could blast this damned roadblock out of here in no time.

It was at times and places like this that infantry forgot its contempt for aviation or the gunners and even for the tanks. Combat reordered the priorities. They could sure use a tank here. Or a small mortar, a .60 or, better still, an .81. There were limitations as to what even the best infantry could do alone up against the rice bags of Seoul. An ordinary rifleman could see that and put aside biases.

Ollie scanned the wrecked roundhouse. Looked like a South Bend bar on a football Saturday night. But if he was frustrated, just think of platoon sergeant Mueller. His lieutenant was down, his 35 or 40 men were pared to 17 ór 18 capables, and it was *his* platoon. Mueller knew these men, had served with them at Pendleton, crossed the Pacific and fought at Pusan beside them. They'd come over the freaking seawall at Inchon together. And now? Half of them were out there sprawled dead or dying on the crummy streets and sidewalks of a warehouse district of a lousy town they'd never heard of three months ago, had never even seen until day before yesterday.

A town that Douglas ("Himself") MacArthur had already informed everyone was now in friendly hands, with the locals cheering and strewing flowers and singing Te Deums at the cathedral. And unless they and their hotshot colonel figured out some way around those rice bags, Mueller and the rest of the platoon would be sprawled dead on the sidewalk.

"Whomp!"

The first shell from the T–34 ripped through one wall of the roundhouse, passing just over the locomotive and out the building's other side, smashing brick as it flew.

Sergeant Buggy, standing at Cromwell's side, ducked instinctively, if a bit late, before lifting up to remark appreciatively, "Looks like they got this place ranged in pretty good, Colonel. That was a nice shot for a first one."

"Yes, it was, Buggy. Very nice."

There was little point to yelling at poor Peachy. He'd heard the tank shell come through considerably closer to him and his two colliers up there in the cab than to Colonel What'shisname or anyone else down there on the roundhouse floor at track level. That shell could have decapitated Peachy and his stokers both. In combat everything is relative, the street-level concrete floor safer than the engine cab. In a firefight there are no rear-echelon pogues, are there?

Finally, to the accompaniment of Buggy's grumbling and the impatient pacing of Colonel Cromwell, the first heavy panting of the huge engine began, its first sign of life. That was Peachy and his shovelers, while other Marines leaned sweating on the manual winches that were easing the reluctant roundtable into position so the set of tracks heading out would be aligned with those atop the table.

"Still no radio, sir."

"Shit!" What else was there to say?

Just then, with steam getting up, a second high-velocity Russian tank shell streaked through the old roundhouse only inches too high, and as Ollie's stomach fell sickeningly, at that very instant the roundtable creakily and grudgingly was swiveling, positioning the locomotive to barrel out of here at top speed for the enemy strong point holding up the Marine advance and the liberation of Seoul, South Korea.

The capital city MacArthur said we captured yesterday.

"Colonel!" Peachy cried. "We're lined up, and we got steam!"

"Good man, Peachy. You can drive my locomotive anytime, anywhere."

Then, "Buggy!"

"Yessir."

"Get 'em aboard, you and Sergeant Mueller. Everyone, locked and loaded. And as many grenades as they've got."

"Aye aye, Colonel."

"The wounded?" That was Buggy asking.

"We'll come back after we take the rice bags. Get 'em next trip."

"Aye aye, sir." Buggy noticed Cromwell's face, split in a lopsided and slightly goofy half-scowl, half-grin. The colonel was having fun.

"Get it rolling, Peachy. Just ram it through the damned door and don't slow or stop. I don't care if they shoot hell out of this thing! Just go and keep going!"

"We'll be high-ballin', Colonel. We'll get the bastards."

"Man sounds like he means it, Sergeant Buggy."

"He surely does, Colonel."

And with a great and faster series of noisy pants, the old engine began to roll ahead, pausing momentarily as it came up against the big overhead door. Then, as the door splintered, broke and shattered into pieces at either side, the engine burst through into the sunshine and rolled powerfully ahead and with increasing speed toward the deadly barricade of rice bags and its stubborn North Korean defenders, a few of whom were already backing away from something none of them had ever before faced—a full-sized steam locomotive under power and heading for them, with American Marines hanging all over it, firing and lobbing grenades as they came, covering the hundred yards or so in what seemed a few seconds.

"By the Christ!" shouted Buggy happily as they smashed into and then through the rice bags. "They never seen nothing like this, I'll bet!"

"No one else ever has either, Sergeant. No one," Cromwell shouted above the deafening roar and the gunfire, every bit as excited as his sergeant, who was by now cursing in tongues.

Both sides were still firing, the Russki tank and the crazy Marines, the ragtag remnants of Mueller's battered rifle platoon and its temporary commanding officer, James T. Cromwell, late of Carlson's Raiders.

Though you couldn't hear individual guns or make out the shouted words, the yelling and the manic laughter—not over the thunder and metallic ripping and escaping steam of the crash as the giant steam engine crunched through the rice bags and headed straight on for the muzzle of the T-34's big gun, Cromwell and all of them squeezing off shots at the fast-closing Russian tank.

"Meat and drink, men!" Ollie yelled joyously, echoing the late Gunny Arzt. "It's meat and drink."

Colonel Cromwell was back in the war.

▪ 43 ▪

REMEMBERING RICHARD LIONHEART GOING OVER THE WALLS OF ACRE
AGAINST SALADIN.

There wasn't much pain. Ollie had been wounded before, and he knew about pain and tolerated it reasonably well. But with a wound like this, he would have expected to feel much worse. Maybe the nurses were spoiling him, boosting the dosage of painkillers without telling him. Maybe without doctors' orders? He recalled Adelaide, the hospital there after Saipan, and the little redhead with freckles. She took pretty good care of him, too. Nurses, even the most professional of them, empathized with all their patients but had a weakness for a certain breed of man. Or was that just Ollie fantasizing? He had no fever, not that he knew of, certainly no symptoms of fever—sweats and shaking—so it couldn't be hallucinations, could it?

He was on the hospital ship *Consolation,* anchored a couple of miles off Inchon—a big, white-painted floating hospital of six hundred beds. The *Consolation* could treat you for cardiac, cure a social disease, remove your tonsils, saw off a limb, do root canal, or perform an autopsy—could probably deliver a baby. Being a field-grade officer, a Marine colonel, Ollie had a room to himself, complete with porthole, through which from his bed he could just see the shore. Korea. Wolmi-do, and the seawall. Peaceful now in the autumn haze. Nothing like that morning Marines scaled the wall with the ladders and dove or rolled over the top, making themselves small under fire, the way men always tried to do in an opposed assault. They never quite succeeded in getting small enough. He wondered if Richard Lionheart's crusaders, with their siege ladders going over the walls of Acre against Saladin and his boys, tried to make themselves small as well.

He supposed they did. Wars changed in the details; soldiers pretty much stayed the same.

On the upper decks of *Consolation,* the less seriously wounded and the convalescent took the air. The mood was cheerful; these were the survivors. Summer was ended; so too the long campaign these men had fought in sapping heat and drenching rains, and now in early autumn nurses and orderlies bundled them in blankets and pullovers against a cool breeze off the Yellow Sea. It wasn't cold yet, not really, but October meant the cold was coming. The summer campaign was over, and, if the brass had any sense, winter quarters beckoned. Cromwell's nurses chattered about the changing weather, and so did ambulatory woundeds who dropped by his stateroom to see the colonel and to inquire, politely of course, had Ollie really driven a locomotive through that enemy roadblock? Or was that just the usual Marine grabass? There was talk of a decoration, perhaps even the Navy Cross. That, for sure, wasn't just grabass. Hooked up to the intravenous and other tubes, Ollie was at the mercy of visitors and the staff, beached here in his room. He wished he could get out there himself into the open air on deck. Catch a little sun, maybe sneak a smoke.

Ollie tried to roll over in the bed, couldn't, accepted the fact, and just lay there. Remembering.

When you're really sick (that malaria after the 'Canal) or badly hurt as he was now and had been before, you shelter in the past. The present being too painful, too real. So to console himself he thought instead of Coach Kennedy at Regis and how his pitted, pleasant face grinned when you made a good play or the small school's teams took a game they had no business winning. Thought, too, of waking at the Breakers with Winter lying next to him and the Palm Beach sun coming through windows and the morning ocean just outside and beckoning. Of that night in the Berlin *brauhaus* when he and his dad drew close and tipsily sang the "Du, du" song. Ollie thought of Nan Murdoch pedaling him on her bike to the beach at Adelaide and telling him about her husband and "best mate" dead at Monte Cassino. Of Gunny Arzt and his Studebaker. Of San Diego with the fleet in. And of the dead Japanese everywhere and hatchet-faced Evans Carlson and the sun off Jimmy Roosevelt's bald dome. He thought of Darcy's little red M.G. speeding across the Golden Gate Bridge. And of a young Ben Sweet coming at him in the campus gloom, feet shuffling through the damp leaves of a South Bend dusk.

He fell asleep just where he was. Might as well dream for awhile. He'd had sufficient reality for now.

▪ 44 ▪

Colonel, you have a visitor."

PFC McGraw came into the room looking shy, helmet in hand, a rifle still slung. Ollie wondered how he got on a hospital ship under arms. Weren't there Geneva Conventions . . . ?

"Lonesome! How the hell did you get out here? I thought you had to be shot up or at least be an admiral to get aboard *Consolation*."

"Well, sir, I ain't shot, and I'm still bucking for corporal."

"Then, how . . . ?

"Oh, I give 'em a sob story. Colonel Cromwell got me out of reform school and into the Crotch, saved my life half-a-dozen times between Pusan and Seoul, rescued me from drowning on the mudflats that morning we came over the seawall. How if I ever had a kid we'd name the little bastard for you. The usual crap Marines tell swabbies."

The nurse, one of those with a few miles on her, and protective of the naval service, cleared her throat.

"I'll be back in ten minutes, Colonel. Then he's out of here and smartly, too."

"Take a pew, Lonesome. She won't be back for awhile."

"Nossir, I got to get back to the division, or I'll miss the boat and get shot for going over the hill. We're heading up somewhere in North Korea by ship to finish off the Commies and win the damned war. But I wanted to say good-bye and that I hope you're okay and thanks for everything. I'm sorry I never made corporal so you'd be proud of me. . . ."

"Hell, I'm proud of you as you are. But I wouldn't be surprised if you didn't make corporal before year's out. Maybe get you a Bronze Star or something, too. For coming up with that idea about the steam engine. Where's Buggy? He okay?"

"Not exactly, Colonel."

"What's that mean, Lonesome?" Ollie tensed, knowing something bad was coming.

"Well, you remember how we run off them Commie bastards in the steam engine? Sergeant was laughing and telling everyone that was the damnedest thing he ever saw. Riding locomotives to the freaking war like we was kings . . ."

"Yes . . . ?" Cromwell knew the boy would get to the point eventually, and he appreciated that he'd come.

"Yessir, well, after you got shot, you was yelling too. And cursing up a storm. Something about Roosevelt's bald head and Japs shooting at it. I asked what that was all about, did the colonel really serve with the president, and sergeant, he told me to shut the hell up, that if Colonel Cromwell had stuff on his mind, it must be important."

Ollie waited, then, "What about Buggy? What about the sergeant?"

"Well, sir, him and some of the others thought, after you got hit, that the steam engine deal worked so good the first time on that Russki tank, they ought to try it again. The steam was up, and the engine was still running, and ol' Buggy, he was pissed off about you getting hit, and all for it."

"Yes?" He liked it that Buggy was sore he'd been hit. Sometimes these old sergeants didn't really care about anyone but themselves and doing the job.

"I ast him, 'Sarge, is the Colonel gonna die?' and he says, 'No, there's some sons of bitches you can't kill.'

"Yessir, that Buggy, he just went nuts then, cursing out them Commies and yelling in lingos I never heard."

"It's called 'the gift of tongues,' Lonesome," Ollie said, being gentle about it.

"But this time," Lonesome continued, "we didn't know about that there was a surprise coming at the next corner. We just kept rolling like to win the freaking war all by ourselves, Sergeant and ol' Peachy and them two boys shoveling and you lying there on the deck moaning, and the rest of us hanging on for dear life and raising hell. And just when that Peachy got her cranked up and locked and loaded, rolling even faster along them tracks, firing BARs and machine guns and lobbing what grenades we got left, with Commies falling and twitching all about, and the ones we didn't hit throwing down their weapons and bugging out, like they was our lousy ROKs and scared as hell, not like good Commie regulars . . . our loco-motive was booming along now, doing twenty, maybe thirty miles an hour, and Buggy pulling on that whistle, *woooooeeeee,* when another big ol' T-34 we never seen nor even knew about just came out of nowhere, around the corner, where the train slowed to make the curve, and they blew the shit out of our flank, the locomotive you liberated, just hammered it. Sergeant

Buggy and ol' Peachy went up, both of 'em with the same damned shot. The shovel boys are okay, though, Colonel. Them and the rest of us jumped off the worse for wear and dragging you with us, while she was on fire and still rolling amid burning black smoke and the stinking coal. You never saw nothing like it, Colonel."

"So the sergeant's dead."

"Yessir, Colonel, him and Peachy. Which is why I come. I didn't want you to hear the bad news from no one else but only from someone that thought highly of Will Buggy, like the way the colonel did, sir."

Lonesome fell silent, having talked himself out, and Ollie wanted to cheer him a little and get his mind off the dead Buggy. So he asked him about the division going north, chasing the Commies all the way to the Chinese border.

"Wish I could go with you, Lonesome. The boys hot to trot, are they?"

"Some are, sure, Colonel. Like always, the crazy ones. But a lot of us, we think maybe General MacArthur's pressing his luck, getting us in over our heads. I dunno, but that's what some are saying."

"They said that about Inchon, too."

"Yessir," the Marine said, but grudgingly.

Cromwell lay there after he left, thinking about Buggy blowing the train whistle and clearing the grade crossings with Peachy driving the bastard and those boys shoveling coal into the furnace, and about how young Lonesome had come to deliver a proper eulogy, when the floor nurse, this one a young blonde and pretty, came in to put him to sleep.

"I'll be giving you a shot now, Colonel."

"Yes, ma'am," he said obediently. And starting to hurt.

The other nurse woke him early next morning, the battle-ax, sounding peevish:

"Why they let you have so many visitors, I can't understand."

This latest sickroom visitor was General O. P. Smith, commanding general of the 1st Marine Division, maybe that was why.

"Cromwell, there are too many of my officers dead or aboard this ship. Just when the division is boarding ship and heading north, some of my best men aren't going with me."

"Like nothing better, General."

"How are you? They treating you okay?"

"Just fine, General. I could do without the bedpan and these tubes in me. But the nurses are fine. A few of them pretty nice to look at, too."

Smith, unlike Lonesome, pulled a straight-backed chair up to the bed-side.

"We're going north, Cromwell, and I wish we weren't. Too late in the year to mount a major offensive into mountains with winter coming on. You're well out of it."

"So MacArthur will have his way."

"He will," said Smith. "They're afraid of him in Washington. Even the joint chiefs, even Bradley, saintly old Omar Bradley, 'the GI's general.' Can't bring themselves to discipline an officer so senior to all of them, even one who's part-mad but has numbers on them. God knows, he was the only one who saw the potential in Inchon and had the guts to pull it off and the sense to let the Marines do it. But for every brilliant stroke, there's another out of madness, a John Brown raid on Harper's Ferry, to cancel it out. Ego, arrogance, and ambition. Dangerous combination."

Smith paused, as if wondering how much he should say about his commanding officer.

"And there's talk the Republicans will nominate him the next time."

"I know, General. I see the *Chicago Trib* occasionally."

"Ah, yes. Your pal Ben Sweet."

"Yessir, my 'pal' Ben . . ." His tone of voice told General Smith he could go ahead and talk.

"You heard what MacArthur did to the Marines when he and Rhee took the salute and declared the capital taken and set free?"

"Nossir, I must have been out of it."

"There're two versions. One is, he told Almond, 'Have the Marines throw a skirmish line of security around the ceremonies. But make sure they're not seen on camera so everything looks peaceful and secure.' " Smith paused.

"That version would have made sense. But the other version's the one most of us believe. He's supposed to have told Almond, 'With all these cameras around, I don't want to see any Marines in tomorrow's newspapers.' "

"MacArthur said that?" Ollie asked.

Uneasy he'd said too much already and criticized a superior officer, Smith drew on an unlit pipe and changed the subject to operations. Ollie, flattered to have this much of Smith's severely rationed time, pulled himself more upright against the pillows, giving as best he could a facsimile of sitting at attention.

Some of the news was bad. Smith said just that final day's fighting for Seoul had cost another sixty Marines dead. What could either officer say about such losses, and for such an empty gesture, beyond rueful cliché? Better to speak of tomorrow and not yesterday.

The 1st Marine Division was boarding ship to be transported by sea to land well above the 38th Parallel at the North Korean seaport of Wonsan on the east coast. It was a sort of second Inchon, but this time against a fleeing, dispirited, probably defeated enemy. Meanwhile, Eighth Army under Walton Walker would be advancing north by land in the western half of the country. The idea was to drive the North Korean army into the hills, cut them up there, and end the war, so that, as a MacArthur aide would famously remark, "The boys can be home by Christmas."

Both halves of the UN army—X Corps under Ned Almond and spearheaded by the Marines and Eighth Army under Walker—would push north to the Yalu River border with China on parallel but distinctly separate routes.

"Wish I could go with you, General," Cromwell said, and he meant it.

"Yes, yes, of course," Smith said almost distractedly. Then, once again focused, he spoke with intensity.

"I don't like it, Ollie. We'll lose a week at sea while the enemy gets to take a breather and reorganize before resuming the fight. When you get them on the run, you stay on their tails and run them down. Run them to death. Nor do I like to see the army divided in two by a mountain range. And no one is quite sure about the Chinese. MacArthur thinks China is one enormous bluff. But there are a million Chinese soldiers up there in nearby China and Manchuria. And behind them, the Soviets and the Red Army.

"General Cates doesn't like it either," O. P. Smith continued, tossing in the commandant's name, "not one damned bit."

Nor did any of the senior Marine officers trust Ned Almond.

"We don't think he has the stuff to tell MacArthur unpleasant truths."

Ollie chose discretion on this big-picture stuff and kept shut. Smith, in a change of pace, went on:

"I'm curious, Cromwell. I was told you were a fellow who spoke his mind. How did you ever get yourself attached to the diplomatic service?"

"You know, General, I never did quite figure that one out either."

"Mmm," said Smith. He knew that the doctors planned to fly this officer to Japan and then back to a naval hospital in the States. So he'd said more than he might have done with another of his officers. Shouldn't have said he and Cates were uneasy with winter closing down . . .

Smith got up.

"Well, I've got calls to make, Cromwell. You do what they tell you, now."

"Yessir," Ollie said brightly. "Maybe I'll catch up to the division up north, General. Maybe I can make myself useful."

Smith shook his hand and left. Ollie considered it significant the general hadn't even attempted to reply with hearty and quite transparent hopes.

In a way, it was reassuring. You wanted a general of division to know what the hell was going on and not just blow smoke to cheer the troops.

▪ 45 ▪

"MACARTHUR SAID HE'D TAKE THE CITY BY SEPTEMBER 25. AND BY GOD, HE DID."

Colonel Cromwell?"

It was the prettiest and youngest of the floor nurses, and she was smiling more winningly than usual.

"I know you're being released tomorrow, but you've got another visitor, if you're not too tired."

"Not tired at all, Ensign." Even when he flirted, a Marine officer ought to observe the military niceties. "Who is it?"

" 'An old friend from college,' he says." Clearly, she was in on the secret and being playful.

Ben Sweet arrived, smiling through the suntan, a dashing figure in official war correspondent gear, waving and shaking hands. Next he'd be passing out eight-by-ten glossies. Cromwell in his hospital gown felt positively shabby in contrast, but Ben was gracious.

"Ollie! If they've got you in bed, I'd hate to see the other guy."

"Hello, Ben. You're looking prosperous."

"Tips and all, I'm breaking even."

The two men had not met since Ollie was hit, and the locker-room wit was a bit forced.

But here was the self-absorbed Ben visiting the sick. Was that a corporal or spiritual work of mercy? Cromwell once knew such things; the Jesuits had pounded them into him. Ollie's attitude toward Ben? He wasn't quite sure of that, either.

The nurse hovered. Women tended to do that when Ben was in the room. He bestowed smiles on Ollie and the nurse, heartily pumped Cromwell's hand, the one still working pretty well, and pulled up a chair.

"I'll be outside, Colonel," the nurse offered, "in case you want something." She meant, of course, "in case Ben Sweet wants something." Even on hospital ships, and with his carcass hooked up to tubes, Ollie could read women.

"Thank you, Ensign. I'll be safe with Mr. Sweet."

Ben tugged his chair closer to the bedside.

"So they're sending you home."

"Looks like it, Ben. You and MacArthur will have to win the war without me."

"Still sour about him?"

"Some."

"Admit it, Ollie. The man did what he said; he liberated Seoul by the twenty-fifth."

"Were you there at the kill, Ben?"

"Wish I had been. I was in Tokyo at the Dai Ichi when he announced X Corps had taken the capital. Exactly three months to the day. Pretty dramatic stuff."

"I guess," Cromwell said, his tone flat, unenthusiastic.

"You guess? Hell, Ollie, MacArthur said he'd take the city September 25, and he did."

"Killed some good men keeping that date, Ben."

"Yeah," said Ben, setting his face into a facsimile of sorrow, "but didn't your hero Carlson preach that? The faster the battle, the fewer the dead?"

"True," Ollie said, aware of contradictions.

He was aware, too, that from Pusan north, Marine deads had been running at a consistent hundred a week. Significantly higher those last few days taking Seoul. But he didn't push it. Wasn't what you did, win an argument on the backs of the dead.

Instead, he changed course: "What do you hear about the Chinese? They coming in?"

"Forget the Chinese, Ollie. They're all bluff. You're not letting a few laundrymen scare you off, are you?"

"I guess not," Ollie said without much enthusiasm. The remark was pure MacArthur. Or maybe, Ned Almond.

Sweet, a winner who could afford to be generous, did not continue the debate.

It was the same old Ben, Cromwell realized, the handsome devil playing soldier, pretending to know what it was about, killing and being killed, when all he was really was a camp follower, scavenging battlefields and stripping the bodies after the smoke cleared.

Thinking that way, Ollie grew impatient with himself. *Oh, hell! Let's not get pious now, Cromwell. Not everyone goes to soldiering. And maybe it's a good thing we don't.*

So he made an effort to be affable. Sweet had come by when he didn't have to.

"Think you'll get a book out of Korea, Ben?"

"Might. It's all grist for the mill. Look at *A Farewell to Arms*. All that mileage Hemingway got out of fighting in Italy."

Ollie was grinning broadly now, amused that Ben was temporarily putting MacArthur aside, turning to earlier heroes.

"Lot of fighting he did, Ben. When Hemingway got his famous war wounds, he was delivering chocolates and Red Cross smokes to Italian infantry."

Sweet nodded. An old story he knew as well as Ollie did. There was a bland, complacent smile on Ben's famous, empty face, punctuated by the occasional carefully considered look of concern for his old "pal," cruelly wounded in combat.

"Poetic license. A novelist is allowed to invent."

Ollie looked up at him from the pillows, taking a playful tack with the self-serious Sweet.

"Maybe you ought to finesse the novel, Ben. Write the definitive history of the war. You know what they say: 'The generals make wars; the historians make reputations.' "

Sweet looked intrigued. "Yeah, but MacArthur would probably beat me to it. Caesar wrote about his own campaigns; why not MacArthur?"

"Sure, an 'American Caesar.' "

Ben nodded, taking Ollie's playfulness at face value. A history of the war? Maybe Korea would turn out worth his time after all.

So he decided, magnanimously, to let an old pal in on secrets.

"The Army's going north, Ollie. All the way to China. But keep it to youself. Top-secret stuff."

Colonel Cromwell had already been told the same thing by a general and a PFC both.

"Couldn't get it out of me with pliers, Ben. MacArthur himself tell you?"

"Well," he said, striving for modesty, "he invited me along."

"There's a new one. War by invitation only. You and MacArthur up there heading for China . . ."

"I'm still a reporter, Ollie. With a source. General Willoughby."

"Oh?"

"Sure, he says the North Koreans are finished. All that's left is the mopping-up. Some American divisions could be transferred pretty soon to

West Germany for NATO. Might even send a few troops home for Christmas."

Willoughby, the fellow who told MacArthur only what he wanted to hear, the intelligence officer who was supposed to sniff out enemy capabilities and report them accurately to the top brass. But didn't.

"That'll be nice," Ollie said, no longer amused, a deadly chill coming over him. He wasn't hearing Sweet's voice now but Oliver Smith's—his reservations about going north with winter coming. Heard Lonesome's fears as well. The general and the PFC, both professionals, both wary of a northern campaign in the mountains, wary of the Chinese Army, worried about where MacArthur was leading them. While Sweet, the gifted amateur, who boasted that his dope came from a practiced liar named Willoughhby, would lead the cheerleading in American newspapers and magazines.

So instead of making something of it, Cromwell cut their conversation short. This wasn't the debating society at Regis.

"Thanks for coming by, Ben. I appreciate it. I really do."

Sweet got out of his chair to give Ollie a bear hug around the shoulders.

"You take care now, Ollie."

This was Ben at his tough-guy best: the muscular hug, the superior grin from a man who played football at South Bend, patronizing a fellow who hadn't quite made the team.

"Sure, Ben. Thanks."

"Sorry you got hit, Ollie. We take our losses," he added smugly.

Ollie gave a short, bitter laugh. He liked Ben's use of the plural "we," including Sweet in the fraternity of men who fought.

"Sure," Ollie said, not calling him on it, letting it ride.

Then Ben went on for one remark too many, meaning to console but coming off condescending, patronizing, "Fortunes of war, Ollie. Fortunes of war."

With his visitor standing there smiling his good-byes, Cromwell repeated Sweet's final words, unable not to:

"War, Ben? Fortunes of war?"

"Yeah, why?"

Ollie turned his head away from his visitor and toward the single porthole, so that he would no longer see the sleek, satisfied face. He was looking instead back at Inchon, at the distant shore where men now dead had gone over the seawall. And, talking easily and low, stifling anger, maintaining cool, Ollie uttered his own quiet, dismissive farewell:

"When it comes to war, Ben, you don't know squat."

■

After a justifiably huffy Pulitzer laureate had stomped from the hospital room, Ollie painfully and with difficulty hunched his buttocks higher against the pillows so he could sit upright and grin his enjoyment. He was slightly ashamed of having run his mouth. But every so often, with a guy peddling stuff like that, you had to call him on it, you had to say *something*!

Maybe it really would be Ben Sweet who wrote the history of this war. If so, Ollie wouldn't have much of a role. Whoever the author, Mac-Arthur or some tenured, scholarly Toynbee on a campus somewhere, the material was surely there: the panicky opening act of that terrible summer, the gritty stand at Pusan, the tides at Inchon, the arrogance of demanding Seoul by a date definite, battles yet to fight up in the winter mountains. . . .

Ollie shoved aside these matters, drifting into a pleasant reverie, very much aware that with the summer campaigning over he was still alive when plenty of good, maybe better, men were dead. And that for a final time he'd commanded Marines in combat. Even Carlson never commanded again, not after they broke up the Raider battalions. But Ollie had. Just a rump, shot-up rifle platoon aboard a damned locomotive, but a Marine command in a last firefight.

They were flying Colonel Cromwell to a hospital in Japan for additional patchwork they couldn't do here aboard *Consolation,* some preparatory physical therapy, then shipping him back to the States. He hoped it would be California again, San Diego so that he could live at home and do his out-patient therapy locally.

The house on the oceanfront cliffs of Dana Point was all on the one level so he would be able to get about quite easily, and he could follow the war in the morning paper and on the evening news, could laze and read and sun himself on the patio, watching the kids surf and looking out on the Pacific, and enjoy the morning fogs, delight in the sunsets. The steep cliff-side path down to the sand would be tricky to navigate, but he wasn't much of a beach person. He'd be close to Camp Pendleton, with privileges at the commissary and the PX, and maybe he'd have dinner Saturdays at the "O" Club and swap war stories over a cocktail at the good, long bar where officers drank, the eager young lieutenants and the old farts both.

He'd be again among family and friends, the family of the Corps. And, though he was damaged goods on inactive service, Cromwell would still be an officer of Marines.

The Colonel was skeptical about most things, and that included cheering assurances from doctors. But if what they told him was even marginally true, he would eventually be able to stand again. If a man can stand, he ought to be able to walk. Maybe even march. As for taking one of Carlson's fifty-mile jaunts, well, he was younger then. As were all of them—young and crazy. The Ollie Cromwell of here and now would settle for a stroll in the California sun.

Cromwell would take that stroll. And cheerfully so. If they could somehow rig him a proper new left leg.

AUTHOR'S NOTE

■

Source material includes:

Alexander, Colonel Joseph H., USMC. *A Fellowship of Valor*. New York: HarperCollins.

Blankfort, Michael. *The Big Yankee*. (Biography of Evans F. Carlson.) New York: Little Brown.

Duncan, David Douglas. *This Is War*. Harper and Brothers.

Fruchtman, Jack, Jr. *Thomas Paine*. New York and London: Four Walls Eight Windows.

Goulden, Joseph C. *Korea: The Untold Story of the War*. Times Books.

Leckie, Robert. *Conflict: The History of the Korean War*. Avon Books.

Montress, Lynn, and Captain Nicholas A. Canzona, USMC. *U.S. Marine Operations in Korea*. (Vols. 1 and 2.) Washington, D.C.: Historical Branch, Headquarters, USMC.

Peatross, Oscar F. *Bless 'em All*. Irvine, Calif.: ReView Publications.

Rosenquist, R. G., Martin J. Sexton, and Robert A. Buerlein. *Our Kind of War*. Richmond, Va.: The American Historical Foundation.

Sexton, Martin J., *The Marine Raiders Historical Handbook,* Richmond, Va.: The American Historical Foundation.

Weintraub, Stanley. *MacArthur's War*. New York: Touchstone/Simon and Schuster.

I have also used Lieutenant Le François's published diary extracts about the Makin Raid.